THE EARL'S CONVENIENT WIFE

BY
MARION LENNOX

Our policy is to use papers that are natural, renewable and recyclable products and made from wood grown in sustainable forests. The logging and manufacturing processes conform to the legal environmental regulations of the country of origin.

Printed and bound in Spain
by CPI, Barcelona

MILLS & BOON

Published in Great Britain 2015
by Mills & Boon, an imprint of Harlequin (UK) Limited,
Eton House, 18-24 Paradise Road, Richmond, Surrey, TW9 1SR

© 2015 Marion Lennox

ISBN: 978-0-263-25150-0

23-0715

Marion Lennox has written more than a hundred romances and is published in over a hundred countries and thirty languages. Her multiple awards include the prestigious RITA® Award (twice) and the *RT Book Reviews* Career Achievement Award "for a body of work which makes us laugh and teaches us about love."

Marion adores her family, her kayak, her dog and lying on the beach with a book someone else has written. Heaven.

With thanks to Rose M, my new and
wonderful neighbour and friend.
Gardening will never be the same again.

CHAPTER ONE

MARRY...

There was deathly silence in the magnificent library of the ancient castle of Duncairn. In specially built niches round the walls were the bottles of whisky Jeanie had scraped to afford. Weirdly, that was what she was focusing on. What a waste. How much whisky could she fit in a suitcase?

How many scores of fruitcakes would they make? There was no way she was leaving them behind. For him. For her prospective bridegroom?

What a joke.

She'd been clinging to the hope that she might keep her job. She knew the Lord of Duncairn didn't like her, but she'd worked hard to give Duncairn Castle the reputation for hospitality it now enjoyed.

It didn't matter. Her efforts were for nothing. This crazy will meant she was out on her ear.

'This must be a joke.' Alasdair McBride, the sixteenth Earl of Duncairn, sounded appalled. It was no wonder. She stood to lose her job. Alasdair stood to lose his...fiefdom?

'A last will and testament is never a joke.' Edward McCraig, of the prestigious law firm McCraig, McCraig & McFerry, had made the long journey from Edinburgh to be at today's funeral for Eileen McBride—Alasdair's grandmother and Jeanie's employer. He'd sat behind Jeanie in the Duncairn Kirk and listened to the eulogies with an air of supressed impatience. He wished to catch the last ferry back to the mainland. He was now seated in one of the library's opulent chairs, reading the old lady's wishes to her only surviving grandson—and to the live-in help.

He shuffled his papers and pushed his glasses further down his nose, looking at neither of them. Crazy or not, Eileen's will clearly made him uncomfortable.

Jeanie looked at Alasdair and then looked away. This might be a mess, but it had little to do with her, she decided. She went back to counting whisky bottles. Maybe three suitcases? She only had one, but there were crates in the castle cellars. If she was brave enough to face the dark and the spiders…

Could you sell whisky online?

She glanced back at Alasdair and found his gaze was following hers, along the line of whisky. With an oath— a mixture of fury and shock—he took three glasses from the sideboard and poured.

Soda-sized whiskies.

The lawyer shook his head but Jeanie took hers with gratitude. The will had been a nasty shock. It was excellent whisky and she couldn't take it all with her.

But it did need to be treated with respect. As the whisky hit home she choked and sank onto one of the magnificent down-filled sofas. A cloud of dog hair rose around her. She really had to do something about Eileen's dogs.

Or not. This will said they were no longer her problem. She'd have to leave the island. She couldn't take the dogs and she loved them. This castle might be over-the-top opulent, but she loved it, too. She felt…befuddled.

'So how do we get around this?' Clearly the whisky wasn't having the same effect on Alasdair that it was on her. His glass was almost empty. She looked at him in awe. Actually she'd been looking sideways at Alasdair all afternoon. Well, why not? He might be arrogant, he might have despised her from the first time he'd met her, but he'd always been worth looking at.

Alasdair McBride was thirty-seven years old, and he was what Jeanie's granny would have described as a man to be reckoned with. Although he didn't use it, his hereditary title fitted him magnificently, especially today. In honour of his grandmother's funeral he was wearing full highland regalia, and he looked awesome.

Jeanie always had had a weakness for a man in a kilt, and the Duncairn tartan was gorgeous. Okay, the Earl of Duncairn was gorgeous, she conceded. Six foot two in his stockinged feet, with jet-black hair and the striking bone structure and strength of the warrior race he'd so clearly descended from, Alasdair McBride was a man to make every eye in the room turn to him. The fact that he controlled the massive Duncairn financial empire only added to his aura of power, but he needed no such addition to look what he was—a man in control of his world.

Except…now he wasn't. His grandmother's will had just pulled the rug from under his feet.

And hers. *Marry?* So much for her quiet life as the Duncairn housekeeper.

'You can't get around it,' the lawyer was saying. 'The will is inviolate.'

'Do you think…?' She was testing her voice for the first time since the bombshell had landed. 'Do you think that Eileen might possibly have been…have been…?'

'Lady McBride was in full possession of her senses.' The lawyer cast her a cautious look as if he was expecting her to disintegrate into hysterics. 'My client understood her will was slightly…unusual…so she took steps to see that it couldn't be overturned. She arranged a certificate of medical competency, dated the same day she made the will.'

Alasdair drained the rest of his whisky and poured another, then spun to look out of the great bay window looking over the sea.

It was a magnificent window. A few highland cattle grazed peacefully in the late-summer sun, just beyond the ha-ha. Further on, past rock-strewn burns and craggy hills, were the remnants of a vast medieval fortress on the shoreline. Two eagles were soaring effortlessly in the thermals. If he used binoculars, he might even see otters in the burns running into the sea, Jeanie thought. Or deer. Or…

Or her mind was wandering. She put her glass down, glanced at Alasdair's broad back and felt a twist of real sympathy. Eileen had been good to her already, and in death she owed her nothing. Alasdair's loss, however, was appalling. She might not like the man, but he hadn't deserved this.

Oh, Eileen, what were you thinking? she demanded wordlessly of her deceased employer—but there was nothing Jeanie could do.

'I guess that's it, then,' she managed, addressing herself to the lawyer. 'How long do I have before you want me out?'

'There's no rush,' the lawyer told her. 'It'll take a while to get the place ready for sale.'

'Do you want me to keep trading? I have guests booked until the end of next month.'

'That would be excellent. We may arrange for you to stay even longer. It'd be best if we could sell it as a going concern.'

'No!' The explosion was so fierce it almost rocked the room. Alasdair turned from the window and slammed his glass onto the coffee table so hard it shattered. He didn't seem to notice.

'It can't happen.' Alasdair's voice lowered, no longer explosive but cold and hard and sure. 'My family's entire history, sold to fund…dogs' homes?'

'It's a worthy cause,' the lawyer ventured but Alasdair wasn't listening.

'This castle is the least of it,' he snapped. 'Duncairn is one of the largest financial empires in Europe. Do you know how much our organisation gives to charity each year? Sold, it could give every lost dog in Europe a personal attendant and gold-plated dog bowl for the rest of its life, but then it's gone. Maintained, we can do good— we *are* doing good. This will is crazy. I'll channel every penny of profit into dog care for the next ten years if I must, but to give it away...'

'I understand it would mean the end of your career—' the lawyer ventured but he was cut off.

'It's not the end of my career.'

If Lord Alasdair had had another glass, Jeanie was sure it'd have gone the way of the first.

'Do you know how many corporations would employ me? I have the qualifications and the skills to start again, but to haul apart my family inheritance on a stupid whim?'

'The thing is,' the lawyer said apologetically, 'I don't think it was a whim. Your grandmother felt your cousin treated his wife very badly and she wished to atone...'

'Here it is again. It all comes back to my wastrel cousin.' Alasdair spun around and stared at Jeanie with a look that was pretty much all contempt. 'You married him.'

'There's no need to bring Alan into this.'

'Isn't there? Eileen spent her life papering over his faults. She was blind to the fact that he was a liar and a thief, and that blind side's obviously extended to you. What was she on about? Marry Alan's widow? You? I'd rather walk on hot coals. You're the housekeeper here—nothing more. Marry anyone you like, but leave me alone.'

Her sympathy faded to nothing. 'Anyone I like?' she retorted. 'Wow. Thank you kindly, sir. As a proposal, that takes some beating.'

'It's the only proposal you're likely to get.'

'Then isn't it lucky I don't want one?'

He swore and turned again to the window. Jeanie's brief spurt of anger faded and she returned to shock.

Marriage…? To Alasdair? What *were* you thinking, Eileen? she demanded again of the departed Lady McBride.

Was she thinking the same as when she'd coerced Alan into marrying Jeanie? At least it was out in the open this time, she conceded. At least all the cards were on the table. The will spelt it out with startling clarity. It was an order to Alasdair. *Marry Jeanie, collect your inheritance, the only cost—one year of marriage. If not, inherit nothing.*

Oh, Eileen.

'I believe the time for angry words is not now.' The lawyer was clearing his papers into a neat pile, ready to depart, but his dry, lawyer's voice was sounding a warning. 'You need to be quite clear before you make rash decisions. I understand that emotions are…high…at the moment, but think about it. Neither of you are married. My Lord, if you marry Mrs McBride, then you keep almost the entire estate. Mrs McBride, if you marry His Lordship, in twelve months you get to keep the castle. That's a substantial amount to be throwing away because you can't get on.'

'The castle belongs to my family,' Alasdair snapped. 'It has nothing to do with this woman.'

'Your grandmother treated Jeanie as part of your family.'

'She's not. She's just as bad as—'

'My Lord, I'd implore you not to do—or say—anything in haste,' the lawyer interrupted. 'Including making statements that may inflame the situation. I suggest you take a couple of days and think about it.'

A couple of days? He had to be kidding, Jeanie thought. There was only one decision to be made in the face of this craziness, and she'd made it. She looked at Alasdair's broad back, at his highland kilt, at the size of him—he was practically blocking the window. She looked at the tense set of his shoulders. She could almost taste his rage and his frustration.

Get this over with, she told herself, and she gave herself a fraction of a second to feel sorry for him again. No more, though. Protect yourself, she scolded. Get out of here fast.

'Alasdair doesn't want to marry me and why should he?' she asked the lawyer. 'And I surely don't want to marry him. Eileen was a sweetheart but she was also a conniving matriarch. She liked pulling the strings but sometimes… sometimes she couldn't see that the cost was impossibly high. I've married one of her grandsons. I'm not marrying another and that's an end to it. Thank you for coming, sir. Should I ring for the taxi to collect you, in, say, fifteen minutes?'

'That would be excellent. Thank you. You've been an excellent housekeeper to Duncairn, Mrs McBride. Eileen was very fond of you.'

'I know she was, and I loved her, too,' Jeanie said. 'But sometimes…' She glanced again at Alasdair. 'Well, the family has always been known for its arrogance. The McBrides have been ordering the lives of Duncairn islanders for generations, but this time Eileen's taken it a step too far. I guess the Duncairn ascendancy is now in freefall but there's nothing I can do about it. Good afternoon, gentlemen.'

And she walked out and closed the door behind her.

She was gone. Thankfully. Alasdair was left with the lawyer.

Silence, silence and more silence. The lawyer was giving him space, Alasdair thought, and he should be grateful. He wasn't.

His thoughts went back to his grandfather, an astute old

man whose trust in his wife had been absolute. He'd run the Duncairn financial empire with an iron fist. Deeply disappointed in his two sons—Alasdair's and Alan's respective fathers—the old man had left control of the entire estate in the hands of Eileen.

'By the time you die I hope our sons have learned financial sense,' he'd told her. 'You can decide who is best to take over.'

But neither of his sons had shown the least interest in the estate, apart from persuading Eileen to give them more money. They'd predeceased their mother, one in a skiing accident, one from a heart attack, probably caused by spending his life in Michelin-starred restaurants.

No matter. That was history. Eileen had come from a long line of thrifty Scots, and in Alasdair she'd found a family member who shared her business acumen and more.

As they'd turned the company into the massive empire it now was, Alasdair had tried to talk his grandmother into making it a public entity, making it safe if anything had happened to either of them. She'd refused. 'I trust you,' she'd told him but she'd maintained total ownership.

And now this…

'Surely it's illegal,' he said, feeling bone weary.

'What could be illegal?'

'Coercing us into marriage.'

'There's no coercion. The way your grandmother worded it…'

'You helped her word it.'

'Mr Duncan McGrath, the firm's most senior lawyer, helped her draft it, to make sure there were no legal loopholes.' The lawyer was suddenly stern. 'She was very clear what she wanted. The will states that the entire financial empire plus any other assets she owns are to be liquidated and left in equal parts to a large number of canine charities.

As an aside, she states that the only way the intentions of the will can be set aside is if you and Mrs McBride marry.'

'That woman is not a McBride.'

'She's Mrs McBride,' the lawyer repeated sternly. 'You know that she is. Your grandmother loved her and treated her as family, and your grandmother wanted to cement that relationship. The bequest to the canine charities can only be set aside if, within a month of her death, you and Mrs Jeanie McBride are legally married. To each other.'

'We both know that's crazy. Even…Mrs McBride… didn't consider it for a moment.' He ran his fingers through his hair, the feeling of exhaustion intensifying. 'It's blackmail.'

'It's not blackmail. The will is set up so that in the— admittedly unlikely—event that you marry, your grandmother provides for you as a family.'

'And if we're not?'

'Then she's done what any lonely old woman in her situation might do. She's left her fortune to dogs' homes.'

'So if we contest…'

'I've taken advice, sir. I was…astounded at the terms of the will myself, so I took the liberty to sound out a number of my colleagues. Legal advice is unanimous that the will stands.'

More silence. Alasdair reached for his whisky and discovered what he'd done. The table was covered with broken glass. He needed to call someone to clean it up.

Mrs McBride? Jeanie.

His cousin's wife had operated this place as a bed and breakfast for the past three years. As cook, housekeeper and hostess, she'd done a decent job, he'd had to concede. 'You should see how it is now,' his grandmother had told him, beaming. 'Jeanie's the best thing that's happened to this family.'

That wasn't true. Even though he conceded she'd looked

after this place well, it was by her first actions he'd judged her. As Alan's wife. She'd run wild with his cousin and she'd been beside him when he'd died. Together she and Alan had broken Eileen's heart, but Eileen had never been prepared to cut her loose.

Marrying Alan had branded her, he conceded, but that brand was justified. Any fool could have seen the crazy lifestyle his cousin had been living was ruinous. The money she and Alan had thrown round... That was why she was still looking after the castle, in the hope of inheriting something more. He was sure of it. For an impoverished island lass, the McBride fortune must seem seductive, to say the least.

Seduction... By money?

If she'd married for money once before...

His mind was suddenly off on a crazy tangent that made him feel ill.

Marriage... But what was the alternative?

'So what if we *did* marry?' he demanded at last, goaded into saying it.

'Then everything reverts to how it's been,' the lawyer told him. He was watching him cautiously now, as if he half expected Alasdair to lob whisky at him. 'If you and Mrs McBride marry and stay married for a period of no less than one year, you'll legally own the Duncairn empire with all it entails, with the exception of the castle itself. Mrs McBride will own that.'

'Just this castle?'

'And the small parcel of land on the same title. Yes. They're the terms of the will.'

'Does she have a clue how much this place costs to maintain? What she gets with the bed and breakfast guests couldn't begin to touch it. And without the surrounding land...'

'I'd imagine Mrs McBride could sell,' the lawyer said,

placing his papers back in his briefcase. 'Maybe to you, if you wish to continue the Duncairn lineage. But right now, that's immaterial. If you don't marry her, the castle will be part of the whole estate to be sold as one. Mrs McBride needs to consider her future with care, but maintenance of the castle is immaterial unless you marry.'

And there was the only glimmer of light in this whole impossible situation. If he didn't inherit, neither would she. It'd be great to be finally shot of her.

He didn't need this inheritance. He didn't. If he walked away from this mess, he could get a job tomorrow. There were any number of corporations that'd take his expertise.

But to walk away from Duncairn? His ancestral home…

And the company. So many people… He thought of the firm most likely to buy if he no longer had control and he felt ill. They'd merge. All his senior management… All his junior staff…Scotland was struggling after the global financial crisis anyway. How could they get new jobs?

They couldn't, and there was nothing he could do about it.

Unless…unless…

'She *has* been married before,' he said slowly, thinking aloud. He didn't like the woman one bit. He didn't trust her, but if he was careful… Initial revulsion was starting to give way to sense. 'She married my cousin so I'm assuming money's important to her. I guess—if it got me out of this mess, I might be prepared to marry. In name only,' he added hastily. 'As a business deal.'

Marriage… The idea made him feel ill. But Lords of Duncairn had married for convenience before, he reminded himself. They'd married heiresses to build the family fortunes. They'd done what had to be done to keep the estate safe.

And the lawyer was permitting himself a dry smile, as if his client was now talking like a sensible man. 'I've considered that option,' he told him. 'It would meet the requirements of the bequest—as long as you lived together.'

'Pardon?'

'Lady Eileen was very sure of what she wanted. She has…all eventualities covered.'

He exhaled and took a while to breathe again. Eventualities… 'Explain.'

'You and Mrs McBride would need to live in the same residence for a period of at least one year before the estate can be settled. However, Lady Eileen was not unreasonable. She acknowledges that in the course of your business you do need to travel, so she's made allowances. Those allowances are restrictive, however. In the twelve months from the time of your marriage there's an allowance for no more than thirty nights spent apart.'

Alasdair said nothing. He couldn't think what to say.

He'd loved his grandmother. None of what he was thinking right now had any bearing on that love. If he had her in front of him…

'She's also taken steps to ensure that this arrangement was kept.' The lawyer coughed apologetically. 'I'm sorry, but you would need to keep to…the intent of the will.'

'You mean she'd have us watched?'

'There are funds set aside to ensure the terms are being adhered to.'

He stared at the lawyer in horror. 'You're out of your mind. Next you'll be saying you'll be checking the sheets.'

'I believe,' the lawyer said and allowed himself another wintry smile, 'that your sleeping arrangements within the one residence would be entirely up to you and your…your wife. Mind…' he allowed the smile to widen '…she's an attractive wee thing.'

'Of all the…'

'Though it's not my business to say so, sir. I'm sorry.'

'No.' Though she was, Alasdair conceded, his thoughts

flying sideways again. He'd been astounded when his cousin had married her. Jeanie McBride was petite and freckled and rounded. Her soft brown shoulder-length curls, mostly tugged back into a ponytail, were nothing out of the ordinary. She didn't dress to kill. In fact, the first time he'd met her, he'd thought how extraordinary that the womanising Alan was attracted to such a woman.

But then she'd smiled at something his grandmother had said, and he'd seen what Alan had obviously seen. Her smile was like the sun coming out after rain. Her face lit and her freckles seemed almost luminescent. She had a dimple at the side of her mouth, and when she'd chuckled…

He hadn't heard that chuckle for a long time, he thought suddenly. He hadn't seen her smile, either.

In truth, he'd avoided her. His grandmother's distress over Alan's wasted life had been enough to make him avoid Jeanie and all she represented. He'd known she was caring for the castle and he acknowledged she'd seemed to be making a good job of it. She'd steered clear of him these past few months when he'd come to visit his grandmother. She'd treated him formally, as a castle guest, and he'd treated her like the housekeeper she was.

But she wasn't just a housekeeper. Right after Alan's death Eileen had said, 'She seems like a daughter to me,' and he'd thought, Uh-oh, she'll stick around until the old lady dies and hope to inherit, and now he was proved right.

She must be as shocked as he was about the will's contents. She'd get nothing unless they married…

That could be used to his advantage. His mind was racing. The only cost would be the castle.

And a year of his life…

The lawyer had risen, eager to depart. 'I'm sorry, sir. I understand I'm leaving you in a quandary but my task here was purely as messenger. I can see the taxi approaching. Mrs McBride has been efficient as always. Will you bid her farewell for me? Meanwhile, if there's anything else myself or my partners can do…'

'Tear up the will?'

'You and I both know that we can't do that. The will is watertight. From now on there's only a decision to be made, and I have no place here while you make it. Good luck, sir, and goodbye.'

CHAPTER TWO

THERE WAS TOO much to get his head around.

Alasdair paced the library, and when that wasn't big enough he took himself outdoors, through the great, grand castle entrance, across the manicured lawns, down the ha-ha and to the rough pastures beyond.

The shaggy highland cattle were still where they'd been while the lawyer had been making his pronouncements. The day had been warm and they were feeling the heat. If it got any hotter, they'd be wandering down to the sea and standing belly deep in the water, but for now they were lying on the rich summer grass, grazing where they could reach.

He loved the cattle. More, he loved this whole estate. His grandparents had made one small section of the castle liveable when his grandfather inherited, and they'd brought him here as a boy. He'd wandered the place at will, free from the demands his socialite parents put on him, free of the restrictions of being known as a rich kid. He'd fished, climbed, roamed, and when his grandmother had decided on restoration he'd been delighted.

Only that restoration had brought Jeanie into their lives.

If it hadn't been Jeanie, it would have been someone else, he thought grimly, striding down the line of battered fencing towards the bay. His grandmother's two dogs,

Abbot and Costello, elegant spaniels, beautiful, fast and dumb, had loped out to join him. The smell of rabbits would be everywhere, and the dogs were going nuts trying to find them.

Alan's wife…Jeanie…

His grandmother had said she'd loved her.

He'd thought his grandmother had loved him.

'So why treat us like this?' he demanded of his departed grandmother. 'If we don't marry, we'll have nothing.'

It was blackmail. Marry… The thing was nonsense.

But the knot of shock and anger was starting to untwist. Jeanie's assessment was right—his grandmother was a conniving, Machiavellian matriarch—so he might have expected something like this. Marriage to Alan's widow… Of all the dumb…

Eileen had loved reading romance novels. He should have confiscated every one and burned them before it was too late.

He reached the bay and set himself down on a great smooth rock, a foundation stone of an ancient fortress. He gazed out to sea but his mind was racing. Option one, no inheritance. Nothing. Walk away. The thought made him feel ill.

He turned and gazed back at the castle. He'd hardly been here these past years but it had always been in his mind. In his heart?

There'd been McBrides at Duncairn Castle since almost before the dinosaurs. Would he be the one to let it go?

The woodchip industry would move in, he thought. The pastures included with the castle title were mostly wild. The castle was heritage-listed, but not the land.

There were deer watching cautiously just above the horizon, but money was in woodchips, not deer. The land would go.

Which led—sickeningly—to option two.

Marriage. To a woman he couldn't stand, but who also stood to gain by the inheritance.

He gazed around again at the cattle, at the distant deer, at the water lapping the shores, the dogs barking in the distance, the eagles…

His land. Duncairn.

Was the thing impossible?

And the more he calmed down, the more he saw it wasn't. His apartment in Edinburgh was large, with separate living quarters for a housekeeper. He'd bought the place when he and Celia were planning marriage, and afterwards he'd never seen the point of moving. He worked fourteen-, fifteen-hour days, especially now. There were things happening within the company he didn't understand. Nebulous but worrying. He needed to focus.

He still could. He could use the Edinburgh house simply to sleep. That could continue and the terms of the will would be met.

'It could work,' he reasoned. 'The apartment's big enough for us to keep out of each other's way.'

But what will she do while you're away every day? The question came from nowhere, and he briefly considered it.

'She can shop, socialise, do what other wives do.'

Wives…

He'd have a wife. After Celia's betrayal he'd sworn…

Eileen had known that he'd sworn. That was why she'd done this.

He needed to suppress his anger. What he'd learned, hard and early, was that emotion got you nowhere. Reason was everything.

'It's only for a year,' he told himself. 'There's no choice. To walk away from everything is unthinkable.'

But walking away was still an option. He had money independent of Duncairn—of course he did. When he'd first started working in the firm, his grandmother had insisted on a salary commensurate with other executives of his standing. He was well-qualified, and even without this dubious inheritance he was wealthy. He could walk away.

But Duncairn…

He turned and looked back again at the castle, a great grey mass of imposing stone built by his ancestors to last for centuries. And the company… The financial empire had drawn him in since his teens. He'd worked to make it the best in the world, and to let it go…

'I'd be able to buy the castle from her when the year's up,' he told himself. 'You can't tell me she's not in for the main chance. If I'm the highest bidder, she'll take the money and run.'

Decision made. He rose and stretched and called the dogs.

'I'll do this,' he said out loud, addressing the ghost of his absent grandmother. 'Fine, Grandmother, you win. I'll talk to her and we'll organise a wedding. But that'll be it. It might be a wedding but it's not a marriage. If you think I'll ever be interested in Alan's leavings…'

Don't think of her like that.

But he couldn't help himself. Alan's betrayal, his gut-wrenching cruelty, was still raw after all these years and Jeanie was Alan's widow. He'd stayed away from this castle because he'd wanted nothing to do with her, but now…

'Now we'll have to share the same front door in Edinburgh,' he told himself. For a year. But a year's not so long when what's at stake is so important. *You can do it, man. Go take yourself a wife.*

She was in the kitchen. The kitchen was her solace, her joy. Cooks had been baking in this kitchen for hundreds of years. The great range took half the wall. The massive oak table, twenty feet long, was pocked and scratched from generations of chopping and rolling and kneading. The vast cobbled floor was worn from hundreds of servants, feeding thousands.

Eileen had restored the castle, making it truly sumptuous, but she'd had the sense to leave the kitchen free from modern grandeur. Jeanie had an electric oven tucked discreetly by the door. There was even a microwave and dishwasher in the vast, hall-like pantry, but the great stove was still lit as it seemed to have stayed lit forever. There was a sumptuous basket on each side for the dogs. The effect was old and warm and breathtaking.

Here was her place, Jeanie thought. She'd loved it the first time she'd seen it, and she'd found peace here.

She was having trouble finding peace now.

When in doubt, turn to scones, she told herself. After all these years she could cook them in her sleep. She didn't provide dinner for the castle guests but she baked treats for occasional snacks or for when they wandered in after dinner. She usually baked slices or a cake but right now she needed something that required no thought.

She wasn't thinking. She was *not* thinking.

Marriage...

She shouldn't care. She hadn't expected to inherit anything, but to tie the estate up as Eileen had... It didn't matter how much she disliked Alasdair; this was cruel. Had Eileen really been thinking it could happen?

And even though her thoughts should be on Alasdair, on the injustice done to him, there was also a part of her that hurt. No, she hadn't expected an inheritance, but she hadn't expected this, either. That Eileen could possibly think she could organise her down that road again... Try one grandson, if that doesn't work, try another?

'What were you thinking?' she demanded of the departed Eileen.

And then she thought: Eileen hadn't been thinking. She'd been hoping.

Those last few months of her life, Eileen had stayed at the castle a lot. Her normally feisty personality had turned inward. She'd wept for Alan, but she'd also wept for Alasdair.

'His parents and then that appalling woman he almost married…they killed something in him,' she'd told Jeanie. 'If only he could find a woman like you.'

This will was a fanciful dream, Jeanie thought, kneading her scone dough. The old lady might have been in full possession of her faculties, but her last will and testament was nothing more than a dream.

'She mustn't have thought it through,' she said to herself. 'She could never have thought we'd walk away from what she saw as irresistible temptation. She'd never believe we could resist.'

But Eileen hadn't had all the facts. Jeanie thought of those facts now, of an appalling marriage and its consequences, and she felt ill. If Eileen knew what she'd done, it'd break her heart.

But what could she do about it now? Nothing. Nothing, nothing and nothing. Finally she stared down and realised what she'd been doing. Kneading scone dough? Was she out of her mind?

'There's nothing worse than tough scones,' she told the world in general. 'Except marriage.'

Two disastrous marriages… Could she risk a third?

'Maybe I will,' she told herself, searching desperately for the light side, the optimistic bit of Jeanie McBride that had never entirely been quenched. 'Eventually. Maybe I might finally find myself a life. I could go to Paris—learn to cook French pastries. Could I find myself a sexy Parisian who enjoys a single malt?'

She almost smiled at that. All that whisky had to be useful for something. If she was honest, it wasn't even her drink of choice.

But since when had she ever had a choice? There was still the overwhelming issue of her debt, she thought, and the urge to smile died. Alan's debt. The bankruptcy hung over her like a massive, impenetrable cloud. How to be optimistic in the face of that?

She glanced out of the window, at the eagles who soared over the Duncairn castle as if they owned it.

'That's what I'd really like to do,' she whispered. 'Fly. But I'm dreaming. I'm stuck.'

And then a deep masculine response from the doorway made her almost jump out of her skin.

'That's what I'm thinking.'

Her head jerked from window to doorway and he was standing there. The Lord of Duncairn.

How long had he been watching? Listening? She didn't know. She didn't care, she told herself, fighting for composure as she tossed her dough into the waste and poured more flour into her bowl. McBrides...

But this man was not Alan. She told herself that, but as she did she felt a queer jump inside.

No, he wasn't Alan. He was nothing like him. They'd been cousins but where Alan had been out for a good time, this man was rock solid. Judgemental, yes. 'Harsh' and 'condemnatory' were two adjectives that described him well—and yet, gazing at the man in the doorway, she felt the weird inside flutter that she'd felt in the library.

Attraction? She had to be joking.

He was her feudal lord, she told herself harshly. She was a peasant. And when peasantry met gentry—run!

But for now she was the cook in this man's castle. She was forced to stay and she was forced to listen.

'Jeanie, my grandmother's treated us both badly,' he said and his tone was one of conciliation. 'I don't know what you wanted but you surely can't have expected this.'

She started at that. The anger she'd heard from him had

disappeared. What came through now was reason and caution, as if he wasn't sure how to proceed.

That made two of them.

'She hasn't treated me badly.' She made herself say it lightly but she knew it was true. Eileen had had no cause to offer her a job and a livelihood in this castle. There'd been no obligation. Eileen's action had been pure generosity.

'Your grandmother has been very, very good to me,' she added, chopping butter and starting to rub it into the new lot of flour. The action was soothing—an age-old task that calmed something deep within—and almost took her mind off the sex-on-legs image standing in the doorway. Almost. 'I've loved living and working here but jobs don't last forever. I don't have any right to be here.'

'You were married to Alan. You were… You *are* family.'

It was as if he was forcing himself to say it, she thought. He was forcing himself to be nice?

'The marriage was brief and it was a disaster,' she said curtly. 'I'm no longer your family—I'm your grandmother's ex-employee. I'm happy to keep running the castle until it's sold but then… Then I'm happy to go.' Liar, liar, pants on fire, she added silently to herself. It'd break her heart to leave; it'd break her heart to see the castle sold to the highest bidder. She had so little money to go anywhere, but there was no way she was baring her heart to this man.

Right now she was almost afraid of him. He was leaning against the doorjamb, watching her. He looked a warrior, as fierce and as ruthless as the reputation of the great lineage of Duncairn chieftains preceding him.

He was no such thing, she told herself fiercely. He was just a McBride, another one, and she needed to get away from here fast.

'But if we married, you could keep the castle.'

Jeanie's hands stilled. She stood motionless. In truth, she was counting breaths, or lack of them.

He'd said it as if it were the most reasonable thing in the world. *If you give me a penny, I'll give you an apple.* It was that sort of statement.

Ten, eleven, twelve... She'd have to breathe soon.

'Maybe it's reasonable,' Alasdair continued while she wondered if her breathing intended starting again. 'Maybe it's the only sensible course of action.' He'd taken his jacket off and rolled his sleeves. His arms were folded. They were great, brawny arms, arms that gave the lie to the fact that he was a city financier. His kilt made him seem even more a warrior.

He was watching her—as a panther watched its prey?

'It'd get us both what we want,' he said, still watchful. 'Alone, we walk away from everything we've worked for. Eileen's will is a nightmare but it doesn't have to be a total disaster. We need to work around it.'

'By...marrying?' Her voice came out a squeak but she was absurdly grateful it came out at all.

'It's the only way you can keep the castle.'

'I don't want the castle.'

That stopped him. His face stilled, as if he wasn't sure where to take it from there.

'No matter what Eileen's will says, the castle should never be my inheritance,' she managed. She was fighting to keep her voice as reasonable as his. 'The castle's my job, but that's all it is. You're the Earl of Duncairn. The castle's your ancestral home. Your grandmother's suggestion might be well-meant, but it's so crazy I don't believe we should even talk about it.'

'We need to talk about it.'

'We don't. I'm sorry your grandmother has left you in such a situation but that's for you to sort. Thank you, Lord Duncairn, for considering such a mad option, but I have scones to cook. I'm moving on. I'll work until the lawyer asks me to leave and then I'll be out of your life forever.'

* * *

Whatever he'd expected, it wasn't this. A straight-out refusal to even talk about it.

Okay, it was how he'd reacted, he decided, but he'd had an hour's walk to clear his head. This woman clearly hadn't had time to think it through.

To walk away from a castle... *This* castle.

What else was she angling for?

He watched her work for a bit while she ignored him, but if she thought he'd calmly leave, she was mistaken. This was serious.

Keep it as a business proposition, he told himself. After all, business was what he was good at. Business was what he was *all* about. Make it about money.

'I realise the upkeep would be far too much for you to keep the castle long-term,' he told her, keeping his voice low and measured. Reasoning as he talked. Maybe she was still shocked at not receiving a monetary inheritance. Maybe there was anger behind that calm façade of hers.

'The company has been funding long-term maintenance and restoration,' he continued, refusing to see the look of revulsion on her face. Revulsion? Surely he must be misreading. 'We can continue doing that,' he told her. 'If at the end of the year this inheritance goes through and you don't wish to stay, the company can buy the castle from you.'

'You could afford that?' she demanded, incredulous?

'The company's huge. It can and it seems the most sensible option. You'll find I can be more than generous. Eileen obviously wanted you looked after. Alan was my cousin. I'll do that for him.'

But at that she flashed him a look that could have split stone.

'I don't need looking after,' she snapped. 'I especially don't need looking after by the McBride men.'

He got it then. Her anger wasn't just encompassing Eileen and her will. Her anger was directed at the McBride family as a whole.

She was holding residual anger towards Alan?

Why?

He and Alan had never got on and their mutual dislike had meant they never socialised. He'd met Jeanie a couple of times before she and Alan had married. Jeanie had worked as his grandmother's part-time assistant while she was on the island. On the odd times he'd met her she'd been quiet, he remembered, a shadow who'd seemed to know her place. He'd hardly talked to her, but she'd seemed… suitable. A suitable assistant for his grandmother.

And then Alan had married her. What a shock and what a disaster—and Jeanie had been into it up to her neck.

Until today he'd seen her as a money-grubbing mouse. The fire in her eyes now suggested the mouse image might possibly be wrong.

'Jeanie, this isn't about looking after—'

'Don't Jeanie me.' She glowered and went back to rubbing butter. 'I'm Mrs McBride. I'm Duncairn's housekeeper for the next few weeks and then I'm nothing to do with you.'

'Then we've both lost.'

'I told you, I've lost nothing. The castle's my place of employment, nothing more.'

'So you wouldn't mind moving to Edinburgh?'

Her hands didn't even pause. She just kept rubbing in the already rubbed-in butter, and her glower moved up a notch.

'Don't talk nonsense. I'm moving nowhere.'

'But you *are* moving out of the castle.'

'Which is none of your business.'

'I'm offering you a job.'

'I don't want a job.'

'If you don't have the castle, you need a job.'

'Don't mess with me, Alasdair McBride. By the way, the kitchen's out of bounds to guests. That's what you are now. A guest. The estate's in the hands of the executors, and I'm employed here. You have a bed booked for the night. The library, the dining room and your bedroom and sitting room are where you're welcome. Meanwhile I have work to do.'

'Jeanie…'

'What?' She pushed the bowl away from her with a vicious shove. 'Don't play games with me, Alasdair. Your cousin messed with my life and I should have moved away then. Right away.'

'I want to help.'

'No, you don't. You want your inheritance.'

'Yes,' he said and he lost it then, the cool exterior he carefully presented to the world. 'Yes, I do. The Duncairn financial empire is colossal and far-reaching. It's also my life. To break it up and use it to fund dogs' homes…'

'There are some very deserving dogs,' she snapped and then looked under the table to where Eileen's two dopey spaniels lay patiently waiting for crumbs. 'These two need a home. You can provide for them first.'

'Look!' He swore and hauled his phone from his sporran —these things were a sight more useful than pockets—and clicked the phone open. He flicked through a few screens and then turned it to face her. 'Look!'

'I have flour on my hands.' She glowered some more and she looked…sulky. Sulky but cute, he thought, and suddenly he found himself thinking…

Um…no. Not appropriate. All this situation needed was a bit of sensual tension and the thing was shot. He needed to stay calm, remember who she was and talk sense.

'Just look,' he said patiently and she sighed and rubbed her hands on her apron and peered at the screen.

'What am I looking at?'

'At a graph of Duncairn's listed charitable donations made in the last financial year,' he told her. 'The figure to the left represents millions. It scrolls off the screen but you can see the biggest beneficiaries. My grandfather and my grandmother after him refused to make Duncairn a listed company, so for years now the profits have either been siphoned back into the company to expand our power base, or used to fund worthwhile projects. AIDS, malaria, smallpox… Massive health projects have all been beneficiaries. Then there are smaller projects. Women's refuges, otter conservation, even dogs' homes.'

And Jeanie seemed caught. 'Those bars are…millions?' she whispered.

'Millions.'

'Then what was Eileen thinking, to leave the lot to just one cause?'

'You know what she was thinking,' Alasdair said wearily. 'We both do. She was blackmailing us into marriage, and as far as I can see, she's succeeded. I have no choice.' He sighed. 'The value of the castle ought to be enough for you, but if it's not, I'll pay you what you ask. I'll mortgage what I have to. Is that what you're after? You can name your terms but look at the alternative to us both. Use your head. I have no expectations of you, and I'll expect nothing from you as my wife. Eileen's will says we have to share a house for one full year before the inheritance is finalised, but I have a huge place in Edinburgh. I'll fund you well enough so you can be independent. Jeanie, do this, if not for the charities I represent, then for you. You'll earn even more than the castle this way. You've won. I concede. We'll marry and then we'll move on.'

And then he stopped. There was no more argument to present.

There was total silence and it lasted for a very long time.

* * *

Marriage…

Third-time lucky? The thought flashed through her mind and she put it away with a hollow, inward laugh. Lucky? With this man?

What he was proposing was purely business. Maybe that was the way to go.

This was a marriage for sensible, pragmatic reasons, she told herself, fighting desperately for logic. She could even feel noble, saving the Duncairn billions for the good of all the charities it assisted.

Noble? Ha. She'd feel sullied. Bought.

He thought she'd walk away with a fortune. If he only knew… But there was no point in telling him about the bankruptcy hanging over her head.

'Would you like to see through the place in Edinburgh?' he said at last. 'It's good, and big enough for us never to see each other. I'll have contracts drawn up that'll give you a generous income during the year, and of course we'll need a prenuptial agreement.'

'So I don't bleed you for anything else?'

'That wasn't what I was thinking.' But of course it was. It was an easy supposition—a woman who'd angled for the castle would no doubt think of marriage in terms of what she could get. 'But the castle will be worth—'

'Shut up and let me think.'

Whoa.

This woman was the hired help. She could see him thinking it. She was his cousin's leavings. The offer he'd made was extraordinary. That she would tell him to shut up…

He opened his mouth to reply, she glared—and he shut up.

More silence.

Could she? she thought. Dared she?

She thought suddenly of Maggie, her best friend on the island. Maggie was a fisherman's wife now, and the mother of two bright boys. Maggie was solid, sensible. She imagined Maggie's reaction when…if…she told her the news.

You're marrying another one? Are you out of your mind?

She almost grinned. It'd almost be worth it to hear the squeal down the phone.

But…

Act with your head. Do not be distracted, she told herself. You've done this in haste twice now. Get this right.

Marriage.

For a year. For only a year.

She'd have to live in Edinburgh, on Alasdair's terms.

No. Even the thought left her exposed, out of control, feeling as she'd vowed never to feel again. No and no and no.

She needed time to think, but that wasn't going to happen. Alasdair was leaning back, watching her, and she knew if she left this kitchen without making a decision the memory of this man would make her run. Physically, he was a stronger, darker version of Alan.

Alan had betrayed her, used her, conned her, but until that last appalling night he'd never frightened her. But this man… It was almost as if he were looking straight through her.

So leave, she told herself. It'd be easy, to do what she'd first thought when the terms of the will were spelled out. She could stay with Maggie until she found a job.

A job, on Duncairn? There weren't any.

She glanced around her, at the great kitchen, at the big old range she'd grown to love, at the two dopey dogs at her feet. This place had been her refuge. She'd built it up with such care. Eileen had loved it and so had Jeanie.

It would have broken Eileen's heart if she'd known Alasdair was forced to let it go. Because of her? Because she lacked courage?

What if…? What if…?

'Think about it overnight,' Alasdair said, pushing himself away from the door. 'But I'm leaving in the morning. I need a decision by then.'

'I've made my decision.'

He stilled.

She'd poured the milk into the flour and turned it to dough without noticing. Now she thumped the dough out of the bowl and flattened it. She picked up her cutter and started cutting, as if perfectly rounded scones were the only thing that mattered in the world.

'Jeanie…'

She shook her head, trying to figure how to say it. She finished cutting her scones, she reformed and flattened the remaining dough, she cut the rest, she arranged them on the tray and then she paused.

She stared down at the scone tray. They were overworked, too. They wouldn't rise properly. She should give up now.

But she wouldn't give up. She'd loved Eileen. Okay, Eileen, you win, she told her silently and then she forced herself to look at the man before her.

'I'll do it if I can stay here,' she managed.

He didn't get it. He didn't understand where this was going, but business acumen told him not to rush in. To wait until she spelled out terms.

She was staring down at her scones. She put her hands on her waist and her head to one side, as if considering. She was considering the scones. Not him.

She had a tiny waist, he thought irrelevantly, for one so…curvy. She was wearing a tailored suit under her apron—for the funeral. Her suit had showed off her neat figure, but the tight ribbons of the apron accentuated it even more. She was curvy at the bottom and curvy at the top... Um, very curvy, he conceded. Her hair was tied up in a knot but wisps were escaping.

She had a smudge of flour on her cheek. He'd like to...

Um, he wouldn't like. Was he out of his mind? This was business. Stick to what was important.

He forced himself to relax, walking forward so he had his back to the fire. Moving closer.

He felt rather than saw her flush.

Inexplicably, he still had the urge to remove that smudge of flour, to trace the line of her cheekbone, but the stiffening of her spine, the bracing of her shoulders, told him he might well get a face covered in scone dough for his pains.

'We'd need to live in Edinburgh,' he said at last, cautiously.

'Then there's not even the smidgeon of a deal.'

'Why the hell...?'

And at that she whirled and met his gaze full on, her green eyes flashing defiance. She was so close...

She was so angry.

'Once upon a time I ached to get off this island,' she snapped. 'Once upon a time I was a fool. The islanders—with the exception of my father—support and care for me. In Edinburgh I have no one. I'd be married to a man I don't know and I can't trust. I've married in haste before, Alasdair McBride, and I'll not do so again. You have much more to gain from this arrangement than I have, so here are my terms. I'll marry you for a year as long as you agree to stay in this castle. Then, at the end of the year, I'll inherit what the will has decreed I inherit. Nothing more. But meanwhile, you live in this castle—in my home, Alasdair—and you live on my terms for the year. It's that or nothing.'

'That's ridiculous.' He could feel her anger, vibrating

in waves, like electric current, surging from her body to his and back again.

'Take it or leave it,' she said and she deliberately turned her back, deliberately broke the connection. She picked up her tray of unbaked scones and slid them into the trash. 'I'm trying again,' she told him, her back to him. 'Third-time lucky? It might work for scones.'

He didn't understand. 'I can't live here.'

'That's your decision,' she told him. 'But I have some very fine whisky I'm willing to share.'

'I'm not interested in whisky!' It was an explosion and Jeanie stilled again.

'Not?'

'This is business.'

'The whole year will be business,' she retorted, turning to the sink with her tray. 'I'm thinking it'll be shortbread for the guests tonight. What do you think?'

'I don't care what you give your guests.'

'But, you see, they'll be your guests, too, Lord Duncairn,' she told him. 'If you decide on marriage, then I'll expect you to play host. If you could keep wearing your kilt—a real Scottish lord playing host in his castle—I'll put you on the website. It'll pull the punters in in droves.'

'You're out of your mind.'

'And so was Eileen when she made that will,' Jeanie told him, still with her back to him. 'So all we can do is make the most of it. As I said, take it or leave it. We can be Lord and Lady of the castle together or we can be nothing at all. Your call, Lord Duncairn. I need to get on with my baking.'

CHAPTER THREE

Four weeks later Lord Alasdair Duncan Edward McBride, Sixteenth Earl of Duncairn, stood in the same kirk where his grandmother's funeral had taken place, waiting for his bride.

He'd wanted a register office. They both had. Jeanie was deeply uncomfortable about taking her vows in a church, but Eileen's will had been specific. Marriage in the kirk or nothing. Jeanie had felt ill when the lawyer had spelled it out, but then she'd looked again at the list of charities supported by the Duncairn foundation, she'd thought again of the old lady she'd loved, and she'd decided God would forgive her.

'It's not that I don't support dogs' homes,' she told Maggie Campbell, her best friend and her rock today. 'But I feel a bit of concern for AIDS and malaria and otters as well. I'm covering all bases. Though it does seem to the world like I'm buying myself a castle with marriage.' She hadn't told Maggie of the debt. She'd told no one. The whole island think this deal would be her being a canny Scot.

'Well, no one's judging you if you are,' Maggie said soundly, hugging her friend and then adjusting the spray of bell heather in Jeanie's simple blue frock. 'Except me. I would have so loved you to be a bride.'

'I should have worn my suit. I'm not a bride. I'm half a

contract,' Jeanie retorted, glancing at her watch and thinking five minutes to go, five minutes left when she could walk out of here. Or run. Honestly, what was she doing? Marrying another McBride?

But Maggie's sister was a lawyer, and Maggie's sister had read the fine print and she'd got the partners in her firm to read the fine print and then she'd drawn up a prenuptial agreement for both Jeanie and Alasdair to sign and it still seemed…sensible.

'This is business only,' she said aloud now, and Maggie stood back and looked at her.

'You look far too pretty to be a business deal. Jeanie, tomorrow you'll be the Lady of Duncairn.'

'I… He doesn't use the title.' She'd tried joking about that to Alasdair. She'd even proposed using it in castle advertising but the black look on his face had had her backing right off. You didn't joke with Lord Alasdair.

Just Alasdair. Her soon-to-be husband.

Her…lord?

'It doesn't stop the title being there, My Ladyship.' Maggie bobbed a mock curtsy as she echoed Jeanie's thoughts. 'It's time to go to church now, m'lady. If m'lady's ready.'

Jeanie managed a laugh but even to her ears it sounded hollow. She glanced at her watch again. Two minutes. One.

'Ready, set, go,' Maggie said and propelled her to the door.

To marry.

Third-time lucky?

He was standing at the altar, waiting for his bride. He'd never thought he'd be here. Marriage was not for him.

He hadn't always believed that, he conceded. Once upon a time he'd been head over heels in love. He'd been twenty-two, just finishing a double degree in law and commerce, eager to take on the world. Celia had been a socialite, five years his senior. She was beautiful, intelligent, a woman who knew her way around Scottish society and who knew exactly what she wanted in a marriage.

He couldn't believe she'd wanted him. He'd been lanky, geeky, unsure, a product of cold parents and too many books, knowing little of how relationships worked. He'd been ripe for the plucking.

And Celia had plucked. When she'd agreed to marry him, he'd thought he was the luckiest man alive. What he hadn't realised was that when she was looking at him she was seeing only his title and his inheritance.

But she'd played her part superbly. She'd held him as he'd never been held. She'd listened as he'd told her of his childhood, things he'd never told anyone. He'd had fun with her. He'd felt light and free and totally in love. Totally trusting. He'd bared his soul, he'd left himself totally exposed—and in return he'd been gutted.

For a long time he'd blamed his cousin, Alan, with his charm and charisma. Alan had arrived in Edinburgh a week before he and Celia were due to marry, ostensibly to attend his cousin's wedding but probably to hit his grandmother for more money. He hadn't been involved with Jeanie then. He'd had some other bimbo on his arm, but that hadn't cramped his style. Loyalty hadn't been in Alan's vocabulary.

And it seemed it wasn't in Celia's, either.

Two days before his wedding, Alasdair had realised he'd left his briefcase at Celia's apartment. He'd had a key so he'd dropped by early, before work. He'd knocked, but of course no one had answered.

It was no wonder they hadn't answered. He'd walked in, and Celia had been with Alan. *With*, in every sense of the word.

So now he was about to marry…another of Alan's leavings?

Don't think of Alan now. Don't think of Celia. He said it savagely to himself but the memory was still sour and heavy. He'd never trusted since. His personal relationships were kept far apart from his business.

But here he was again—and he was doing what Celia had intended. Wedding for money?

This woman was different, he conceded. Very different. She was petite. Curvy. She wasn't the slightest bit elegant.

She was Alan's widow.

But right now she didn't look like a woman who'd attract Alan. She was wearing a simple blue frock, neat, nice. Her shoes were kitten-heeled, silver. Her soft brown curls were just brushing her shoulders. She usually wore her hair tied back or up, so maybe this was a concession to being a bride—as must be the spray of bell heather on her lapel—but they were sparse concessions.

Celia would have been the perfect bride, he thought tangentially. That morning, when he'd walked in on them both, Celia's bridal gown had been hanging for him to see. Even years later he still had a vision of how Celia would have looked in that dress.

She wouldn't have looked like this. Where Celia would have floated down the aisle, an ethereal vision, Jeanie was looking straight ahead, her gaze on the worn kirk floorboards rather than on him. Her friend gave her a slight push. She nodded as if confirming something in her mind—and then she stumped forward. There was no other word for it. She stumped.

A romantic bride? Not so much.

Though she was…cute, he conceded as he watched her come, and then he saw the flush of colour on her cheeks and he thought suddenly she looked…mortified?

Mortified? As if she'd been pushed into this?

It was his grandmother who'd done the forcing, he told himself. If this woman had been expecting the castle to fall into her lap with no effort, it was Eileen who'd messed with those plans, not him. This forced marriage was merely the solution to the problem.

And mortified or not, Jeanie had got what she wanted. She'd inherit her castle.

He'd had to move mountains to arrange things so he could stay on the island. He'd created a new level of management and arranged audits to ensure he hadn't missed anything; financial dealings would run smoothly without him. He'd arranged a satellite Internet connection so he could work here. He'd had a helipad built so he could organise the company chopper to get him here fast. So he could leave fast.

Not that he could leave for more than his designated number of nights, he thought grimly. He was stuck. With this woman.

She'd reached his side. She was still staring stolidly at the floor. Could he sense…fear? He must be mistaken.

But he couldn't help himself reacting. He touched her chin and tilted her face so she had no choice but to meet his gaze.

'I'm not an ogre.'

'No, but—'

'And I'm not Alan. Business only.'

She bit her lip and his suspicion of fear deepened.

Enough. There were few people to see this. Eileen's lawyer was here to see things were done properly. The minister and the organist were essential. Jeanie's friend Maggie completed the party. 'I need Maggie for support,' Jeanie had told him and it did look as if she needed the support right now. His bride was looking like a deer trapped in headlights.

He took her hands and they were shaking.

'Jeanie…'

'Let's…let's…'

'Not if you're not sure of me,' he told her, gentling now, knowing this was the truth. 'No money in the world is worth a forced marriage. If you're afraid, if you don't want it, then neither do I. If you don't trust me, then walk away now.'

What was he saying? He was out of his mind. But he'd had to say it. She was shaking. Acting or not, he had to react to what he saw.

But now her chin was tilting in a gesture he was starting to recognise. She tugged her hands away and she managed a nod of decision.

'Eileen trusted you,' she managed. 'And this is business. For castle, for keeps.' She took a deep breath and turned to the minister. 'Let's get this over with,' she told him. 'Let's get us married.'

The vows they spoke were the vows that were spoken the world over from time immemorial, between man and woman, between lovers becoming man and wife.

'I, Alasdair Duncan Edward McBride, take thee, Jeanie Margaret McBride… To have and to hold. For richer or for poorer. In sickness and in health, for as long as we both shall live.'

He wished—fiercely—that his grandmother hadn't insisted on a kirk. The minister was old and faded, wearing Wellingtons under his well-worn cassock. He was watching them with kindly eyes, encouraging them, treating them as fresh-faced lovers.

For as long as we both shall live…
In his head he corrected himself.
For twelve months and I'm out of here.

For as long as we both shall live…
The words were hard to say. She had to fight to get her tongue around them.

It should be getting easier to say the words she knew were just words.

The past two times, she'd meant them. She really had. They were nonsense.

Stupidly she felt tears pricking at the backs of her eyelids and she blinked them back with a fierceness born of an iron determination. She would not show this man weakness. She would not be weak. This was nothing more than a sensible proposition forced on her by a crazy will.

You understand why I'm doing it, she demanded silently of the absent Eileen. You thought you'd force us to become family. Instead we're doing what we must. You can't force people to love.

She'd tried, oh, she'd tried, but suddenly she was remembering that last appalling night with Alan.

'Do you think I'd have married you if my grandmother hadn't paid through the nose?'

Eileen was doing the same thing now, she thought bleakly. She was paying through the nose.

But I'm doing it for the right reasons. Surely? She looked firmly ahead. Alasdair's body was brushing hers. In his full highland regalia he looked…imposing. Magnificent. Frightening.

She would not be frightened of this man, she told herself. She would not. She'd marry, she'd get on with her life and then she'd walk away.

For as long as we both shall live…

Somehow she made herself say the words. How easy they'd been when she'd meant them but then they'd turned out to be meaningless. Now, when they were meaningless to start with, it felt as if something were dying within.

'You may kiss the bride,' the minister was saying and she felt like shaking her head, turning and running. But the old man was beaming, and Alasdair was taking her hands again. The new ring lay stark against her work-worn fingers.

Alasdair's strong, lean hands now sported a wedding band. Married.

'You may kiss the bride...'

He smiled down at her—for the sake of the kindly old minister marrying them? Surely that was it, but, even so, her heart did a back flip. What if this was real? her treacherous heart said. What if this man really loved...?

Get over it. It's business.

But people were watching. People were waiting. Alasdair was smiling, holding her hands, ready to do what was right.

Kiss the bride.

Right. She took a deep breath and raised her face to his.

'Think of it like going to the dentist,' Alasdair whispered, for her ears alone, and she stared up at him and his smile widened.

And she couldn't help herself. This was ridiculous. The whole thing was ridiculous. Jeanie Lochlan marrying the Earl of Duncairn. For a castle.

She found herself chuckling. It was so ridiculous she could do it. She returned the grip on his hands and she even stood on tiptoe so he could reach her.

His mouth lowered onto hers—and he kissed her.

If only she hadn't chuckled. Up until then it had been fine. Business only. He could do this. He could marry her, he could keep his distance, he could fulfil the letter of the deal and he could walk away at the end of twelve months feeling nothing. He intended to feel nothing.

But that meant he had to stay impervious to what she was; to who she was. He couldn't think of her as his wife at all.

But then she chuckled and something happened.

The old kirk. The beaming minister. The sense of history in this place.

This woman standing beside him.

She was in this for profit, he told himself. She was sure of what she wanted and how she was going to get it. She was Alan's ex-wife and he'd seen how much the pair of them had cost Eileen. He wanted nothing to do with her.

But she was standing before him and he'd felt her fear. He'd felt the effort it had cost her to turn to the minister and say those vows out loud.

And now she'd chuckled.

She was small and curvy and dressed in a simple yet very pretty frock, with white lace collar, tiny lace shoulder puffs and a wide, flouncy skirt cinched in at her tiny waist. She was wearing bell heather on her lapel.

She was chuckling.

And he thought, She's enchanting. And then the thought flooded from nowhere.

She's my wife.

It hit him just as his mouth touched hers. The knowledge was as if a floodgate had opened. This woman…

His wife…

He kissed her.

She'd been expecting…what? A cursory brushing of lips against lips? Or less. He could have done this without actually touching her. That would have been better, she thought. An air kiss. No one here expected any more.

She didn't get an air kiss. He'd released her hands. He put his hands on her waist and he lifted her so her mouth was level with his.

He kissed her.

It was a true wedding kiss, a lordly kiss, the kiss of the Lord of Duncairn claiming his bride. It was a kiss with strength and heat and passion. It was a kiss that blew her fragile defences to smithereens.

She shouldn't respond. She shouldn't! They were in a kirk, for heaven's sake. It wasn't seemly. This was a business arrangement, a marriage of convenience, and he had no right...

And then her mind shut down, just like that.

She'd never been kissed like this. She'd never felt like this.

Fire...

His mouth was plundering hers. She was raised right off her feet. She was totally out of control and there was nothing she could do but submit.

And respond? Maybe she had no choice. Maybe that was the only option because that was what her body was doing. It was responding and responding and responding.

How could it not? This was like an electric charge, a high-voltage jolt that had her locked to him and there was no escape. Not that she wanted to escape. The fire coursing through her body had her feeling...

Here was her home? Here was her heart?

This was nonsense. Crazy. Their tiny audience was laughing and cheering and she fought to bring them into focus. She fought desperately to gather herself, regain some decorum, and maybe Alasdair felt it because finally, finally he set her on her feet. But his dark eyes gleamed at her, and behind that smile was a promise.

This man was her husband. The knowledge was terrifying but suddenly it was also exhilarating. Where were smelling salts when a girl needed them? she thought wildly, and she took a deep, steadying breath and turned resolutely back to the minister. Get this over with, she pleaded silently, and let me get out of here.

But the Reverend Angus McConachie was not finished. He was beaming at her as a father might beam at a favourite daughter. In fact, the Reverend Angus had baptised her, had buried her mother, had caught her and her friends stealing strawberries from his vegetable patch, had been there for all her life. She'd tried to explain to him what this wedding was about but she doubted he'd listened. He saw what he wanted to see, the Reverend Angus, and his next words confirmed it.

'Before I let you go...' he was beaming as if he'd personally played matchmaker, and happy families was just beginning '... I wish to say a few words. I've known our Jeanie since the time she turned from a twinkle in her father's eye into a pretty wee bairn. I've watched her grow into the fine young woman she is today. I know the Lady Eileen felt the same pleasure and pride in her that I do, and I feel the Lady Eileen is looking down right now, giving these two her blessing.'

Okay, Jeanie thought. That'll do. Stop now. But this was the Reverend Angus and she knew he wouldn't.

'But it's been my sorrow to see the tragedies that have befallen our Jeanie,' the minister continued, his beam dipping for a moment. 'She was devoted to her Rory from the time she was a wee lass, she was a fine wife and when the marriage ended in tragedy we were all heartbroken for her. That she was brave enough to try again with her Alan was a testament to her courage—and, dare I say, it was also a testament to the Lady Eileen's encouragement? I dare say there's not an islander on Duncairn whose heart didn't break with her when she came home after such trouble.'

'Angus...' Jeanie hissed, appalled, but Angus's beam was back on high and there was no stopping him.

'And now it's three,' he said happily. 'Third-time lucky. I hear the Lady Eileen has her fingers in the pie this time, too, but she assured me before she died that this one would be a happy ever after.'

'She told you?' Alasdair asked, sounding incredulous.

'She was a conniving lass, your grandmother.' Angus beamed some more. 'And here it is, the results of that conniving, and the islanders couldn't be happier for you. Jeanie, lass, may third time be more than lucky. May your third time be forever.'

Somehow they made it outside, to the steps of the kirk. The church sat on the headland looking over Duncairn Bay. The sun was shining. The fishing fleet was out, but a few smaller boats were tied on swing moorings. Gulls were wheeling overhead, the church grounds were a mass of wild honeysuckle and roses, and the photographer for the island's monthly newsletter was asking them to look their way.

'Smile for the camera… You look so handsome, the pair of you.'

This would make the front cover of the *Duncairn Chronicle*, she knew—*Local Lass Weds Heir to Duncairn*.

Her father would be down in the pub now, she thought, already drinking in anticipation of profits he'd think he could wheedle from her.

'This is the third time?' Alasdair sounded incredulous.

'So?' Her smile was rigidly determined. Alasdair's arm was around her waist, as befitted the standard newlywed couple, but his arm felt like steel. There was not a trace of warmth in it.

'I assumed Alan was the only—'

'You didn't ask,' she snapped. 'Does it matter?'

'Hell, of course it matters. Did you make money from the first one, too?'

Enough. She put her hand behind her and hauled his arm away from her waist. She was still rigidly smiling but she was having trouble…it could so easily turn to rictus.

'Thanks, Susan,' she called to the photographer. 'We're

done. Thanks, everyone, for coming. We need to get back to the castle. We have guests arriving.'

'No honeymoon?' Susan, the photographer, demanded. 'Why don't you go somewhere beautiful?'

'Duncairn is beautiful.'

'She won't even close the castle to guests for a few days,' Maggie said and Jeanie gritted her teeth and pushed the smile a bit harder.

'It's business as usual,' she told them. 'After all, this is the third time I've married. I'm thinking the romance has worn off by now. It's time to get back to work.'

Alasdair drove them back to the castle. He'd bought an expensive SUV—brand-new. It had been delivered via the ferry, last week before Alasdair had arrived. Alasdair himself had arrived by helicopter this morning, a fact that made Jeanie feel as if things were happening far too fast—as if things were out of her control. She'd been circling the SUV all week, feeling more and more nervous.

She wasn't a 'luxury-car type'. She wasn't the type to marry a man who arrived by helicopter. But she had to get used to it, she told herself, and she'd driven the thing down to the kirk feeling…absurd.

'It's gorgeous,' Maggie had declared. 'And he's said you can drive it? Fabulous. You can share.'

'This marriage isn't about sharing, and my little banger is twenty years old. She's done me proud and she'll keep doing me proud.'

'Och, but I can see you sitting up beside your husband in this, looking every inch the lady.' Maggie had laughed and she'd almost got a swipe to the back of her head for her pains.

But now… She was doing exactly that, Jeanie thought. She was sitting primly in the front passenger seat with her hands folded on her lap. She was staring straight ahead and beside her was…her husband.

'Third time…'

It was the first time he'd spoken to her out of the hearing of their guests. As an opening to a marriage it was hardly encouraging.

'Um…' Jeanie wasn't too sure where to go.

'You've been married three times.' His mind was obviously in a repetitive loop, one that he didn't like a bit. His hands were clenched white on the steering wheel. He was going too fast for this road.

'Cattle and sheep have the right of way here,' she reminded him. 'And the cattle are tough wee beasties. You round a bend too fast and you'll have a horn through your windscreen.'

'We're not talking about cattle.'

'Right,' she said and subsided. His car. His problem.

'Three…' he said again and she risked a glance at his face. Grim as death. As if she'd conned him?

'Okay, as of today, I've been married three times.'

He was keeping his temper under control but she could feel the pressure building.

'Did my grandmother know?' His incredulity was like a flame held to a wick of an already ticking bomb.

But if he thought he had sole rights to anger, he had another thought coming. As if she'd deceive Eileen…

'Of course she knew. Eileen knew everything about me. I…loved her.'

And the look he threw her was so filled with scorn she flinched and clenched her hands in her lap and looked the other way.

Silence. Silence, silence and more silence. Maybe that's what this marriage will be all about, she thought bleakly. One roof, but strangers. Silence, with undercurrents of…

hatred? That was what it felt like. As if the man beside her hated her.

'Was he rich, too?' Alasdair asked and enough was enough.

'Stop.'

'What…?'

'Stop the car this instant.'

'Why should I?'

But they were rounding a tight bend, where even Alasdair had to slow. She unclipped her seat belt and pushed her door wide. 'Stop now because I'm getting out, whether you've stopped or not. Three, two…'

He jammed on the brakes and she was out of the door before they were completely still.

He climbed out after her. 'What the…?'

'I'm walking,' she told him. 'I don't do dinner for guests but seeing you live at the castle now you can have the run of the kitchen. Make yourself what you like. Have a happy marriage, Alasdair McBride. Your dislike of me means we need to be as far apart as we can, so we might as well start now.'

And she turned and started stomping down the road.

She could do this. It was only three miles, and if there was one thing Jeanie had learned to do over the years, it was walk. She loved this country. She loved the wildness of it, the sheer natural beauty. She knew every nook and cranny of the island. She knew the wild creatures. The sheep hardly startled at her coming and she knew each of the highland cattle by name.

But she was currently wearing a floaty dress and heels. Not stilettos, she conceded, thanking her lucky stars, but they were kitten heels and she wasn't accustomed to kitten heels.

Maybe when Alasdair was out of sight she'd slip them off and walk barefoot.

Ouch.

Nevertheless, a girl had some pride. She'd made her bed and she needed to lie on it. Or walk.

She walked. There was no sound of an engine behind her but she wasn't looking back.

And then a hand landed on her shoulder and she almost yelped. Almost. A girl had some pride.

'Don't,' she managed and pulled away to keep stomping. And then she asked, because she couldn't help herself, 'Where did you learn to walk like a cat?'

'Deerstalking. As a kid. My grandpa gave me a camera for my eighth birthday.'

'You mean you don't have fifty sets of antlers on your sitting-room walls back in Edinburgh?' She was still stomping.

'Nary an antler. Jeanie—'

'Mrs McBride to you.'

'Lady Jean,' he said and she stopped dead and closed her eyes. *Lady Jean...*

Her dad would be cock-a-hoop. He'd be drunk by now, she thought, boasting to all and sundry that his girl was now lady of the island.

His girl.

Rory... She'd never been her father's girl, but Rory used to call her that.

'My lass. My sweet island lassie, my good luck charm, the love of my life...'

That this man could possibly infer she'd married for money...

'Go away,' she breathed. 'Leave me be and take your title and your stupid, cruel misconceptions with you.'

And she started walking again.

To her fury he fell in beside her.

'Go away.'

'We need to talk.'

'Your car's on a blind bend.'

'This is my land.'

'*Your* land?'

There was a moment's loaded pause. She didn't stop walking.

'Okay, *your* land,' he conceded at last. 'The access road's on the castle title. As of marrying, as of today, it's yours.'

'You get the entire Duncairn company. Does that mean you're a bigger fortune hunter than me?'

'I guess it does,' he said. 'But at least my motive is pure. How much of Alan's money do you have left?'

And there was another statement to take her breath away. She was finding it hard to breathe. Really hard.

Time for some home truths? More than time. She didn't want sympathy, but this…

'You'd think,' she managed, slowly, because each word was costing an almost superhuman effort, 'that you'd have done some homework on your intended bride. This is a business deal. If you're buying, Alasdair McBride, surely you should have checked out the goods before purchase.'

'It seems I should.' He was striding beside her. What did he think he was doing? Abandoning the SUV and hiking all the way to the castle?

'I have guests booked in at four this afternoon,' she hissed. 'They'll be coming round that bend. Your car is blocking the way.'

'You mean it's blocking your profits?'

Profits. She stopped mid-stride and closed her eyes. She counted to ten and then another ten. She tried to do a bit of deep breathing. Her fingers clenched and re-clenched.

Nothing was working. She opened her eyes and he was

still looking at her as if she was tainted goods, a bad smell. He'd married someone he loathed.

Someone who married for profit... Of all the things she'd ever been accused of...

She smacked him.

She'd never smacked a man in her life. She'd never smacked anyone. She was a woman who used Kindly Mousers and carried the captured mice half a mile to release them. She swore they beat her back to the castle but still she kept trying. She caught spiders and put them outside. She put up with dogs under her bed because they looked so sad when she put them in the wet room.

But she had indeed smacked him.

She'd left a mark. *No!*

Her hands went to her own face. She wanted to sink into the ground. She wanted to run. Of all the stupid, senseless things she'd done in her life, this was the worst. She'd married a man who made her so mad she'd hit him.

She'd mopped up after Rory's fish for years. She'd watched his telly. She'd coped with the meagre amount he'd allowed her for housekeeping—and she'd never once complained.

And Alan... She thought of the way he'd treated her and still... She'd never once even considered hitting.

But now... What was she thinking? Of all the stupid, dumb mistakes, to put herself in a situation where she'd ended up violent...

Well, then...

Well, then what? A lesser woman might have burst into tears but not Jeanie. She wasn't about to show this man tears, no matter how desperate things were.

Move on, she told herself, forcing herself to think past the surge of white-hot anger. Get a grip, woman. Get yourself out of this mess, the fastest way you can. But first...

She'd smacked him and the action was indefensible. Do what comes next, she told herself. Apologise.

'I'm sorry.' Somehow she got it out. He was staring at her as if she'd grown two heads, and who could blame him? How many times had the Lord of Castle Duncairn been slapped?

Not often enough, a tiny voice whispered, but she wasn't going there. No violence, not ever. Had she learned nothing?

'I'm very sorry,' she made herself repeat. 'That was inexcusable. No matter what you said, I should never, ever have hit you. I hope... I hope it doesn't hurt.'

'Hurt?' He was still eyeing her with incredulity. 'You hit me and ask if it hurts? If I say no, will you do it again?' And it was almost as if he was goading her.

She stared at him, but her stare was blind.

'I won't...hit you.'

'What have I possibly said to deserve that?'

'You judged me.'

'I did. Tell me what's wrong about my judgement.'

'You want the truth?'

'Tell me something I don't know,' he said wearily and her hand itched again.

Enough. No more. Say it and get out.

He wanted the truth? He wanted something he didn't know? She took a deep breath and steadied.

Let him have it, then, she told herself. After all, the only casualty was her pride, and surely she ought to be over pride by now.

'Okay, then.' She was feeling ill, cold and empty. She hated what she was about to say. She hated everything that went with it.

But he was her husband, she thought bitterly. For now. For better or for worse she'd made the vows. The marriage would need to be annulled and fast, but meanwhile the truth was there for the telling. Pride had to take a back seat.

'I make no profit. I won't inherit the castle, no matter how married I am,' she told him. 'Believe it or not, I did this for you—or for your inheritance, for the Duncairn legacy Eileen cared so much about. But if I can't see you without wanting to hit out, then it's over. No lies are worth it, no false vows, no inheritance, nothing. I've tried my best but it's done.'

Done? The world stilled.

It was a perfect summer's day, a day for soaking in every ounce of pleasure in preparation for the bleak winter that lay ahead. But there was no pleasure here. There was only a man and a woman, and a chasm between them a mile deep.

Done.

'What do you mean?' he asked at last.

'I mean even if we managed to stay married for a year, I can't inherit,' she told him, in a dead, cold voice she scarcely recognised. 'I've checked with two lawyers and they both tell me the same thing. Alan left me with massive debts. For the year after his death I tried every way I could to figure some way to repay them but in the end there was only one thing to do. I had myself declared bankrupt.'

'Bankrupt?' He sounded incredulous. Did he still think she was lying? She didn't care, she decided. She was so tired she wanted to sink.

'That was almost three years ago,' she forced herself to continue. 'But bankruptcy lasts for three years and the lawyers' opinions are absolute. Because Eileen died within the three-year period, any inheritance I receive, no matter when I receive it, becomes part of my assets. It reverts to the bankruptcy trustees to be distributed between Alan's creditors. The fact that most of those creditors are any form of low-life you care to name is irrelevant. So that's it—the only one who stood to gain from this marriage was you. I agreed to marry you because I knew Eileen would hate the estate to be lost, but now… Alasdair, I should never have agreed in the first place. I'm sick of being judged. I'm tired to death of being a McBride, and if it's driving me to hitting, then I need to call it quits. I did this for Eileen but the price is too high. Enough.'

She took off her shoes, then wheeled and started walking.

Where was a spacecraft when she needed one? 'Beam me up, Scotty…' What she'd give to say those words.

Her feet wouldn't go fast enough.

'Jeanie…' he called at last but she didn't even slow.

'Take your car home,' she threw over her shoulder. 'The agreement's off. Everything's off. I'll see a lawyer and get the marriage annulled—I'll do whatever I need to do. I'd agreed to look after the castle for the next few weeks but that's off, too. So sue me. You can be part of my creditor list. I'll camp in Maggie's attic tonight and I'm on the first ferry out of here tomorrow.'

'You can't,' he threw after her, sounding stunned, but she still didn't turn. She didn't dare.

'Watch me. When I reach the stage where I hit out, I know enough is enough. I've been enough of a fool for one lifetime. Foolish stops now.'

CHAPTER FOUR

THERE WAS ONE advantage to living on an island—there were only two ferries a day. Actually it was usually a disadvantage, but right now it played into Alasdair's hands. Jeanie might be heading to Maggie's attic tonight but she'd still be here in the morning. He had time.

He needed time. He needed to play catch up. Jeanie was right: if she'd been a business proposition, he would have researched before he invested.

An undischarged bankrupt? How had he not known? The complications made his head spin.

The whole situation made his head spin.

He tried to get her to ride home with him but she refused. Short of hauling her into the SUV by force he had to let her be, but he couldn't let her walk all the way. He figured that was the way to fuel her fury and she was showing enough fury as it was. He therefore drove back to the castle, found her car keys hanging on a nail in the kitchen, drove her car back along the track until he reached her, soundlessly handed her the keys, then turned and walked back himself.

She must have spent a good hour trying to figure out how not to accept his help, or maybe she didn't want to pass him on the track. Either way, he was back at the castle when her car finally nosed its way onto the castle sweep.

Maybe he should have talked to her then, but he didn't have all the facts. He needed them.

Luckily he had help, a phone call away.

'Find anything there is to find out about Jeanie Lochlan, born on Duncairn twenty-nine years ago,' he told his secretary. Elspeth was his right-hand woman in Edinburgh. If anyone could unearth anything, it was her.

'Haven't you just married her?' Elspeth ventured.

'Don't ask. Just look,' he snapped and whatever Elspeth heard in his voice he didn't care.

Jeanie was back in her rooms downstairs. He was in his sitting room right over hers. He could hear her footsteps going back and forth, back and forth. Packing?

Finally he heard her trudge towards the front door.

He met her at the foot of the castle stairs and tried to take an enormous suitcase from her.

'I can manage.' Her voice dripped ice. 'I can cope by myself.'

And what was it about those few words that made him flinch?

She was shoving her case into the back of her battered car and he was feeling as if...feeling as if...

As if maybe he'd messed something up. Something really important.

Yes, he had. He'd messed up the entire Duncairn empire, but right now it felt much more personal.

She closed the lid of the boot on her car and returned. He stood and watched as she headed for the kitchen, grabbed crates and wads of newspaper and headed for the library.

He followed and stood at the door as she wrapped and stowed every whisky bottle that was more than a third full.

The B & B guests would come back tonight and be shattered, he thought. Half the appeal of this place on the web was the simple statement: *'Genuine Scottish Castle,*

*with every whisky of note that this grand country's ever
made free to taste.'*

He'd seen the website and had congratulated his grandmother on such a great selling idea.

'The whisky's Jeanie's idea,' Eileen had told him. 'I told
her I thought the guests would drink themselves silly, but
she went ahead and bought them anyway, out of her own
salary. She lets me replenish it now, but the original outlay
and idea were hers. So far no one's abused it. The guests
love it, and you're right, it's brilliant.'

And the guests were still here. They'd want their
whisky.

'And don't even think about claiming it,' she snapped
as she wrapped and stowed. 'I bought the first lot out of
my wages so it's mine. Be grateful I'm only taking what's
left. Alasdair, you can contact Maggie if you want my for-
warding address…for legalities. For marriage annulment.
For getting us out of this final foolishness. Meanwhile
that's it. I'm done and out of here. From this day forth I'm
Jeanie Lochlan, and if I never see a McBride again, it'll
be too soon.'

She picked up her first crate of whisky and headed to
the car. Silently he lifted the second and carried it after her.

She shoved both crates into the back seat and slammed
the door after them. Her little car shuddered. It really was
a banger, he thought.

Alan's wife. An undischarged bankrupt. Alan… He
thought of his cousin and he felt ill.

'Jeanie, can we talk?'

'We've talked. Goodbye.' She stuck out her hand and
waited until he took it, then shook it with a fierceness that
surprised him. Then she looked up at his face, gave one
decisive nod and headed for the driver's seat.

'I'm sorry about the castle,' she threw at him. She could
no longer see him. She was hauling on her seat belt, mov-

ing on. 'And I'm sorry about your company. On the up-side, there are going to be some very happy dogs all over Europe.'

He stood and watched her as she headed out of the castle grounds, along the cliff road towards the village. When she disappeared from view he watched on.

His entire financial empire had just come crashing down. He should be gutted.

He was gutted but what was uppermost in his mind right now was that he'd hurt her. She'd hit him but the next moment she'd drawn back as if he'd been the one who'd hit her.

He had made assumptions, he thought, but those assumptions had been based on facts. He knew how much money Eileen had withdrawn from the company when Jeanie and Alan had married. 'It'll set them up for life,' Eileen had told him. 'I know Alan's not interested in the company but he is my grandson. He wants his inheritance now, and if it helps him settle, then he should have it.'

The amount she'd given the pair had been eye-watering. And yes, Alan's lifestyle had been ruinous but his death must have meant most of the capital was intact. Surely Alan couldn't have gambled that much?

Surely?

He'd always thought Jeanie's decision to come back here to the castle was an attempt to ingratiate herself with his grandmother. The contents of Eileen's will had proved him right.

The sight of her heading away in her ancient car gave him pause.

An undischarged bankruptcy…

If it was true, then the castle was forfeit no matter whether they married or not.

And with that thought came another. He'd loved the castle since he was a child, even when it was little more than a ruin. Eileen's restoration had made it fabulous. She'd been overwhelmingly proud of it—and so was he. He gazed up now at the turrets and towers, the age-old battlements, the great, grand home that had sheltered so many generations of his family. That had provided work for so many islanders...

He was the Lord of Duncairn. Even though he no longer used it, the title, but the castle and the island were still important to him. Desperately important. With her leaving, Jeanie had sealed the castle's fate. It would leave the family forever.

He was forcing his mind to think tangentially. If what she'd just told him was based on facts, then it wasn't Jeanie who'd sealed the castle's fate. It had been Alan.

He thought suddenly of the night Alan had been killed. He'd been driving a brand-new sports car, far too fast. A clear road. An inexplicable swerve to the left, a massive tree.

Jeanie had been thrown clear, suffering minor injuries. Alan had died instantly.

He'd thought until now it had been alcohol or drugs that had caused the crash, but now... Had it been suicide? Because of debt?

Had he tried to take Jeanie with him?

He'd been too caught up with Eileen's grief to ask questions. What sort of fool had he been?

A car was approaching, a low-slung, crimson sports car. The couple inside wore expensive clothes and designer sunglasses. The car spun onto the driveway, sending up a spray of gravel. The pair climbed out, looking at the castle in awe.

And they also looked at Alasdair. He was still in his wedding finery. Lord of his castle?

He'd lose the castle. Alan had gambled it away.

And he'd gambled more than the castle away. Jeanie…
He'd gambled with her life.

'Hi, there.' The young man was clearly American, and
he was impervious to the fact that Alasdair's gaze was
still following Jeanie's car. He flicked the boot open and
pointed to the baggage, then turned back to his partner.
'This looks cool,' he told her. 'And check out the doorman.
Great touch.' And he tossed the car keys to Alasdair, who
was so stunned that he actually caught them.

'This is just what we ordered—real Scotland,' he continued. 'Wow, look at those ruins down by the sea. You
can put them on the Internet, honey. And check out the
battlements. I've half a mind to put in an offer for the place,
doorman and all. But first, my love, let's check out this
whisky.' He glanced back at Alasdair. 'What are you waiting for, man? We need our bags straight away.'

'Carry your own bags,' Alasdair snapped. 'I don't work
in this place. I own it.'

Only he didn't.

'As far as short marriages go, this must be a record.'

Down in the village, Maggie had chosen a top-of-the-
range bottle from Jeanie's crates and had poured two
whiskies. They were sitting at Maggie's kitchen table, surrounded by the clutter of Maggie's kids, Maggie's fisherman husband and the detritus of a busy family. The ancient
stove was giving out gentle warmth but Jeanie couldn't
stop shaking. Maggie's hug had made her feel better, the
whisky should be helping, but she had a way to go before
shock lessened.

'So the marriage lasted less than an hour,' Maggie continued. 'I'm guessing…not consummated?'

'Maggie!'

'Just asking.' Maggie grinned and raised her glass.
'You might need to declare that to get an annulment—

or am I thinking of the bad old days when they checked the sheets?'

'I can hardly get a doctor to declare me a virgin,' Jeanie retorted, and Maggie's smile broadened. But behind her smile Jeanie could see concern. Real concern.

'So what happened? Did he come on too fast? Is he a brute? Tell me.'

If only, Jeanie thought, and suddenly, weirdly, she was thinking of her mother. Heather Lochlan had died when Jeanie was sixteen and Jeanie still missed her with an ache that would never fade.

'He's not a brute. He's just…a businessman.' She buried her face in her hands. 'Mam would never have let me get myself into this mess,' she whispered. 'Three husbands… Three disasters.'

'Your mam knew Rory,' Maggie retorted. 'Rory was no disaster. Your mam would have danced at your wedding.'

She well might have, Jeanie thought. Rory had been an islander, born and bred. He'd been older than Jeanie by ten years, and he'd followed his father and his grandfather's way to the sea. He'd been gentle, predictable, safe. All the things Jeanie's dad wasn't.

She'd been a mere sixteen when her dad had taken control of her life.

Her mam's death had been sudden and shocking, and Jeanie's dad had turned to drink to cope. He'd also pulled Jeanie out of school. 'Sixteen is well old enough to do the housework for me. I'm wasting no more of my money.'

She'd been gutted, but then Rory had stepped in, and amazingly he'd stood up to her father. 'We'll marry,' he'd told her. 'You can work in the fish shop rather than drudge for your father. You can live with my mam and dad.'

Safe… That was what Rory was. She'd thought she loved him, but…

But working in the fish shop, doing an online accountancy course because she ached to do something other than serve fish and clean, waiting for the times Rory came home from sea, fitting in with Rory's life…sometimes she'd dreamed…

It had never come to a point where she'd chafed against the bonds of loving, for Rory had drowned. She'd grieved for him, honestly and openly, but she knew she should never have married him. Safety wasn't grounds for a marriage. She'd found a part-time job with the island solicitor, and she'd begun to think she might see London. Maybe even save for a cruise…

But it had been so hard to save. She'd still been cleaning for her in-laws. She'd been earning practically nothing. Dreams had seemed just that—dreams. And then Eileen had come and offered her a job, acting as her assistant whenever she was on the island. And with Eileen… Alan.

Life had been grey and drab and dreary and he'd lit up everything around him. But…

There was that *but* again.

'Mam would have told me not to be a fool,' she told Maggie. 'Maybe even with Rory. Definitely with Alan and even more definitely with this one.'

'Maybe, but a girl has to follow her heart.'

'My heart doesn't make sense. I married Rory for safety. I married Alan for excitement. I married…this one…so he could keep his inheritance. None of them are the basis for any sort of marriage. It's time I grew up and accepted it.'

'So what will you do now?' Maggie was watching her friend with concern.

'I'm leaving the island. I never should have come back after Alan's death. I was just…so homesick and battered, and Eileen was kind.' She took a deep breath. 'No matter. I've enough money to tide me over for a few weeks and there are always bookkeeping jobs.' She raised her whisky to her friend. 'Here's to an unmarried future,' she said.

'Och,' Maggie exclaimed, startled. 'You can't expect me to drink to that.'

'Then here's to an unmarried Jeanie Lochlan,' Jeanie told her. 'Here's to just me and that's how it should be. I'm on my own and I'm not looking back.'

Alasdair was not on his own. He was surrounded by eight irate guests and two hungry dogs. Where did Jeanie keep the dog food? He had no idea.

He'd stayed in the castle off and on when his grandmother was ill, and after his grandmother's funeral. During that time the castle had been full of women and casseroles and offers of help. Since that time, though, he'd been back in Edinburgh, frantically trying to tie up loose ends so he could stay on the island for twelve months. He'd arrived this morning via helicopter, but the helicopter was long gone.

He was stuck here for the night, and the castle was full, not with offers of help, but with eight guests who all wanted attention.

'Where's the whisky, fella? We only came for the whisky.' That was the American, growing more and more irate.

'Jeanie has shortbread.' That was the shorter of two elderly women in hiking gear. 'I'm Ethel, and Hazel and I have been here a week now. We know she made it, a big tin. Hazel and I ate three pieces each last night, and we're looking forward to more. If you could just find it… Oh, and Hazel needs a hot-water bottle. Her bunion's playing up. I told her she should have seen the doctor before she came but would she listen? She's ready for a drop of whisky, too. When did you say Jeanie would be back?'

He'd assumed Jeanie had some help. Someone other than just her. These people were acting as if Jeanie were their personal servant. What the…?

'I'll ring the village and get whisky delivered,' he said and the American fixed him with a death stare.

'That's not good enough, man. It should be here now.'

'We've had a problem.'

'Is something the matter with Jeanie?' The lady called Ethel switched to concern, closely followed by visions of disaster. 'Where is she? And the whisky? You've lost it? Were you robbed? Is Jeanie hurt? Oh, she's such a sweetheart. If anything happened to her, we'd never forgive ourselves. Hazel, Jeanie's been hurt. Oh, but if it's robbery, should we stay here...?'

'It's not robbery.'

'It'll be that father of hers,' Hazel volunteered. 'He came when we were here last year, blustering his way in, demanding money. He took her whisky. Oh, she'll be mortified, poor lass.'

'But where's *our* whisky?' the American demanded and Hazel swung around and raised her purse.

'If you say one more word about whisky when our Jeanie's in trouble, this'll come down on your head,' she told him. 'My bunion's killing me and I could use something to hit. Meanwhile Mr... Mr...' She eyed Alasdair with curiosity.

'McBride,' Alasdair told her.

And with the word, the elderly lady's face sagged into relief. 'You're family? Oh, we're so glad. Ethel and I worry about her being here in this place all alone. We didn't know she had anyone. Is she really all right?'

'I... Yes. She just...needs to stay in the village tonight. For personal reasons.'

'Well, why shouldn't she?' the lady demanded. 'All the times we've stayed here, we've never known her to take a night off, and she works so hard. But we can help. The doggies need their dinner, don't you, doggies? And we can make our own hot-water bottles. If you light the fire in the sitting room, Ethel and I will feed the doggies and find the shortbread. Oh, and we'll take the breakfast orders, too, so you'll have them all ready.' Her face suddenly puckered. 'But if Jeanie's not back by the morning…Ethel and I come for Jeanie's porridge. We can cope without whisky but not without our porridge.'

The guests headed to the village for dinner, and by the time they returned Alasdair had whisky waiting. It wasn't enough to keep the Americans happy, but the couple had only booked for one night and for one night Alasdair could cope with bluster.

But one night meant one morning. Breakfast. Ethel and Hazel had handed him the menus, beaming confidence. He'd glanced through them and thought there was nothing wrong with toast.

He couldn't cope with breakfast—and why should he? This marriage farce was over. All he had to do was accept it. He could contact the chopper pilot, get him here first thing and be back in Edinburgh by mid-morning.

He'd be back in charge of his life—but Hazel and Ethel wouldn't get their porridge and the Duncairn empire was finished.

He glanced again at the menus. Porridge, gourmet omelettes, black pudding…Omelettes were easy, surely. Didn't you just break eggs into a pan and stir? But black pudding! He didn't know where to start.

Did Jeanie do it all? Didn't she have anyone to help?

The memory flooded back of Jeanie in the car. What had he said to her? That his car was…'*blocking your profits…*'

The moment he'd said it he'd seen the colour drain from her face. The slap had shocked her more than it had shocked him.

An undischarged bankruptcy?

He didn't know anything about her.

What had she said? *'This is a business deal. If you're buying, Alasdair McBride, surely you should have checked out the goods.'*

He'd set Elspeth onto a background check. Yes, he should have done it weeks ago but he'd assumed...

Okay, he'd assumed the worst—that Jeanie was as money-grubbing as her ex-husband. It had just seemed a fact.

He thought back to the one time—the only time—he'd seen Jeanie together with Alan. They'd just married. Alan had brought his new bride to the head offices of the Duncairn Corporation and introduced her with pride.

'Isn't she gorgeous?' he'd demanded of Alasdair and Alasdair had looked at Jeanie's short, short skirt and the leather jacket and boots and the diamond earrings and he'd felt nothing but disgust. The demure secretary he'd seen working with Eileen had been a front, he'd thought. The transformation made him wonder just how much his grandmother had been conned.

He was about to find out. 'You know what this means,' Alan had told him. 'I'm respectable now. The old lady thinks the sun shines out of Jeanie. She's already rethinking the money side of this business. Half this company should be mine and you know it. Now Eileen's thinking it, too.'

Eileen hadn't been thinking it, but she had settled an enormous amount on the pair of them. 'It's easier than to have the inheritance of the company split when I die, and Jeanie's excellent with money. She'll manage it.'

The next time he'd seen Jeanie, she'd been back here and his grandmother had been dying. There'd been no sign of the tight-fitting clothes or the jewels then. There'd been no sign of the brittle, would-be sophisticate—and there'd been no sign of the money.

On impulse he headed upstairs to the room his grand-mother had kept as her own. Eileen had spent little time here but when she'd known her time was close she'd wanted to come back. He had to clear it out—sometime. Not now. All he wanted to do now was look.

He entered, wincing a little at the mounds of soft pillows, at the billowing pink curtains, at the windows open wide to let in the warm evening air. Jeanie must still be caring for it. All signs of the old lady's illness had gone but the room was still Eileen's. Eileen's slippers were still beside the bed.

There were two photographs on the dresser. One was of him, aged about twelve, holding his first big salmon. He looked proud fit to burst. The other was of Alan and Jeanie on their wedding day.

Jeanie was holding a posy of pink roses. She was wearing a dress similar to the one she had on today. Alan was beaming at the camera, hugging Jeanie close, his smile almost…triumphant.

Jeanie just looked embarrassed.

So the tarty clothes had come after the wedding, he thought.

So the marriage to Alan had been almost identical to the one she'd gone through today?

Maybe it was. After all, he was just another McBride.

He swore and crossed to Eileen's desk, feeling more and more confused. The foundations he'd been so sure of were suddenly decidedly shaky.

What he was looking for was front and centre—a bound ledger, the type he knew Eileen kept for every transaction she had to deal with. This was the castle ledger, dealing with the day-to-day running of the estate. Jeanie would have another one, he knew, but, whatever she did, Eileen always kept a personal account.

He flicked through until he found the payroll.

Over the past couple of months there'd been a few on the castle staff. There'd been nurses, help from the village, the staff Alasdair had seen when he'd come to visit her. But before that... Leafing through, he could find only two entries. One was for Mac, the gillie. Mac had been gillie here for fifty years and must be close to eighty now. He was still on full wages, though he must be struggling.

The castle wasn't running as a farm. The cattle were here mostly to keep the grass down, but still... He thought of the great rhododendron drive. It had been clipped since the funeral. There was no way Mac could have done such a thing, and yet there was no mention of anyone else being paid to do it.

Except Jeanie? Jeanie, who was the only other name in the book? Jeanie, who was being paid less than Mac? Substantially less.

What was a good wage for a housekeeper? He had a housekeeper in Edinburgh and he paid her more than this—to keep house for one man.

His phone rang. Elspeth.

'That was fast,' he told her, but in truth he was starting to suspect that what she had to find was easy. He could have found it out himself, he thought. His dislike of Alan had stopped him enquiring, but now... Did he want to hear?

'I thought I'd catch you before you start enjoying your wedding night,' Elspeth said and he could hear her smiling. 'By the way, did you want more of those financial records sent down? I'm not sure what you're worried about. If you tell me, I can help look.'

'I'm not worried about the business right now,' he growled and heard Elspeth's shocked silence. What a statement!

But she regrouped fast. She was good, was Elspeth. 'I've been busy but this has been relatively simple,' she told him. 'From what I've found there's nothing to get in the way of having a very good time. No criminal record. Nothing. There's just one major hiccup in her past.'

And he already knew it. 'Bankruptcy?'

'You knew?'

'I… Yes.' But how long for? Some things weren't worth admitting, even to Elspeth. 'But not the details. Tell me what you have. As much as you have.'

'Potted history,' she said. Elspeth had worked for him for years and she knew he'd want facts fast. 'Jeanie Lochlan was born twenty-nine years ago, on Duncairn. Her father is supposedly a fisherman, but his boat's been a wreck for years. Her mother sounds like she was a bit of a doormat.'

'Where did you get this information?' he demanded, startled. This wasn't facts and figures.

'Where does one get all local information?' He could hear her smiling. 'The post office is closed today, so I had to use the publican, but he had time for a chat. Jeanie's mother died when she was sixteen. Her father proceeded to try to drink himself to death and he's still trying. The local view is that he'll be pickled and stuck on the bar stool forever.'

So far he knew…well, some of this. He knew she was local. 'So…' he said cautiously.

'When she was seventeen Jeanie got a special dispensation to marry another fisherman, an islander called Rory Craig,' Elspeth told him. 'I gather she went out with him from the time her mam died. By all reports it was a solid marriage but no kids. She worked in the family fish shop until Rory drowned when his trawler sank. She was twenty-three.'

And that was more of what he hadn't known about. The details of the first marriage. He'd suspected…

He'd suspected wrong.

'I guess she wouldn't be left all that well-off after that marriage,' he ventured and got a snort for his pains.

'Small family fishing business, getting smaller. The trawler sank with no insurance.'

'How did you get all this?' he demanded again.

'Easy,' Elspeth said blithely. 'I told the publican I was a reporter from Edinburgh and had heard Lord Alasdair of Duncairn was marrying an islander. He was happy to tell me everything—in fact, I gather the island's been talking of nothing else for weeks. Anyway, Rory died and then she met your cousin. You must know the rest.'

'Try me.'

'You mean you don't?'

'Eileen didn't always tell me...' In fact, she'd never told Alasdair anything about Alan. There'd been animosity between the boys since childhood and Eileen had walked a fine line in loving both. 'And Jeanie keeps herself to herself.'

'Okay. It seems your gorgeous cousin visited the island to visit his gran—probably to ask for money, if the company ledgers are anything to go by. He met Jeanie, he took her off the island and your grandmother paid him to marry her.'

'I...beg your pardon?'

'I'm good,' she said smugly. 'But this was easy, too. I asked Don.'

Don.

Alasdair had controlled the day-to-day running of the firm for years now, but Don had been his grandparents' right-hand man since well before Alasdair's time. The old man still had a massive office, with the privileges that went with it. Alasdair had never been overly fond of him, often wondering what he was paid for, but his place in his grandparents' affections guaranteed his place in the company, and gossip was what he lived for.

'So Don says…' Elspeth started, and Alasdair thought, This is just more gossip, I should stop her—but he didn't. 'Don says soon after Alan met Jeanie, he took her to Morocco. Eileen must have been worried because she went to visit—and Alan broke down and told her the mess he was in. He was way over his head, with gambling debts that'd make your eyes water. He'd gone to the castle to try to escape his creditors—that's when he met Jeanie—and then he'd decided to go back to Morocco and try to gamble his way out of trouble. You can imagine how that worked. But he hadn't told Jeanie. She still had stars in her eyes— so Eileen decided to sort it.'

'How did she sort it?' But he already knew the answer.

'I'd guess you know.' Elspeth's words echoed his thoughts. 'That was when she pulled that second lot of funds from the company, but she gave it to Alan on the understanding that no more was coming. She was sure Jeanie could save him from himself, and of course Alan made promise after promise he never intended to keep. I'm guessing Eileen felt desperate. You know how she loved your cousin, and she saw Jeanie as the solution. Anyway, after his death Eileen would have helped Jeanie again— Don says she felt so guilty she made herself ill—but Jeanie wouldn't have any of it. She had herself declared bankrupt. She accepted a minimal wage from Eileen to run the castle, and that's it. End of story as far as Don knows it.' She paused. 'But, Alasdair, is this important? And if it is, why didn't you ask Don before you married her? Why didn't you ask *her*?'

Because I'm stupid.

No, he thought grimly. It wasn't that. He'd known Alan gambled. He knew the type of people Alan mixed with. If he'd enquired… If he'd known for sure that Jeanie was exactly the same as Alan was, with morals somewhere between a sewer rat and pond scum, he'd never have been able to marry her.

Except he had believed that. He'd tried to suppress it, for the good of the company, for the future of the estate, but at the back of his mind he'd branded her the same as he'd branded Alan.

'She still married him,' he found himself muttering. How inappropriate was it to talk like this to his secretary about…his wife? But he was past worrying about appropriateness. He was feeling sick. 'She must have been a bit like him.'

'Don said Eileen said she was a sweet young thing who was feeling trapped after her husband died,' Elspeth said. 'She was working all hours, for Eileen when your grandmother was on the island but also for the local solicitor, and cleaning in her husband's family's fish shop as well. Being paid peanuts. Trying to pay off the debt left after her husband's trawler sank with no insurance. She was bleak and she was broke. Don thinks Alan simply seduced her off the island. You know how charming Alan was.'

He knew.

He sat at the chair in front of Eileen's dresser and stared at himself in the mirror. The face that looked back at him was gaunt.

What had he done?

'But it's lovely that you've married her,' Elspeth said brightly now. 'Doesn't she deserve a happy ending? Don said she made Eileen's last few months so happy.'

She had, he conceded. He'd been a frequent visitor to the castle as his grandmother neared the end, and every time he'd found Jeanie acting as nursemaid. Reading to her. Massaging her withered hands. Just sitting…

And he'd thought… He'd thought…

Yeah, when the will was read he'd expected Jeanie to be mentioned.

That was what Alan would have done—paid court to a dying woman.

'Is there anything else you need?' Elspeth asked.

Was there anything else he needed? He breathed out a few times and thought about it.

'Yes,' he said at last.

'I'm here to serve.' He almost smiled at that. Elspeth was fifty and bossy and if he pushed her one step too far she'd push back again.

'I need a recipe for black pudding,' he told her.

'Really?'

'Really.'

'I'll send it through. Anything else?'

'Maybe a recipe for humble pie as well,' he told her. 'And maybe I need that first.'

CHAPTER FIVE

MIDNIGHT. THE WITCHING HOUR. Normally Jeanie was so tired that the witches could do what they liked; she couldn't give a toss. Tonight the witches were all in her head, and they were giving her the hardest time of her life.

'You idiot. You king-size madwoman. To walk back into the McBride realm…'

Shut up, she told her witches, but they were ranting and she lay in the narrow cot in Maggie's tiny attic and held her hands to her ears and thought she was going mad.

Something hit the window.

That'll be more witches trying to get in, she told herself and buried her head under the pillow.

Something else hit the window. It sounded like a shower of gravel.

Rory used to do this, so many years ago, when he wanted to talk to her and her father was being…her father.

The ghost of Rory? That's all I need, she thought, but then another shower hit the window and downstairs Maggie's Labrador hit the front door and started barking, a bark that said terrorists and stun grenades were about to launch through the windows and a dog had to do its duty. Wake up and fight, the dog was saying to everyone in the house. No, make that everyone in the village.

There was an oath from Maggie's husband in the room

under Jeanie's, and, from the kids' room, a child began to cry.

And she thought…

No, she didn't want to think. This was nothing to do with her. She lay with her blanket pulled up to her nose as she heard Maggie's husband clump down the stairs and haul the door open.

'What do you think you're doing?' Dougal's shout was as loud as his dog's bark. 'McBride… It's McBride, isn't it? What the hell…? You might be laird of this island, but if you think you can skulk round our property… You've woken the bairns. Shut up!' The last words were a roar, directed at the dog, but it didn't work the way Dougal intended. From under her window came a chorus of frenzied barks in response.

Uh-oh. Jeanie knew those barks. Abbot and Costello! Alasdair was here and he'd brought Eileen's dogs for the ride.

And then it wasn't just Maggie's dog and Eileen's dogs. The neighbours' dog started up in response, and then the dogs from the next house along, and then the whole village was erupting in a mass of communal barking.

Lights were going on. Maggie's two kids were screaming. She could hear a child start up in the house next door.

Should I stay under the pillows? Jeanie thought. It had to be the wisest course.

'I need to speak to my wife.' It was Alasdair, struggling to make himself heard above the din.

His wife. She needed more pillows—the pillows she had didn't seem to be effective.

'Jeanie?' That was Maggie, roaring up the stairs. 'Jeanie!'

'I'm asleep!'

'Jeanie, you know how much I love you, but your man's

roaring in the street and he's woken the bairns. Either you face him or I will, and if it's me, it won't be pretty.'

Alasdair wasn't roaring in the street, Jeanie thought helplessly, but everyone else was. Everyone in Duncairn would know that the Earl of Duncairn was under Maggie's window—wanting his wife.

Everyone knew everything on this island, she thought bitterly as she hauled on jeans and a sweatshirt and headed downstairs. Why broadcast more? As if the whole mess wasn't bad enough… She didn't want to meet him. She did not. She'd had enough of the McBrides to last her a lifetime.

Dougal was still in the doorway, holding the dog back. He'd stopped shouting, but as she appeared he looked at her in concern. 'You sure you want to go out there, lass?'

She glowered. 'Maggie says I have to.'

There was a moment's pause while they both thought about it. 'Then better to do what Maggie says,' he said at last. Dougal was a man of few words and he'd used most of them on Alasdair. 'Tell him to quiet the dogs. I'll be here waiting. Any funny business and I'm a call away. And don't be going out there in bare feet.'

Her shoes were in the attic, two flights of stairs away. At home…at the castle…she always left a pair of wellies at the back door, but here it hadn't been worth her unpacking.

The only Wellingtons on the doorstep were Dougal's fishing boots.

But a girl had to do what a girl had to do. She shoved her feet into Dougal's vast fishing wellies and went to meet her…her husband.

He'd found out where Maggie lived. That had be_____
the island boasted one slim phone book wit_____
included. He hadn't meant or wanted to w_____
but she'd told him she'd be sleeping in th_____

wanted was for her to put her head out to investigate the shower of stones, he'd signal her down and they could talk.

The plan hadn't quite worked. Now the whole village was waiting for them to talk, and the village wasn't happy. But as a collective, the village was interested.

'Have you run away already, love?' The old lady living over the road from Maggie's was hanging out of the window with avid interest. 'Well, it's what we all expected. Don't you go letting him sweet-talk you back to his castle. Just because he's the laird… There's generations of lairds had their way with the likes of us. Don't you be trusting him one inch.'

She might not be trusting him, he thought, but at least she was walking towards him. She was wearing jeans, an oversize windcheater and huge fishermen's boots. Her curls were tumbled around her face. By the light of the street lamp she looked young, vulnerable…and scared.

Heck, he wasn't an ogre. He wasn't even really a laird. 'Jeanie…'

'You'd better hush the dogs,' she told him. 'Why on earth did you bring them?'

'Because when I tried to leave they started barking exactly as they're barking now.' He needed to be calm, but he couldn't help the note of exasperation creeping in. 'And your guests have already had to make do with half a shelf of whisky instead of a full one, and bought biscuits instead of home-made. What did you do with the shortbread? If the dogs keep barking, we'll have the castle empty by morning.'

'Does that matter?' But she walked across to the SUV and yanked open the door. 'Shush,' she said. They shushed.

It was no wonder they shushed. Her tone said don't mess with me and the dogs didn't. She was small and cute and fierce—and the gaze she turned on him was lethal.

glowered and then hesitated, glancing up at the lit

window over the road. 'It's all right, Mrs McConachie, I have him… I have things under control. Sorry for the disturbance, people. You can all go back to bed now. Close your windows, nothing to see.'

'You tell him, Jeanie,' someone shouted, and there was general laughter and the sound of assorted dogs faded to silence again.

But she was still glowering. She was looking at him as if he were five-day-old fish that had dared infiltrate the immaculate castle refrigerators.

Speaking of food… Why not start off on neutral territory?

'I don't know how to make black pudding,' he told her and her face stilled. The glare muted a little, as if something else was struggling to take its place. Okay. Keep it practical, he told himself, and he soldiered on. 'Two of your guests, Mr and Mrs Elliot from Battersea, insist they want black pudding for their breakfast. And Ethel and Hazel want porridge.'

'Hector and Margaret adore their black pudding,' she said neutrally, and he thought, Excellent, this was obviously the way to lead into the conversation they had to have.

'So how do you make it?'

'I don't. Mrs Stacy on the north of the island makes them for me and she gets her blood from the island butcher. I have puddings hanging in the back larder. You slice and fry at need. The shortbread's on top of the dresser—I put it where I can't reach it without the step stool because otherwise I'll be the size of a house. The porridge is more complicated—you need to be careful not to make it lumpy but there are directions on the Internet. I'm sure you can manage.'

'I can't.'

'Well, then…' She stood back, hands on her hips, looking as if he was a waste of space for admitting he couldn't make porridge. 'That's sad, but the guests need to find somewhere else as a base to do their hill climbing. They might as well get disgusted about their lack of black pudding and porridge tomorrow, and start looking elsewhere immediately.'

Uh-oh. This wasn't going the way he'd planned. She looked as if she was about to turn on her heels and retreat. 'Jeanie, there was a reason you agreed to marry me.' He needed to get things back on a sensible course now. 'Believe it or not, it's still the right thing to do. It was a good decision. You can't walk away.'

'The decision to marry? The right thing?'

'I believe it still is, even though…even though your reasons weren't what I thought they were. But long-term, it still seems sensible.'

'It did seem sensible.' She still sounded cordial, he thought, which had to be a good sign, or at least she still seemed neutral. But then she continued: 'But that was before I realised you think I'm a gold-digging harpy who's spent the last three years sucking up to Eileen so I can inherit the castle. Or maybe I did know that, but it got worse. It was before you inferred I'd married twice for money, three times if you count marrying you. You thought I was a tart the first time you saw me and—'

'I didn't.'

'Come off it. When Alan introduced us you looked like you'd seen lesser things crawl out of cheese. I concede the way I was dressed might have swayed you a little—'

'A little!' He still remembered how he'd felt as Alan had ushered her into his office. Appalled didn't begin to cut it.

'Alan said it was a joke,' she told him, a hint of defensiveness suddenly behind her anger. 'He said you were a judgemental prude, let's give you a heart attack. He said you were expecting him to marry a tart so let's show him one. I was embarrassed to death but Alan wanted to do it and I was naïve and I thought I was in love and I went along with it. It even seemed…funny. It wasn't funny, I admit. It was tacky. But Alan was right. You were judgemental. You still are. Eileen kept telling me you were nice underneath but then she loved Alan, too. So now I've been talked into doing something against my better judgement—again. It has to stop and it's stopping now. I'll get the marriage annulled. That's it. If you don't mind, my bed's waiting and you have oats to soak. Or not. Lumpy porridge or none at all, it's up to you. I don't care.'

And she turned and walked away.

Or she would have walked away if she hadn't been wearing men's size-thirteen Wellington boots. There was a rut in the pavement, her floppy toe caught and she lurched. She flailed wildly, fighting for balance, but she was heading for asphalt.

He caught her before she hit the ground. His arms went round her; he swung her high into his arms and steadied. For one moment he held her—he just held.

She gasped and wriggled. He set her on her feet again but for that moment…for that one long moment there'd been an almost irresistible urge to keep right on holding.

In the olden days a man could choose a mate according to his status in the tribe, he thought wryly. He could exert a bit of testosterone, show a little muscle and carry his woman back to his cave. Every single thing about that concept was wrong, but for that fleeting moment, as he held her, as he felt how warm, how slight, how yielding her body was, the urge was there, as old as time itself.

And as dumb.

But she'd felt it, too—that sudden jolt of primeval need. She steadied and backed, her hands held up as if to ward him off.

Behind them the door swung open. Dougal was obviously still watching through the window and he'd seen everything. 'You want me to come out, love?'

'It's okay, Dougal.' She sounded as if she was struggling for composure and that made two of them. 'I...just tripped in your stupid wellies.'

'They're great wellies.' That was Maggie, calling over Dougal's shoulder. 'They're special ones I bought for his birthday. They cost a fortune.'

'I think they're nice, too,' Alasdair added helpfully and she couldn't help but grin. She fought to turn it back into a glower.

'Don't you dare make me laugh.'

'I couldn't.'

'You could. Go away. I'm going to bed.'

Enough. He had to say it. 'Jeanie, please come back to the castle,' he said, pride disappearing as the gravity of the next few moments hit home. 'You're right, I've been a judgemental fool. I've spent the last few hours trawling through Eileen's financial statements. I can see exactly what she has and hasn't given you. I can see what a mess Alan left you in. I can see...what you've given Eileen.'

She stilled. 'I don't know what you mean.'

'For the last three years you've made this castle a home for her,' he told her. 'I know Eileen's official home was in Edinburgh, and she still spent too much time in the office, trying to keep her fingers on the company's financial affairs. But whenever she could, she's been here. When she became ill she was here practically full-time, only returning to Edinburgh long enough to reassure me there was no need for me to keep an eye on her. I thought she was staying here because she needed to keep an eye on you. I thought this was simply another financial enterprise. But tonight I spent a little time with your guests and some rather good whisky—'

'I didn't leave any good stuff behind.'

'I made an emergency dash. I spent a little time with them and they talked about why they've come back every year since you started running the B & B. They talked about how they and my grandmother talked about you and they talked about fun. How you and Eileen enjoyed each other's company, but that they'd always been welcome to join you. How Eileen sat in the library like a queen every night and presided over the whisky and talked about the estate as it's been, about my grandfather's ancestors and hers. It seems it didn't matter how often they heard it, they still loved it. And they talked about you, Jeanie, always in the background, always quietly careful that Eileen didn't do too much, that she didn't get cold, that she didn't trip on her stupid dogs. And then I looked at the wages and saw how little you've been paid. And Elspeth…'

'Who's Elspeth?' She sounded winded.

'My secretary. I asked her to do some long-overdue background checks. With the information you gave me this afternoon the rest was easy to find. She tells me that, as well as almost killing you that last night in his unpaid-for sports car, Alan died in debt up to his ears. He left you committed to paying them, even though most of them were to gambling houses and casinos. But somehow you seem to have become jointly responsible. I know Eileen would have paid them off, but they were vast debts, eye-watering debts, and you refused to let her help. You declared yourself bankrupt and then you accepted a minimal wage to stay on at the castle.'

'You have—'

'Been learning. Yes, I have. I've learned that this marriage arrangement gives you one more year in the castle but that's all it gives you. I'm still not sure why you agreed to marry me, but I'm pathetically grateful you did. Jeanie, I'm so sorry I misjudged you. Please come home.'

'It's not my home.'

'It is a home, though,' he said, gently now. 'That's what I didn't get. You made it Eileen's home and for that I can never thank you enough.'

'I don't want your thanks. Eileen let me stay. That was enough.'

'And I know I don't have the right, but I'm asking you to stay longer.'

'But not as your wife.'

'Legally as my wife. We both know that's sensible.'

'I don't do…sensible. I'm not very good at it. I have three dumb marriages to prove it.'

'Then do gut instinct,' he told her. 'Do what you think's right. Think back to the reasons you married me in the first place.'

'That's blackmail again.'

'It's not. I know I stand to gain a fortune by this transaction. You stand to gain nothing. That's what I hadn't understood. But we can work things out. If the company ends up in my name, I can buy the castle from the bankruptcy trustees. I intended to buy it from you anyway, but I can arrange for you to be paid more—'

'I don't want anything,' she snapped. 'Don't you get it? Don't you understand that there's nothing you can offer me that I want?'

'You do want another year in the castle. At the end of the year—'

'Don't even say it,' she told him. 'I will not be bought.'

Silence. What else could he say?

He could fix things if she let him. Duncairn Enterprises was extensive enough to soak up the purchase of the castle at market price. He could also settle a substantial amount on Jeanie when her bankruptcy was discharged, but he knew instinctively that saying that now would count for nothing. Right now, he had enough sense to know it would make things worse.

This woman—*his wife*—had married for a reason. She knew the good the company did. She knew how much the castle and the company meant to Eileen. He just had to hope those reasons were still strong enough.

'Jeanie, do you really want to get on that ferry tomorrow?' he asked. 'The dogs want you back at the castle. The guests want you. This does seem like cutting off your nose to spite your face. Please?'

'So…it's not just the porridge.'

'Not even the black pudding.'

'Alasdair…'

'There'll be no strings,' he said and held up his hands. 'I promise. Things will be as you imagined them when you agreed to this deal. You'll have a year's employment. You can use the year to sort what you want to do next and then you can walk away. There'll be no obligation on either of our parts.'

'No more insults?'

'I won't even comment on your footwear.'

She managed to smile again at that. It was faint but it was there.

And then there was silence. It was so deep and so long that Dougal opened the door again. He stood uncertainly on the doorstep. He made to say something but didn't. The silence lengthened. Finally he was dragged inside again by Maggie.

Maggie, at least, must understand the value of silence, Alasdair thought. The last light went off inside. Even if, as Alasdair suspected, Maggie was still lurking, she was giving them the pretence that they were alone.

The night was still and warm. The numbers of nights like this on Duncairn could be counted on less than a man's fingers. Everyone should be out tonight, he thought. The stars were hanging brilliant in the sky, as if they existed in a separate universe from the stars he struggled to see back in Edinburgh. The tide was high and he could hear the waves slapping against the harbour wall. Before dawn the harbour would be a hive of activity as the island's fishermen set to sea, but for now the village had settled back to sleep. There was no one here but this woman, standing still and watchful.

Trying to make her mind up whether to go or stay.

'Can I have the dogs?' she said at last, and he blinked.

'The dogs?'

'At the end of the year. That's been the thing that's hurt most. I haven't had time to find a job where I can keep them, and I can't see them living in an apartment in Edinburgh with you. If I stay, I'll have twelve months to source a job where they can come with me.'

'You'd agree to keeping on with the marriage,' he said, cautiously because it behoved a man to be cautious, 'for the dogs?'

'What other reason would there be?'

'For the company? So Duncairn Enterprises will survive?'

'That's your reason, not mine. Dogs or nothing, My Lord.'

'Don't call me that.'

She tilted her chin. 'I need something to hold on to,' she said. 'I need the dogs.'

He stared around at the two dogs with their heads hanging out of the window. Abbot was staring down at the road as if considering jumping. He wouldn't. Alasdair had been around this dog long enough to know a three-foot jump in Abbot's mind constituted suicide.

A moth was flying round Costello's nose. Costello's nose was therefore circling, too, as if he was thinking of snapping. He wouldn't do that, either. Risk wasn't in these two dogs' make-up and neither was intelligence.

'They're dumb,' he said, feeling dumbfounded himself.

'I like dumb. You know where you are with dumb. Dumb doesn't leave room for manipulation.'

'Jeanie...'

'Dumb or not, it's yes or no. A year at the castle, no insults, the dogs—and respect for my privacy. The only way this can work is if you keep out of my way and I keep out of yours.'

'We do still need to share the castle.'

'Yes, we do,' she agreed. 'But you'll be treated as a guest.'

'You mean you'll make the porridge?'

Her expression softened a little. 'I kind of like making it,' she admitted.

'So we have a deal?'

'No more insults?' she demanded.

'I can't think of a single insult to throw.'

'Then go home,' she told him. 'I'll be there before breakfast.'

'Won't you come back now?'

'Not with you,' she said flatly. 'I'll follow separately, when I'm ready. From now on, Alasdair McBride, this is the way we do things. Separately or not at all.'

How was a man to sleep after that? He lay in the great four-poster bed in the opulent rooms his grandmother had done up for him during the renovation and he kept thinking...of Jeanie.

Why hadn't his grandmother told him of her plight?

Because he'd never asked, he conceded. Eileen had known of the bad blood between the cousins. Revealing the mess Alan had left Jeanie in would have meant revealing even more appalling things of Alan than he already knew.

So she'd let him think Jeanie was a gold-digger?

No. Eileen wouldn't have dreamed he'd think Jeanie was

mercenary, he conceded, because anyone who met Jeanie would know that such a thing was impossible.

Except him. He'd met her, he'd judged her and he'd kept on judging her. He'd made the offer of marriage based on the assumption that she was out for what she could get, and he'd nearly destroyed his chances of success in doing it.

Worse, he'd hurt her. He'd hurt a woman who'd done the right thing by Eileen. A woman Eileen had loved. A woman who'd agreed to a marriage because…because he'd told her of the charities Duncairn supported? Because she could spend another year acting as a low-paid housekeeper? Because she loved two dopey dogs?

Or because she'd known Eileen would have wanted him to inherit. The realisation dawned as clear as if it were written in the stars.

She'd done it for Eileen.

Eileen had loved her and he could see why. She was a woman worthy of…

Loving?

The word was suddenly there, front and centre, and it shocked him.

Surely he was only thinking of it in relation to Eileen— but for the moment, lying back in bed in the great castle of his ancestors, he let the concept drift. Why had Eileen loved her?

Because she was kind and loyal and warm-hearted. Because she loved Eileen's dogs—why, for heaven's sake? Because she was small and cute and curvy and her chuckle was infectious.

There was nothing in that last thought that would have made Eileen love her, he decided, but it surely came to play in Alasdair's mind.

When she'd almost fallen, when he'd picked her up and held her, he'd felt…he'd felt…

As if she was his wife?

And so she was, he thought, and maybe it was the vows he'd made in the kirk so few hours ago that made him feel like this. He'd thought he could make them without meaning them, but now…

She was coming back here. His wife.

And if he made one move on her, she'd run a mile. He knew it. Alan had treated her like dirt and so had he. Today he'd insulted her so deeply that she'd run. This year could only work if it was business only.

He had to act on it.

There was a whine under the bed and Abbot slunk out and put his nose on the pillow. The dogs should be sleeping in the wet room. That was where their beds were but when he'd tried to lock them in they'd whined and scratched and finally he'd relented. Were they missing Jeanie?

He relented a bit more now and made the serious mistake of scratching Abbot's nose. Within two seconds he had two spaniels draped over his bed, squirming in ecstasy, then snuggling down and closing their eyes very firmly—*We're asleep now, don't disturb us.*

'Dumb dogs,' he told them but he didn't push them off. They'd definitely be missing Jeanie, he thought, and he was starting—very strongly—to understand why.

Why was she heading back to the castle? She was out of her mind.

But she'd packed her gear back into her car and now she was halfway across the island. Halfway home?

That was what the castle felt like. Home. Except it wasn't, she told herself. It had been her refuge after the Alan disaster. She'd allowed Eileen to talk her into staying on, but three years were three years too many. She'd fallen in love with the place. With Duncairn.

With the Duncairn estate and all it entailed?

That meant Alasdair, she reminded herself, and she

most certainly hadn't fallen in love with Alasdair. He was cold and judgemental. He'd married her for money, and he deserved nothing from her but disdain.

But he'd caught her when she'd fallen and he'd felt… he'd felt…

'Yeah, he'd felt like any over-testosteroned male in a kilt would make you feel,' she snapped out loud.

Her conversation with herself was nuts. She had the car windows open and she'd had to stop. Some of the scraggy, tough, highland sheep had chosen to snooze for the night in the middle of the road. They were moving but they were taking their time. Meanwhile they were looking at her curiously—listening in on her conversation? She needed someone to talk to, she decided, and the sheep would do.

'I'm doing this for your sakes,' she told them. 'If I go back to the castle, he can buy it from the bankruptcy trustees at the end of the year and it'll stay in the family.'

Maybe he'll let me stay on as caretaker even then?

That was a good thought, but did she want to stay as housekeeper/caretaker at Duncairn for the rest of her life?

'Yes,' she said out loud, so savagely that the sheep nearest her window leaped back with alarm.

'No,' she corrected herself, but maybe that was the wrong answer, too. That was the dangerous part of her talking. That was the part of her that had chafed against being part of Rory's family business, doing the books, cleaning the fish shop, aching to get off the island and do something exciting.

Well, she had done something exciting, she told herself bitterly. She'd met and married Alan and she'd had all the excitement a girl could want and more.

'So it's back in your box to you, Jeanie McBride,' she told herself and thought briefly about her name. Jeanie McBride. She was that. She was Alan's widow.

She was Alasdair's wife.

'At the end of the year I'm going back to being Jeanie Lochlan,' she told the last sheep as it finally ambled off the road. 'Meanwhile I'm going back to being house-keeper at Duncairn, chief cook and bottle washer for a year. I'm going back to taking no risks. The only thing that's changed for the next twelve months is that the house has one permanent guest. That guest is Alasdair McBride but any trouble from him and he's out on his ear.'

And you'll kick him out how?

'I won't need to,' she told the sheep. 'I hold all the cards.

'For a year,' she reminded herself, wishing the sheep could talk back. 'And for a year…well, Alasdair McBride might be the Earl of Duncairn but he's in no position to lord it over me. For the next year I know my place, and he'd better know his.'

CHAPTER SIX

ALASDAIR WOKE AT DAWN to find the dogs had deserted him. That had to be a good sign, he told himself, but he hadn't heard Jeanie return.

His room was on the ocean side of the castle. The massive stone walls would mean the sound of a car approaching from the land side wouldn't have woken him.

That didn't mean she was here, though.

He wanted—badly—to find out. The future of Duncairn rested on the outcome of the next few minutes but for some reason he couldn't bear to know.

He opened his laptop. He didn't even know if she'd returned but it paid a man to be prepared.

It paid a man to hope?

By eight o'clock he'd formed a plan of action. He'd made a couple of phone calls. He'd done some solid work, but the silence in the castle was starting to do his head in. He couldn't put it off any longer. He dressed and headed down the great staircase, listening for noise—listening for Jeanie?

He pushed open the door to the dining room and was met by…normal. Normal?

He'd been in this room often but this morning it was as if he were seeing it for the first time. Maybe it was because last night he'd almost lost it—or maybe it was because this morning it was the setting for Jeanie. Or he hoped it was.

Regardless, it was some setting. The castle after Eileen's amazing restoration was truly luxurious, but Eileen—and Jeanie, her right-hand assistant—had never lost sight of the heart of the place. That heart was displayed right here. The massive stone fireplace took half a wall. A fire blazed in the hearth, a small fire by castle standards but the weather was warm and the flame was there mostly to form a heart—and maybe to form a setting for the dogs, who lay sprawled in front of it. Huge wooden beams soared above. The vast rug on the floor was an ancient design, muted yet glorious, and matching the worn floorboards to perfection.

There were guests at four of the small tables, the guests he'd given whisky to last night. They gave him polite smiles and went back to their breakfast.

Porridge, he thought, checking the tables at a glance. Black pudding. Omelettes!

Jeanie *must* be home.

And almost as he thought it, there she was, bustling in from the kitchen, apron over her jeans, her curls tied into a bouncy ponytail, her face fixed into a hostess-like beam of welcome.

'Good morning, My Lord. Your table is the one by the window. It has a fine view but the morning papers are beside it if you prefer a broader outlook. Can I fetch you coffee while you decide what you'd like for your breakfast?'

So this was the way it would be. Guest and hostess. Even the dogs hadn't stirred in welcome. Jeanie was home. They had no need of him.

Things were back to normal?

'I just need toast.'

'Surely not. We have eggs and bacon, sausages, porridge, black pudding, omelettes, pancakes, griddle cakes… whatever you want, My Lord, I can supply it. Within reason, of course.' And she pressed a menu into his hands and retreated to the kitchen.

* * *

He ate porridge. No lumps. Excellent.

He felt…extraneous. Would he be served like this for the entire year? He'd go nuts.

But he sat and read his paper until all the guests had departed, off to tramp the moors or climb the crags or whatever it was that guests did during their stay. The American couple departed for good, for which he was thankful. The rest were staying at least another night. Jeanie was obviously supplying picnic baskets and seeing each guest off on their day's adventures. He waited a few moments after the last farewell to give her time to catch her breath, and then headed to the kitchen to find her.

She was elbow deep in suds in front of the sink. Washed pots and pans were stacked up to one side. He took a dishcloth and started to dry.

'There's no need to be doing that.' She must have heard him come in but she didn't turn to look at him. 'Put the dishcloth down. This is my territory.'

'This year's a mutual business deal. We work together.'

'You've got your company's work to be doing. There's a spare room beyond the ones you're using—your grandmother set it up as a small, private library for her own use. It has a fine view of the sea. We'll need to see if the Internet reaches there—if not you can get a router in town. Hamish McEwan runs the electrical store in Duncairn. He'll come out if I call him.'

Business. Her voice was clipped and efficient.

She still hadn't looked at him.

'We need to organise more than my office,' he told her. 'For a start, we need a cleaning lady.'

'We do not!' She sounded offended. 'What could be wrong with my cleaning?'

'How many days a year do you take guests?'

'Three-sixty-five.' She said it with pride and scrubbed the pan she was working on a bit harder.

'And you do all the welcoming, the cooking, the cleaning, the bed-making…'

'What else would I do?'

'Enjoy yourself?'

'I like cleaning.'

'Jeanie?'

'Yes.'

'That pan is so shiny you can see your face in it. It's time you stopped scrubbing.'

There were no more dishes. He could see her dilemma. She needed to stop scrubbing, but that would mean turning—to face him?

He lifted the pan from her hands, set it down and took her wet hands in his.

'Jeanie…'

'Don't,' she managed and tugged back but he didn't let her go.

'Jeanie, I've just been on the phone to Maggie.'

She stilled. 'Why?'

'To talk to her about you. You didn't tell her you were coming back here. She thought you'd gone to the ferry.'

He didn't tell her what a heart-sink moment that had been. She didn't need emotion getting in the way of what he had to say now.

'I thought I'd ring her this morning.' She sounded defensive. 'I thought… To be honest, when I left Maggie's I wasn't sure where I was going. I headed out near the ferry terminal and sat and looked over the cliffs for a while. I wasn't sure if I should change my mind.' She looked down at their linked hands. 'I'm still not sure if I should.'

'You promised me you'd come back.'

'I stood in the kirk and wed you, too,' she said sharply.

'Somewhere along my life I've learned that promises are made to be broken.'

'I won't break mine.'

'Till death do us part?'

'I'll rethink that in a year.'

'You have to be kidding.' She wrenched her hands back with a jerk. 'It's rethought now. Promises mean nothing. Now if you'll excuse me, I have beds to make, a castle to dust, dogs to walk, then the forecourt to mow. You go back to sorting your electrics.'

'Jeanie, it's the first day of our honeymoon.'

'Do you not realise I'm over honeymoons?' She grabbed the pan he'd just taken from her and slammed it down on the bottom shelf so hard it bounced. 'What were you thinking? A jaunt to a six-star hotel with a casino on the side? Been there, done that.'

'I thought I'd take you out to see the puffins.'

And that shocked her. She straightened. Stared at him. Stared at him some more. 'Sorry?'

'Have you seen the puffins this year?'

'I… No.'

'Neither have I. I haven't seen the puffins since my grandfather died, and I miss them. According to Dougal, they're still there, but only just. You know they take off midsummer? Their breeding season's almost done so they'll be leaving any minute. The sea's so calm today it's like a lake. You have all the ingredients for a picnic right here and Dougal says we can use his *Mary-Jane*.'

'*Dougal will lend you his boat?*'

'It's not his fishing boat. It's just a runabout.'

'I know that, but still…he won't even trust Maggie with his boat.'

'Maybe I come with better insurance than Maggie.'

'Do you even know how to handle a boat?'

'I know how to handle a boat.'

She stared at him, incredulous, and then shook her head. 'It's a crazy idea. As I said, I have beds—'

'Beds to make. And dusting and dog-walking and grass to mow.' He raised his fingers and started ticking things off. 'First, beds and general housework. Maggie's mam is already on her way here, bringing a friend for company. They'll clean and cook a storm. They're bringing Maggie's dog, too, who Maggie assures me keeps Abbot and Costello from fretting. They'll walk all the dogs. Maggie's uncle is bringing up the rear. He'll do the mowing, help Mac check the cattle, do anything on the list you leave him. He'll be here in an hour but we should be gone by then. Our boat's waiting. Now, can I help you pack lunch?'

'No! This is crazy.'

'It's the day after your wedding. It's not crazy at all.'

'The wedding was a formality. I told you, I don't do honeymoons.'

'Or six-star hotels, or casinos. I suspected not. I also thought that if I whisked you off the island you might never come back. But, Jeanie, you do need a holiday. Three years without a break. I don't know what Eileen was thinking.'

'She knew I wouldn't take one.'

'Because you're afraid?' he said gently. He didn't move to touch her. In truth, he badly wanted to but she was so close to running… 'Because you've ventured forth twice and been burned both times? I know you agreed to marry so I could inherit, but there's also a part of you that wants another year of safe. Jeanie, don't you want to see the puffins?'

'I…'

'Come with me, Jeanie,' he said and he couldn't help himself then, he did reach out to her. He touched her cheek, a feather-light touch, a trace of finger against skin, and why it had the power to make him feel…make him feel…

As if the next two minutes were important. Really important. Would she pull away and tell him to get lost, or would she finally cut herself some slack? Come play with him...

'I shouldn't,' she whispered, but she didn't pull back.

'When did you last see puffins?'

She didn't reply. He let his hand fall, though it took effort. He wanted to keep touching. He wanted to take that look of fear from her face.

What had they done to her? he wondered. Nice, safe Rory, and low-life Alan...

There was spirit in this woman and somehow it had been crushed.

And then he thought of the slap and he thought, No, it hadn't quite been crushed. Jeanie was still under there.

'Not since I was a little girl,' she admitted. 'With my mam. Rory's uncle took us out to see them.'

'Just the once?'

'I... Yes. He took tourists, you see. There were never places—or time—to take us.'

What about your own dad? he wanted to ask. Jeanie's father was a fisherman. He'd had his own boat. Yes, it was almost two hours out to the isolated isles, the massive crags where the puffins nested, but people came from all over the world to see them. To live here and not see...

His own grandparents had taken him out every summer. When he'd turned sixteen they'd given him a boat, made sure he had the best instruction, and then they'd trusted him. When his grandfather had died he'd taken Eileen out there to scatter his ashes.

'Come with me,' he said now, gently, and she looked up at him and he could see sense and desire warring behind her eyes.

'It's not a honeymoon.'

'It's a day trip. You need a holiday so I'm organising a series of day trips.'

'More than one!'

'You deserve a month off. More. I know you won't take that. You don't trust me and we're forced to stay together and you don't want that, but for now…you've given me an amazing gift, Jeanie Lochlan. Allow me to give you something in return.'

She compressed her lips and stared up at him, trying to read his face.

'Are you safe to operate a boat out there?' she demanded at last.

'You know Dougal. Do you think he'd lend me the *Mary-Jane* if I wasn't safe?'

Dougal's uncle had taught him how to handle himself at sea. Once upon a time this island had been his second home, his refuge when life with his parents got too bad, and sailing had become his passion.

'He wouldn't,' Jeanie conceded. 'So we're going alone?'

'Yes.' He would have asked Dougal to take them if it would have made Jeanie feel safer but this weather was so good every fisherman worth his salt was putting to sea today. 'You can trust me, Jeanie. We're interested in puffins, that's all.'

'But when you touch me, I feel…'

And there it was, out in the open. This *thing* between them.

'If we're to survive these twelve months, we need to avoid personal attraction,' he told her.

Her face stilled. 'You feel it, too.'

Of course I do. He wanted to shout it, but the wariness in her eyes was enough to give a man pause. That and reason. Hell, all they needed was a hot affair, a passionate few weeks, a massive split, and this whole arrangement would be blown out of the water. Even he had the sense to see hormones needed to take a back seat.

'Jeanie, this whole year is about being sensible. You're an attractive woman...'

She snorted.

'With a great smile and a big heart,' he continued. 'And if you put a single woman and a single man together for a year, then it's inevitable that sparks will fly. But we're both old enough and sensible enough to know how to douse those sparks.'

'So that's what we're doing for the next twelve months. Dousing sparks?' She ventured a smile. 'So do I pack the fire extinguisher today?'

'If we feel the smallest spark, we hit the water. The water temperature around here is barely above freezing. That should do it. Will you come?'

There was a moment's hesitation and then: 'Foolish or not, I never could resist a puffin,' she told him. 'My only stipulation is that you don't wear a kilt. Because sparks are all very well, Alasdair McBride, but you put a kilt on that body and sparks could well turn into a wildfire.'

He was free to make of that as he willed. She turned away, grabbed a picnic basket and started to pack.

He couldn't just manage a boat; he was one with the thing.

Jeanie had been in enough boats with enough men—she'd even worked as crew on Rory's fishing trawler—to recognise a seaman when she saw one.

Who could have guessed this smooth, suave business-man from Edinburgh, this kilted lord of all he surveyed at Duncairn, was a man who seemed almost as at home at sea as the fishermen who worked the island's waters.

The *Mary-Jane* was tied at the harbour wharf when they arrived, with a note from Dougal to Alasdair taped to the bollard.

Keep in radio contact and keep her safe. And I don't mean the boat.

Alasdair had grinned, leaped lightly onto the deck and turned to help Jeanie down. She'd ignored his hand and climbed down herself—a woman had some pride. And she was being very wary of sparks.

The *Mary-Jane* was a sturdy cabin cruiser, built to take emergency supplies out to a broken-down fishing trawler, or as a general harbour runabout. She was tough and serviceable—but so was the man at the helm. He was wearing faded trousers, heavy boots and an ancient sweater. He hadn't shaved this morning. He was looking…

Don't think about how he looks, she told herself fiercely, so instead she concentrated on watching him handle the boat. The Duncairn bar was tricky. You had to know your way, but Alasdair did, steering towards the right channel, then pausing, waiting, watching the sea on the far side, judging the perfect time to cross and then nailing it so they cruised across the bar as if they'd been crossing a lake.

And as they entered open water Jeanie found herself relaxing. How long since she'd done this? Taken a day just for her? Had someone think about her?

He wanted to see the puffins himself, she told herself, but a voice inside her head corrected her.

He didn't have to do this. He didn't have to bring me. He's doing it because I need a break.

It was a seductive thought all by itself.

And the day was seductive. The sun was warm on her face. Alasdair adjusted his course so they were facing into the waves, so she hardly felt the swell—but she did feel the power of the sea beneath them, and she watched Alasdair and she thought, There's power there, too.

He didn't talk. Maybe he thought she needed silence.

She did and she was grateful. She sat and let the day, the sea, the sun soak into her.

This was as if something momentous had happened. This was as if she'd walked through a long, long tunnel and emerged to the other side.

Was it just because she'd taken the day off? Or was it that she'd set her future for the next twelve months, and for the next year she was safe?

It should be both, but she knew it wasn't. It was strange but sitting here in the sun, watching Alasdair, she had an almost overwhelming sense that she could let down her guard, lose the rigid control she'd held herself under since the appalling tragedy of Alan, let herself be just…Jeanie.

She'd lost who she was. Somewhere along the way she'd been subsumed. Jeffrey's daughter, Rory's girlfriend and wife, then Alan's woman. Then bankrupt, with half the world seeming to be after her for money owed.

Then Eileen's housekeeper.

She loved being the housekeeper at Duncairn but the role had enveloped her. It was all she was.

But today she wasn't a housekeeper. She wasn't any of her former selves. Today she was out on the open sea, with a man at the helm who was…

Her husband?

There was nothing prescribed for her today except that she enjoy herself, and suddenly who could resist? She found herself smiling. Smiling and smiling.

'A joke?' Alasdair asked softly, and she turned her full beam onto him.

'No joke. I've just remembered why I love this place. I haven't been to sea for so long. And the puffins…I can't remember. How far out?'

'You mean, are we there yet?' He grinned back and it was a grin to make a girl open her eyes a little wider. It was a killer grin. 'Isn't that what every kid in the back seat asks?'

'That's what I feel like—a kid in the back seat.' And then she looked ahead to the granite rock needles that seemed to burst from the ocean floor, isolated in their grandeur. 'No, I don't,' she corrected herself. 'I feel like I'm a front-seat passenger. It's one of these rocks, isn't it, where the puffins are found?'

'The biggest one at the back. The smaller ones are simply rock but the back one has a landmass where they can burrow for nests. They won't nest anywhere humans can reach. It means we can't land.'

'We'd need a pretty long rope ladder,' Jeanie breathed, looking at the sheer rock face in awe. And then she forgot to breathe… 'Oh-h-h.'

It was a long note of discovery. It was a note of awe.

For Alasdair had manoeuvred the boat through a gap in the island rock face and emerged to a bay of calm water. The water was steel grey, fathoms deep, and it was a mass of…

Puffins. Puffins!

Alasdair cut the motor to just enough power to keep clear of the cliffs. The motor was muted to almost nothing.

The puffins were everywhere, dotted over the sea as if someone had sprinkled confetti—only this confetti was made up of birds, duck-sized but fatter, black and white with extraordinary bright orange bills; puffins that looked exactly like the ones Jeanie had seen in so many magazines, on so many posters, but only ever once in real life and that so long ago it seemed like a dream.

Comical, cute—beautiful.

'They have fish,' she breathed. 'That one has… It must be at least three fish. More. Oh, my…I'd forgotten. There's another. And another. Why don't they just swallow them all at once?'

'Savouring the pleasure?' Alasdair said, smiling just as

Aladdin's genie might have done in the ancient fairy tale. Granting what he knew was a wish...

'You look like a benevolent Santa,' Jeanie told him and he raised his brows.

'Is that an accusation?'

'I... No.' Because it wasn't. It was just a statement.

Though he didn't actually look like Santa, Jeanie conceded. This was no fat, jolly old man.

Though she didn't need to be told that. His skill at the wheel was self-evident.

Sex on legs...

The description hit her with a jolt, and with it came a shaft of pure fear. Because that had been how she'd once thought of Alan.

Life with Rory had been...safe. He'd lived and dreamed fishing and would never have left the island. He was content to do things as his father and grandfather had done before him. His mother cooked and cleaned and was seemingly content, so he didn't see that Jeanie could possibly want more.

He was a good man, solid and dependable, and his death had left Jeanie devastated. But two years later Alan had blasted himself into her life. She'd met him and she'd thought...

Yep, sex on legs.

More. She'd thought he was everything Rory hadn't been. He was exciting, adventurous, willing and wanting to try everything life had to offer. He'd taken her off the island and exposed her to a life that...

That she never wanted to go back to. A life that was shallow, mercenary, dangerous—even cruel.

Alan was a McBride, just as this man was.

Sex on legs? Get a grip, she told herself. Have you learned nothing? The only one who'll keep yourself safe is yourself.

But she didn't *want* to be safe, a little voice whispered, and she looked at Alasdair and she could see the little voice's reasoning but she wasn't going there. She wasn't.

'If you want to know the truth, I read about them last night,' Alasdair told her. He was watching the puffins—thankfully. How much emotion could he read in her face? 'They can carry up to ten small fish in their beaks at a time. It's a huge genetic advantage—they don't waste energy swallowing and regurgitating, and they can carry up to ten fish back to their burrows. Did you know their burrows can be up to two feet deep? And those beaks are only bright orange in the breeding season. They'll shed the colour soon and go back to being drab and ordinary.'

'They could never be ordinary,' she managed, turning to watch a puffin floating by the boat with…how many fish in its beak? Five. She got five.

She was concentrating fiercely on counting. Alasdair was still talking…and he usually didn't talk. He'd swotted up for today, she thought. Was finding out how many fish a puffin could hold a seduction technique?

The thought made her smile. No, she decided, and it settled her. He was taking her out today simply to be nice. He wasn't interested in her, or, if he was, it'd be a mere momentary fancy, as Alan's had been.

So get yourself back to basics, she told herself. Eileen had offered Alan money to marry her. She knew that now. The knowledge had made her feel sick, and here was another man who'd been paid to marry her.

Sex on legs? Not so much. He was a husband who was hers because of money.

Hold that thought.

'Will we eat lunch here?' she asked, suddenly brisk, unwinding herself from the back seat on the boat and heading for the picnic basket. 'Can you throw down anchor or should we eat on the way back?'

'We have time to eat here.' He was watching her, his brows a question. 'Jeanie, how badly did Alan hurt you?'

'I have sandwiches and quiche and salad and boiled eggs. I also have brownies and apples. There's beer, wine or soda. Take your pick.'

'You mean you're not going to tell me?'

'Past history. Moving on…'

'I won't hurt you.'

'I know you won't,' she said briskly. 'Because I won't let you. This is a business arrangement, Alasdair, nothing more.'

'And today?'

'Is my payment for past services.' She was finding it hard to keep her voice even but she was trying. 'You've offered and I've accepted. It's wonderful—no, it's magic—to be eating lunch among the puffins. It's a gift. I'm very, very grateful but I'm grateful as an employee's grateful to her boss for a day off. Nothing more.'

'It's not a day off. It's a week almost completely off and then I'm halving your duties for double the wages.'

Whoa? Double wages?

She should refuse, she thought, but then…why not just be a grateful employee? That was what she was, after all.

'Excellent,' she said and passed the sandwiches. 'Take a sandwich—sir.'

Employer/employee. That was a relationship that'd work, he thought, and it was fine with him—wasn't it?

He was grateful to Jeanie. She'd agreed to marry him, and in doing so she'd saved the estate. More, she'd made Eileen's last years happy. He was doing what he could to show he was grateful and she was accepting with pleasure.

It should be enough.

Their puffin expedition was magic. For Alasdair, who'd seen them so often in the past, they should feel almost commonplace, but in watching Jeanie watch them he was seeing them afresh. They were amazing creatures—and Jeanie's reaction was magic.

She tried hard to be prosaic, he thought. Her reactions to him were down-to-earth and practical, and she tried to tone down her reactions to the birds, but he watched her face, he watched the awe as she saw the birds dive and come up with beaks stuffed with rows of silver fish, he watched her turn her face to the sun and he thought, Here was a woman who'd missed out on the joy of life until now.

It was a joy to be able to share.

They returned to the castle late afternoon to find all the tasks done, the castle spotless, the grass mowed, the cattle tended. Jeanie entered the amazing great hall and looked up at the newly washed leadlight, the carpets beaten, the great oak balustrades polished, and he thought he detected the glimmer of tears.

But she said nothing, just gave a brisk nod and headed for her kitchen.

The baking was done. A Victoria sponge filled with strawberries and cream and a basket of chocolate brownies were sitting on the bench. Jeanie stared at them blankly.

'What am I going to do now?' she demanded.

'Eat them,' Alasdair said promptly. 'Where's a knife?'

'Don't you dare cut the sponge. The guests can have it for supper. You can have what's left.'

'Aren't I a guest?'

'Okay, you can have some for supper,' she conceded. 'But not first slice.'

'Because?'

'Because you're the man in the middle. Guest without privileges.'

'Guest with brownie,' he retorted and bit into a still-warm cookie. 'So tomorrow…otters?'

'What do you mean, otters?'

'I mean Maggie's mam and her friends are hired to come every weekday until I tell them not, and I haven't seen the Duncairn otters for years. They used to live in the burns running into the bay. I thought we could take a picnic down there and see if we can see them. Meanwhile I'm off to work now, Jeanie. You can go put your feet up, read a book, do whatever you want, whatever you haven't been able to do for the last few years. I'll see you at dinner.'

'Guests eat out,' she said blankly, but he shook his head.

'Sorry, Jeanie, but as you said, I'm the man in the middle. I'm a guest, but I'm also Lord of this castle. I'm also, for better or for worse, your husband.'

'There was nothing in the marriage contract about me feeding you.'

'That's why I'm feeding you,' he told her and at the look on her face he grinned. 'And no, I'm not about to whisk you off to a Michelin-ranked restaurant, even if such a thing existed on Duncairn, but Maggie's mam has brought me the ingredients for a very good risotto and risotto is one of the few things in the world I'm good at. So tonight I'm cooking.'

'I don't want—'

'There are lots of things we don't want,' he said, gentling now. 'This situation is absurd but there's nothing for it but for us both to make the most of it. Risotto or nothing, Jeanie.'

She stared at him for a long moment and then, finally, she gave a brisk nod. 'Fine,' she said. 'Good. I...I'll eat your risotto and thank you for it. And thank you for today. Now I'll...I'll...go do a stocktake of...of the whisky. There's all the new stuff you've bought. I keep a ledger. Call me when dinner's ready...sir...'

'Alasdair,' he snapped.

'Alasdair,' she conceded. 'Call me when dinner's ready. And thank you.'

She fled and he stood staring after her.

She was accepting his help. It should be enough.

Only it wasn't.

She felt weird. Discombobulated. Thoroughly disoriented. For the first time in over three years she had nothing to do.

Except think of the day that had just been.

Except think of Alasdair?

He was her husband. She should be used to having husbands by now. He was nothing different.

Except he was. He'd spent today working for nothing except her enjoyment.

He'd seen puffins many times before—the way he looked at them told her that. He also had work to do. She'd heard him at the computer almost all the time he'd been here. She'd heard the insistent ring of his telephone. Alasdair McBride was the head of a gigantic web of financial enterprises, and one look at the Internet had told her just how powerful that web was.

He'd spent the day making her happy.

'Because I agreed to keep our bargain,' she told herself. 'I'm saving his butt.

'The best way for him to keep his butt safe is for him to keep a low profile.' The dogs, well-fed and exercised, were sprawled in front of the kitchen range. They were fast asleep but she needed someone—anyone—to talk to. 'He must know that, and yet he risked it…

'To make me happy?' She thought of Rory doing such a thing. Rory was always too tired, she conceded. He had long spells at sea and when he was home he wanted his armchair and the telly. He'd taken time to spend with her before they were married but afterwards…it was as if he no longer had to bother.

And Alan? That was the same thing multiplied by a million. Pounds. He'd had well over a million reasons to marry her but when he had what he wanted, she was nothing.

And Alasdair? He, too, had more than a million reasons to marry her, she thought, way more, but she'd agreed to his deal. He'd had no reason to spend today with her.

'Maybe he thinks I'll back out,' she told the dogs but she knew it wasn't that.

Or maybe it was that she hoped it wasn't that.

'And that's just your stupid romantic streak,' she told herself crossly. 'And, Jeanie Lochlan, it's more than time you were over that nonsense.'

Her discussion with herself was interrupted by her phone. Maggie, she thought, and sure enough her friend was on the line, and Maggie was almost bursting with curiosity.

'How did it go? Oh, Jeanie, isn't he gorgeous? I watched you go out through the entrance with the field glasses—I imagine half the village did. Six hours you were out. Six hours by yourself with the man! And the amount he's given Dougal for the *Mary-Jane*, and what he's paying Mam and her friends… Jeanie, what are you doing not being in bed with your husband right now?'

She took a deep breath at that. 'He's not my real husband,' she managed but Maggie snorted.

'You could have fooled me. And Mam says he was just lovely on the phone and he's thanked her for the sponge cake and the brownies as though she wasn't even paid for them, and he's organised her to go back tomorrow and he says he's taking you to see otters. Otters! You know the old cottage down by the Craigie Burn? There's otters down there, I'm sure of it. You could light a fire and—'

'Maggie!'

'It's just a suggestion. Jeanie, you married the man and if you aren't in bed with him already you should be. Oh, Jeanie, I know he's not like Alan, I know it.'

'You've hardly met him.'

'The way he said his vows…'

'We were both lying and you know it.'

'I don't know it,' Maggie said stoutly. 'You went home last night, didn't you? One night married, three hundred and sixty-four to go—or should I multiply that by fifty years? Jeanie, do yourself a favour and go for it. Go for him.'

'Why would I?'

There was a moment's silence while Maggie collected her answer. One of the guest's cars was approaching. Jeanie could see it through the kitchen window. She took a plate and started arranging brownies. This was her job, she told herself. Her life.

'Because he can afford—' Maggie started but Jeanie cut her off before she could finish.

'He can afford anything he wants,' she conceded. 'But that's thanks to me. I told you how Eileen's will works. He gets to keep his fortune and I… I get to keep my independence. That's the way I want it, Maggie, and that's the way it's going to be.'

'But you will go to see the otters tomorrow?'

'Yes,' she said, sounding goaded. Which was how she felt, she conceded. She'd been backed into a corner, and she wasn't at all sure she could extricate herself.

By keeping busy, she told herself, taking the brownies off the plate and rearranging them more…artistically.

One day down, three hundred and sixty-four to go.

CHAPTER SEVEN

THEY DID GO to look for otters, and Alasdair decreed they would go to Craigie Burn. It was the best place to see otters, he told her, the furthest place on the estate from any road, a section of the burn where otters had hunted and fished for generations almost undisturbed. The tiny burnside cottage had been built by a long-ago McBride who'd fancied fishing and camping overnight in relative comfort. But at dusk and dawn the midges appeared in their hordes and the fishing McBride of yore had soon decided that the trek back to the comforts of the castle at nightfall was worth the effort. The cottage had therefore long fallen into disrepair. The roof was intact but the place was pretty much a stone shell.

Jeanie hadn't intended telling Alasdair about Craigie Burn—but of course he knew.

'I spent much of my childhood on the estate,' he told her as they stowed lunch into the day pack. 'I had the roaming of the place.'

'Alan, too?' she asked because she couldn't help herself. Alan had hardly talked of his childhood—he'd hardly talked of his family.

'My father and Alan's father were peas in a pod,' he said curtly. 'They were interested in having a good time and not much else. They weren't interested in their sons. Both our childhoods were therefore lonely but Alan thought he was lonelier here. The few times Eileen brought him here he hated it.'

He swung the pack onto his back and then appeared to check Jeanie out—as she checked the guests out before they went rambling, making sure boots were stout, clothing sensible, the wildness of the country taken into account when dressing. He gave a curt nod. 'Good.' The dogs were locked in the wet room. Maggie's mam would see them walked, for if the dogs were with them the possibility of seeing otters was about zero. 'Ready?'

'Ready,' she said, feeling anything but. What was she doing traipsing around the country with this man when she should be earning her keep?

But Alasdair was determined to give her a...honeymoon? Whatever it was called, it seemed she had no choice but to give in to him. She was still getting over sitting at the kitchen table the night before eating the risotto he'd prepared. It was excellent risotto, but...

But the man had her totally off balance.

They set off, down the cliff path to the rocky beach, then along the seafront, clambering over rocks, making their way to where Craigie Burn tumbled to the sea.

The going was tough, even for Jeanie, who was used to it. Alasdair, though, had no trouble. A few times he paused and turned to help her. She shook off his offer of assistance but in truth his concern made her feel...

As she had no right to feel, she told herself. She didn't need to feel like the 'little woman'. She'd had two marriages of being a doormat. No more.

'Tell me about your childhood here,' she encouraged as she struggled up one particularly rocky stretch. She asked more to take Alasdair's attention away from her heavy breathing than out of interest—she would not admit she was struggling.

But instead of talking as he climbed, Alasdair turned

and gazed out to sea. Did he sense how much she needed a breather? He'd better not, she thought. I will not admit I'm a lesser climber than he is.

But…without admitting anything…she turned and gazed out to sea with him.

'I loved it,' he said at last, and it had taken so long to answer she'd almost forgotten she'd asked. But his gaze was roving along the coastline, rugged, wild, amazing. 'My father and my uncle hardly spent any time here. They hated it. My grandparents sent them to boarding school in England and they hardly came back. They both married socialites, they lived in the fast lane on my grandparents' money and they weren't the least bit interested in their sons. But Alan loved their lifestyle—from the time he was small he wanted to be a part of it. He loved the fancy hotels, the servants, the parties. It was only me who hated it.'

'So you came back here.'

'We were dumped,' he told her. 'Both of us. Our parents dumped us with Eileen every school holidays and she thought the castle would be good for us. Alan chafed to be able to join his parents' lifestyle.' He gave a wry smile. 'Maybe I was just antisocial even then, but here…'

He paused and looked around him again. A pair of eagles was soaring in the thermals. She should be used to them by now, she told herself, but every time she saw them she felt her heart swell. They were magnificent and Alasdair paused long enough for her to know he felt it, too.

'Here was home,' Alasdair said at last. 'Here I could be myself. Eileen usually stayed when Alan and I were here. You saw the place before she renovated. She and my grandfather didn't appear to notice conditions were a bit…sparse. I don't think I noticed, either. I was too busy, exploring, fishing, trying not to think how many days I had left before I went back to school. Alan was counting off the days until he could leave. I wanted to stay for the rest of my life.'

'You didn't, though. You ended up based in Edinburgh. You hardly came here until…until Eileen got sick at the end.'

She was trying hard not to make her words an accusation but she didn't get it right. It sounded harsh.

There was a long silence. 'I didn't mean to be accusatory,' she ventured at last and he shook his head.

'I know you didn't. But I need to explain. At first I didn't come because I was immersed in business. I took to the world of finance like a duck to water, and maybe I lost perspective on other things I loved. But then… When Eileen started spending more time here, I didn't come because you were here.'

That was enough to give a girl pause. To make her forget to breathe for a moment. 'Did you dislike me so much?' she asked in a small voice and he gave an angry shrug.

'I didn't know you, but I knew Alan. I knew I hated him.'

'Because?'

'Because he was the sort of kid who pulled wings off flies. I won't sugar coat it. My father was older than his, so my father stood to inherit the title, with me coming after him. Alan's father resented mine and the resentment was passed on down the line. I don't know what sort of poison was instilled in Alan when he was small but he was taught to hate me and he knew how to hurt.'

Whoa. He hadn't talked of this before. She knew it instinctively and who knew how she knew it, but she did. What he was saying was being said to her alone—and it hurt to say it.

His eyes went to a point further along the coast, where the burn met the sea. 'It came to a head down here,' he told her, absently, almost as if speaking to the land rather than her. Apologising for not being back for so long? 'I loved the otters, and I used to come down here often. One day Alan followed me. I was lying on my stomach watching the otters through field glasses. He was up on the ridge, and he'd taken my grandfather's shotgun. He killed three otters before I reached him. He was eighteen months older than me, and much bigger, and I went for him and he hit me with the gun. I still carry the scar under my hairline. I was dazed and bleeding, and he laughed and walked back to the castle.'

'No…'

His mouth set in a grim line. 'Thinking back…that blow to my head… He nearly killed me. But I was twelve and he was fourteen, and I was afraid of him. I told Grand-mother I'd fallen on the cliffs. Soon after that his parents decided he was old enough to join them in the resorts they stayed at, so I didn't have to put up with him any more. I never told Eileen what happened. In retrospect, maybe I should have.' And then he paused and looked at her. 'But you… You loved him?'

'No.'

'It doesn't matter. It's none of my business, but these last years… Just knowing you were here in the castle was enough to keep me away.'

'I'm so sorry.'

'You shouldn't have to apologise for your husband's faults.'

'But as you said, I married him.'

'I can't see you killing otters.'

'Is that why you took me to look at the puffins first?' she asked. 'To see how I reacted?'

'I was hardly expecting a gun.'

'I'd guess you weren't expecting a gun from Alan, ei-ther.' She sighed and took a deep breath—and it wasn't only because she needed a few deep breaths before tackling the rise in front of her. 'Okay, I understand. Alasdair, we don't need to go there any more. I'll stop judging you for not spending more time with your grandmother if you stop judging me for being married to Alan. I know I'm still… tainted…but we can work around that. Deal?'

He looked at her for a long moment, seeming to take in every inch of her. And then, slowly, his face creased into a smile.

It was an awesome smile, Jeanie thought. It was dark turning to light. It lit his whole face, made his dark eyes glint with laughter, made him seem softer, more vulnerable…

A warrior exposed?

That shouldn't be how she saw him, but suddenly it was. He was the Earl of Duncairn, and he wore armour, just as surely as his ancestors wore chain mail. His armour might be invisible but it was still there.

Telling her about the otters, telling her about Alan, had made a chink in that armour, she thought, and even though he was smiling she could see the hint of uncertainty. As if telling her had left him vulnerable and he didn't like it.

She had a sudden vision of him as a child, here in this castle. It was wild now; it would have been wilder then. Eileen had told her she'd brought both boys here during their school holidays. Jeanie had envisaged two boys with a whole estate to explore and love.

But later Eileen had said she'd often had to leave the boys with the housekeeper when she'd had to go back to Edinburgh, and Jeanie saw that clearly now, too. A twelve-year-old boy would have been subjected to the whims and cruelty of his older cousin. It wouldn't just have been the otters, she thought grimly. She knew Alan. There would have been countless cruelties during the years.

'This next bit's rough,' Alasdair was saying and he held his hand out. 'Let me help you.'

She looked down at his hand.

He was a McBride. He was yet another man who'd caught her at a weak moment and married her.

But the day was magic, the hill in front was tough and Alasdair was right beside her, smiling, holding out his hand.

'If I had one more brain cell, it'd be lonely,' she muttered out loud, to no one in particular, but Alasdair just raised his brows and kept on smiling and the sun was warm on her face and the otters were waiting, and a woman was only human after all.

She put her hand in his and she started forward again.

With Alasdair.

What followed was another magic day. Duncairn's weather was unpredictable to say the least, but today the gods had decided to be kind—more, they'd decided to put on Scotland at her most splendid. There was just enough wind to keep the midges at bay. The sky was dotted by clouds that might or might not turn to rain, but for now the sun shone, and the water in the burn was crystal clear.

Without hesitation Alasdair led them to a ledge near the cottage, a rocky outcrop covered with a thick layer of moss. It stretched out over the burn, but a mere ten feet above, so they could lie on their stomachs and peer over the edge to see what was happening in the water below.

And for a while nothing happened. Maybe it wouldn't, Alasdair conceded. Otters were notoriously shy. They could well have sensed their movement and darted back under cover, but for now they were content to wait.

Alasdair was more than content.

It was a strange feeling, lying on the moss-covered rock with Jeanie stretched out by his side.

His life was city-based now, mostly spent in Edinburgh but sometimes London, New York, Copenhagen, wherever the demands of his company took him. Under the terms of Eileen's will he'd need to delegate much of that travel for the next year. He'd thought he'd miss it, but lying next to Jeanie, waiting for otters to grace them with their presence, he thought suddenly, *Maybe I won't*.

What other woman had he ever met who'd lie on her stomach on a rock and not move, not say a word, and somehow exude a quality of complete restfulness? After half an hour the otters still hadn't shown themselves. He knew from past experience that half an hour wasn't long for these shy creatures to stay hidden, but did Jeanie know that? If she did, she didn't mind. She lay with her chin resting on her hands, watching the water below, but her eyes were half-closed, almost contemplative.

Her hair was tumbling down around her face. A curl was blocking his view. He wanted to lift it away.

She'd been Alan's wife.

Surely it didn't matter. He wanted to touch…

But if he moved he'd scare the otters, and he knew…he just knew that this woman would be furious with him—not just for touching her but for spoiling what she was waiting for.

She was waiting for otters, not for him.

Right. Watch on. He managed to turn his attention back to the water rippling beneath them.

'There…' It was hardly a whisper. Jeanie was looking left to where a lower overhang shaded the water, and there it was, a sleek, beautiful otter slipping from the shadows, with a younger one behind.

'Oh,' Jeanie breathed. 'Oh…'

She was completely unaware of him. All her attention was on the otters.

They were worth watching. They were right out from under the shadows now, slipping over the burn's rocky bed, nosing through the sea grasses and kelp, hunting for the tiny sea creatures that lived there.

'They eat the kelp, too,' Jeanie whispered but Alasdair thought she was talking to herself, not to him.

'They're stunning,' he whispered back. 'Did you know their coat's so thick not a single drop of water touches their skin?'

'That's why they're hunted,' she whispered back. 'You will…keep protecting them? After I've left?'

And there it was again—reality, rearing its ugly head. At the end of this year, this castle would go to Jeanie's creditors. He'd buy it and keep it—of course he would. He'd keep it safe. But he glanced at Jeanie and saw her expression and he thought, She's not sure.

He'd promised—but this woman must have been given empty promises in the past.

She was resting her chin on her hands and he could see the gold band he'd placed on her finger two days ago. For a year they were required to be officially married, and officially married people wore rings.

But now… What worth was a promise? Jeanie didn't trust him and why should she?

He glanced down at the otters, hunting now in earnest, despite the humans close by. They must sense their shadows, but they'd waited for almost an hour before resuming hunting. They'd be hungry. They'd be forced to trust.

As Jeanie had been forced to trust. She'd been put into an impossible situation. How to tell her…?

The ring…

One moment she was lying watching otters, worrying about their future, thinking would Alasdair really keep this estate? Would he keep caring for these wild creatures she'd come to love?

The next moment he'd rolled back a little and was tugging at his hand. Not his left hand, though, where she'd placed the wedding ring that meant so little. Instead he was tugging at his right hand.

At the Duncairn ring.

She'd seen this ring. It was in every one of the portraits of the McBride earls, going back in time until the names blurred and Eileen's history lesson had started seeming little more than a roll call.

Each of those long-dead earls had worn this ring, and now it lay on Alasdair's hand. It was a heavy gold signet, an intricate weaving, the head of an eagle embossed on a shield, with the first letters of the family crest, worn but still decipherable, under the eagle's beak: LHV.

Loyalty, honour, valour.

Alan had mentioned this ring, not once, but often. 'He's a prig,' he'd said of Alasdair. 'And he's younger than me. He thinks he can lord it over me just because he wears the damned ring…'

The 'damned ring' was being held out to her. No, not held out. Alasdair was taking her hand in his and sliding the ring onto the middle finger of her right hand. It fitted—as if it was meant to be there.

She stared down at it, stunned. So much history in one piece of jewellery… So many McBride men who'd worn this ring…

'Wh-what do you think you're doing?' she stammered at last, because this didn't make sense.

'Pledging my troth.'

'Huh?' Dumb, she thought, but that was how she was feeling. Dumb. And then she thought: she shouldn't be here. Her fragile control felt like crumbling. This man seemed as large and fierce and dangerous as the warriors he'd descended from.

Loyalty, honour, valour…

This was the McBride chieftain. He was placing a ring on her finger, and the ring took her breath away.

'Jeanie, I have nothing else to show you I'm serious.' In the kirk, Alasdair's vows had been businesslike, serious, but almost…clinical. Here, now, his words sounded as if they came from the heart. 'I'm promising you that at the end of this year of marriage I will make your life secure. As well, I will buy this castle for what it's worth and Alan's creditors will be paid. I'll treat it as the last of Alan's share of the estate. He was, after all, just as much Eileen's grandson as I was.'

'You don't have to make me secure,' she managed, still staring at the ring. 'And Alan wasn't worth—'

'I'm not judging,' he told her. 'And I refuse to think of Alan after this. To be honest, it took courage to come here. I haven't been back to this place since that day he hurt the otters. But I have come, to find life has moved on. But it needs faith to face it. So here's my faith in you, and I'm hoping you can find that faith in me. At the end of the year I'll take on this estate and I'll care for it as Eileen would have wanted it cared for. And as I suspect you want it cared for. And I will ensure your future…'

'I don't want anything.'

'I know you don't. You don't seem to put yourself into the equation at all, but I'm putting you there. It seems you canna keep the castle, Jeanie lass, no matter what Eileen's will says, but you can keep the heart of it. As long as you wear this ring, this estate will be safe, our Jeanie. I promise you. Hand on this ring, I swear.'

He'd lapsed into broad Scottish, the voice of his ancestors, the voice of his people. He was lying full-length on a bed of moss over a rippling burn, he was looking at her as no man had ever looked at her, and the way he spoke… It was as if he were kneeling before a throne, head bowed, swearing fealty to his king.

Swearing fealty to…her?

'Alasdair…' It was hard to breathe, much less speak.

She had to fight for the words. 'There's no need,' she managed. 'You don't have to do this. Besides…' She stared at the intricate weaving of gold on her finger and her heart failed her. 'I'll probably lose it in a pudding mix.'

He smiled then, but his smile was perfunctory, the gravity of the moment unchanged. 'I know you won't. I trust you with it, Jeanie, as you trust me with the castle.' His hand closed over hers, folding her fingers, the ring enclosed between them. 'I'm asking that you trust me back.'

'I can… I can trust you without the ring.'

'Why would you?'

'Because…' How to say it? There were no words.

And the truth was that until now, until this moment, she hadn't trusted. Yes, he was Lord of Duncairn but he was just another man, like her father, like Rory, like Alan. A man to be wary of. A man who sought to control.

Was this ring another form of control? She searched for the control angle, and couldn't find it.

She had no doubt as to the significance of this ring. She could hear it in his voice—that it meant as much to him as it had to every other earl who'd ever worn it.

Trust… He was offering it in spades.

'I'll give it back,' she managed. 'At the end of the year.'

'You'll give it to me when you've seen what I intend doing with this place,' he told her. 'When you see me hand the wilderness areas over to a trust to keep it safe in perpetuity. When you have total faith, Jeanie McBride, then you can give it back.'

'I have faith now.'

'You don't,' he said softly and his hold on her hand tightened. 'You can't. But you will.'

And then it rained.

She'd been so caught up, first with the otters and then with…well, with what she'd been caught up with, that she hadn't noticed the clouds scudding in from the west. Now, suddenly, the sun disappeared and the first fat droplets splashed down.

And Alasdair was tugging her to her feet, smiling, as if something had been settled between them that made going forward easy.

Maybe it had.

And maybe, Jeanie thought as she scrambled with Alasdair to reach the shelter of the cottage, as she didn't quibble about the feel of his hand still holding hers, as she fought to regain her breath and composure, maybe something had settled inside her as well.

Trust? She'd never trusted. She'd walked into this marriage blind, knowing only that circumstances once again had thrust her into making vows. But now… For some reason it was as if a weight was lifting from her shoulders, a weight she hadn't known she was carrying.

This year could work. This year could almost be…fun? Such a word was almost nonexistent in her vocabulary. As a child of a dour, grim fisherman and then as Rory's wife, a man under the thumb of his family, a man with limited horizons and no ambition to change, life had been hard and pretty much joyless. Life with Alan, so tantalising at first, had ended up filled with nothing but terror, and since that time she'd been subsumed with guilt, with debt, with responsibilities.

Today, though…today she'd lain in the sun and watched otters and this man had given her his ancestral ring. He'd given her trust…

And then he pushed open the cottage door and all thoughts of trust went out of the window.

She'd been in this cottage before. She'd walked this way with the dogs—it was a fair trek from the castle but at times during the past three years she'd needed the effort it required. Sometimes trekking the estate was the only way to get rid of the demons in her head, but even when she was fighting demons she still liked staying dry. On the west coast of Scotland rain came sudden and fierce. She'd walked and watched the sky—as they hadn't today—and she'd used this cottage for shelter.

She knew it. Any furniture had long gone, the windows were open to the elements and the place seemed little more than a cave.

But today… Someone had been in here before them. The room they walked into was a combination of kitchen/living, with a hearth at one end. The hearth had always been blackened and empty, but now… It contained a massive heap of glowing coals. Firewood was stacked beside it. The stone floor in front of it had been swept of debris and a rug laid in front. With the fire at its heart, the room looked almost cosy.

She hadn't noticed smoke from the chimney. Why?

She'd been too aware of Alasdair, that was why. Of all the stupid…

'How on earth…?' she managed, staring at the fire in disbelief, and Alasdair looked smug.

'Insurance,' he told her. 'There's never a day on this island when you're guaranteed of staying dry, and I'm a cautious man. I never take risks without insurance.' But he was frowning at the rug. 'I didn't ask for the rug, though. That's a bit over the top.'

'You think?' Her voice was practically a squeak. 'Who did this? Not you. Surely…'

'You don't think I could have loped up here before breakfast?'

'No!' And her tone was so adamant that he grinned.

'That's not a very complimentary way to talk to your liege lord.'

She told him where he could put his liege lord and his grin widened. 'I talked to Mac about getting the fire lit,' he confessed. 'Mac can't walk up here himself any more—I need to do something about gillie succession planning— but he does know a lad, who came up here and lit it for him.'

'A lad?' Jeanie breathed. And then she closed her eyes. 'No.' It was practically a groan. 'It won't be one lad. It'll be two. He'll have asked Lachlan and Hamish McDonald, two of the biggest wastrels this island's ever known. They're twins, they're forty, their mother still irons their socks and they do odd jobs when they feel like it. And they gossip. Mac's their uncle. Do you realise what you've done? This'll be all over the island before we get back to the castle that you and I have lain by the fire here and…and…'

'And what, Jeanie?' His smile was still there but his eyes had become…watchful?

'And nothing,' she snapped and walked forward and grabbed the backpack from his shoulders and started to unpack. 'We'll eat the sandwiches I made and then we'll go home. And why did you pack wine? If you think I could climb these crags after a drink…'

'I could carry you.' He sounded almost hopeful.

'You and whose bulldozer? Get real.' She was totally flustered, trying to haul the lunch box from the backpack, trying not to look at him. She tugged it free with a wrench and shoved it down onto the hearth.

Alasdair stooped. His hand came over hers before she could rise again and his laughter died.

'I'm not into seduction,' he told her. His words echoed into the stillness. 'You're safe, Jeanie. This fire's here to keep us warm and dry, nothing more. I won't touch you.'

There was a long pause. 'I never said you'd try,' she said at last.

'You look like you expect it.'

She was struggling, trying to get it right, trying to explain this…panic. 'It's this ring,' she said at last. She stared

down at the magnificent Duncairn signet and she felt…
small. Frightened? At the edge of a precipice?

But still Alasdair's hand was over hers, warm, steady,
strong. They were crouched before the fire. His face in the
firelight was strong and sure.

'The ring is simply a promise,' he told her. 'It's a promise to keep the faith, to keep your faith. You needn't fear.
I'm not into taking women against their will.'

'Not even…' Her voice was scarcely a whisper. 'Not
even the woman you've taken as your wife?'

'You're not my wife,' he said, evenly now. 'We both
know that this is a business relationship, despite what
Hamish and Lachie may well have told the islanders. So
let's have our sandwiches, and I intend to drink at least
one glass of this truly excellent wine—my grandmother
kept a superb cellar. You can join me or not, but whatever
you do, my Jeanie, know that seduction is off the agenda.'

Which was all very well, she thought crossly as she did
what was sensible. She ate her sandwiches and she drank
one glass—only one—of wine, and she thought she should
have settled, but why did he have to have called her *my
Jeanie*? And *Jeanie lass*?

It was merely familiar, she told herself as she cleared
their debris into the backpack. Any number of the older
folk on the island called her Jeanie lass. Any number of
islanders referred to her as our Jeanie.

But Alasdair McBride was not a member of the island's
older folk. Nor was he really an islander.

It shouldn't matter. It didn't matter.

It did. It made her feel…

Scared.

'It does seem a shame to waste the rug. Do you want a
nap before we head back?' Alasdair was watching her—
and the low-life was laughing again. But not laughing out

loud. It was more a glint behind his eyes, a telltale quiver of the corners of his mouth, the way his eyes met hers…

Laughter never seemed too far away. What did this man have to laugh about? she demanded of herself. Didn't he know life was hard?

But it wasn't hard for him. This man was the Earl of Duncairn. He could laugh at what he wanted.

He could laugh at her if he wanted. She couldn't afford to respond.

'It's stopped raining and we're getting out of here fast,' she said with acerbity. 'I wouldn't be surprised if there are field glasses trained on this doorway right now. There's no way I'm having the islanders conjecturing about my supposed love life.'

'They're conjecturing already,' he told her. 'And there's hardly shame attached. We are married.'

'We're not married,' she snapped again. 'Do you want to see the otters again before we head back?'

'Yes.' The sun was shining again. 'Why not?'

'Then let's go,' she told him. 'But keep twenty paces distant, Alasdair McBride, and no closer or this ring gets tossed in the burn.'

'You wouldn't.' She'd touched him on the raw then; his face had even paled. She relented. Some things were too precious to even joke about.

'No. I wouldn't. Are you sure you don't want it back?'

'I don't want it back,' he told her. 'I trust you. And you can trust me, Jeanie, whether it's at twenty paces or a whole lot closer.'

A whole lot closer? There was the crux of the matter, she decided. He was too gorgeous for his own good.

Her problem was, she thought as she lay in bed that night and stared up into the darkness…her major problem was that she wouldn't mind getting a whole lot closer to Alasdair.

Or just a bit?

No. At three in the morning her mind was crystal clear and there was no way she could escape honesty. A whole lot closer was what she wanted.

She was out of her mind. A whole lot closer was exactly what sensible Jeanie would never allow herself to think about.

Except she was thinking about it. She was lying sleepless in the small hours. Alasdair's wedding band lay on one finger, his ancestral signet lay on another and she felt…she felt…

'Like a stupid serving maid having ideas above my station,' she told herself crossly and threw back the covers and went to stare out of the window.

She could see the sea from her bedroom. The moon was almost full, sending streams of silver across the water, almost into her room. It felt as if she could walk out of the bedroom and keep on walking…

'As maybe you should if you feel like this,' she told herself. 'Use some brains.

'I don't want to.'

Above her, in the vast, imposing bedroom that had been the bedroom of Earls of Duncairn for centuries past, lay the current Earl of Duncairn. The four-poster bed was enormous. His bedroom was enormous. Eileen had giggled when she'd been making decisions about restoring the castle and she'd told Jeanie she wanted a bedroom fit for a lord. Together they'd chosen rich velvet drapes, tapestries, rugs, furnishings…

To say it was lavish was an understatement. Apart from the servants' rooms she used and had—with some difficulty—kept free from Eileen's sumptuous plans, this castle was truly astonishing.

'It's enough to make its lord feel he can snap his fingers and any servant girl will come running,' she said out loud and then she caught her breath with where her thoughts were taking her.

This servant girl wouldn't mind running—but this servant girl should turn and run as far from this castle as possible.

'I was good today,' she told herself. 'I was sensible.

'Excellent,' she told herself. 'That's two days down, three hundred and sixty-three to go.'

But... There was a voice whispering in the back of her head and it wasn't a small voice, either. You're married to him. It wouldn't hurt.

'Are you out of your mind? Of course it'll hurt.' She ran her fingers through her tangled curls and the signet ring caught and hurt. 'Excellent,' she told herself. 'Just keep doing that. Pull your hair whenever you think of being an idiot.

'And he doesn't want you, anyway.'

She let her mind drift back to her mind-set when she'd married Rory. She'd still been a kid when she'd married him. He'd been safe, he'd been kind, and when she'd taken her vows she'd felt...as if a new net had been closing over her? He'd protected her from her father, and she'd been grateful, but that hadn't stopped her lying in bed at night after a wild night watching the telly feeling...was this all there was?

Which was why, two years after Rory's death, she'd been ripe for the picking. She had no doubt now that the only reason Alan had been attracted to her was to persuade his grandmother to give him money, but the means he'd used to attract... Excitement, adventure, travel had seemed a wild elixir, a drug impossible to resist, and by the time she'd woken to reality she'd been in so far it had been impossible to extricate herself.

And now here she was, wanting to…wanting to…

'I want nothing,' she told herself. 'For heaven's sake, Jeanie, grow a little sense. Put your head in a bucket of cold water if you must, but do not walk headlong into another emotional mess.'

'Get some sense.' On the floor above, in a bedroom so vast it made him feel ridiculous, Alasdair was staring at the slivers of moonlight lighting the dark and he was feeling pretty much the same.

'If you sleep with her, how the hell are you going to extricate yourself? You'll be properly married.

'There's no thought of sleeping with her.'

But there was. No matter how much his head told him it was crazy, his body was telling him something else entirely.

'It's just this stupid honeymoon idea,' he told himself. 'I never should have instigated it. Leave her to get back to her work and you get back to yours.'

Except…how long since she'd had a holiday? Yesterday and today she'd lit up. Clambering up the scree today, lying on the moss-covered rocks, watching the otters, she'd seemed younger, happier…free.

What had two husbands done to her? What had they done *for* her?

Saddled her with debt and regrets, that was what. Hell, she deserved a break.

'But not with me.' He said it out loud.

He should call off this honeymoon idea. But no, he couldn't do that. He'd told her they'd have a week.

She could have a week, he thought. She could do whatever she wanted, just not with him.

That's not a honeymoon.

'Right.' He was talking into the dark. 'It's not and it's not supposed to be.

'You'll tell her how?

'Straight out. She'll be relieved.

And what was there in that that made his gut twist?

Honesty. He could at least give her that. She deserved no less.

She deserved…

That he think seriously about what he was letting himself in for.

CHAPTER EIGHT

SHOULD ONE MAKE a special dinner to celebrate a one-month anniversary?

The weather had closed in, the sleet was driving from the north and she had no guests booked for the night. Jeanie was staring into the refrigerator, vacillating between sausages or something fancy. She had beef in the freezer. She had mushrooms for guests' breakfasts. She had excellent red wine, bought by Eileen and stocked in the castle larder.

Beef Bourguignon was hardly Scottish, but she could serve the rest of the red wine alongside, and make a lovely mash, and maybe make a good apple pie as well. She had clotted cream…

'And he'll eat it at his desk as he's eaten his dinner at his desk every night for the last month.' She slumped down at the table. The two dogs put their noses on her knee and whined.

'Yeah, the weather's getting to you, too,' she told them, but she knew it wasn't that. She'd grown up with Duncairn weather. She usually enjoyed the gales that blasted the island, donning wellies and mac and walking her legs off, the dogs at her side.

She'd walked her legs off this afternoon but it hadn't stopped the feeling of…desolation?

'Which is dumb,' she told the dogs and gave herself a mental shake. 'As is making any kind of anniversary dinner when all it means is that we've put up with each other for a month.

'And it's working okay,' she added after a moment, as if she was reassuring herself.

It was. Sort of. After the dumb idea of the honeymoon, which had lasted two days before he'd pulled out and she'd agreed with relief, Alasdair had decreed she have one day a week completely off. But not with him.

Their lives had settled into a pattern. She cared for the castle and the guests. Alasdair worked in his rooms or he headed to Edinburgh for the day. When that happened his chopper would arrive at dawn and bring him back before dusk, so one of his precious nights of freedom wouldn't be used up.

He walked but he walked alone. He kept himself to himself and she did the same.

He'd spent three nights in Hong Kong and it shouldn't have made any difference, but it did. The castle was empty for his going.

And now he was back. Today he was spending the entire day here. The weather was too rough for the chopper.

He was trapped—and that was how she felt, too. She worked on but she was so aware of him overhead. It was as if the entire month had been building. Every sense was tuned...

'And I'm getting stupid in my old age,' she told the dogs. 'I'm not a needy woman. I'm not.' She stared around the kitchen in frustration. She needed more to do. Anything. Fast.

Then the kitchen door swung open. Alasdair was standing there, in his casual trousers and sweater, his hair ruffled as if he'd raked it and raked it again.

'Jeanie?'

'Mmm?' Somehow she made herself sound non-committal. Somehow.

'This weather's driving me nuts.'

'You *are* on Duncairn.'

'I am,' he told her. 'And I'm thinking at the end of eleven months I'll be back in Edinburgh full-time and what will I have to show for these months? So I'm thinking... Jeanie, would you teach me to cook something other than spaghetti or risotto?'

If Duncairn had split in two and drifted in different directions in the sea, she couldn't have been more astonished.

'Cook,' she said blankly and he gave her a lopsided smile.

'If you would.'

'Why?'

Why? The question hung in the air between them. It needed an answer and Alasdair was searching for one.

The fact that Jeanie was in the kitchen wasn't enough—though it was certainly a factor.

For the past month he'd put his head down and worked. Duncairn Enterprises took all his time and more. There seemed to be some sort of financial leak at head office. It was worrying, but over the past few weeks he'd almost welcomed it, sorting painstakingly through the remaining financial web his grandmother had controlled, rejecting the inclination to do anything else.

This afternoon he'd thought, Why? He could call in outside auditors to do what he'd been doing. He wasn't happy about letting outsiders look at possible financial problems of his grandmother's making, but then his grandmother was past caring, and Jeanie was downstairs.

So why not go downstairs and join her? It had been an insistent niggle and this afternoon it had become a roar. Because he didn't want to get emotionally involved? He'd spent a month telling himself to form any sort of relationship would be courting catastrophe. If it didn't work out and she walked, it would be a disaster. He knew the way forward was to move with caution.

But for the past month he'd lived in the same house with Jeanie. He'd watched the dogs fly to meet her every time she left the house. He'd watched from his windows whenever she took them out, striding out across the pasture, stopping to speak to the cattle, the dogs wild with excitement at her side.

He'd listened to her sing as she did the housework. He'd heard her laugh with the guests, or empathise with them about bad roads or lost suitcases or general travel fatigue.

He'd eaten while he worked, separate from the other guests, working through a pile of papers a foot high, and he'd been aware of the aromas coming from the kitchen. He'd watched the dogs fly back and forth…

And this afternoon he'd cracked. He stood at the kitchen door and felt mildly foolish but hell, he was here, he'd said it and he was seeing this through.

And she'd asked why.

'I'm fed up with playing Lord of the castle,' he told her and she looked up at him and smiled.

'You can hardly knock back the title. It's what you are.'

'While you play servant.'

'That's what I am.'

'No.' It was an explosion that had the dogs starting out from under the table. Abbot even ventured a feeble bark.

'Your grandmother employed me to housekeep for the castle,' Jeanie said mildly. 'That's what I've been doing for the last three years. I have one more year to go.'

'You were Alan's wife. You deserve—'

'I deserve nothing for marrying Alan.'

'My grandmother thought you did.' Why was he getting into this conversation? He surely hadn't intended to.

'Your grandmother was kind and sentimental and bossy.

She felt sorry for me, end of story. Now if you'll excuse me, I need to get on…'

'Cooking. What do you intend to cook?'

'You're the only guest in the house tonight. What would you like me to cook?'

'I'm not a guest.'

'No, but in my mind that's how I'm seeing you. It keeps me sane. Now…requests? Sausages? Beef Bourguignon? Anything else that strikes your fancy?'

She was wearing a pink, frilly apron over her jeans and windcheater. It was tied with a big bow at the back, almost defiantly, as if she knew the bow was corny but she liked it anyway. She really was impossibly cute, he thought. Jeanie Lochlan, Domestic Goddess. Jeanie McBride…

His wife.

'Singing hinnies,' he told her. 'And I want to make them.'

'You're serious?'

'Do you know how to make them?' he asked.

'You're asking me, an islander born and bred, if I know how to make singing hinnies?'

'I'm sorry. Of course you do.'

'My granny's singing hinnies were famous.'

'Is the recipe a family secret?'

'Possibly.' She eyed him thoughtfully. 'Though some might say you're family now.'

And what was there in that to give him hope? He almost took the apron Jeanie took from the pantry and offered him. But it was pink, too. Did she expect him to wear a bow as well?

'You'll get batter on your lovely sweater.'

'I have more.'

'Of course you do,' she retorted and he looked at her—just looked.

'Oops,' she said and out peeped one of her gorgeous

smiles. 'Servant giving master lip. Servant needs to learn to shut up.'

'Jeanie?'

'Yes…sir?'

'Teach me to cook,' he demanded and she saluted and her smile widened. 'What do I do?'

'What you're told, My Lord,' she retorted. 'Nothing else.'

He made singing hinnies and 'awesome' was too small a word for it. There was no explaining it. Either he was a natural-born cook or…

Or Jeanie was the world's best teacher. She certainly was good. She stood and instructed as he rubbed the butter into flour, as he made the perfect batter, as he heated the griddle on the stove, greased it with lard and finally popped his hinnie on to cook. It hissed and spluttered and rose. He flipped it over and it was done. Perfection! He placed it on a plate in the range's warming drawer and went on to make another, feeling about ten feet tall.

Closing a million-dollar deal against a business rival had never felt this good.

And then, when the last hinnie was on the plate, Jeanie put a teapot, mugs and butter and jam on a plate.

'My sitting room or yours?' she asked and that was a statement to give a man hope as well. He'd never been in Jeanie's tiny apartment. He'd seen it on the plans, a bedroom with a small living space specifically designed for a housekeeper. To be invited… Boundaries were certainly being shifted.

The castle was magnificent, lavish, amazing. Jeanie's apartment…wasn't. He stepped through the door and blinked. Gone were the opulent colours, drapes, rugs, furnishings of the ancient and historical treasure that was Duncairn Castle. This was just…home.

The dogs bounded in before him and nosedived to the

hearth. The fire was crackling, emitting a gentle heat. The room was faded, homey, full of books and magazines and odds and sods: seashells in chipped bowls, photos in unmatched frames, ceramic dogs and the odd shepherdess—what was it with ceramic shepherdesses?—an old cuckoo clock, squashy furniture… All discards, he thought, from the rest of the castle, removed as Eileen had spent a fortune on redecorating.

He thought of his magnificent living quarters upstairs and suddenly it had lost its appeal.

'Get your cooking into you before it's cold,' Jeanie told him, still smiling, so he sat in one of her squashy armchairs and he ate four singing hinnies and drank two cups of tea, and Jeanie sat on the mat with the dogs and ate two singing hinnies and drank one cup of tea and then they were done.

Done? Jeanie cleared the cups and lifted the tray to one side. To safety? The world steadied—waiting to see what would happen?

The way he was feeling… She was so… Jeanie. There was no other word to describe her. Jeanie.

He slid down onto the mat beside her. The action was deliberate. One more boundary crossed?

He shouldn't be pushing boundaries. He, of all people, knew how important boundaries were, but maybe this one could be…stretched?

'Jeanie,' he said softly and he reached out and took her hand, not the hand wearing the wedding ring because for some reason the wedding ring was not where promises were to be made, but her right hand where lay the heavy signet of the Duncairn line.

'Jeanie,' he said again, and then, because he couldn't help himself, 'I'd really like to kiss you. No pressure. If you say no, then I won't ask you again.'

'Then I'd best say yes,' she said, softly, amazingly, wonderfully. 'Because I can't stand it one moment longer. I'd really, really like it if you kissed me.'

She was out of her mind. She should not be doing this—she should not!

She was and she had no intention of stopping.

They were on the rug before the fire. His hands cupped her face, he looked into her eyes for a long, long moment, the world held its breath—and then he drew her mouth to his and kissed her.

And she'd never been kissed like this. Never. It was as if she'd found her home. Her centre. Her heart.

There was all the tenderness in the world in his kiss, and yet she could feel the strength of him, the heat, the need. The sheer arrant masculinity of him.

How could a kiss be a life changer? How could a kiss make her feel she'd never been alive until this moment?

How could a kiss make her feel as if her world were melting, the outside fading to nothing, that everything were disappearing except this man, this moment, this kiss?

The heat…the strength…the surety… For that was what it was, she thought in the tiny part of her mind that was still available for rational thought. Surety?

Home.

She was twenty-nine years old. She'd spent twenty-nine years failing at this relationship business. She'd had a weak mother, a bully for a father, a husband who was no more than a mirror of his family's business, then another who was vain and selfish and greedy.

This man might be all those things underneath, she thought, but there was no hint of it in his kiss. Her head should override what her body was telling her, what his kiss was telling her, but this kiss couldn't be ignored. This kiss was making her body feel as if it were no longer hers.

Rightly or wrongly, all that mattered was that, for this

moment, Alasdair McBride wanted her and she wanted him, as simple as that. One man, one woman and a desire so great that neither could pull back. Sense had no place here. This desire was as primeval as life itself and she'd gone too far to pull back.

Too far to pull back? That was crazy. It was only a kiss. She could break it in a moment.

But she had no intention of breaking it. This kiss was taking her places she'd never been, places she hadn't known existed. Her hands had somehow found their way to his hair, her fingers sliding through the thick thatch of jet black, her hands drawing him closer so she could deepen…deepen…

She heard a tiny sound from far away and she thought, That's me. Moaning with desire? What sort of dumb thought was that?

Dumb maybe, but the time for asking questions was over. If this moment was all she had of this man, her body knew she'd take it.

Weak perhaps? Stupid? Was it Jeanie being passive? Was this the Jeanie of old?

No. She felt her world shift and shift again and she knew this was no passive submission. Her hands held him even tighter and then tugged until his arms came around her and he drew her up to him, so his dark eyes could gleam into hers.

'Jeanie McBride, can I take my wife to bed?'

If the dogs hadn't been there, they might have made love right where they were—he certainly wanted to—but the dogs were gazing on with interest and, even though they were only dogs, it was enough to make a man take action.

Or maybe it was because he wanted to take this woman to bed with all the honour he could show her? Maybe this moment was too important to rush?

He wasn't sure what the reason was. Hell, his brain was mush, yet he knew enough to gather her into his arms and sweep her against his chest and carry her up the great, grand staircase to his rooms, to his bedroom, to the massive four-poster bed that was the place the Earls of Duncairn had taken their brides for generations past.

His bride?

She'd married him a month ago and yet a month ago she hadn't felt like this. He hadn't felt like this. As if this was his woman and he'd claim her and honour her and protect her from this day forth.

What had changed?

Nothing…and everything.

He'd spent the past month watching her. He'd come to her with preconceptions, prejudiced beyond belief by her marriage to his cousin. Those prejudices had been smashed by Jeanie, by her laughter, her courage, by everything about her. Every little thing.

He'd spent a month waiting for this new image to crack. Waiting for the true Jeanie to emerge.

It hadn't happened, or maybe…maybe it had. For the image he'd built up was a woman with a brave heart and an indomitable spirit.

What he held in his arms now was a woman of fire. A woman who, as he laid her down on his bed, as he hauled off his sweater and drew her to him, took the front of his shirt in her two hands and ripped…

'If you knew how long I've wanted to do this,' she murmured. And then she stopped because his chest was bare and she was gazing at him in awe…and then shifting just slightly so she could kiss…

She was adorable, he thought. She was stunning, beautiful, wild. She still had a smear of flour on her face from cooking. He'd never seen anything so beautiful in his life.

'If you've wanted to see me naked,' he said and he couldn't get his voice steady for the life of him, 'how do you think I've wanted to see you?'

And then she smiled, a smile of sheer transparent happiness, a smile that shafted straight to his heart.

Jeanie woke as the first rays of light crept over the sea through the window.

She woke and she was lying in the arms of the man she loved.

The knowledge almost blindsided her. She couldn't move. She could hardly breathe. She was lying tucked under his arm. He was cradling her—even in sleep? Her skin was against his skin. She could feel his heartbeat.

Her man. It was a feeling so massive it threatened to overwhelm her.

When she was young she'd loved Rory, large, dependable Rory, who'd wanted to please and protect her—as long as it hadn't interfered with his routine. She had loved him, she thought, but never like this. Never with this overwhelming sense of belonging.

For a short time she'd also thought she'd loved Alan. How long had it taken her to find the true Alan under the sham of the charming exterior? Too long.

But now… With Alasdair…

True waters run deep?

Where had that saying come from? She didn't know. She didn't even know if she had it right, but the words came to her now and she felt almost overwhelmed by their rightness.

This man was deep, private, a loner. She knew the story of his parents. She knew from Eileen about his solitary childhood and she'd learned more from him.

And now… She'd learned more in the past hours than she could even begin to understand. He'd wanted her but this was more than that. The words he'd murmured to her through the night, the way he'd held her, the way he'd looked at her…

He'd shed his armour, she thought. Her great warrior had come home.

'Penny for them.' His voice startled her. It was still sleepy, but there was passion behind the huskiness. There was tenderness, too, and she thought last night wasn't just…last night. The armour was still discarded.

He was still hers.

'I was feeling like we should advertise singing hinnies as the world's new aphrodisiac,' she managed. 'Known only to us.'

'Let's keep it that way,' he said and gathered her closer. 'Just between us. It feels…excellent. Jeanie…'

'Mmm?' She lifted her face so she was pillowed on his chest. She liked his chest. As chests went, his was truly magnificent. The best?

'I don't know if I'm going to be any good at this.'

'At…'

'At marriage.'

She thought about that for a moment, assembling ideas and discarding them until she found the right one.

'Just lucky we're not, then.'

'We are.'

'No.' She pushed herself up so she was looking down at him, into his beautiful dark eyes, so she could see him clearly, all of him. He was her husband, her body was screaming at her—but she knew he wasn't.

'Alasdair, I've been down that path,' she said, slowly but surely, knowing that, no matter what her body was telling her, what she said was right. 'Twice now I've taken wedding vows and meant them. This time we spoke them but we didn't mean them. They were lies from the start so maybe that's the way it's meant to be. We've made the vows but now we need to prove them. We shouldn't even think of marriage before…unless…we fall in love.'

'Jeanie, the way I feel—'

'Hush,' she told him and put a finger to his lips. 'We both feel,' she told him. 'And maybe for you it's the first time, but for me… Alasdair, if this is for real, then it has to feel real. I won't have you held to me by vows we made when we were under duress. Let's leave this for a year.'

'A year…' He shook his head, his eyes darkening. He lifted one of her curls and twisted it and the sensation of the moving curl was enough to drive her wild all by itself. 'I have news for you. I don't think I can wait a minute.'

She was struggling to keep her voice even, to say what needed to be said. 'That's the way I feel, too, and I think… I think that's okay.'

'It has to be okay—wife.'

'No.' She drew back, still troubled. She had to make him see. 'I'm not your wife, Alasdair. For now I'm your lover, and I'd like… I'd like to stay your lover. Last night was…'

'Mind-shattering,' he said and she wanted to melt but she mustn't. She mustn't.

'We didn't go into last night with vows, though,' she managed. 'Alasdair…'

'Jeanie?'

He was driving her wild with wanting, but she had to say it. 'If at the end of the year we still want to marry, then…then we can think about it, but no pressure. We're not married until then.'

'So we're merely lovers?'

'I don't think merely comes into it.'

'Neither do I,' he said and he smiled and tugged her back to him. 'Maybe you're right,' he told her. 'A year of self-enforced courtship. A year where I'm locked in Duncairn Castle with my Jeanie, and at the end—'

'I'm not your Jeanie, and we'll worry about the end at the end.'

'But for the next few moments?'

And finally she managed to smile. Finally she let herself relax and savour being where she most wanted to be in the world. 'Let's just take each few moments as they come.'

'Starting now?'

And he smiled back at her, a dark, dangerous smile that had her heart doing back flips. He tugged her closer and he didn't need to wait for a response.

'Yes,' she breathed and then she could scarcely breathe at all.

CHAPTER NINE

LIFE HAD TO RESTART, a new norm had to be established, the world had to realign on its axis.

Lovers but not husband and wife?

It was working, Jeanie conceded as week followed week, as summer faded to autumn, as the castle settled to its new routine. Duncairn guests were now welcomed by a host as well as a hostess. Alasdair drew back on his visits to Edinburgh. He still worked during the day, sometimes from dawn, but at five every afternoon he kitted himself out in full highland regalia and came down the massive stairway to greet their guests.

Their guests. That was what it felt like. It was even fun, Jeanie conceded, sitting in the great library watching guests sipping their whisky, listening to Alasdair draw them out, listening to them tell of their travels, watching them fall under his spell.

It was also excellent for business. Although she nobly didn't advertise it, it was soon all over the web that the Earl of Duncairn Castle greeted his guests in person, and bookings went up accordingly.

'By the time you get your castle back it might be paying for itself,' she teased him that night.

For the nights were theirs. Their lives had fallen into a pattern. They walked the dogs at midday or when there was a break in the weather. They greeted the guests together. They had a brief dinner together. They came together at night.

Every night he was hers.

'We'll get the castle valued and add to your wages accordingly,' he told her. 'You needn't worry about the effort you're putting in not being appreciated.'

'I'm not worried about value.'

'You should be.'

But how to explain to him she didn't give a toss? How to say that she was living for the moment, and if, at the end of the year, this wasn't a marriage, then she'd not want anything to remind her of what could have been?

For she'd fallen in love, she conceded, as the weeks wore on. Alasdair might be able to hold himself apart, segment his life into times he could spend with her and times he couldn't, but there was no way she could.

He'd thought this could be a marriage, but Jeanie knew what bad marriages were, and she wanted more.

Did he think of her at all when he was elbow deep in his endless paperwork, phone calls, negotiations, flying trips to Edinburgh, fast international flights for imperative meetings? she wondered.

Did he fly back to her thinking, I want to get back to Jeanie? Or did he fly back thinking he had to get back to fulfil the stipulations of his grandmother's will?

At night, held in his arms, cocooned in the mutual passion, he felt all hers. But at dawn he was gone again.

She rose each day and got on with her work but she couldn't help listening for when the dogs' pressure got too much and she'd hear his study door open.

'Walk?'

How could she ever say no? It'd be like cutting her heart from her body. She donned her mac and her walking boots, they set off in whatever direction the dogs led them and she thought as she walked that she'd never been happier.

Except…

Except this was still compartmentalised. While they walked they talked of the castle, of the guests they'd had the night before, of the eagles, the otters, the wild things that crossed their path.

She tried, a few times, to ask about his work. Each time he answered politely, telling her what she wanted to know but no more.

The message was clear. His work was one compartment. She was another.

In those times she knew he wasn't hers completely. She could see it in his eyes—this was a midday walk between business sessions. His mind was on deals, plans, business she had no part in.

And she was part of his plans for the castle. As the weeks wore on she realised that. His decision to dress and come down to greet their guests was a business decision and a good one. She was part of that section of his business dealings but not the rest.

'I should be happy,' she told the dogs, because there was no one else to talk to. 'How many wives know their husband's business?'

She'd known Rory's—he'd bored her to snores with details of every last fish.

She'd been forced to know Alan's. He'd involved her in it to the point where she'd thought she was drowning.

Alasdair kept his business separate. She thought…she guessed…there was something worrying him about the business but she wasn't permitted to know what.

'It's his right to keep to himself,' she told the dogs. 'We could still… We might still be married, even if…'

Even if…

'He has less than a year to let me in,' she whispered. She was sitting by her hearth, supposedly reading, but she'd given the book up to hug the dogs. She needed hugging.

It was late at night, she was tired and soon she'd go to bed but she could hear the distant murmur of Alasdair on the phone. Who was he talking to? Who knew?

Should she go to bed and wait?

'Of course I will,' she told the dogs. She had to be up early in the morning to get the guests' breakfasts, but, no matter how early she rose, Alasdair would rise earlier.

Ten more months to make a marriage?

'It's not going to work,' she said bleakly.

'So tell him,' she told herself.

'How can I?' She hugged the dogs tighter. 'How can I?' she asked them again. 'He's given me so much…how can I ask for more?'

It was working better than he'd thought possible. Somehow he seemed to have succeeded at this marriage business. Somehow he'd got it right.

For it was working. He spent his days immersed in doing what he'd been doing ever since his grandfather had taken him into the company's headquarters. That had always been his way of blocking out…life? He'd hated his parents' life, the life he'd been born to. His engagement to Celia had been an unmitigated disaster. When he'd realised how much she'd taken from him and how stupid he'd been, he'd backed into his world of business and he loved it. The cut and thrust of the financial world, where he knew the odds, where he held the cards, where he knew when to play and when to walk away… It was where he wanted to be.

The financial leaks he was dealing with now were troubling but intriguing. They were taking most of his attention, but gloriously, unexpectedly, Jeanie was fitting into the edges. She didn't intrude. She kept to herself but when he wanted her she was there. His perfect woman…

And then Elspeth dropped her bombshell.

* * *

If Jeanie Lochlan was Alasdair's perfect wife, Elspeth was his perfect secretary. She was the one person in his business world he trusted absolutely, and when she rang one afternoon and asked could she see him, the answer had to be 'of course'. The chopper was in Edinburgh. 'It'll be quicker if I come to you,' she told him. 'I need to talk face-to-face.'

The vague worries he'd been confronting for the past few weeks coalesced into a knot of trouble.

'I'll talk when I get there. There are too many ears in this place.' She disconnected and he stared at nothing.

The dogs were waiting for their walk and Jeanie was waiting with them. He joined her and he walked but his mind was all over the place.

'Is something wrong?' Jeanie asked as they reached the clifftops and he realised he hadn't spoken since they'd left the castle.

'I… No. My secretary's flying in at two. If needs be, can we put her up for the night?'

'Of course.'

'Thank you.'

'It's your castle,' she said gently, but he was no longer listening. He was playing scenarios out in his mind. Something was badly wrong. He knew it.

'Can I help?' she asked and he shook his head again and managed a smile.

'That'd be like me offering to fix your burned scones.'

'You can share my burned scones,' she told him, but she said it so lightly he hardly heard and his mind was off on tangents again.

She said little more. They returned to the house. She headed for the kitchen and closed the door behind her. He hesitated and then followed her.

'Jeanie, I might not be down to play host this evening.'

'We can cope without you,' she said, giving him a bright

smile. 'The dogs and I put on a glorious welcome all by ourselves.'

'You lack the kilt.'

'We lack the title, too,' she said and her smile became a little more relaxed. 'The punters want to see the Earl of Duncairn, but they'll have to cope with portraits today. Isn't that the chopper landing?'

It was. He nodded and headed out to see it land.

He'd been right to be worried. Elspeth was distressed. As soon as he met her he could see the rigidity in her face, the fact that this was bad. He led her inside.

'Can I get you some tea? Jeanie could make us—'

'I don't want your wife bothered. Does she know about the business?'

'No.'

'Then let's leave it like that. The less people who know about this, the better. Alasdair, it's Don.'

'Don?' His grandmother's friend? 'What on earth…?'

'You know your grandparents gave him total trust? Last month you asked for the accounts to be audited, for everything your grandmother oversaw to be checked to make sure there weren't any gaps that hadn't been filled. The accounts that went through your grandmother's office were the only ones not subject to company scrutiny. Now it seems…' She took a deep breath. 'It seems you were right in your suspicions. You've been wondering for years how the Antica Corporation seem to be second-guessing us. They haven't been guessing. There's been an income stream from them flowing straight to Don's bank account.'

'Straight…'

'Well, not straight.' Elspeth handed over a folder. 'He couldn't do that, because the tax people would have caught him, so he's been streaming cash through the company accounts. Until Eileen's death the order's always been to leave Don's affairs to Don—maybe it was a measure of your grandparents' trust in him. So Don's financial dealings with the company have been audited for the first time ever. He's hidden it incredibly carefully. They've had to probe and probe, but finally it's exposed, and it's a hornet's nest. There's talk of insider trading—Don's been buying shares of companies we've dealings with and he's been buying them with money coming from Eileen's charity funds. There's so much… This has ramifications as far as the eye can see. The auditors want to call in the police. They need to talk to you but I thought it best I talk to you first.'

She watched them leave.

'I'll be back in a couple of days,' Alasdair said curtly, his face blank.

'What's wrong?'

'It's nothing to concern you. Apologise to the guests.'

Fine, she told herself. Life went on. She didn't need him.

She greeted the guests. She took the dogs for another walk. She made dinner for herself and had to force herself to eat, but the look on his face stayed with her. And with it came other doubts.

It's nothing to concern you.

She'd thought she had a marriage.

No, she conceded as the night wore on to the small hours and sleep wouldn't come. Until this afternoon she'd tried to pretend she had a marriage but as he'd left, with his face still impassive, revealing nothing of the turmoil she guessed was underneath, she'd felt…

Ill.

'Unless he comes back and tells me about it…' she whispered to the dogs, but she knew he wouldn't.

Because reality was finally sinking in.

They didn't have a marriage at all.

What followed was messy, nasty, heartbreaking. At least Eileen wasn't alive to see it, Alasdair thought. He wouldn't press charges—how could he? It'd make the company seem lax, and as well as that…it'd show the world he'd trusted.

Do not trust.

'Thank God I have Jeanie,' he told himself as the auditors unravelled the web of financial deceit and he saw the full extent of the betrayal of his grandparents' trust. 'Thank God I can go back to Jeanie. I can trust her. Separation of worlds is the only way to go. If I keep our lives separate, it'll work. It's the only way it can.'

He was away for two days. He returned late in the afternoon, the chopper flying in low from the east, setting him down and taking off almost as soon as he'd cleared the blades.

Jeanie was working in the kitchen. She saw the chopper land through the window. She let the dogs out and watched them race hysterically towards him. She watched him set down his bulging briefcase so he could greet them—and she thought maybe she should be doing the same.

The little wife, welcoming her husband home after his foray into the big, bad world.

He'd gone away looking as if he'd been slugged with a shock that was almost unbearable. He hadn't phoned. He'd told her nothing.

She wiped her hands slowly on the dishcloth and went to the door to greet him.

He looked exhausted. He looked…bleak. She wanted to put her arms around him and hug—but he was still in his business suit. His face said he still belonged to that other world.

And then he saw her waiting, and his face changed.

She saw it. He'd left here shocked and disoriented. Something bad had happened—she didn't have to be Einstein to figure that out. He'd been immersed in whatever it was for two days, and now he was home.

Now she watched him slough off whatever had made him look as if he'd come back from a war and turn into Alasdair. Into the man who took her to his bed.

His face creased into the smile she knew and loved. He reached her in three long strides, he had her in his arms and he swung her round and round as if she were a featherweight rather than a slightly too-curvy housekeeper who liked her own cooking.

His face radiated pleasure, and when finally he stopped swinging he set her down, cupped her face and kissed her.

A girl could drown in that kiss.

Not. She would not. For somewhere in the back of her head there was a place where passion couldn't reach. And it was ringing alarm bells that she'd heard before.

Once upon a time she'd fancied she was in love with Rory. He'd been the answer to her prayers, she'd been joyous when he'd asked her to marry him, but a tiny part of her had voiced doubts.

Do you want to spend the rest of your life cleaning his fish and watching football on the telly?

She'd ignored the voice. And then with Alan... That same little voice as she'd left the island with him, as she'd headed off to the world she'd dreamed of, the same voice had been whispering...

What does a man like this want with a girl like me? This doesn't make sense. Why is Eileen looking like she's worried?

And now that same dratted voice was no longer whispering. It was shouting.

He's in trouble and he's not telling me. I'm just the little wife, not to be worrying her head about such things. I'm just the cook and bottle washer, and a warm body in his bed.

'Alasdair,' she managed. 'What's happened?'

'Nothing that need concern you. Give me thirty minutes. I need to make a couple of calls and I'll be with you.'

'I'll be in the kitchen.'

He must have heard the strain in her voice. 'Is something wrong?'

'Nothing that need concern you.'

'Jeanie—'

'Go and get changed,' she told him, feeling suddenly weary beyond belief. 'I'll see you when you're ready.'

The calls stretched to an hour. He hadn't meant them to, but if Don's fraud wasn't to hit the front pages of the financial papers, there were people he had to placate. He'd used an outside auditor and outside audit firms had their own leaks. Rumours were swirling and they had to be settled.

The legal problems were another matter. They were still a minefield to be faced.

When finally he reached the kitchen he was beyond exhaustion. Jeanie was waiting. He smiled at seeing her, hoping like hell she wouldn't ask what was wrong again, immeasurably thankful for her presence.

She was making shortbread, pressing dough into wooden moulds with thistles carved into them, then tapping the shaped dough out onto trays. He sank into a chair and watched. She let him be for a while. Three moulds. Four.

'Do you enjoy making them?' It was a bit of an inane question but he was feeling inane right now.

'I'm good at it.' She looked down at the perfect circles. 'It's supposed to be what a good Scottish housewife does.'

That was a jarring note. 'You'd rather be doing something else?'

'Learning to fly,' she said, unexpectedly. She gestured to the window where, in the distance, he could see the eagles soaring in the thermals. 'Like those guys. But each to his own. They fly. I make shortbread. Alasdair, I need to ask you again. What's wrong?'

'Just a problem at headquarters.'

'A big problem.' It wasn't a question.

'Maybe.' His tone said no more questions.

She looked at him for a long moment and then filled a couple more moulds. The shortbread shapes looked beautiful, perfect circles with a thistle etched on top. He hardly noticed.

It was enough that she was here. That was all he wanted, Jeanie, a safe haven where he could bury the outside world.

He glanced outside at the eagles and thought he was very glad she wasn't out there flying. He wanted her here.

A good Scottish housewife?

'Alasdair, let me in,' she said and his thoughts focused. The almost animal instinct to relax, to let himself be… just disappeared.

'How do you mean?'

'You know what I mean.' She took a deep breath and steadied. 'Something's happened, something bad. I could read Elspeth's face. I could see your shock. You left looking like death. I've heard nothing from you for two days and you return looking like you've been through the wringer. You say it's nothing to concern me. You have me worried.'

'Don't worry.'

'You lie in my arms every night and I shouldn't worry for you?'

He didn't want this conversation. He was too tired. 'Jeanie, you're separate. You're here, you're part of this place and that's all that matters. I can't believe what we've managed to forge. If you knew how much I've been aching to come back to you…'

'You're back and you're hurting.' Her tone was neutral. 'But you don't want to tell me why?'

'You're not part of that world.'

'And you don't want me to know about it?'

'I don't want to have to trust…'

And as soon as he said it, he knew he'd killed something. He saw it in her face. He might just as well have slapped her.

If he hadn't been so tired, he would have phrased it better, thought of some way round it, thought of how he could deflect it. But the words had been said, and they seemed to hang over his head, like a sword, about to come crashing down.

'You don't trust,' she said, softly now, as if she, too, feared the sword.

'I do. I can.'

'You mean you can trust me with the parts of your world you allow me to share. The part that likes hinnies and shortbread and walking the dogs and holding me at night. But there are parts you won't entrust to me.'

'No. I…'

'Are they state secrets? Stuff that'd bring down countries, stuff worth so much secret agents might torture me to make me confess?'

He managed a smile. 'Hardly. Jeanie—'

'Then what?' She ran a hand through her curls, leaving a wash of flour she didn't notice. 'What's so important?'

'It's just that our worlds are different.' He was too tired to explain. He couldn't get it right. 'I don't interfere with your life—'

'As I see it, you've interfered a lot.' Her voice was calm, but the shuttered look was down. 'You married me to save your inheritance. You're walking in and out of my world as you like, but it's all one-way.'

'You don't want to be part of my world.'

'Part of your business world?'

'Right. It has nothing to do with you.'

'And if it did…I'd likely betray something? Do you really think that?'

'No.' It was he who was raking his hair now. He was so tired he couldn't get this right, but he had to. What to say?

And in desperation he said it. 'Jeanie, I've fallen in love with you.' The words were out and they didn't sound so bad. In fact, they sounded okay. Good, even. This house, this woman, this home… 'This is everything I want,' he told her. 'And I don't want to mess with that.'

He'd just told a woman he loved her. It was big. It was momentous—but Jeanie was staring at him as if he'd offered poison. 'So…sharing might mess with it?'

'I don't know,' he said honestly. 'Maybe. All I know is that I love what we have here. Can you not just accept that?'

'I already have accepted it.' But her voice was dead. Whatever response he'd been hoping for, he knew it wasn't this.

'You mean you love me?'

'No. Or maybe. But it doesn't matter. It can't matter.' She was looking stricken. She took two steps back from the table as if she needed to put distance between them. 'I mean I've been married before, Alasdair. Married, but not *married*. Married on just the terms you're offering.'

And that got him. 'How can you compare me to Alan?'

'Or Rory?' she added. 'I'm not comparing men. I'm comparing marriages. They've been three very different… disasters but the same each time. They say some people go on repeating the same mistake for the rest of their lives. It's time I stopped.'

'Jeanie…'

'Rory was older than me,' she said, still in that cold, dead voice. He wanted to go to her but the look on her face was a shield all by itself. 'He was like my big brother. When my mam died, I was gutted but Rory stood up for me. He stood up to my bully of a father. He made me feel safe and when he married me I thought I was the luckiest woman on the island. The problem was, that's who I was. The little woman, to be protected. I never shared Rory's world. I was a tiny part of it. I was the woman who kept the home fires burning, who cleaned and cooked and worked for his parents, but when he wanted to talk he went out with the boys. I never knew anything that troubled him. I was his wife and I knew my place.'

'I don't—'

'Think you're like that? No? And then there was Alan.' She was talking fast now, her hands up as if to prevent him interrupting. Or taking her in his arms? Her hands said do neither. 'Alan blew me away with his fun, his exuberance, the way he embraced...everything. I was still young and I was stupid and I'd been bogged down by grief at Rory's death for so long that I fell for him like a ton of bricks. And when he asked me to marry him I was dazzled. But Alan, too, had his secrets. The biggest one was that he was up to his neck in debt. He was desperate for his grandmother to bail him out and he thought by marrying someone she was fond of he'd get her to agree. She did, but at what cost? I was trapped again, a tiny part of a life I couldn't share.'

'This is nothing like that.' He was on his feet now, angry. That she would compare him to his cousin...

'I know you're not.' Her voice softened. 'I know you're nothing like Alan. But you have your demons, too. You've let me close enough to see them, but, Alasdair, whether I see them or not is irrelevant. You won't share.'

'I want to be married. This can work.'

'You don't want to be married.' She shook her head, as if trying to work it out for herself. 'The thing is that I have a different definition of marriage from you. Marriage is supposed to be the joining together of two people—isn't it? That's what I want, Alasdair. That's what I dream of. But you…you see marriage as the joining together of the little bits you want to share.'

'You don't want to know about my business.'

'Maybe I don't,' she said slowly. 'But that's not what I'm talking about. You don't want to trust. You don't want to share because it'll make you somehow more exposed. And I don't want that sort of semi-commitment. More, I'll run a mile before I risk it. I'm sorry, Alasdair, but it has to end. The vows we took were only mock. You say you love me. It's a wonderful compliment but that's all it is—a compliment. We need to work out a way forward but the little loving we've been sharing isn't the way to go. It has to end and it will. Right now.'

He looked ill but she wouldn't allow herself to care. She mustn't. Something inside was dying but she couldn't let herself examine it. Like a wounded creature of the wild, she needed to be left alone. She wanted to find a place where she could hide.

To recover? How did she recover? She felt dead inside. Hopeless.

'Alasdair, you're too tired to take this in.' She forced herself to sound gentle—to play the concerned wife? No. She was a concerned friend now, she told herself. Nothing more. 'How long since you slept?'

'I can't—'

'Remember? Go up and sleep. We'll talk later.'

'We'll talk now.' It was a possessive growl and instinctively she backed away.

'Not now. There's nothing to say until you've thought it through.'

'You won't leave while I sleep?'

'No.'

'And after that?'

'We'll talk tomorrow. Go to bed.'

'Jeanie…'

'Alasdair, I have guests arriving in half an hour and I have work to do. Please…leave me be.' She turned to put trays of her shortbread into the oven.

If he came up behind her, she thought, if he touched her, how could she keep control? She was so close to the edge…

But he didn't come. She waited, every nerve in her body, every sense tuned to the man behind her. If he touched her…

She'd break. She'd said what she had to say. She'd meant it but her body didn't mean it. Her body wanted him.

She wanted him, but the cost was too high. The cycle had to be broken, right here, right now.

Please… It was a silent prayer and in the end she didn't know whether it was for him to leave or for him to stay. Please…

And in the end who knew whether the prayer was answered?

He left.

He was too tired to think straight. He was too tired to fight for what he wanted.

The mess in Edinburgh had needed a week to sort, but, with only twenty-eight nights away from the castle permissible under the terms of the will, he'd had to get home. So he'd worked through, forty-eight hours straight.

His head was doing weird things. It was as if Jeanie's words had been a battering ram, and he'd been left concussed.

It must be exhaustion, he told himself. He should have stayed another night in Edinburgh—he could have managed it in his schedule—but he'd wanted to get home.

To Jeanie.

She was downstairs and she wasn't coming up. She intended to sleep in her own apartment. He'd be going to bed alone.

Maybe it was just as well. He needed time to think. He had to get it sorted.

Maybe she was talking sense. Maybe the type of relationship she was demanding wasn't something he could give?

His head hurt.

He showered and his head didn't clear. The night was closing in. All he saw was fog.

He headed for his bedroom and there was a bowl of soup and toast and tea by his bed.

'Try to eat,' the note beside it said. 'Things will look better in the morning.'

How could they look better?

Was she talking about Don? About the betrayal?

He hadn't told her about Don. He hadn't let her close.

He stared down at the simple meal, thinking he wanted her to be here while he ate it.

He wanted her as an accessory to his life?

It was too hard. He couldn't make his mind work any more. He managed half the meal. He put his head on the pillow and slept.

She shouldn't have cooked for him. The little wife preparing supper for her businessman husband, home after a frantic two days at the office? Ha.

But this much was okay, she told herself. She'd waited until she heard the sound of his shower and then slipped his meal in unseen, as she'd done a hundred times for guests who'd arrived late, who hadn't been able to find a meal in town or who were ill or in trouble.

He was a guest, she told herself. That was the way it was now. He was a guest in the bed and breakfast she worked in. Nothing more.

CHAPTER TEN

HE WAS TROUBLED by dreams but still he slept, his body demanding the rest it so badly needed. He hadn't set his alarm and when he woke it was nine o'clock and he could hear the sound of guests departing downstairs.

He lay and let the events of the past two days seep back into his consciousness. He allowed them in piece by piece, assessing, figuring out what had gone wrong, how he could have handled things better.

The financial and legal mess Don had left would have ramifications into the future. He should let his mind dwell on that as a priority. Instead his brain skipped right over and moved on...

To Jeanie.

There was a scratch at the door. The dogs. He rose to let them in and found an envelope had been slipped under the door. Like a checkout slip from a hotel? *Thank you for your patronage—here's the cost?*

He snagged the envelope, let the dogs in and went back to bed. Abbot and Costello hit the covers with joy. He patted them but his pat was perfunctory.

'Nice to see you, too, guys. Settle.'

And they did settle, as if they, too, knew the contents of the envelope were important.

He lay back on the bed, reluctant to open it but it had

to be done. It contained two pages of what looked like…
a contract?

Note first.

Dear Alasdair,
You'll be worried by now that I'm going to leave. If
I do, then of course things revert to their former disaster. I won't do that to you. Just because my emotional needs don't match yours, there's no need to
bring down the Duncairn Empire.

Alasdair, your grandmother's will was fanciful
—an old lady's wish born out of fondness for me.
But she's already done so much for me—more than
enough—so this is how it will be.

I'll stay until the end of the twelve months, as your
housekeeper. I'll accept a decent wage, but that's all.
At the end of the year I'll walk away and I'll take
nothing. The following contract, signed by me and
witnessed by the guy who delivered this morning's
groceries, grants you every right to the castle.

I know Alan's creditors will still claim it, but you
can then pay them out if you wish. Or not. It's nothing to do with me. All I want—and I do want this—
is the dogs. Oh, and what's left of my whisky. I've
given up the idea of selling it online so I'll be making awesome Christmas cakes for generations. That's
my own little Duncairn Legacy.

Meanwhile, if you sign the contract, that's what
it says and that's where we'll leave it. It's as professional as I can make it.

It's been lovely, Alasdair, but we should never
have mixed business with pleasure. You're right—
our lives are separate.

Oh, and your ring is in the safe in your grandmother's room. I have no right to it, and it's too precious to lose.

Yours back to being formal.

Jeanie

He lay and stared at the ceiling while the dogs settled, draped themselves over him, slept.

Our lives are separate.

Downstairs he heard Jeanie start to hoover. In a while she started to hum and then to sing.

If he didn't know better, he'd think she was happy. She wasn't. He'd lived in the same castle as this woman for almost two months. He could hear the note of determined cheerfulness. The courage.

She had a great voice, he thought inconsequentially. With the hoover in the background it was the best…

Jeanie…

Too precious to lose?

Hell.

The dogs were letting him go nowhere—or maybe it was his mind letting him go nowhere. What he'd learned in a crisis was to get all the facts before he made a move and he didn't have all the facts before him yet. Or he did, but they weren't in the proper order. He needed to marshal them, set them in a line, examine them.

But they wouldn't stay in line. They were jumping at him from every which way, and overriding all of them was the sound of Jeanie singing.

The contract fell off the coverlet, onto the floor. He let it lie.

Done. Dusted. Sorted. Jeanie had told him the end of this particular story. Move on.

It'd been all right when he'd thought he'd been buying her out, he thought savagely. Why wasn't it okay now?

His phone interrupted. It was his chief lawyer, calling

to talk about Don. Listening to what the man was telling him, he felt some relief—but suddenly the lawyer was talking about something else. Jeanie's bankruptcy?

What he told him made Alasdair pay more attention than all the details of Don's betrayal.

Why tell him this now? he demanded, but it had only been after a long examination of all the contracts that the lawyers had felt sure.

He disconnected feeling…discombobulated. Talk about complications! What was he going to do with this?

He needed to walk. He needed to get his mind clear before he talked to her.

'Come on, guys,' he told the dogs, tossing back the covers. 'Let's go discuss this with the otters.'

She hoovered every inch of the castle and then some. Halfway through the hoovering she heard Alasdair come down the stairs, the dogs clattering after him. She held her breath but she heard them head straight for the wet room. The back door slammed and then she heard silence.

He'd taken the dogs for a walk? Good.

'But I'm taking the dogs when I go,' she muttered and she tried to make herself sound angry but in the end all she felt like was crying.

But she would not cry. Not again. Not over a man— even if he was Alasdair. She had to keep it together and get the next ten months over with. For ten months she had to live in the castle so their mock marriage could stay intact. She had to stay sane.

She would.

She sniffed and sniffed again, and then walked determinedly to the back door. Alasdair and the dogs were over the brow of the first hill. Out of earshot? Excellent. She took a deep breath, stood on the top step and let fly.

'Don't you dare get attached to those dogs,' she yelled,

to the departing Alasdair, to the world in general. 'They're mine. I don't have a right to your castle, but your grandma's dopey dogs are mine, and I'll fight for them.'

And the whisky?

'And the whisky, too,' she yelled but he was long gone and nobody heard.

She wouldn't cry. *She would not.*

Instead she went back inside and returned to her hoovering. 'Back to being the char,' she told herself and then she forced a mocking smile. 'But back to being your own woman as well. It's about time you learned how.'

He headed along the cliffs, to Craigie Burn, to the place where he and Jeanie had watched the otters. The dogs were wild with excitement, but then they were always wild with excitement. They raced deliriously around him but finally settled to his gentle amble, keeping him in sight but leaving him to himself. When he paused at the point where the burn cut him off from wild woods beyond, the dogs found a rabbit warren and started digging. Next stop China, he thought, as he watched the dirt flying. Any Duncairn rabbit was safe from this pair. They were closer to burying each other than catching anything.

He left them be. He headed for the cottage, sat on the rock above the water and stared at nothing in particular. He had things to be thinking, things to be working out, but his mind seemed to have gone into shutdown.

Jeanie had given him what he wanted—hadn't she? It was selfish to want more.

The dogs were yapping in the distance and he found himself smiling. Stupid dogs.

At the end of the year he wouldn't have them.

He could buy others. He could find dogs with a bit more intelligence.

He could find…another woman?

And there his thoughts stopped.

Another woman?

A wife?

He didn't want a wife. He wanted Jeanie.

Two different things.

But he'd treated her as…just a wife, he conceded, thinking of the past few weeks. *A housewife.* He'd played the businessman, and Jeanie was his appendage. Each had their clear delineation of responsibility. Each only interacted on a need-to-know basis.

Except Jeanie hadn't treated their marriage like that, he thought. She hadn't compartmentalised as he had. She'd welcomed him into her kitchen, into her bed, into her life.

She'd told him everything he wanted to know about this business, this island, her life. She'd opened herself to him, whereas he…

He'd done what would work. He'd resisted the temptation to trust because trust only led to trouble.

A movement by the water's edge caught his eye. Welcoming the diversion from thoughts that were taking him nowhere, he let himself be distracted. The pocket of his hiking jacket always held a pair of field glasses. He hauled them out and focused.

A pair of sea otters were at the water's edge beneath him, devouring the end of what looked like the remains of a rather large fish. He watched, caught by their beauty and their activity, welcoming the diversion.

What was a group of sea otters called? A raft? He found himself wondering why.

And then he found out. The fish finished, the otters slipped back into the water and drifted lazily out midstream. They stayed hard up against each other and he focused his glasses to see more clearly.

They were linked. Hand in hand? Paw in paw? They floated on the surface, their faces soaking up the rays of the weak autumn sun, replete, relaxed, ready for sleep? Together they made a raft of two otters. Their eyes were closed. They were only two, but their raft was complete.

Jeanie would like to see this.

And then he thought: I can show her—but at the end of the year she'll walk away.

Because he couldn't trust? No, because he didn't want to trust. He didn't want to risk…

Risk what? Losing his business? She'd saved that for him. This estate? It'd survive as well.

What, then?

Did trust have to mean betrayal?

In his world, it did. His parents had shown him no loyalty whatsoever. They'd dumped him whenever they could. He'd had one disastrous engagement, which had ended in betrayal. He'd been humiliated to the core. And now Don… An old family friend. A man his grandparents had trusted completely.

He'd lost through betrayal. His parents. His fiancée. Don. The hurt from his parents was ongoing. His father had died without ever showing him affection. His mother… she was with someone in the US. Someone fabulous, someone rich, someone who didn't want anything to do with her past.

And now… If his grandmother had known about Don, it would have broken her heart, he thought. Oh, Eileen, you should have learned. Counter betrayal by not trusting. Don't leave yourself open to that devastation.

Eileen had loved Jeanie. She'd trusted her completely.

Was that why she'd engineered this marriage—because she'd trusted Jeanie to love her grandson? What an ask.

The otters were drifting further downstream, seemingly asleep, seemingly oblivious to their surroundings. Were they pups? he wondered. A mother and her offspring? A mating pair?

Did otters mate and stay mated? He needed to find out.

He watched them float and found himself thinking that what he was seeing was perfect trust. They were together and that seemed all that mattered.

But…they were floating towards the point where the burn met the incoming sea.

The burn was running gently, but the sea was not so gentle. There must have been a storm out in the Atlantic not long since, because the sea was wild. The breakers were huge and the point where the waves washed into the mouth of the burn was a mass of white water.

The otters were almost there.

Were they pups? Didn't they know? Dumb or not, he found himself on his feet, staring helplessly at them, wanting to yell…

His glasses were still trained on their heads. Just as they reached the point where the wash of surf could have sucked them in, he saw one stir and open its eyes…

What followed was a swift movement—a nudge? They were both awake then, diving together straight into the wash, surfacing on a wave, cruising on its face across the surf—then back into the safety and relative calm of the burn.

He watched them glide sleekly back up the burn, past him, then drift together again, once more forming a raft—then close their eyes and proceed to do it all over again.

Trust…

And suddenly it was as if invisible cords were breaking from around him. He felt light, strange—free.

Thoughts came after the sensation. It was as if his body already knew what his mind would think. He had to watch the otters for a while as his mind caught up.

But catch up it did.

The otters trusted.

Rafted together, two lots of senses looked onto the outside world. Who knew if otters hunted together, but, if they did, two must be able to work more effectively than one. Two had devoured a truly excellent salmon that might well have been too much for one. Rafted together, they seemed a larger animal, a bigger presence to possibly deter predators.

Rafted together, they could have fun?

Fun.

Trust. Dependence.

Love.

The thoughts were almost blindsiding him. He wasn't sure what to do with them but when he finally rose there was only one thing he knew for certain.

He had to share.

CHAPTER ELEVEN

'COME AND SEE.'

Three words. He said them but he hardly knew whether she'd accept or not.

He'd brought the dogs home, settled them, given them a bone apiece. He'd fetched another pair of field glasses and then put a rug into a backpack and a bottle of wine. Hopeful, that. Then he'd searched for Jeanie. She was in the library, wiping her whisky bottles clean. She was polishing…for the sake of polishing?

'Come where?' She didn't turn to face him. There must be a smear on the bottle she had in her hand. It was taking all her concentration.

'To Craigie Burn. I need you to come, Jeanie. Please.'

She shouldn't come. She shouldn't go anywhere near this man. He…did things to her. He touched her without touching her.

He made her feel exposed and raw, and open to a pain that seemed to have been with her all her life.

'Please,' he said again and she set down the whisky bottle with a steadying clink.

'The guests arrive at four. I'll be back by then?'

'You will.' It was a promise and it steadied her.

'Give me five minutes to change.'

What did he want? Why was she going? She was an

idiot, she told herself as she went to fetch a sweater and coat. A blind idiot.

Come and see, he'd said, so she went.

'I was born a fool,' she told herself as she headed for the back door where he stood waiting. 'Have you no idea how to defend yourself?'

Come and see, he'd said and she had no weapons at all.

The otters were gone. Of course they were; they were wild creatures who went where they willed. They'd hunted and eaten and moved on. Who knew where they were now? Alasdair stood on the cliff and surveyed the water below.

No otters.

It didn't matter.

'Come and see...what?' Jeanie asked beside him. They'd walked here in almost total silence. Who knew what she was thinking? It was enough that she trusted him to take her here, he thought. He wouldn't ask more.

'I want you to see the otters,' he told her. 'They were here this morning. They're not here now but I still want you to see them.'

She looked at him in silence for a long moment. 'Right,' she said. 'You know they might not appear again for a week?'

'They'll appear if you close your eyes and let yourself see.'

There was another silence, longer this time. And then she closed her eyes.

'I'm watching.'

Trust...

It took his breath away. It was a small thing, doing what he'd asked, coming with him, closing her eyes on demand, but that she would put her trust in him...

He wanted to take her into his arms, tell her he loved her, sweep her into the moment.

Instead he made himself take his time. He spread his blanket on the ground, took her arms and pressed her gently to sit.

'What can you hear?'

'The burn,' she said, promptly. 'The water rippling down over the rocks. The waves in the distance. There's a bird somewhere…a plover? If it's thinking about swooping while I have my eyes closed…'

'It's not thinking about swooping. You're safe.'

'I trust you. Thousands wouldn't. What do you want me to see, Alasdair?'

And there was a note of restraint in her voice that told him this was hard for her. Trust was hard?

She had no reason to trust him. No reason at all.

'I want you to see the otters,' he told her, gently now. He sank down beside her and took her hand. He felt her stiffen, he felt the sharp intake of her breath and then he felt her consciously force herself to relax.

'Word picture?' she said and she had it. He had to smile. He might have guessed this woman would know what he was about.

'I watched them this morning,' he told her. 'Imagine them just below this overhang, on the great rock covered with weed. Two otters. I don't know if they were young or old, male or female, mother and cub, but I'm imagining… something in them was like us. Two creatures blessed with having all Duncairn as our domain.'

'I won't—'

'Stay with your eyes closed, Jeanie. Keep seeing the otters, but while you do I need you to listen to what I want to tell you. I need to say this first because I can't talk of the future without clearing the past. Jeanie, I would never marry you for the castle. I'm asking you to accept that. I've been thinking of this all night. Thinking it makes it impossible to ask…but today, looking at the otters, I thought, maybe I *can* ask you to trust. But before I ask… Jeanie, the castle is yours.'

Her forehead wrinkled. 'I don't understand.'

He put his finger to her lips. 'Hush, then. Hear me out. This has nothing to do with you or me. It's a legal opinion. I've had Duncairn's best legal minds look at the mess that Alan left you with. He assigned you his debt, he died and you were somehow lumbered with it. You'd signed contracts…'

'I know. I was stupid.'

'He was your husband. You weren't stupid, you were trusting and you were intimidated. But you were also conned. But the lawyers have demanded copies and it's taken time. The contracts contain pages of small print, but on all of them your name appears only on the first page. Did you read all those contracts?'

'I didn't even see the rest,' she confessed. 'Alan only ever gave me one page. There was no hint of more. He said it was so he could use the house Eileen had given us as security for business dealings. I thought…it was Alan's right—Eileen's gift had been to Alan.'

'Eileen wanted to keep you safe, but that's beside the point. The lawyers say there was no financial advantage to you included in the contracts Alan had you sign. If you'd initialled each page, if there was proof you'd read them in full, then the contracts could have held water, but as it is… Jeanie, those debts aren't binding. There was no need for you to be declared bankrupt. If Eileen had given you a decent lawyer instead of offering you a place here as housekeeper, she would have been doing you a much bigger service.'

'But I love it here.' She still had her eyes closed. She was feeling the salt in the autumn air, listening to the ocean, to the water rippling over the rocks. What he was saying seemed almost dreamlike. She didn't want to think of Alan and contracts and debt. Or even the castle. They all seemed a very long way away. 'What are our otters doing now?'

'They've just caught fish,' he told her. 'A fish apiece. They're eating them slowly, savouring them. They must be sated—the fishing must have been good this morning. Jeanie, we can discharge your bankruptcy right now. The lawyers are already instigating proceedings. As of now you're free of debt, and if we can manage to stay together for the next ten months, then Eileen's wishes are granted. You get the castle. I get the remainder.'

She had to force herself to focus. 'I don't want the castle. You're the Earl of Duncairn. It's your right.'

'I don't have rights. The otters are finishing their fish, right now. They're doing a little grooming.'

'I love watching otters groom. Are they sleek? Are they beautiful?'

'The sun's shining on their coats. The one on the left has fish caught in his whiskers. He's using his paws to get himself clean, then grooming his paws as well. How can we train the dogs to do that?'

'That's…my problem.'

'I'd like it to be ours.' He said it almost nonchalantly, as if it didn't matter at all. 'They've finished grooming now. They're slipping back into the water. They're slipping under, doing a few lazy circles, maybe getting rid of the last trace of fish. Jeanie, I had to tell you about the castle. I don't mean I'm reluctant to tell you. It's just that you need to know before…before I ask you something else.'

'Why?'

It was a tiny word, half whispered.

'Because what I'm about to say demands trust,' he told her. 'Because if I ask you to marry me properly, then you might think that I'm doing it now because of the castle. For castle, for keeps. I wouldn't do that, Jeanie.'

'I don't—'

'The otters have come together now,' he told her and he took her hands in his. She was shaking. Hell, *he* was shaking. She tugged away but when he went to release her she seemed to change her mind. Her hands held his as if he were an anchor in a drifting world.

'They're floating,' he told her. 'But the burn is running down to the sea. They'll end up on the rocks where the surf breaks.'

'They'll turn.'

'I know they will.' His grip on her hands tightened. What happened in the next few moments was so important—all his life seemed to be hanging in the balance. 'But look what they're doing now. They're catching paws. Catching hands.'

'I've seen them do that,' she whispered, unsure where he was going but willing to still see his otters. 'It's called rafting. A raft of otters.'

'So have I but I didn't get it until this morning,' he told her. 'I'm watching them float almost into the surf. They have their eyes closed, as yours are closed now, but one's aware. Just as the rocks grow sharp and jagged, just before they're in peril, his eyes fly open, and he moves and his partner's nudged and they dive away to safety. And then watch them, Jeanie. They disappear under the water, they glide unseen…and then they're upstream and they're rafting again and they're floating down, loving the water, loving the sun on their faces, but this time it's the other otter who stays aware, who does the nudging. Who keeps them both safe.'

'Why are you telling me this?' She seemed breathless. Her face was turned to the sun. Her eyes were still closed as if she didn't want to let go the vision.

'Because they've learned to trust, Jeanie,' he said softly. 'And because they trust, they can have fun. Because they trust, they can eat together, hunt together, float together. And as I lay on this rock this morning and I watched them, I thought of the way I've compartmentalised my life. I thought of how you've been hurt in the past by just such compartments and here I was doing it all over again. I've hurt you, Jeanie, and I'm sorry.'

He was finding it hard to keep talking. So much depended on this moment. So much…

'Jeanie, now, with the castle, you must know that it's yours,' he told her. 'You know the only way I can have any claim on it is to marry you properly so I need to say it upfront. For you need to know that I want to marry you no matter what you do. If you want to sell the castle to care for all the dogs of Europe, then it has to be okay with me. As long as you let me share your life. As long as you let me take your hand and let me float beside you.'

Her eyes were still closed. He was watching her face and he saw a tiny tic move at the corner of her mouth. Revulsion? Anger?

'You want me to float?' she demanded at last.

'With me.'

'In the burn? You'd be out of your mind. It's freezing.'

And the tic was laughter. Laughter! 'Metaphorically,' he said, with all the dignity he could muster.

'You don't really want to float with me?'

'If you want to float, then I'll float,' he said heroically and the tic quivered again.

'In your kilt?'

'If you ask it of me.'

'For castle, for keeps,' she mused and he couldn't bear it.

'Jeanie, open your eyes.'

'I'm still watching otters. They're having fun.'

'We could have fun.'

'You'd want to share my whisky.'

'Guilty as charged. And your dogs. I'd want to share your dogs.'

'I might want more.'

'Okay.' He was ready to agree to anything. Anything at all. 'But…can we get smart ones?' he suggested, cautiously, and then even more cautiously… 'And maybe eventually a bairn or two?'

The tic quivered. 'Bairns! With you spending thirty days a year away from the castle?'

'I've been thinking about that. Jeanie, I do need to travel to keep the company viable. I'd like the castle to stay as our home—if you're happy to share—but if I need to leave… would you fancy travelling with me?'

'Floating, you mean?'

'It would be my very great honour to keep you safe from rocks and rapids, but I'm looking forward now, Jeanie, and I can't see rapids. If you agreed to marry me, if we can both find it in ourselves to trust, then I can't see a rock in sight. But right now I'm thinking about flying.'

'Flying…'

'If you'd truly like to learn to fly—and you can't make shortbread forever—then flying's an option. Jeanie, what I've been doing for the last few days is complicated. I'll explain it all to you later, in all the detail you want, but, in a nutshell, Eileen's best friend in the company has betrayed her trust, a thousand-fold, leaving a legal and financial nightmare. That's why I had to leave in such a hurry. For a while I thought the foundations of the company might give, but we've done some massive shoring up, and this morning's legal advice is that we'll survive. The insider trading Don was involved in will fall on his head, not the company's. We might well need to adopt economies, however, so combining roles might be just what Duncairn Enterprises needs.'

'How…how do you mean?'

'Your role, for instance.' He wanted to tug her into his arms. It took an almost superhuman effort not to, but he had to keep control. So much hung on what he had to say right now.

'If you would like to reach for the sky,' he managed, 'how about a new role? Not Jeanie McBride, Alasdair's wife. How about Jeanie McBride, pilot and partner? You'd need lessons—lots of lessons—and that could be…fun?'

'Lessons?'

'Flying lessons. If that's your dream, Jeanie, I don't see why you shouldn't have it.'

'You'd teach me to fly?' Her eyes flew wide.

'Not me,' he said hurriedly. 'I'd sit in the passenger seat with my eyes closed. It's not a good look for a teacher. But we could find someone to teach you, and if you were flying, I'd be right with you. Trusting you like anything.'

She shook her head in wordless astonishment and he had to force himself to keep going. All he wanted to do was to kiss her, but he had this one chance. Don't blow it, he told himself. Say it like it is.

'It's not for castle, for keeps, Jeanie love,' he said, gently but urgently. 'If you agree…it's for *us*, for keeps. It's for us, for fun. For us, forever. Jeanie McBride, I love you. Whatever you do or say now, that's unchanged—I love you whatever you decide to do. But I do need to ask. Jeanie, I'd like to say our vows again, but this time for real. This time I'd like to say those vows aloud, and, if you let me, I'd like to mean them for the rest of our lives.'

There was a long, long silence. She blinked in the sunlight. Her gaze was a long, in-depth interrogation where he couldn't begin to guess the outcome.

'You'd trust me,' she said at last. 'With the bad things as well as the good?'

'I might try to protect—'

'No protection. Just trust.'

'Okay,' he said humbly. 'Trust first.'

'Really with the flying?'

'Really with the flying.' And then he added honestly, 'Unless you end up stunt flying, in which case no love in the land is big enough.'

'Coward.'

'I'd rather be a chicken than a dead hen.'

She grinned at that. 'I can't see the Lord of Duncairn as a dead hen.'

'And you can't expect the Lord of Duncairn to be a complete doormat,' he agreed. 'I might try to protect, but I'll do my best to let you fly free, stunt flying not included. Any other exclusions you want, just say the word. Meanwhile, if there's any company details you might like to know, just ask. Jeanie, I've been thinking, watching our otters...'

'Are you sure there were otters?'

'There were otters. Jeanie, I really would like to share. I'm not sure how to yet, but I need to try. If you trust me, that is. If you'd trust me to share, to love you, to hold you in honour...'

'And make me watch invisible otters? And help me fly?'

'Yes. Yes and yes and yes.'

There was another silence then, longer than the last. The whole world seemed to be holding its breath. Alasdair had almost forgotten how to breathe. This slip of a woman, this sprite, his amazing Jeanie, she held his heart in the palm of her hand.

'I don't suppose,' she said, diffidently now, gesturing to the dilapidated cottage behind them, 'that you thought to lay the fire?'

'No,' he said, reluctantly. 'This morning got a bit busy.'

'You so need a partner.' And amazingly her eyes twinkled with laughter and he felt his heart lurch with the beginnings of joy. 'I guess...we could make do without. It's not raining. The pasture up here is nice and soft, and if we wander around the next headland, the curve of the cove makes it private.'

'Are you suggesting what I think you might be suggesting?'

'I might be,' she said demurely. 'Though we'll need to ring Maggie's mam to deal with the guests.'

'I already did,' he said and he smiled at her and she smiled right back. Shared laughter…the best part of loving bar none.

But then she turned and looked towards the faraway castle, high on the headland in the distance, and her face twisted with something he didn't understand.

'Lady of Duncairn Castle,' she said softly, at last. 'I don't think I'll be very good at it.'

'No castle ever had a lady more worthy. Jeanie, I love you.'

'I love you, too,' she said softly. 'Otters or not. Wealth or not. Castle or not. Eileen would be pleased.'

'I'll bet she knows,' he told her and, enough, it was time. A man had to do what a man had to do. He was the Lord of Duncairn and this was his lady. His wife. He swept her up and held her in his arms and stood for a long, long moment on the crag over the burn, looking out over the sea.

And something settled in his heart, something so deep and so pure that he felt almost as if he were being reborn.

'If I was Tarzan right now, I suspect I'd beat my chest and yodel,' he told his love, and she chuckled and looped her arms around his neck and held.

'Don't you dare drop me.'

'I wouldn't,' he told her and he kissed her then, long and deep and hard, with all the love in his heart, with all the tenderness he could summon, with all the joy of the future in the link between them.

And then he turned and carried his lady to the waiting wild grasses of Duncairn Island.

The two eagles soared on the thermals, and two otters drifted lazily downstream again, at one with their world, at peace.

It didn't matter. The world continued apace. The Lord and Lady of Duncairn might know in their hearts that all was well on their estate, but for now they weren't watching. They were otherwise engaged.

And they were otherwise engaged for a very long time.

* * * * *

"You just have to promise me one thing," Jake said.

Running the pad of her index finger over his tempting bottom lip, her wrist rubbed against the sexy stubble on his cheeks. Her body reacted with a warming shiver. He opened his mouth and gently caught her finger between his teeth. Nipped at it and sucked on it for a moment.

It felt like she'd been waiting her entire life for this moment. Despite his words, he certainly didn't seem to be in a hurry to get away. Yeah, he wasn't going anywhere.

Not right now, at least.

"Anything," Anna said.

She wasn't going to let him tell her he wasn't good enough for her.

She knew what she wanted, and he'd just slipped his arms around her again.

"No regrets," he said.

"No regrets," she answered. "But tell me something. How do you know that you're not good for me—that we're not good together—if we've never… tried it out?"

* * *

Celebrations, Inc:
Let's get this party started!

HOW TO MARRY A DOCTOR

BY
NANCY ROBARDS THOMPSON

Published in Great Britain 2015
by Mills & Boon, an imprint of Harlequin (UK) Limited,
Eton House, 18-24 Paradise Road, Richmond, Surrey, TW9 1SR

© 2015 Nancy Robards Thompson

ISBN: 978-0-263-25150-0

23-0715

Harlequin (UK) Limited's policy is to use papers that are natural, renewable and recyclable products and made from wood grown in sustainable forests. The logging and manufacturing processes conform to the legal environmental regulations of the country of origin.

Printed and bound in Spain
by CPI, Barcelona

National bestselling author **Nancy Robards Thompson** holds a degree in journalism. She worked as a newspaper reporter until she realized reporting "just the facts" bored her silly. Much more content to report to her muse, Nancy loves writing women's fiction and romance full-time. Critics have deemed her work "funny, smart and observant." She resides in Florida with her husband and daughter. You can reach her at nancyrobardsthompson.com and facebook.com/nancyrobardsthompsonbooks.

This book is dedicated to everyone who
believes in happily ever after.

Chapter One

Anna Adams parked her yellow VW Beetle in Jake Lennox's driveway, grabbed her MP3 player and took a moment to make sure it was loaded and ready to go.

She was about to hold an intervention and music—just the right song—was the key component of this quirky job.

Today, she was going to save Jake, her lifelong best friend, from himself. Or at least from drowning in the quicksand of his own sorrow.

This morning, Celebration Memorial Hospital had been abuzz with rumors that Jake's girlfriend, Dorenda, had dumped him. Anna might've been a little miffed that she'd had to hear about his breakup through the nursing staff grapevine, but the sister of one of Dorenda's friends was an LPN who worked the seven-to-three shift at the hospital and she'd come in positively brimming over with the gossip.

Jake had been scarce today. He hadn't been around for lunch. Another doctor had done rounds today. When she'd tried to phone Jake after work, the call had gone to voice mail.

The radio silence was what made Anna worry. She hadn't realized that he'd been so hung up on *Miss Texas*. That's what everyone called Dorenda, even though no one was sure if she'd actually held the title or if she'd gotten the nickname simply because she was tall and beautiful and looked like she should've worn a crown to her day job. Poor schlubs like Anna did well to make it to their shifts at the hospital wearing mascara and lipstick.

Anna wasn't sure what the real story was. When Jake had a girlfriend, he tended to disappear into the tunnel of love. Or at least he never seemed to bring his girlfriends around her. And Dr. Jake Lennox usually had a girlfriend.

Anna didn't celebrate Jake's breakups, but she had to admit she did relish the intervals between his relationships, because, for as long as she'd known him, that was when she'd gotten her friend back. Sure, they usually saw each other daily at the hospital. It was not as if he completely disappeared. But in those times between relationships, he always gravitated to her.

She would take the spaces in between any day. Because those spaces ran deeper than the superficial stretches of time he spent with the Miss Texases of the world.

Anna rapped their special knock—*knock, knock-knock, knock, knock*—on Jake's front door, then let herself in.

He never locked the door, but then again, they never waited to be invited into each other's homes. "Jake? Are you here?"

Really, she wasn't surprised when he didn't answer. In fact, she had a pretty good idea of where he was. So, she closed the door and let herself in the backyard gate and followed the mulch path down to the lake, the crowning jewel of his property.

Yep, if he was back here brooding, it clearly called for an intervention or, as they'd come to call it over the years, the Sadness Intervention Dance.

It was their private ritual. Whenever one of them was blue about something, the other performed the dumbest dance he or she could come up with for the sole reason of making the other person smile. The dance was always different, but the song was *always* the same: "Don't Worry, Be Happy" by Bobby McFerrin.

Jake had invented it way back in elementary school. Gosh, it was so long ago—back when the song had just hit the airwaves—she couldn't even remember what she'd been upset about that had compelled him to make a fool of himself to jolt her out of it. But it stuck and stayed with them over the years and now, even though they were both in their thirties, it was still their ritual. The SID was as much a part of them as all those New Year's Eves their families had rung in together or all those Fourths of July at the lake they'd shared. Back in the day, the mere gesture was always enough to push the recipient out of his or her funk. Or, on the rare occasion that it didn't, the SID was the kickoff of the pity party and the guest of honor was officially put on notice that he or she had exactly twenty-four hours to get over whatever was bringing him or her down. Because whatever it was, it wasn't worth the wasted emotion.

Nowadays, it was usually performed at the end of a love affair, as was the case today and the time that Jake had basically saved her life when her marriage had ended—metaphorically speaking, of course. But then again, he was a doctor. Saving lives was second nature to him.

Love was no longer second nature to Anna.

Sure, once upon a time, she'd believed in true love.

She'd believed in the big white dress and the happily-ever-after. She'd believed in spending Saturday nights snuggling on the couch, watching a movie with her husband. She'd believed in her wedding vows, especially the part where they'd said *'til death do us part* and *forsaking all others*. From that day forward, the promises she and Hal had made were etched on her soul.

Then it all exploded right in front of her face.

After nearly four years of marriage, she discovered Hal, who had also looked her in the eyes and made the same vows on their wedding day, had been sleeping with his office manager.

That was when Anna had stopped believing in just about everything. Well, everything except for the one person in the world who had ever been true to her: Jake Lennox.

Jake had been her first friend, her first kiss, and the

first guy to stick around after they realized they were much better friends than anything more.

He'd never stopped believing in her.

After finding out about Hal's infidelity, the only thing Anna had wanted to do was to numb the pain with pints of Ben and Jerry's and curl up into the fetal position in between feedings. Jake, however, was having none of that. He'd arrived on her doorstep in San Antonio and pulled her out of her emotional sinkhole and set her back on her feet. Then one month ago, after the divorce was final, he'd come back to San Antonio, single-handedly packed Anna's belongings and moved her to Celebration. He'd even helped her find a house and had gotten her a nursing job at Celebration Memorial Hospital.

But before he'd done any of this, he'd done the SID.

There he stood: a tall, handsome thirty-four-year-old man doing the most ridiculous dance you could ever imagine to "Don't Worry, Be Happy."

Was it any wonder that Anna felt duty-bound to be there for him on a day like today?

It was her turn to perform the SID. As humiliating as it was—well, that was the point. Anna was fully prepared to make a colossal fool of herself.

The gardenia bushes were in full bloom. Their heady scent mixed with the earthy smell of the lake perfuming the humid evening air. She swatted away a mosquito who had decided she was dinner.

Instinct told her she'd find Jake on the dock, most likely sitting on the ground with his feet in the water and a beer in his hand. Her intuition didn't let her down.

There he sat, with his back to her, exactly as she had imagined. His lanky body was silhouetted by the setting sun. She could just make out his too-long brown hair that looked a little mussed, as if he'd recently raked his fingers through it. He was clad in blue jeans and a mint-green polo shirt. A symphony of cicadas supplied the sound track to the sunset, which had painted the western sky into an Impressionistic masterpiece in shades of orange, pink and blue.

A gentle wind stirred, rippling the lake water and providing welcome relief to the oppressive heat.

Obviously, Jake hadn't heard her coming.

Good. The element of surprise always helped with the SID.

She took advantage of the moment to ready herself, drawing in a couple of deep breaths and doing some shoulder rolls. With one last check of the volume on her MP3 player, she pushed Play and Bobby McFerrin's whistling reggae strains preempted the cicadas' night song.

Jake's head whipped around the minute he heard the music. Then he turned the rest of his body toward her, giving her his full attention.

Anna sprang into action attempting to do something she hoped resembled the moonwalk. Thank goodness she didn't have to watch herself and the shameless lengths she was going to tonight.

Once she'd maneuvered off the grass and was dancing next to him on the dock, she broke into alternate moves that were part robot and part Charleston and part something…er…original.

As she danced, trying her best to coax a full-on smile from him, she tried to ignore the sinking feeling that maybe he'd been more serious about Dorenda than the others. That his most current ex had sent him into a Texas-sized bad humor.

She reminded herself that was exactly why she was here today. For some quality time with her best bud. To bring him out of his post-breakup funk. She knew she looked ridiculous in her pink nurse's scrubs that were slightly too big and clunky white lace-up shoes, but Jake's initial scowl was beginning to morph into a lopsided smile, despite himself. She could actually see him trying to fight it.

Oh, yeah, he was fighting it, but he couldn't fool her. She knew him much too well.

In fact, it only made her unleash the most ridiculous of her dance moves: the sprinkler, the cotton-swab, and the Running Man. Dignity drew the line at dropping down onto her stomach and doing the worm. Although that move hadn't been below Jake a month ago when he'd been there after she'd signed her divorce papers.

That intervention had been a doozy and a true testament to the depth of their friendship.

But he wouldn't have to perform another intervention for her anytime soon.

After losing herself and getting burned so badly, Anna wasn't in any hurry to get involved again.

For now, she was happy to serve as Jake's intervener.

Sprinkler-two-three-four, *cotton-swab*-two-three-four, *Running Man*-two-three… She was just getting into a groove, ready to transition from the Running

Man back to the robot when, in the middle of possibly the best sequence yet, her foot hit an uneven plank on the dock, causing her to lose her balance.

She saw the fall coming in slow motion and she would have face-planted if not for Jake's quick reflexes. Instead of kissing the dock, she found herself safe in the strength of his strong arms, looking up into his gorgeous blue eyes.

Anna smelled good.

The kind of *natural good* that made him want to pull her closer, bury his face in her neck and breathe in deeply.

But this was *Anna*, for God's sake.

He couldn't do that.

He respected her too much and owed her so much more than that.

Especially after she'd gone to such crazy lengths to cheer him up. Did he dare tell her that he really didn't need cheering up? Not in the way she thought he did. Sure, Dorenda had ended things, but the breakup had come as more of a relief than anything.

Before he did something stupid that would be awkward for both Anna and him, he set her upright and took a step back, allowing both of them to reclaim their personal space.

"That was graceful," he said, hoping humor would help him regain his equilibrium.

"You know me," Anna said. "Grace is my middle name." Actually, it really was. "I aim to please. How are you doing, Jake? You okay?"

Her long auburn hair hung at her shoulders in loose waves. Her clear, ivory skin was virtually makeup-free. She had this look in her blue eyes that warmed him from the inside out.

He tried not to think about the strange impulse he'd had just a minute ago, an impulse that lingered even if he was trying not to acknowledge it.

"I'm great," he said. "Want a beer? I'd like to toast your latest choreography. You're getting really good at it. I'll give your Running Man a nine-point-five. I have to take off a half point since you didn't stick the landing."

She swatted him and quickly crossed her arms in front of her.

"Yes, I'd love a beer. Thank you. I need one after that."

He smiled. "Come on. Let's go back up to the house. I have five of a six-pack in the fridge."

She was eyeing him again. "Well, good. I was afraid that maybe you'd been at home all day drowning your sorrows."

"I was seeing patients all day. In case you haven't noticed, I usually don't take off midweek to go on a bender."

He and Anna both worked at Celebration Memorial Hospital, but she was an OB nurse on the third-floor maternity ward and he was a hospitalist on the general medical-surgical floors. Unless they sought each other out, their paths usually didn't cross at work.

"I must say, you're taking this awfully well," she said.

"What?"

"The breakup. If I didn't know better, I'd swear that you were fine."

"Do I act like I'm not fine?"

"Well, no. That's what I just said. You seem remarkably unfazed by Miss Texas's departure. Sorry, by *Dorenda's* breaking up with you."

He pulled open the back door for her and stepped aside so she could enter the house first.

"Dorenda was a great woman, but our relationship had run its course. I'll miss her, but it was time to move on."

He shrugged and stepped inside behind her.

"Are you telling me that *you* broke up with *her*?"

Throwing her a glance over his shoulder as he walked toward the kitchen, he said, "No, she's the one who dropped the bomb. Actually, it was more of an exploding ultimatum. I saw it coming a mile away."

He reached into the fridge, grabbed a beer and twisted off the bottle cap.

"She gave you an ultimatum? Really? Well, but then again, how long were the two of you together?"

"Four or five months or so. Do you want a mug? I have some in the freezer."

"Yes, please. Had it really been five months? I mean, I've only been back a month."

He nodded as he poured the beer down the inside of the mug, careful to create just the right amount of foam on top. "She reminded me of that more than a few times last night. She was talking five-year plans that involved marriage and kids and bigger houses. She kept saying she needed some assurance about our future, needed to know where we were going. I'm not going to lie to her. I enjoyed her company, but I wasn't going to marry her."

He handed the beer to Anna.

"Why not?" Anna asked. "She was beautiful. You seemed like you were really into her."

Jake nodded. "She was nice. Pretty. But…I couldn't see myself spending the rest of my life with her. That's the bottom line."

Anna squinted at him, her brows drawn together, as she sipped her beer.

"What's wrong? Is the beer not good? You don't have to drink it if you don't like it."

She set down the mug on the kitchen counter. "No, I like it. But I have two questions for you."

"Okay. Shoot."

"First question. If you're *fine* with everything, how come you let me keep dancing and make a fool of myself?"

Her voice was stern.

He laughed out loud. He couldn't help it. "Are you kidding? Watching you was the most fun I've had in months. No way was I going to stop you. For the record, you didn't make a fool of yourself. You're adorable. In fact, you'd been away so long down there in San Antonio, I'd almost forgotten how adorable you are."

She rolled her eyes, but then smiled.

"So happy to have cheered you up," she said.

"What's the second question?" he asked.

She looked at him thoughtfully for a long moment.

"Why, Jake? Why do you keep dating the same type of women? I don't mean to be judgmental and I know I haven't been around for the last decade or so. But think of this as tough love. You keep dating the same type of women, expecting to get different results, but it always turns out the same way. Always has, always will."

He crossed his arms, feeling a little defensive, but knowing she was right. Sometimes her friendship felt like the only real thing in the world. But still, he didn't want to get into this right now.

"I don't exactly see you out there blazing trails in the dating world," he countered.

She sighed. "The divorce has only been final for a month."

"But you were separated for nearly two years."

"This isn't about me, Jake. This is about you. What are you looking for?"

He shook his head.

"*Company*. Companionship? That's why, when I know the relationship has run its course, I end it. Or in today's case, I let Dorenda do the honors. I don't string them along."

"But you do sort of string them along. You dated Dorenda for four months. That's a significant amount of time in the post-twenties dating world."

Overhead, the fluorescent lights buzzed. He glanced out the kitchen window. Inky dusk was blotting out the last vestiges of the sunset.

"I don't know what you want me to say, Anna."

"Say that you'll let me fix you up with a different type of woman."

Different?

"Define *different*."

"Don't take this the wrong way, but maybe you should consider women who are a little more down-to-earth than the Miss Texases of the world."

He knocked back the last of his beer and debated grabbing another, but his stomach growled, reminding him he really should think about getting some food into his system first.

"Down-to-earth, huh? I wouldn't even know where to begin to look for someone down-to-earth."

"Exactly. That's why I want you to let me fix you up."

"I don't know, Anna. Blind dates aren't really my thing."

He returned to the fridge, pulled open the door and surveyed the meager contents.

"When was the last time you went on a blind date?"

"Better question," he countered. "When was the last time *you* even went on a date?"

He looked back over his shoulder to gauge her reaction. She didn't seem to like being in the line of fire any more than he did.

"This isn't about me, Jake."

"It's been nearly two years since you and Hal broke up. So, while we're on the subject, it's high time for *you* to get back in the saddle and try again."

She put her hands on her hips and shook her head, looking solemn. "Okay, you're changing the subject, and I don't know if I even want to date. You, on the other hand, obviously do like getting involved. I know you so well, and if you'll just let me help you, I'll bet I can make it a much more rewarding experience for you. Or at least one that has the potential to last, maybe even change your mind about marriage. Come on. Be a sport."

"Why are women always trying to change me?"

"The right woman wouldn't change you, but she might make you want to see other possibilities.

He took out a carton of eggs, some butter, various veggies and the vestiges of a package of turkey bacon. It was all he had. When all else failed, breakfast for dinner always worked. It was his favorite go-to meal when the pickings were slim. He really should go to the grocery store later tonight. The rest of his week was busy.

"You'd really wager that you could fix me up with someone who is better for me than my usual type?"

She raised her chin. "You bet I could. In fact, I'll bet I could introduce you to your soul mate if you gave me a fair chance."

He chuckled. "You are the eternal optimist. Do you want to stay for dinner? I'll make us an omelet."

She put her hand on her stomach. "That sounds great. I'm starving. We can talk more about this wager. How can I help with dinner?"

"You can wash and dice the onions and red peppers."

She stepped up to the sink to prep the peppers, but first she began by putting some dirty dishes into the dishwasher and hand-washed several pieces of flatware.

"You don't have to do that," he said. "I didn't have time to clean up this morning before I left for work. I'll do those later when I clean up the dinner dishes."

"Actually, it's sort of hard to wash the peppers with dishes in the way. I don't mind, really. You are fixing me dinner. And we're going to need forks to eat with."

Jake left her to do what she needed to do because God knew she would anyway.

He took a bowl out of one of the cupboards and began cracking eggs into it. "Since when did you become a matchmaker? And what makes you think you can find me the right woman? I've been trying all these years and I haven't been successful."

"That's easy. A—I know you better than you know yourself, and B—you are attracted to the wrong women. Your judgment is clouded. Mine is not."

She might've had a point. But after just getting out of a relationship, he wasn't very eager to jump back into anything serious. So looking at it from that perspective, what harm would a few dates do? Other than take up what little free time he had away from the hospital. He could indulge Anna. She meant that much to him. Then again, could he ever really expect to find his soul mate or anyone long-term when he never wanted to get married?

That was something he'd known for as long as he'd had a sense of himself as an adult. He did not want to get married. Marriage was the old ball and chain. It took something good, a relationship where two people chose to be together, and turned it into a contractual obligation. He'd witnessed it firsthand with his parents. All he could remember was the fighting, his mom leaving and his father's profound sadness. Sadness that drove him to seek solace in the bottle. Anna knew his family history. Sure, she'd have good intentions. She'd think she was steering him toward someone who made him happy, but what was the point?

Jake vowed he'd never give a woman that much power over him.

So he said, "Before we go any farther, I have a stipulation."

"Jake, no. If we're going to do this and do it right, you have to play by my rules. You can't give me a laundry list of what you want. That's where you get into trouble with all these preconceived notions. Maybe we can talk about deal breakers, such as must not be marriage-minded or must not want kids, etcetera, but we're not getting into the superficial. You're just going to have to trust me."

He poured a little milk into the eggs, a shake of salt, a grind of black pepper and began to beat them. Even though they'd spent a lot of time apart, Anna still knew him so well. A strange warmth spread through him and he whisked the eggs a little faster to work off the weird sensation.

"I wasn't going to get superficial. In fact, my stipulation wasn't even about me. I want to propose a double wager. Since we both need dates to the Holbrook wedding, I'll let you fix me up, if you'll let me fix you up."

The daughter of Celebration Memorial Hospital's chief executive officer Stanley Holbrook was getting married in mid-July. Jake had his eye on a promotion and attending his boss's daughter's wedding was one of the best ways to prove to the man he was the guy for the job. Since Holbrook was a conservative family man, Anna's offer to fix him up with a woman of substance wasn't a bad idea.

She was looking at him funny.

"Deal?" he said.

She opened her mouth, but then clamped it shut before saying anything. Instead, she shook her head. "No. Just...*no*."

"Come on, Anna, fair is fair. I know Hal hurt you, but you're too young to put yourself on a shelf. You want to get married again. You want to have kids. There are good guys out there, and I think I know one or two who would be worthy of you."

She stopped chopping. "Worthy of me?" Her expression softened. "That's the sweetest thing anyone has said to me in a very long time."

"Case in point of why you need to get out more, my dear. Men should be saying many *nice* things to you."

She made short order of chopping the peppers, scraping the tiny pieces into a bowl and then drying her hands.

"Okay, I'll make a deal with you," she said. "We'll do this until Stan Holbrook's daughter's wedding. Between now and then, I'll bet I can match you with your soul mate and cure you of your serial monogamy issues."

He winced. "What? As in something permanent?"

She shrugged. "Just give me a chance."

"Only if you'll let me do the same for you. Do we have a deal?"

She nodded.

"So what are we betting?"

She shrugged. "I didn't really mean it as a serious bet."

"I think making a bet will make this more interesting. We don't have to decide the prize right away. Let's just agree that the first one who succeeds in making a match for the other wins."

Anna wrinkled her nose. "Knowing you, you'll let a good woman go just to win the challenge. You're so competitive."

"But if you think about it," he said, "who will be the real winner? One will win the bet, but the other will win love."

"That's extremely profound for a man who has such bad taste in women." She gave him that smile that always made him feel as if he'd come home. He paused to just take it in for a moment.

Then Jake shook her smooth, warm hand, and said, "Here's to soul mates."

Chapter Two

Soul mates.

Why did hearing Jake say that word make her stomach flip? Especially since she wasn't even sure if she believed in such a thing as *soul mates*. After all she'd been through with Hal, she still believed in love and marriage enough to try again…someday. But *soul mates*? That was an entirely different subject. The sparkle had dulled from that notion when her marriage died.

"I'm done chopping." Anna set the bowl on the granite counter next to the stove where Jake was melting butter in a frying pan. Then she deposited their empty beer bottles into the recycle bin in the garage.

"Now what can I do?" she said when she got back into the kitchen.

"Just have a seat over there." With his elbow, he gestured toward the small kitchen table cluttered with mail and books. "Stay out of my way. Omelet-flipping is serious business. I am a trained professional. So don't try this at home."

"I wouldn't dream of it," she said, eyeing the mess on the table's surface. "That's why I have you. So you can fix me omelets. Apparently, I will repay you by setting the table for us to eat. And after I've excavated a space to put the plates and silverware, then I might clean the rest of your house, too. I thought you had a housekeeper. Where has she been?"

"Her name's Angie and she's been down with the flu. Hasn't been available to come in for two weeks."

Anna glanced around the room at the newspapers littering the large, plush sectional sofa in the open-plan living room. There were mugs and stacks of magazines and opened mail on the masculine, wooden coffee and end tables. Several socks and running shoes littered the dark-stained, hardwood living room floor.

"Wow. Well…" In fact, it looked as if Jake had dropped everything right where he'd stood. "God, Jake, I didn't realize you were such a slob."

Jake followed her gaze. "I'm not a slob," he said. "I'm just busy. And I wasn't expecting company."

Obviously.

Anna thought about asking why he didn't simply walk a few more steps into the bathroom where he could deposit his socks into the dirty clothes hamper rather than leaving them strewn all over the floor. Instead, she focused on being part of the solution rather than nagging him and adding to the problem. She quickly organized the table clutter into neat piles, revealing two placemats underneath, and set out the silverware she'd just washed and dried.

"Where are your napkins?" she asked.

He handed her a roll of paper towels.

This was the first time in the month that she'd been home that they'd cooked at his place. Really, it was just an impromptu meal, but it was just dawning on her how little she'd been over at his place since she'd been back. That was thanks in large part to Jake's girlfriend. She wondered if Dorenda had seen the mess—or had helped create it—but before she could ask, she realized she really didn't want to know.

"It must be a pretty serious case of the flu if Angie has been down for *two* weeks. Has she been to the doctor?"

Jake gave a one-shoulder shrug. "She's fine. I ran into her at the coffee shop in downtown the other day. She looked okay to me. She'll probably be back next week."

Anna balked. "Why do you keep her?"

She crossed the room to straighten the newspapers and corral the socks. She couldn't just stand there while Jake was cooking and the papers were cluttering up the place and in the back of her mind she could hear him toasting soul mates.

Even that small act of picking up would help work off some of her nervous energy.

"I don't have time to find someone else," he said. "Besides, it's not that bad around here."

She did a double take, looking back at him to see if he was kidding.

Apparently not.

But even if it looked as if Jake had simply dropped things and left them where they fell, the house wasn't dirty. It didn't smell bad. In fact, it smelled like *him*— like coffee and leather and something else that bridged the years and swept her back to a simpler time before she'd married the wrong man and Jake had become a serial monogamist. She breathed in deeper, wondering if they were still the same people or if the years and circumstances had changed them too much.

She bent to pick up a dog-eared issue of *Sports Illustrated* that was sprawled on the floor facedown. As she prepared to close it back to its regular shape, she nearly dropped it again when she spied the tiny, silky purple thong hidden underneath. Like a lavender spider. Only it didn't get up and crawl away.

"Eww." Anna grimaced. "I think Miss Texas forgot something."

Jake gave a start as his gaze fell to where Anna pointed.

She reached over and grabbed the poker from the fireplace tool set on the hearth and used it to lift the thong off the ground.

"This is classy. How does a woman forget her underwear?"

He smiled that adorable lopsided smile that always suggested something a little bit naughty. There was no doubt why women fell for him. Heck, she'd fall for him if he weren't her best friend.

"She carried a big purse," Jake said. "It was like a

portable closet. She probably didn't leave here commando." His gaze strayed back to the panties. "Then again, maybe she did."

Anna raised the poker. The thong resembled a scanty purple flag, which she swiftly disposed of in the trash can.

"She might want that back," Jake protested.

"Really? You think she's going to call and ask if you found her underwear?"

They locked gazes.

"If she does—" Anna scowled at him and pointed to the garbage "—it's right here."

He was quiet as he pulled out the toaster and put in two slices of whole wheat bread.

Anna returned the poker to its stand.

"Jake, this is why we need to have a heart-to-heart talk about what you want in a woman. It's no wonder you can't seriously consider spending the rest of your life with a woman who leaves her panties on your living room floor. Even if she lived here, *leaving* her panties lying around in the living room wouldn't be a good sign."

"I leave my socks on the floor," he said as he transferred the omelet from the frying pan onto the two plates Anna had set out.

"Yeah, and it wouldn't take that much more effort to put them in the laundry hamper," she said. "Do you want orange juice? I need orange juice with my eggs."

"Sorry, I'm out. I have coffee and there's more beer. I need to go to the grocery store. I really should go tonight because I'm not going to have time to go later with everything going on this weekend."

She passed on the beer. Not her favorite thing to drink with eggs. Even if it was dinner. It was one of those combos that just didn't sound appetizing. She opted for making herself a quick cup of coffee in his single-serving coffee brewer. As she pushed the button selecting the serving size, it dawned on her that even if they had been apart for a long time, she still felt at home with Jake. She could raid his K-Cups and brew herself a cup without asking. Even in the short amount of time that she'd spent here, she knew which cabinet contained the coffee, and that he stored his dinner plates in the lower cabinet to the right of the sink because they stacked better there.

"I need some groceries, too," she said. "How about if we shop together after we do the dishes? We can talk as we shop and figure out where the happy medium is between the nice women you *should* be dating and the ones who leave their underwear all over town."

Jake's brows knit together as he set the dinner plates on the table.

"Don't look at me like that," Anna said as she slid into her seat at the table. "You know I'm right. If you keep doing what you're doing, you'll keep getting what you're getting and you'll keep repeating the same pattern. You need to look a little deeper than a pretty face."

He sat down, speared some of the omelet and took a bite, watching her as he chewed. She wished he'd say something. Not with food in his mouth, of course. But that was the thing about Jake—he may be a manly guy's guy who didn't know how to pick up after himself, but he still had manners. He didn't talk with his mouth full, he said please and thank-you; Jake Lennox was a gentleman.

He knew how to treat a lady. He just didn't know how to choose the right lady.

"So what are the deal breakers, Jake?"

"Deal breakers?"

"You know, the qualities in a woman that you can't live with."

"Why don't we focus on the good? The attributes that I'm attracted to?"

"Because attraction is what gets you in trouble. Attraction is what caused Miss Texas to leave her thong on your living room floor."

Ugh. She sounded like such a harpy. She knew that even before she saw the look on his face and consciously softened her tone.

"I don't mean to be a nag. Really, I don't. It's just that sometimes it helps if you work backward."

She wasn't going to pressure him. That was the fastest way to suck all the fun out of the bet. This was supposed to be *fun*, not an exercise in browbeating.

She was prepared to change the subject when he said, "Anyone I date has to be comfortable with the fact that I don't want to get married and I don't want kids. I don't want anyone who thinks they can change my mind. That's a deal breaker. It's what started things going south with Dorenda. She was Miss Independent for the first couple of months. Then she started in with the *five-year plan*, which eventually turned into an ultimatum."

Anna realized it was the first time she'd ever been on Dorenda's side. Who could blame her for wanting more? Especially when it involved more Jake. But she wasn't going to argue with him. This anti-marriage/anti-family stance was new. Or at least something that had developed during the time that they were apart. Probably the reason he'd been involved in his string of relationships. Jake had grown up in a single-parent household. His mom had left the family when Jake was in first grade.

One night before they left for college, when she and Jake were having one of their famous heart-to-hearts, he'd opened up about how hard it had been on him and his brothers when their mom left the family.

Yet he'd never mentioned that he didn't want to get married.

Actually, though, when she thought about it, it was a good thing he was being so up front about everything. That's just how Jake was. He knew himself, and he was true to himself. Maybe if Hal had been more honest with both of them, they might have avoided a world of hurt.

So yeah, considering *that*, Jake's candid admission was a good thing.

Now, her mind and its deductive reasoning just had to convince her heart that was true, because she hated the thought of Jake ending up alone years down the road.

"So you want someone who is family-oriented, funny, kind, honest and smart," Jake recapped as he pushed the shopping cart down the canned goods aisle in the grocery store. "You don't want to date a doctor, because of Hal. So what about looks? What's your type?"

Anna stopped to survey a row of black beans lined up like soldiers on a shelf.

"I thought we agreed that we weren't going to concentrate on the physical. That's where we get into trouble. We need to get past that."

"What? Should I disqualify a guy if he is good-looking?"

She quirked a brow at him as she set two cans in the otherwise empty cart. "I'd love to hear your idea of a good-looking guy."

He scowled back at her. "I don't know. Beauty is in the eye of the beholder, as they say. I have no idea what makes a guy attractive to a woman."

"I was just teasing, Jake. You know you're my ideal. If I can't have you, then…"

She made a *tsk*ing sound and squeezed his arm as she walked farther down the aisle to get something else on her list.

If he didn't know her so well, he might've thought her harmless flirtation had started a ripple of *something* inside him. But that was utterly ridiculous. This was *Anna*, and that's why he couldn't put his finger on the *something* she'd stirred. Maybe it was pride, or actually, more like gratitude that pulled at him. He looked at her in her scrubs that were a little too big for her slight frame. Her purse, which she'd slung across her body, proved that there were curves hidden away under all that pink fabric.

He averted his gaze, because *this was Anna*. Dammit, he shouldn't be looking at her as if she was something he'd ask the butcher to put on a foam tray and wrap up in cellophane. As the thought occurred to him, he realized his gaze had meandered back to where it had no business straying.

He turned his body away from her and toward the shelf of black beans Anna had just pored over. He didn't know what the hell to do with canned black beans, but he took a couple of cans and added them to the cart as he warred with the very real realization that he didn't want to fix her up with just anyone. Certainly not most of his buddies, who if they talked about Anna the way they talked about other women he'd have no choice but to deck.

"Excuse me." Jake looked over to see a small, silver-haired woman holding out a piece of paper. "Your wife dropped this list." The woman hooked her thumb in Anna's direction at the other end of the aisle. "I'd go give it to her myself, but I'm going this way."

My wife?

Jake smiled at the woman and started to correct her, to explain that he and Anna weren't married, but the words seemed to stick in his throat. He found himself reaching out and accepting the paper—a grocery list— and saying, "Thanks, I'll give it to her."

She nodded and was on her way before Jake could say anything else.

Hmm. My wife.

He tried to see what the woman saw—Anna and him together...as a couple. But in similar fashion to not being able to look at her curves in good conscience, he couldn't fully let his mind go there.

It wasn't that the thought disgusted him—or anything negative like that. On the contrary. And that brought a whole host of other weirdness with it. The only way around it was to laugh it off.

"You dropped your list," he said as he stopped the cart next to her. "The nice lady who found it thought you were my wife."

Anna shot him a dubious look. "Oh, yeah? Did you set her straight?"

She deposited more canned goods into the basket and then took the list from his hand.

"No. I didn't. I need bread. Which aisle is the bread in?"

She let the issue drop. He almost wished she would've said something snide like, *That's awkward.* Or, *Me? Married to you? Never in a million years.* Instead, she changed the subject. "Do you want bakery bread or prepackaged? And why don't you know where the bread is?"

He certainly didn't dwell on it.

"I don't know. I guess I don't retain that kind of information. Grocery shopping isn't my favorite sport."

"I can tell," she said. "And if you don't pick up the pace, you're going to get a penalty for delay of game. I'm almost finished. Where's your list? Let me see if I can help move this along."

"I don't have a list," he said. He knew he should make an off-the-cuff comment about her, his pretend wife, being the keeper of the list for both of them, but it didn't feel right.

Since when had anything ever not felt right with Anna?

"I keep the list in my head," he added.

"And of course, you're out of everything. Here, I can help. We'll just grab things for you as we go by them."

She pulled the shopping cart from the front end and turned the corner into the next aisle.

"Do you want cereal?" she asked.

Before he could answer, a couple a few feet away from them broke out into an argument that silenced both Anna and him.

"Look, I'm an adult," said the guy. "If I want to eat sugary cereal for breakfast, I will. In fact, if I want to eat a bowl of pure sugar, I will. You get what you like and I'll get what I want."

"Breakfast is the most important meal of the day, honey." The woman took a cereal box—the bright yellow kind with fake berries—out of the shopping cart and put it back on the shelf. "This won't hold you. You need something with fiber and protein. If you eat this, you'll be raiding the vending machine by ten o'clock."

The guy took the cereal box off the shelf and put it back in the cart. "I grew up eating this stuff. You're my wife, not the food police. So hop off."

Anna and Jake quickened their pace as they passed the couple. They exchanged a look, which the couple obviously didn't notice because now insults were inching their way into the exchange and tones were getting heated.

"We'll come back for cereal," Anna said.

Jake nodded. "When we do, are you going to mock my cereal choice?"

"Why would I do that? I'm not your wife."

There. Good. She said it. The dreaded w word.

"Are you saying it's a wife's role to mock her husband's cereal choice?"

"Of course not. I never told Hal what he could and couldn't eat. Then again, since I was the one who cooked in that relationship, he didn't have much say. But he was completely on his own for breakfast and lunch, free to make his own choices. And you see where that got me. Do you think we would've lasted if I had been more concerned?"

"No. Hal was an ass. He didn't deserve your picking out healthy cereal for him."

"So you're saying the woman picking out the cereal rather than leaving him to his own devices was a good thing?"

"Well, yeah. For the record, in the couple we saw back there, the wife was right. He may have wanted that crap, but he didn't need it. So I'll side with her. Do you want me to go back over there and tell her I'm on her side?"

"Better not. Not if you want to keep all your teeth."

Jake laughed but it sounded bitter—even to his own ears. "Why does that have to happen in relationships? People get married and end up hating each other over the most ridiculous things. They fight and tear each other apart and someone leaves. That marriage is in trouble over Much-n-Crunch and its artificially flavored berries. That's exactly why I don't want marriage."

"So you're saying that the guy should've gotten the cereal he wanted?"

"No. I already said I thought the wife was right. Junk like that *will* kill you. I agree with her. Healthy eating habits are good."

As they strolled past the dairy section, Anna studied him for a minute. "I've just figured out who I'm fixing you up with on your first date. She's a nutritionist. I think the two of you will have a lot in common. I can't believe I didn't think of her until now."

Her response caught him off guard.

"What is she like?" he asked.

Anna raised her brows. "You'll just have to wait and see."

"Okay. Two can play that game," he said. "You'll have to be surprised on your first date, too."

She grimaced. "Go easy on me, Jake. I'm so out of practice. You know how I am. I'm casual. I haven't been out there in so long."

"That's why you need me to fix you up."

He had no idea who he was going to pick for her first date. Who would be worthy of her? Maybe the best place for him to start would be to rule out anyone who was remotely similar to himself. Because Anna deserved so much better.

Chapter Three

"Try this one." Anna's sister, Emily, shoved a royal blue sundress with a white Indian motif on the front through the opening in the fitting room curtain in the Three Sisters dress shop in downtown Celebration. "It looks like the basis of a good first-date outfit."

Anna still wasn't sure who her date was or where they were going, but one thing she did know was they were getting together on Wednesday and she had nothing to wear. It had been so long since she'd worn anything but jeans or hospital scrubs, she didn't have a stitch appropriate for a...date. Plus, she had a busy week ahead and this was Emily's night off. So Anna figured she might as well seize the moment and bring her sister along to help her pick out something nice. If she felt good with what she was wearing, she might feel less nervous on the date, thereby eliminating one potential avenue of stress…or disaster.

She held up the dress her sister had chosen and looked at herself in the mirror. The white pattern running up the front of the dress had a design that might've made a nice henna tattoo. It was a little wild for her taste.

"I don't know, Em, this one looks a little low cut."

"Try it on. You never can tell when it's on the hanger."

Wasn't that the truth? The same rule could apply to men, too. You had to try them on—well, not literally, of course. She couldn't fathom getting intimate with a man. Even if it was a man Jake had picked out for her. Not that she was contemplating life as a born-again virgin. It was just too much to contemplate right now. First, she'd meet the guy or guys—Jake did have until the wedding—and see how she got along with him or them. Then she'd think about…more.

The thought made her shudder a little.

She slipped out of the dress she'd just tried on and hung it up—it was a prim flowery number in primary colors. It was too dowdy—too matronly—too…*something*. Anna couldn't put her finger on it. Whatever it was, it just didn't feel right.

"Who did you fix Jake up with?" Emily asked from the other side of the fitting room curtain.

"Her name is Cheryl Woodly. She's a freelance nutritionist who works with new mothers. I met her at the hospital."

"Oh, yeah? What's she like?"

Anna slipped the dress over her head.

"Nice. Smart. Pretty."

"How is she different from Jake's past girlfriends?"

"Did you not hear me say she's *nice* and *smart*? Miss Texas possessed neither of those qualities."

"Me-ow," said Emily.

"I'm only speaking the truth."

"When are they going out?"

"Friday."

Anna stared at herself in the mirror, tugged up on the plunging halter neckline, trying to give *the girls* a little more coverage. She wasn't so sure she wanted to put everything on display on a first date. The dress was great, but it was decidedly not *her*.

"Anna? Did you try on the one I just gave you?"

"Yeah, but—I don't know."

"Come out. Let's see it."

"Nah. Too much cleavage. Too little dress."

Anna hesitated, turning around to check out the back view. She had to admit it was a snappy little number and it looked great from behind. But the front drew way too much focus to the cleavage and that made her squirm.

"Let me see." Before Anna could protest, Emily's face poked through the split in the curtain.

Anna's had flew up to her chest.

"It looks great," Emily said. "The color is out of this world on you. It brings out your eyes. And move your hand."

Emily swatted away her sister's hand from its protective station.

"I don't know what you're afraid of. It accentuates your tiny waist and you're barely showing any cleavage at all. It's just-right sexy. A far cry from those scrubs you hide in every day."

"My scrubs are for work. They're my uniform." Anna turned back to the mirror and put her hands on her hips. She turned to left and then to the right. "You're just jealous that you don't ever get to dress so comfortably at work."

By day, Emily worked in a bank in Dallas and wore suits to work. Because she was saving for a house, two or three times a week she worked as a hostess at Bistro St. Germaine, where she had to dress in sleek, sophisticated black to fit in with the timeless elegance of the downtown Celebration restaurant. Emily had great taste in clothes. Anna would've asked if she could borrow something from her younger sister—and Emily would've graciously dressed her—but it was time for Anna to add a couple of new pieces to her own wardrobe.

"Scrubs are like wearing jammies to work every day," Emily said.

"You know you would if you could," Anna said.

Emily rolled her eyes. "I think you should buy that dress. If not for a date, for you."

"I'll think about it. Now let me change."

Emily stepped back and let Anna close the curtain. Before Anna took off the dress, she did one last three-sixty. It really was cute, in a boho-sexy sort of way.

"Do you really think Jake has some good prospects in mind for you?"

"Who knows? We just talked about this a couple of days ago."

She slipped off the dress and put it with a cute red dress with a bow that tied in front. As she pulled on her jeans and plain white T-shirt, Emily said, "You don't sound very enthusiastic. Are you sure you want to do this?"

"The ball is already rolling. It's just until the wedding. I'll be surprised if it's even five dates. We'll see what happens."

When Anna opened the curtain, she noticed a certain look on her sister's face.

"What?" Anna asked and gathered the clothes, keeping the red and blue dresses separate from the things she didn't want.

"I have to be honest," Emily said. "I always thought you and Jake would end up together."

Her stomach clenched in a way that bothered her more than her sister's words.

"Emily, why would you say that? Jake and I are friends. Good friends. Nothing more."

"Because for better or worse, you two have always stuck together. I mean, I grew up with him, too, but you don't see him hanging out with me. The two of you have always had a really strong bond. Think about it. You and Jake outlasted your marriage. Why the heck are you fixing him up with someone else?"

"Emily, don't. That's not fair."

Anna walked away from her sister.

"Yes, it is. Why is it not fair?"

Anna set the two dresses she wanted to buy on the counter and handed the hanging clothing she didn't want to the sales clerk. After she paid for her purchases and they were outside the Three Sisters shop, Emily resumed the conversation.

"What's not fair about it?"

"You know I can't date Jake. He's my *friend*. He's always been my friend and that's all we will ever be."

Anna felt heat begin to rise up her neck and bloom on her cheeks.

"Then why are you blushing?" Emily asked.

Anna turned and walked to the next storefront, the hardware store, and studied the display as if she'd find the perfect pair of sandals to go with her first-date dress hidden somewhere among the tool kits, ladders and leaf blowers showcased in the window.

Of course, Emily was right behind her. Anna could see her sister's reflection in the glass. She couldn't look at her own as she tried to figure out exactly what was making her so emotional. It wasn't the fact that she was fixing Jake up with someone who could potentially change his mind about marriage being the equivalent of emotional Siberia. Good grief, she was the one who came up with a plan in the first place.

Now Emily's arm was on Anna's shoulder.

"Hey, I'm sorry. I didn't mean to upset you. I'm just a little puzzled by your reaction. I was half teasing, but you're upset. You want to talk about it?"

Anna ran her hand through her hair, feeling a bit perplexed herself.

"I guess it's just the thought of the dating again. You know, starting over. I'm thirty-three years old. This is not where I thought I would be at this age. Em, I want a family. I want a husband who loves me and kids. I never thought I'd be one of those women who felt her biological clock ticking, but mine feels like a time bomb waiting to explode."

The two sisters stood shoulder to shoulder, staring into the hardware store window.

"Well, I guess that eliminates Jake, since we know his thoughts on marriage. Even if he is the hottest guy in town, you don't need to waste your time there."

Anna drew in a deep breath, hoping it would be the antidote to the prickles of irritation that were beginning to feel as if they would turn into full-blown hives.

"Even if he was the marrying kind, he's my best friend, Emily. There are some things you just don't mess with and that's one of them. Hal used to go on and on about how Jake and I secretly wanted each other. Once he even swore there was something going on between Jake and me. But Hal was my husband. I loved him. I loved our marriage and I never cheated. He couldn't get it through his head that a man and a woman could be friends—that there was nothing sexual about it."

"That's probably because in his eyes he couldn't look at a woman without thinking about sex," Emily said. "You know what they say, people usually yell the loudest about the things they're guilty of themselves."

"So, could you just help me out please and not talk about Jake and me in those terms? He's my friend. End of story. Okay?"

Jake had heard a lot of excuses for getting out of a date, and tonight's ranked up there with the best. Cheryl Woodly had called him thirty minutes before he was supposed to pick her up at her place in Dallas for dinner. Her reason for begging off? Her cat, Foxy, had undergone emergency surgery that day and she wasn't comfortable leaving it alone.

He could understand that. He knew people were as crazy about their animals as they were about their children. In some cases, people's animals were their children.

As he turned his 1969 Mustang GTO around and headed back toward Celebration, he realized he wasn't a bit disappointed that Cheryl Woodly had canceled. In fact, from this vantage point, getting out of the blind date seemed like a blessing in disguise. Cheryl had halfheartedly mentioned that maybe they could have a rain check, and he'd made all the right noises and said he'd call her next week to see if they could get something on the books. He wasn't sure if she was preoccupied with her animal or if she was only being polite in suggesting they reschedule. Either way, she didn't seem very enthusiastic. So he wished Foxy the cat well and breathed a sigh of relief.

Still, there was the matter of what to do with the two tickets he'd bought to the Celebration Summer Jazz Festival. He didn't want them to go to waste. Five minutes later, he found himself parking his car in the street in front of Anna's house.

She lived in a Key West–style bungalow two blocks away from downtown Celebration's Main Street. Jake had helped Anna pick out the house after she'd moved to Celebration and her divorce was final.

The place had been a fixer-upper in need of some TLC. Anna had said it was exactly what she wanted—

a project to sink her heart and soul into while she was getting used to her new life. She'd done a great job. Now the house was neat and a little quirky with its fresh island-blue and sea-green paint job. Its style reflected Anna's unique cheerful personality and it always made Jake smile. The lawn was neatly manicured. She must've recently planted some impatiens in the terracotta pots that flanked the porch steps. The flowers' vibrant pinks, fuchsias and reds added another well-planned accent to the already colorful house.

That was the thing about Anna; she put her heart and soul into her home and the place radiated the care she'd invested.

Her Beetle was in the driveway. He could see the inviting faint glow of a light through the living room window.

Good. She was home.

He was going to razz her about her matchmaking skills being a little rusty, since the first date she'd arranged had essentially stood him up. Technically, Cheryl hadn't left him hanging. But Jake was realizing he could get some mileage out of the canceled date and he intended to use it as leverage to get Anna to go to the jazz festival with him tonight.

He'd have a lot more fun with her anyway.

Jake let himself out of the car and walked up the brick path that led to Anna's house. He rapped on the door. *Knock, knock-knock, knock, knock*, their traditional signal that announced they were about to let themselves inside. Really, the knock was just a formality, to keep the other from being surprised. In case she was having sex in the kitchen or something.

Actually, he hadn't been concerned about walking in on Anna having sex because she'd been living like a nun since her divorce. And funny, now that he thought about it, Anna never seemed to come around as much when he was in a relationship.

Hmm. He'd never realized it until right now.

He tried the handle and her door was unlocked. So he let himself in the side door.

"Hey, Anna? It's me."

He heard a muffled exclamation from the other side of the living room. Then Anna stuck her head out of the bedroom door.

"Jake? What are you doing here? Why aren't you out with Cheryl?"

She was hugging the doorjamb and clutching something to her chest as if she were hiding. It looked like she was wearing a dress.

When was the last time he'd seen Anna in a dress?

"She stood me up. What are you all dressed up for? Don't tell me you have a date."

Anna straightened, moving away from the doorjamb, cocking her head to the side.

"She stood you up? Are you kidding me?"

Whoa. She was definitely wearing a dress and she looked *nice*. He'd never realized she had so much going under those scrubs…so much going on *upstairs*. How had he never noticed that before?

The fact made him a little hot and bothered.

He had to force his gaze to stay on her face. Or on her bare feet. Her toenails were painted a sexy shade of metallic blue that matched the dress. Her legs—how had he never noticed her legs before? They were long and lean and tan and looked pretty damn good coming out of the other end of that skirt, which might've been just a hair short…for Anna.

Damn. She sure did look good. No. She looked *hot.*

If she looked like that, why did she cover herself up?

Because this was *Anna.*

He cleared his throat. "Well, she didn't technically stand me up. She called me when I was on my way to get her to say her cat had surgery today and she didn't feel right about leaving it alone."

Anna put her hands on her hips and grimaced. The movement accentuated the low neckline of her dress and the way her full breasts contrasted with her tiny waist that blossomed into hips… Jake forced himself to look away.

"So you didn't shave before you went out? Are you trying to look cool or are you just too lazy?" she asked.

"What?" He rubbed his hand over the stubble on his jaw. "I'm trying to look cool. The ladies like a little five-o'clock shadow."

She quirked a brow and smiled. "Okay, I'll give you that one. It does look pretty…hot."

Something flared inside of him.

"Well, I mean it would be hot if it wasn't *you.*"

"What do you mean *if it wasn't me?*"

She shot him a mischievous smile that warmed up her whole face.

"You're messing with me, aren't you?" he said.

"Yeah. I am. It's fun. Oh, I forgot to tell you that Cheryl is a major animal lover. I'm not surprised she wanted to stay home with the cat, but it would've been nice if she could have given you a little more notice."

"Ya think? Where are you going, dressed like that?"

Anna blushed and crossed her arms in front of her, suddenly seeming self-conscious again. It was one of the things he found most endearing about her.

"I'm not going anywhere. I bought some new clothes and I was trying them on so I could figure out what I wanted to wear on my date with Joseph. He texted me today and asked what I was doing next Wednesday. So I figured I needed to decide what I was going to wear. What do you think of this dress? I wasn't so sure, but Emily talked me into getting it."

She put her hands back on her hips and struck a pose. The tags were dangling under her arm and he had an urge to suggest she take it back and exchange it for something a little more modest. Something that didn't make her look like such a knockout.

"It's, uhh… It looks great."

Maybe a little too great for a first date with a guy like Joseph Gardner. He and Joe had been roommates in college while Jake was doing his undergraduate work. Joe lived in Dallas now. He was a friend, a good guy, really. That's why he'd decided to fix him up with Anna.

And that was why his own attitude about the dress confused him.

"In fact, since you're dressed, why don't you give it a test run and wear it to the jazz festival with me tonight?"

Anna groaned and shook her head. "No, Jake, I really wasn't up for doing anything tonight—"

"God, you're so boring." He smiled to let her know

he was just kidding. "Besides, since you fixed me up with a dud, don't you think you owe it to me to not let this extra ticket go to waste?"

She sighed and cocked her head to the side. She smiled at him. He could see her coming around.

"In fact, if we leave now, we will have just enough time to grab something to eat and get over to the pavilion for the first act."

She shook her head. "Jake, I took my makeup off when I got home from work. Can you give me a couple of minutes to fix myself up?"

She looked so good he hadn't even realized she didn't have any makeup on. Her skin was clear and her cheeks and lips looked naturally rosy. Standing there with her auburn hair hanging in loose waves around her shoulders... And with just the right amount of cleavage showing, he couldn't imagine that she could make herself any more beautiful.

Something intense flared inside him. It made him flinch. His instinct was to mentally shake it off. When that didn't work he decided to ignore it, pushing it back into the recesses of his brain where he kept all unwelcome thoughts and memories and other distractions that might trip him up or cause him to feel things that were unpleasant.

It was mind over matter.

Right now, what mattered was him getting his head on straight so that they could get to dinner and the jazz festival.

"You look fine," he said. "Besides, it's just me."

"Yeah, you and the hundreds of other people that will be at the jazz festival. You don't want them looking at you and wondering, Who's that homely woman with Jake Lennox?"

Homely? How could she see herself that way? It didn't make sense.

"Darlin', you are a lot of things, but homely isn't one of them."

She rolled her eyes at him. "Okay. Okay. You don't have to lay it on so thick. Let me get my sandals and we can go."

When she turned around to walk back into the bedroom, his eyes dropped to her backside which swayed gently beneath the fabric of her dress.

What was wrong with him?

Nothing.

Just because Anna was his friend and it had never really registered in his brain that she was an attractive woman, didn't mean she wasn't or that he couldn't appreciate her…from afar.

From very far away. If he knew what was good for him.

But why now?

Why, in the wake of this bet, did it feel as if he was seeing her for the very first time?

Chapter Four

One of the things Anna loved most about Jake was his ability to surprise her. Like tonight, for example. When she'd gotten home from work, she thought she would try on her new dresses, figure out which one she wanted to wear on her date with Joseph, then put on her sweats, make a light dinner and settle in with a good book and a cup of tea.

The last thing she thought she'd be doing was sitting on a red plaid blanket in the middle of downtown Celebration at a jazz festival waving at people she knew, talking to others who stopped by.

But here she was.

And she was enjoying herself.

Who knew?

It was a nice night to be outside. As evening settled

over the town, a nice breeze mellowed the heat of the late June day, leaving the air a luxuriously perfect temperature.

Leave it to Jake to completely turn her plans upside down—and she meant that in the best possible way. He was her constant and her variable. He was her rock and the one who challenged her to leap off the high dive when she didn't even want to leave her house. Like with these dates they were fixing each other up on. The prospect of spending the evening with blind dates felt like a huge leap into the unknown. Without the assurance of a safety net. Yet somehow she knew Jake wouldn't steer her wrong.

She trusted him implicitly.

That's probably why spending the evening with him and his five-o'clock shadow at an event like this—which could actually be quite romantic with the right guy— seemed more appealing than being here with...another guy.

They'd staked out a great place on the lawn in downtown Celebration's Central Park—close enough to the gazebo that they could see the members of the various bands that would be performing tonight, but not so close that they wouldn't be able to talk. Jake had purchased tickets for the VIP area that allowed for the best viewing of the concerts. Leave it to him to do it first-class.

The area was packed with people of all ages: couples, families, groups of friends. All around them, people were talking and laughing and enjoying picnic suppers. There was a happy buzz in the air that was contagious. Suddenly, Anna knew she didn't want to be anywhere else tonight except right here in the middle of this crowd, holding down the fort while Jake went to get them a bottle of wine and their own picnic supper from Celebrations Inc. Catering Company, which had set up a tent at the back of the park.

She'd almost forgotten what it was like to feel like part of a community. Living in San Antonio with Hal had been completely different. Houston was a thriving metropolis; Hal had been kind of a stick-in-the-mud, actually. Picnics and jazz festivals weren't his gig. He was more the type to enjoy eighteen rounds on the golf course, dinner at the club with his stuffy doctor friends and their wives. If the men weren't playing golf, they were talking about it or some scholarly study they'd read about in a medical journal. Anna had tried to join in their conversation once when they were discussing risk factors for major obstetric hemorrhage—after all, she was an OB nurse—but they'd acted as if she'd wanted to discuss the merits of Lucky Charms with and without marshmallows.

Later, Hal had been furious with her. He'd claimed she had embarrassed him and asked her to just do her part and entertain the wives. Never mind that she had zero in common with any of them. She worked, they lunched. She didn't know the difference between Gucci and The Gap—and frankly, she didn't care. Still, she was forced to sit there and listen to them prattle on about who had offended whom on the country-club tennis team and who was the outcast this week because she was sleeping with someone else's husband.

Of course, Anna made the appropriate noises in all

the right places. She'd become an expert at smiling and nodding and sleeping with her eyes open as the women went on and on and on about utter nonsense. Funny thing was, it didn't seem to matter that she had nothing to contribute. They were so busy talking and not listening— too busy formulating what they were going to say next while trying to get a foot in on the conversation—that it didn't even matter that Anna sat there in silence.

Until the last dinner. Anna had sensed the shift in the air even before they sat down to order. The women were unusually interested in *her.* Their eyes glinted as they asked her about her job, the hours she worked. Did she ever work weekends? Nights? How long had she and Hal been married now? How on earth did they make their two-career marriage work?

It reminded her of those days back in elementary school when one kid was chosen to be the student of the week and all the bits and pieces of their lives were put on display for all to see. Of course, the elementary school spotlight was kinder and gentler. The interest was sincere, even if the others really didn't have a burning desire to know.

This sudden interest in her personal life was downright creepy. And she'd left the club that night with the unshakable feeling that something was up. Something was different. They knew something, and like a pride of lionesses, they were going to play with their prey— get maximum enjoyment from the game before the kill.

On the way home Anna had tried to talk to Hal about it, but as usual he wasn't interested.

Exactly one week to the day later—after the niggling feeling that something was *different* grew into a gut-wrenching knowledge that something was very wrong, something that everyone but her seemed to know about—she'd checked Hal's email and everything was spelled out right there. Sexy messages from his office manager. Plans for hookups and out-of-town getaways. The jackass had been so smug in his cozy little affair that he'd left it all right there for her. All she had to do to learn what was really going on was type in his email password, which was the month, day and year of their wedding anniversary.

And Hal had had the nerve to accuse her of being more than just friends—or wanting to be more than just friends—with Jake.

Anna's gaze automatically picked out Jake in the midst of the crowd. As he walked toward her carrying a large white bag in one hand and a bottle of wine in the other, she shoved aside the bad memories of Hal, refusing to let him ruin this night.

She watched Jake as he approached. He was such a good-looking man—tall and broad-shouldered, with dark hair that contrasted with blue-blue eyes. But what mattered even more was that he was a good man, an honest man. He might be a serial monogamist, but he broke up with a woman before he began something with someone else. That was more than she could say for her ex-husband.

It hit her that she was luckier than any of Jake's past girlfriends. They had a connection that went deeper than most lovers. As far as she was concerned, she would do whatever it took to keep their relationship constant.

"They had this incredible-looking bow-tie pasta with rosemary chicken, mushrooms and asparagus," Jake said as he lowered himself onto the blanket. "I got an order of that and they had another type with a red sauce. I picked up a couple of salads and some flatbread. And they had tiramisu. So save room for dessert. Unless you don't want yours. I'll eat it."

"I'll bite your arm if you try to take my dessert."

He held up his hands. "Never let it be said that I came between you and your tiramisu."

"You're a smart man."

Yes, he was.

She took the feast out of the bag and set the containers out on the blanket as Jake opened the red wine and poured it into two plastic cups. He handed one to Anna and raised his, touching the rim to hers.

"Thanks for being such a good sport and coming out here with me tonight," he said. "I would've hated for the tickets to go to waste. Cheryl doesn't know what she's missing."

"Poor Cheryl," Anna said. "No, actually, not poor Cheryl. I understand that she needed to take care of her cat. I wish she could've given you a little more notice."

"No problem," said Jake as he began dishing up pasta on two plates. "I'll probably have a better time with you anyway."

"Are you going to give her another chance?"

Jake gave a noncommittal shoulder roll. "We talked about it, but she didn't sound very eager. If I didn't know better I'd think she changed her mind about the date altogether. But hey, that's fine."

Anna tasted a bite of the bow-tie pasta. It was delicious. She hadn't realized how hungry she was until now, and she had to force herself to chew her food slowly to keep from eating too fast. As she chased down the bite with a swallow of wine, she noticed a couple of women who were sitting in lawn chairs a few feet away from them blatantly looking at Jake and talking to each other. Clearly, they were talking about him.

Really?

She wanted to tell them that they were being obvious.

What if he was on a date tonight? For all they knew, she could've been his girlfriend. They were being so obvious it was rude. Through it all, Jake seemed to be oblivious.

Anna reminded herself that she wasn't his girlfriend. She had no right to feel territorial.

Yeah, what was with that anyway?

She may not have liked Miss Texas—er Dorenda—but she never felt…like *this*.

Then again, she'd always done her best to give Jake and his women plenty of space.

Now that he was free, what was she doing? Why was she meddling? Jake certainly did not want for female attention. And he really wasn't looking to settle down into anything permanent. Maybe Cheryl's canceling was a sign that she needed to back off.

Maybe she should simply enjoy this time with him before he got involved with somebody else—maybe she shouldn't be so quick to pair him up with someone new.

Right. But how was she supposed to get out of the bet now?

* * *

"Is that the blind date you're with?" asked Dylan Tyler, an orthopedic doctor who was brand-new to Celebration Memorial Hospital. He'd come over to say hello after Anna had excused herself to find the ladies' room before the music started.

"No, I'm here with my friend Anna Adams. Do you know her? She is a nurse at the hospital. Works up in OB."

"How did I miss her?" Tyler asked. "You're not going out with her?"

Jake shrugged off Dylan's question.

"If not, introduce me. It's nice to meet new people. I'd certainly like to get to know her better."

I'll bet you would.

Since Tyler had moved to the area, Jake got the feeling the two of them might occasionally *fish in the same pond*. He hoped his colleague wasn't the kind of guy who would poach. Because his interest in Anna encroached a little too close to home.

"I don't think so."

"So you are interested?" Tyler asked. "If so, I'll back off. No problem."

No. He just didn't want someone like Tyler messing with Anna.

Still, Jake nodded.

Dylan Tyler was a good doctor, but he was the last person he'd fix up with Anna. Or one of the last. There were others who were probably worse, but Dylan's overenthusiasm had helped Jake make an instantaneous decision that he wanted to keep the hospital a dating-free zone—for both of them. He'd have to talk to Anna about that as they continued to work out the parameters of this bet they had going on.

Besides, she didn't want to date a doctor anyway. So that automatically ruled out Dr. Dylan Tyler and any lecherous ideas he might have in mind as he tried to get his hands on her.

"No problem, bud. I can take a hint. Anyway, here comes your lady. I'll let you get back to business. You're welcome to join us." With a jerk of his head, Tyler gestured to his party of at least fifteen people, who had set up camp a few yards away from Jake and Anna's blanket for two. "Or if you'd rather be alone, have fun *not dating* her."

Tyler smirked and gave Jake a fist bump before he walked away.

"Who was that?" Anna asked, watching Tyler still watching them—or her. Was the guy blatant or what? She waved at him, obviously wanting to let him know that she was aware of him. It wasn't exactly a flirty move, as much as it was an I-see-you-there act of self-assurance. Even though she had a shy side, when it came to things like this she had a wit that Jake loved.

"That's Dylan Tyler. Orthopedics. He's the new kid in town. Only been at the hospital for about ten days. You haven't met him?"

He knew she hadn't. He just wanted to see what she'd say.

"No. I haven't had the pleasure. He's cute."

Something strange and possessive reared inside Jake. "I thought you said you didn't want to date a doctor."

Anna dragged her gaze from Dylan back to Jake. In the evening light, her blue eyes looked like twin sapphires. "Yes. I did say that, didn't I? Maybe I need to reconsider my criteria. Or at least make an exception. Why let Hal...rob me?"

"What? Rob you of that guy?" Jake asked.

"You look like you smell something gross. Is he that bad?"

Dr. Tyler wasn't really *bad*, but Jake wasn't convinced he was good enough for Anna. Hmm...maybe he identified with Tyler just a little too much? That's why he understood his game.

"Look, you can't keep changing your list of deal breakers," Jake said. "If you do, how am I supposed to know what kind of guy to fix you up with?"

He lowered himself onto the blanket and Anna did, too, gracefully curving her legs around to the side and positioning her dress to cover her thighs. Even so, there was still a whole lot of pretty leg showing.

"Who said anything about not being able to change criteria? The list shouldn't be set in stone, Jake. What if we go out with someone and we realize that something else is a deal breaker, or maybe there's a quality we originally thought was a deal breaker that turns out to not be such a bad thing after all?"

It irritated him the way she glanced in Tyler's direction when she said that.

"If you want me to introduce you to him, I will." He hadn't meant for his voice to hold that much edge.

"Someone's a little touchy tonight." She raised a brow at him.

"I'm just saying, how am I ever going to win this bet if you don't know what you want?" With that, he took care to infuse humor into his tone.

"I don't think either of us knows what we want. If we did, there would be no bet."

Touché.

The first musical group up, a Rastafarian reggae-jazz fusion band, took the stage and preempted their conversation. After a short warm-up, they got the party started with a Bob Marley tune, which got most of the crowd to its feet. Some people swayed, while others sang along.

After the first song ended, the singer in his smooth Jamaican accent shouted, "Hello, all of you beautiful people. We are so happy to be here tonight. How are you all feeling?"

As the crowd cheered, Jake and Anna exchanged glances that seemed to call a truce to the discussion they'd had a moment ago.

"We are releasing our first CD next month and we would like to introduce you to the first single from that album. It's all about feeling the love and sharing it. Isn't that a great thought? Wouldn't you like to fill the world with love?"

As the band broke into the first strains of their song, the singer said, "I want to see everybody on their feet. Let's all dance and sing and fill the world with love. I don't want to see anybody sitting down looking sad."

Jake took her Anna's hand and pulled her to her feet.

"Oh, no, you're not—"

"Oh, yes I am."

He pulled her in close, holding one of her hands

down at their sides as she placed her other hand on his shoulder and he placed his hand on the small of her back and sent her out for a twirl. Back in middle school, they had learned to swing dance in PE. It was something that the two of them still loved to do, though he couldn't remember the last time they had gone dancing. Anna's husband, Hal, hadn't been very understanding. So Jake had let it go so as not to rock the boat.

Other than their Sadness Intervention Dance, it had been far too long since they'd done that. They weren't the only ones dancing; it seemed a good part of the crowd had been inspired by the Rastafarian singer as he sang his song of spreading joy and love.

It was funny how even after all these years the steps moved through him and into Anna and back to him, the steps and twirls pulling each other together and breaking them apart, but ultimately reeling them back in.

Maybe it was the wine or the music, or it could have even been the setting sun that was sinking lower in the evening sky and bathing everything in a warm golden glow, but for the first time in a long time Jake felt as if he didn't have a care in the world.

As the song wound down, the Rastafarian hopped down off the bandstand into the audience and was encouraging people to fall in love, "at least for tonight. Love the one you're with and send a message of love and good energy out into the world."

Jake gave Anna one final flourishing spin and reeled her back in so that they stood face-to-face, still in each other's arms. Jake's hands moved slowly up her back and over her shoulders until his fingers cupped her face.

His body knew what he was going to do before his mind could stop him.

He bent his head and covered her lips with his.

She didn't pull away. She accepted the kiss like a gift. A gift that was as much for him as it was her.

Her mouth was soft and yielding.

She sighed, a feminine little shudder of a breath, and he pulled back the slightest bit to allow her to object.

But she didn't.

So, he took that to mean that she had accepted his gift and leaned in and kissed her with hunger, and conviction and a need that made the axis of his world shift.

And she kissed him back.

He didn't care that they were in the middle of downtown Celebration in Central Park where anyone could see. Hell, for all he knew, her parents and sister or his brothers might be watching him kiss his best friend, Anna Adams. But he didn't care. Because, for that moment, they were the only two people in the world.

It was just him wanting her and her kissing him back.

Chapter Five

Jake wasn't avoiding Anna.

But he wasn't at all positive she wasn't avoiding him.

He had no idea what had gotten into him Friday night. One minute they'd been dancing and having a great time, and then they were kissing. He wasn't sure who had started it—or if it even mattered. The thing was, he'd kissed his best friend, and at the time neither of them seemed to mind. In fact, it felt good…as if it worked.

Would they work? The two of them…?

It should've felt like kissing his sister. But it hadn't. It felt warm and ripe and *right*. At least in the moment. Then they had done a damn good job of settling down and pretending as if nothing had happened. They'd watched the rest of the concert with a respectable amount of space between them on the blanket. He'd taken her home, walked her to the door and they'd wished each other a platonic good-night.

To the untrained eye, it might've looked as if nothing had happened between them. But then they'd gone all weekend without talking to each other. Proof positive that all was not well and it simply shouldn't have happened.

Jake couldn't remember the last time he and Anna had gone two days without talking. Not since she'd moved back to Celebration. Even when he'd been dating Dorenda and the women who had come before her, he and Anna had talked. They may not have seen each other every day, but they'd talked. Now everything felt off balance and he knew it would stay that way until one of them broke the ice. And that was exactly what he intended to do.

It was eleven-thirty on Monday morning and he'd be damned if he was going to let this weirdness go on a moment longer. He did his best to isolate the kiss, to box up the memory of it and relegate it to the places in his mind where he kept things he didn't want to think about, the things that got in the way.

With that done, he realized that on a normal day by now, he probably would have already seen her—razzed her about whether or not she'd seen Dr. Dylan Tyler today and probably asked her if she had plans for lunch.

He might've been a little behind schedule, but it wasn't too late to man up and get up to speed.

The elevator opened on the maternity ward on the third floor of the hospital. It wasn't his usual territory.

He generally stayed one floor below on the second floor. But every so often—mostly when he wanted to see Anna—he'd find his way up here.

It must've been a slow morning, because three nurses stood talking behind the main desk. They looked up and one blushed as he approached.

"Hi, Dr. Lennox," said one nurse. Her name was Marissa. He knew that because Anna always spoke highly of her. "How can I help you?"

Jake glanced down the empty hallway toward the patient rooms, but didn't see any sign of his friend. The sound of a newborn crying cut through the air.

"Hi, Marissa, ladies. Is Anna around?"

On the wall behind the desk a bulletin board was full to overflowing with baby and family pictures, thank-you notes and pictures drawn in crayon. A call light came on, signaling that a patient needed help and one of the nurses—he wasn't sure of her name and she wasn't wearing a name tag—excused herself to tend to the woman.

"No, we're pretty slow up here today. But I hear you're hopping downstairs. The chief asked if Anna would come down there and help until y'all are caught up. I'm surprised you didn't see her since that's your floor."

"Really? How long had she been there?"

The two nurses exchanged a glance. "Probably since about ten o'clock," said the one whose name tag read "Patty."

So Anna had been on his floor for an hour and a

half and she hadn't said anything. Okay, this definitely called for an intervention.

"I guess that just shows you how busy we've been," said Jake. "Thanks, ladies."

As he turned to walk away, Patty said, "Did you have fun at the jazz festival Friday night? I saw you there and I wanted to get over to say hello, but…" Patty and Marissa exchanged another look. "You saw for yourself how crowded it was and, well, I didn't want to interrupt. Y'all looked like you were having such a good time."

Patty's words were like a well-landed kick in the gut.

Great. Just great. All they needed was to become a rumor on the hospital grapevine. He should've thought of that before losing his mind Friday night.

He stared at the women for a moment, unsure of what to say. After all, what did one say to a comment so full of insinuation?

It's none of your business?

Quit gossiping?

Get back to work?

What an inappropriate thing for them to say. Celebration Memorial didn't have an uptight work atmosphere, but they still adhered to a certain level of professionalism.

They must've read his irritation on his face, because their smiles gradually faded. He hoped they hadn't been this out of line with Anna. But if Patty felt free enough to be that bold with him, he had a sinking feeling he'd better find Anna fast and make sure everything was okay.

"Ladies." He gave them a curt nod and turned back toward the elevator.

This was case in point of why it was a bad idea to date anybody he worked with. He was sure Anna would tell him the same thing once they had a chance to talk.

Relationships were complicated enough. Things like this made them worse. There may have been one day of gossip when he and Dorenda broke up, but it had faded and everyone went on about their business.

Honestly, he hadn't cared what everyone was saying.

But this was different.

Now every time he and Anna were together, people would be speculating. He didn't worry for himself; he worried about how it would make Anna feel.

The elevator dinged and Jake steeled himself to see someone else who might've been at the festival, someone who would give him a sidelong, raised-eyebrow look. But when the door slid open, a man holding a little girl in one arm and a giant vase of roses in another smiled at him as he stepped out into the hall. Jake smiled back and let them clear out before he got in and pressed the button for the second floor.

To hell with them. To hell with them all. Except Anna.

If he could have a do-over, Friday night would be it. Never in his life had he wanted to take back something so badly. Well, of course the other big do-over would be to go back and make things right with his mother. All those years that she'd lived with that secret and let her sons believe she was the culprit who caused the splintering of their family, when in actuality their dad had given her a very good reason to leave. And he'd been content to take the secret to his grave.

If Jake's indiscretion with Anna was his reason for not dating coworkers, his mom and dad's story was the case against marriage. Marriage could turn everything you believed in into a lie. You thought you knew someone, and it turned out they were a complete stranger. Then you had to wreck a lot of lives to get back to the truth.

Jake scrubbed his eyes with his palm, trying to scour away the regret. He had too much to do today to worry about things he couldn't change.

When he stepped out of the elevator on the second floor, Anna was at the nurses' station. She looked up and their gazes snagged. For a split second, she looked like a deer caught in headlights, but then the warm smile that he loved so much spread across her face and he knew everything was going to be okay.

"There you are," he said as he walked toward the nurses' station.

"Here I am," she said. "I didn't know I was lost."

"Actually, I'm probably the one who is lost. I had no idea you were working down here today. I just went up to three to find you."

Her smile froze and her eyes got large and she didn't have to say a word for him to know that Patty and Marissa had probably given her a more intense grilling than they had given him.

He wondered what she'd said, but this was not the time or the place to ask her.

He looked at his watch. "Hey, I was wondering if you wanted to grab a bite of lunch."

Anna's face fell. "I just got back from lunch. I only

took a half hour since we're so busy. I wish I'd known—
I would've waited."

"Hey, no problem—"

"Excuse me, Dr. Lennox," said Cassie Davis, one
of the surgical floor nurses. "The family of Mr. Garrity, who is in room 236, is here and they have some
questions for you. I told them you probably wouldn't
be able to meet with them right now, but I said I would
ask. But if you're just getting ready to go to lunch, I can
tell them you're busy."

Jake shook his head. "No, I can talk to them now.
It's fine."

Cassie handed Jake the patient's chart. "Thank you,"
he said to her as she walked to the opposite side of the
nurses' station. When she was out of earshot, he said
to Anna, "Let's talk later. Okay?"

She nodded.

"Maybe tonight?" he said. "Do you want to grab a bite
after work?"

Anna closed the computer file she had been working
on. "Actually, I can't. I have a date. Over the weekend,
Joseph Gardner, the guy you set me up with, texted and
asked if we could move our date from Wednesday to
tonight. We're going ice-skating."

Ice-skating in June? That was different. Good. It
meant she would have to cover up. She'd have to wear
something like jeans and a turtleneck. Multiple layers
on top. Maybe even a scarf around her neck.

Anna gave a little shrug. She looked unimpressed.

"Oh, okay. Have fun."

All Jake could think was, thank God she wouldn't be wearing that blue-and-white dress.

Have fun?
Oh, okay. Thanks.
Was that all he had to say?
Then again, what did she want him to say?
"Dr. Lennox is such a great guy," said Cassie. There was a dreamy note in her voice. "Why can't all doctors in this hospital be more like him?"
Anna followed Cassie's gaze and saw her watching Jake disappear into Mr. Garrity's room.
"Nice and so good-looking…" Cassie sighed, looking absolutely smitten. "A rare combination in these halls, wouldn't you say?"
"You've got that right."
Actually, truer words had never been spoken. Anna knew all about good-looking doctors who were not of the nice variety. Her husband, Hal, had been smart and handsome, but sometimes he could be the most insensitive, obtuse SOB you could have ever imagined. When he was irritated or bored, he let his feelings hang out there. He could be caustic and rude.
If he'd been on his way to lunch, the patient's family would've had to wait. His philosophy was, if you didn't set boundaries, coworkers and patients and their families wouldn't set them for you.
On paper, his argument was valid. The only problem was, he didn't seem to realize that other people had boundaries and feelings…and needs.

Jake always seemed to have a moment for anyone who asked, yet he never acted as if he felt compromised.

Anna hoped Friday night hadn't compromised their friendship.

There was no denying that the kiss had blown her mind. She'd never really given much thought to what it would be like to kiss Jake, but now she couldn't get it out of her mind.

All weekend long she'd felt his hands on her body, felt the phantom sensation of his lips moving on hers. He tasted wonderful, like red wine and chocolate-laced espresso from the tiramisu. Flavors that were rich and dark and delicious. Flavors that a girl might start craving once she got a taste.

And she couldn't even believe she was linking cravings and Jake Lennox in the same thought.

What's wrong with me? Am I in high school?

No, because in high school Jake had always been like a brother she'd never had.

Now she'd gone and kissed him. And he wanted to talk.

Talk. That couldn't be good. He hadn't kissed her at the door Friday night—would she have wanted him to? That needy, greedy part of her that could still taste him probably wouldn't have objected if he had. But the logical, sensible Anna knew they were flirting with disaster.

She knew what he was going to say. That the kiss had been a mistake. That they needed to pretend it never happened.

She bit her bottom lip.

They didn't need to discuss it. As far she was concerned it was forgotten.

Ha, ha! Now they'd satisfied that little curiosity, it was time to put it behind them.

She felt her phone vibrate in the pocket of her scrubs, signaling a text. She pulled it out and looked at it. It was from Joseph Gardner, her date tonight.

Maybe he was canceling. *God, wouldn't that be great.*

But then she saw the message he left.

Looking forward to ice-skating tonight and seeing if we might fall for each other.

What?

She cringed. Oh, God, that was a bad pun. Ice-skating and falling.

No. Just no.

"Everything okay?" Cassie asked.

Anna hadn't realized Cassie had walked up behind her. The woman seemed to be the only one in the hospital who hadn't heard about her public display of… friendship with Jake.

"Yes. Fine."

She dropped her phone back into her pocket as if it was a hot potato and took a deep breath.

With her attitude, she probably had no business going out with this poor guy. Really, the text was sweet. Corny, but sweet. Despite the fact that she hadn't even met him in person, it showed that he had a sense of humor. It was the kind of gesture that a woman would find very endearing if she was into the man who'd sent it.

But for the woman who wasn't even looking forward to the date…

Stop it, Anna. What kind of horrible attitude is that?

Joseph Gardner had taken time out of his day to text her. She should consider it a good sign. She should be nice.

Or maybe she should save him the brunt of her bad humor and cancel…

She drummed her fingernails on the desk for a moment, contemplating what to do. Then she pulled her phone out of her pocket again and texted Joseph back.

Anna had insisted on meeting Joseph Gardner at the ice rink in Celebration. Even if this guy was a friend of Jake's and an established investment banker, she didn't know him. Besides, she liked the idea of having an escape in case she wanted to leave.

She arrived at the skating rink right on time, with her socks and her gloves and the determination to come into this evening with a better attitude than she had had today.

She wouldn't think of Jake and his lips and his taste of red wine and chocolate.

Nope. She wasn't gonna invite him along on this date.

She got out of the car and walked up to the window where they sold admission. She looked around, but she didn't see anyone who might remotely be Joseph.

Should she wait for him out here? Or should she go inside and get her skates?

But if she went inside, that meant she would pay for

herself. She had no problem with that; in fact part of her preferred it because then there would be no feelings of anybody owing anyone anything.

But it was awkward. Should she buy his ticket, too? No. That would be weird.

At heart, she was a traditionalist who enjoyed being treated like a lady. But it didn't necessarily mean she wasn't a lady if she paid her own way.

She really was so bad at this.

No. Not bad. Just a little rusty.

And he was late.

Anna got in line. The box office was manned by a lone teenage boy who didn't seem to be in a hurry for anything. It took about five minutes to get to the window.

"One admission, please, for the seven o'clock skating session. I'll need to pay for skate rental, too."

The teenager checked his phone and answered a text before he methodically punched numbers into the cash register. No wonder it was taking so long. But why should she be in a hurry?

"That'll be ten bucks. Four for the skates, six for admission."

As she was fishing her wallet out of her purse, she wondered if she should wait a few minutes longer. What if he didn't show? Did she really want to be stuck here all evening?

It's not like I have to stay if he doesn't show.

As she opened her wallet, someone behind her said, "Anna? Are you Anna Adams?"

She turned around and saw a tall, thin, blond man with sparkling brown eyes.

"Joseph?"

"The one and only. I'm sorry I'm late. You know, when longshoremen show up late for work they get docked."

She blinked at him. She might've even frowned because she had no idea what he was talking about.

"Longshoremen," he repeated. "They get *docked*. It's a joke."

"Oh!" Anna forced a laugh, even though it really wasn't funny. It was kind of sophomoric, actually. But she wanted to be a good sport. "I get it. You're a *punny* guy, aren't you, Joseph?"

His eyes lit up and he opened his mouth and pointed at her. "That was good. I think I'm going to like you. Put your money away. When I ask a woman out, I pay. So this is on me."

She held her breath, waiting for him to deliver another pun, but he didn't. So she stuffed the ten-dollar bill back into her wallet.

"Thank you, Joseph. Do you go by Joseph? Or should I call you Joe?"

He took their tickets and stepped away from the window, motioning toward the door. "Yeah, it's Joseph. And you can call me Joseph."

Umm? Oh. "Okay. Joseph."

"No, actually you can call me Joe. I'm just kidding you."

Was that supposed to be funny?

They waited while a family of four entered the building. Then Joseph held the door for Anna, allowing her to step inside first.

At least he was a gentleman.

Inside, the place was at least thirty degrees cooler than it had been outside; the smell of freshly popped popcorn and hot dogs mingled with the scent of dampness. The sound of video games warred with loud music. The rink was already buzzing with activity, but an uncomfortable silence had wedged itself between Anna and Joe. As they waited in line to get their ice skates, Anna could feel the nervous energy radiating off her date. She sort of felt bad for the guy.

She'd been anxious about meeting him, but now she wanted to take him by the shoulders, look him in the eyes and tell him to take a deep breath. He didn't have to try so hard.

Maybe *she* needed to try a little harder to take a little of the pressure off him.

"What do you do, Joe?"

"I'm an investment banker, but I'm starting to lose interest."

He laughed, then cleared his throat when he noticed that Anna was grimacing.

"So you're a nurse?" he said. "Did you hear about the guy whose entire left side was cut off? He's all *right* now."

Anna winced.

"You better slow down there, buddy. You don't want a use up your best material before they Zamboni the ice for the first time."

He looked a little embarrassed. "Too much, huh?"

Anna held up her thumb and index finger so that they were about an inch apart. "Just a tad."

She didn't want to be mean, but really, was there anything much worse than canned humor? Couldn't he hear himself? A horrifying thought crossed her mind—that he could hear himself, but just couldn't *help* this incessant need to make a joke out of everything.

Was there a name for that sort of disorder? Or was it a defense mechanism?

Either way, at this rate, it was going to be a long night. She sat down on the bench to put on her skates. She'd have to ask Jake if his pal Joe had been the class clown.

In all fairness, she'd told Jake that humor was high on her list. She loved to laugh. Who didn't? But no one liked to be pelted with nonstop rehearsed repertoire.

By the grace of God, Joe managed to contain himself as they finished putting on their skates.

After she put on her gloves, Anna stood, wobbling a little bit. Joe reached out a hand, which she grabbed to steady herself.

"It's been a long time since I've been ice-skating. Hope I can still do it."

She braced herself for another pun, vaguely fearing that she'd left herself wide-open by saying that, but either Joe was out of material or he was showing some restraint.

"Jake told me you were athletic. That's why I thought this would be fun."

Fun. Okay, that was a good sign. If he could stop

with the bad jokes, she could loosen up a little bit and have fun.

They made their way into the rink. He stepped onto the ice first, looking sure of himself and steady. He held out his hand and helped Anna. She wobbled again, but managed to grab the bar attached to the shoulder-high wall surrounding the ice. But soon enough, she found her balance and they began circling the rink. He seemed to understand Anna's need to hug the wall for the first couple of rounds. For the most part, he stayed next to her, but showed off a little bit, skating backward every now and then.

At least he didn't try to hold her hand.

Was it natural for a man in his thirties to be this good at ice-skating?

She gave herself a mental slap for being so judgmental.

When the music changed to a slow song and the DJ dimmed the light and turned on the disco ball, Joe turned around to skate backward and started to reach for her.

"I need a break," Anna said. "How about we sit this one out?"

They made their way to a table in the concession area. Joe got them hot chocolate and a tub of popcorn. Anna had to give him props for getting it to the table without dropping, sloshing or spilling. She wouldn't have been so adroit.

He set the drinks on the table and they sat quietly as they watched the skaters float by in pairs.

"Do you have any hobbies? Or do you play any sports?"

"I like basketball."

It made sense. He was tall and moved well. So, okay. Good. Now they were getting somewhere.

"When I'm playing, I always wonder why the basketball keeps getting bigger, and then it hit me."

She blinked at him. The guy just couldn't stop. She was going to kill Jake. Why in the world would he fix her up with an amateur comedian?

"So I imagine that right about now, you want to throw something at me, don't you?" he said.

Yes.

She smiled and shrugged.

"If you do, I hope you'll make it a soda—"

"Because it's a soft drink," Anna finished. She shook her head.

Okay. That's enough. There was being a good sport and then there was being a martyr. Was this the kind of guy Jake saw her with? Just what part of this did he think she would find attractive? No offense to Joe. He was a good guy and would make the right woman happy—hysterically happy. But he wasn't for her. Clearly, her heart was somewhere else.

"So, Jake told me you're divorced," Joe said. Even though this was a topic Anna generally wouldn't want to talk about with a stranger, and certainly not on a first date, it was Joe's first real attempt to make conversation that wasn't a setup for a pun.

"I am. The divorce was official a month ago, but we've been broken up for about two years now."

Joe stared at his hands for a moment.

When he looked up, Anna saw something that resembled vulnerability in his eyes.

"It's only been six months for me," he said. "Does it get easier?"

So that explained it—his nervousness, his need to cover up by making dumb jokes. Well, maybe that was just part of his personality. But she felt bad for the guy. He was obviously hurting.

"It does. It just takes time. If it makes you feel any better, you are my first date since my divorce."

And Jake was your first kiss.

Knock it off, Anna. Stay in the moment.

Joe's eyes lit up the way they did when he was about to bomb her with a bad joke. Anna held up her hand and he stopped.

"Joe, you're a nice guy, and I can't deny that you are just as rusty at this as I am. But the jokes and the puns… maybe use them like salt and pepper?"

He looked sheepish.

"I don't mean to be a bitch. Really, I don't. Can you just think of it as—?"

She started to say *tough love*, but she didn't want to give him the wrong idea.

"Think of it as a friend being brutally honest."

Had Jake planned on dishing out a heaping helping of brutal honesty when he'd asked her to lunch today?

"You're right," he said. "I appreciate your brutal honesty. I guess it might be a little too soon for me to be getting out there again. Obviously."

"You'll be a fun date when you are finally ready,"

said Anna. She wanted to add, *when you meet the right woman*, but she was sure he already knew that.

The couples' skate ended, the lights were restored to their earlier brightness and a faster, decidedly less romantic tune sounded from the speakers.

"Shall we head back out there?" he asked.

She stood. "I need to go to the ladies' room. How about if I meet you on the ice?"

As she scooted out of the booth, Joe stood—just like a gentleman should. But somewhere between scooting and standing, the toe of her skate connected with something hard and the next thing Anna knew she was pitching forward, sticking her hands out to keep from doing a face-plant.

Her wrists bore the brunt of her fall. As Joe pulled her to her feet, a white-hot pain shot down the fingers of her left hand and up to her elbow. She pulled her hand into her chest, cradling it, but trying to not draw any more attention to herself than she already had.

She must've been a lousy actress.

"Are you okay?" Joe asked, reaching for her hand. "Let me look at that. You didn't break it, did you?"

She could move her fingers, but the movement sent flashes of pain spiraling through her.

"I don't think it's broken, but it hurts."

"Let me get you some ice," he offered. "This place should have plenty."

He was almost to the concession stand before she could object. Then, by the time he returned, she knew the night was over.

"Thank you for the ice, Joe. But I think I should go. I'm sorry."

"Should we go to the hospital and get it x-rayed?" he said. "I'll go with you. I hate it that you got hurt."

"No, thank you for offering, though. I'm a nurse. I'm sure it's not fractured. It's probably just a sprain. But I think I should go and ice it down and take care of it. The last thing I need is to fall on it again. Given my graceful performance tonight, that's not so far-fetched."

Joe looked a little relieved. "Aren't we a pair? You with your sprained wrist and me with my bad jokes."

He didn't have to say any more for Anna to know that he wasn't really feeling the chemistry either. Despite everything, it made the night better. Sort of like negatives canceling each other out to make a positive.

"Let me drive you home, at least," he said. "I'll arrange to get your car tomorrow."

"No. But thank you, Joe. I don't live too far from here. Really, I'll be fine. Thank you for everything."

As she extended her good hand to shake his, she looked into his earnest brown eyes. There was a woman out there who would love Joseph Gardner's quirky sense of humor. He truly was a good guy. Sadly, he just wasn't the guy for her.

Chapter Six

"What did you do to your hand?" Jake wasn't calling Anna to check up on the date. In fact, he hadn't planned on calling her at all that night, but what kind of friend wouldn't have checked on her after learning she'd fallen at the ice-skating rink and had hurt herself?

"Jake? I'm fine. How did you know?"

He explained that Joe had called him and given him the scoop.

"What else is there to tell you?" Anna asked.

"Why don't you let me have a look at your hand?"

He knew what her reaction would be, and that's why he'd driven over before she could tell him not to.

"Jake, you didn't have to drive all the way over here. I'm sore, but I really don't think it's broken."

He got out of the car and started walking up the brick path.

"I was in the neighborhood."

"You and I do not live in the same neighborhood."

"Well, I'm here now. In fact, I'm standing outside your front door. Are you going to let me in or not?"

"Sure."

He would've let himself in like he always had, but now... Now that Anna was dating, he thought it would be best to respect her privacy. Although part of him was a little surprised when she did not comment on the fact that he'd knocked when he'd always let himself in in the past.

He glanced at his watch. It was nearly nine o'clock. She'd probably already locked up for the night. In fact, if she hadn't, he was going to say something. Insist that she be more careful. Celebration was as close to being a crime-free community as one could hope for, but she was a single woman living alone. Just to make sure she wasn't compromising herself, Jake reached out and tried the door.

It was locked. As it should be. *Good.*

The porch light flicked on, followed by the sound of the dead bolt turning and the big wooden door opening. His heart clenched when he saw her standing there with her left arm in a makeshift sling. She was wearing a soft-looking pink T-shirt with blue pajama bottoms patterned with white sheep—or they might have been cumulus clouds. He didn't want to look too closely; besides he was more concerned with the drawn look on her face and the dullness in her eyes that indicated that she was in considerable pain.

"What did you do to yourself?"

She stepped back and let him inside, closing the door behind them.

"I don't know why I thought I could escape tonight unscathed," she said as he followed her into the family room off the kitchen. There was a pregnant pause and for a moment he wasn't sure if she was talking about the date or the ice-skating. He decided to wait for her to continue rather than ask.

"I guess I'm not as young as I thought I was."

"Don't be ridiculous. You are one of the most athletic people I know."

"Obviously, I'm no Tara Lipinski."

She sat down on the couch and gestured for him to take a seat next to her.

"No medals?"

"Only if they gave awards for klutziness—I'd win the gold. I wasn't even on the ice when I fell. If I was going to walk away with battle wounds, at least I could've had a good story to tell—that I landed wrong when I attempted my triple Salchow sequence. But no, I tripped over the leg of the table in the snack bar. There's a story for my grandkids."

Jake knew it was only a figure of speech, but Anna did see grandkids in her future. She wanted them—like most normal, healthy women. And she should have a family—a husband who loved her, a house full of kids and even more grandkids.

He could never give her that.

Not that she was thinking about him that way, he hoped. Everything had just gotten so muddied since the kiss. At least it had for him.

"Let me take a look at that." He reached out and eased the scarf that she was using as a makeshift sling over her head. She smelled good. Like shampoo and that flowery perfume she wore. The closeness and the smell of her and the act of lifting the scarf off her body conjured visions of him leaning in and kissing her again and taking off her shirt—

What the hell was wrong with him?

He was here to help her, not mentally undress her.

Holding her injured hand, he moved his knee away from hers to put a little distance between them. He tried to ground himself firmly in the reality that he was holding her hand because he was a doctor. And she was in pain, for God's sake. Never mind that her fingers were long and slender and her wrist was fine-boned, despite the swelling. He could tell that when he compared it to the one that wasn't injured.

He'd known her all these years, yet he'd never noticed this? How had that happened?

"Can you move your fingers?"

"I can." She demonstrated slowly, but grimaced from the pain.

"How about your wrist?"

"Yep." She lifted her hand from his and circled it in the air. "Ouch."

She lowered her hand back into his, palm side up, and he lightly stroked her skin with his thumb. She was so soft, so—

"I know this hurts," he said. "I'm sorry. But just one more test. Can you make a fist?"

"I can, but I don't want to because it hurts."

"I think we should take you in and get an X-ray," Jake said. "Just as a precaution."

He was still cradling her hand in his. Now he was using his other hand to lightly caress the soft skin on her inner forearm.

"Would you let me take you to the hospital?"

She pulled her hand from his, holding it against her chest.

"No, Jake." She looked almost panicked.

"Why not?"

"Because if we come into the ER together at this time of night, it's just going to perpetuate the rumors."

Oh. God, that's right.

He raked his hand through his hair. "You know what? I don't give a damn what they think. I don't care what they're saying. We are none of their business."

We?

They weren't a *we*. Well, they were, but not *that kind* of we.

Anna sat back on the couch. "Yeah, that's easy for you to say because you don't have to hear what they're saying. Since you're a doctor, they talk about you, but not to you."

He frowned. "Oh, I heard about it all right, from Patty who works with you up in OB."

Okay, so she had a point about the gossip. Yes, if they came in together tonight, the rumors would be flying tomorrow.

"But, Anna, if you need an X-ray, you need an X-ray. As your attending physician, I am suggesting that you get this looked at just to be sure."

"You are not my doctor. You're my—" She shook her head. "You're my friend." She held up her hand. "If it were broken, I couldn't do this." She made a fist with her hand and shook it at him, but no sooner had she done it than she gasped from the pain.

Now he was shaking his head.

"You need an X-ray."

"Not tonight."

"You have to be one of the most stubborn women I've ever met."

She shrugged. "Well, the least you could do is go get me some ice. Even Joe was nice enough to do that. Before you called, I was using that bag of frozen peas." She nodded in the direction of a bag lying atop a magazine on the coffee table. "But I think it's spent. I could probably use a full-fledged ice pack. There's a box of zipper baggies in that drawer in the kitchen. You know where the ice is."

He gave her a look, but he spared her the lecture about refusing physicians' orders. She was right—he wasn't her doctor. And she was a smart woman. She knew her body. Then again, sometimes health-care workers were the worst when it came to taking care of themselves in situations like this.

"Jake. The ice? Please?" Then as if she were reading his mind she added, "If the pain gets any worse, I'll have it x-rayed when I get to work tomorrow."

He came back with the ice and handed it to her.

"Do you want me to go to the pharmacy and get you something for the pain?"

"No, thanks. You know I'm no good on strong meds. I took some ibuprofen when I got home. It's starting to take the edge off."

"Speaking of, how did you get along with Joe?"

He knew she might not be in the mood to talk about it, but it didn't hurt to ask. He was curious, and Joe had been a little tight-lipped on the phone, not really sharing much other than the fact that Anna had fallen and wouldn't let him take her to the hospital.

"He's a nice guy deep down. But did you really think he was my type? He kept cracking these really corny jokes. I mean it was rapid-fire, one right after the other. Did he act like that when you roomed with him in college?"

Had he?

"I guess he was a little annoying, but that was a while ago. Because if I were he, I would've grown up a little by now."

"I think he uses humor to deflect his pain. He hasn't been divorced for that long."

"I guess not. Maybe he's not over his ex. Maybe it was too soon."

"Why would you fix me up with someone who'd recently gone through a divorce?"

Jake rolled his shoulders. What was he supposed to say? *Because the two of you had that in common.* Obviously, he was not a matchmaker. Obviously, he didn't have a clue.

"Not your type, huh?"

"No." He wasn't sure if she was annoyed or if it was the pain bleeding through into her words.

His gaze fell to her bottom lip. He was irrationally relieved that Joe hadn't kissed her. He couldn't quite reconcile that feeling. He knew she was off-limits to him. He'd fixed her up with Joe, thinking they might get along. Or if he thought about it a little more, he realized that she and Joe probably had nothing in common.

"Good to know," he said. "Maybe it's not a bad idea to have a debriefing after each of the dates so that we can figure out what worked and what didn't work, so that the next time, we come closer to getting it right. What do you think?"

"If you'll actually go on the next date I set up for you, you might not need next time."

He had the strongest urge to ask her if she wanted to talk about what happened between them at the jazz festival. He realized it was completely out of context, but here she was still hell-bent on introducing him to the perfect woman.

A voice way back in the recesses of his brain challenged him to consider the possibility that the perfect woman was sitting right here in front of him.

But no. Oh, no. *Hell, no.* He wasn't about to go there. He couldn't.

He lowered himself onto the couch next to her face-forward so he wouldn't have to look at her.

"So, using Joe as a point of reference, what should I do differently when I arrange the next date?"

She thought about it for a moment. She laid her head back on the couch and stared at the ceiling.

"Well, I liked the fact that Joe acted like a gentleman. He got points in that area, but there was zero attraction."

Good.

"And of course there's funny, and then there's annoying. In that area, Joe bordered on annoying. So, next time maybe go with somebody perhaps a bit more intelligent, someone kind and someone who hasn't just come from signing divorce papers."

She sat up and rearranged the ice pack on her wrist inside the sling, then looked at him.

"I have an idea," she said. "One thing that might be making this difficult is that we've never seen each other in action out on a date."

"You saw me with Dorenda."

"I felt like I needed to avert my eyes when you and Dorenda were together. Either that, or tell you to get a room. The PDA was really unbearable."

"So what are you getting at?" he asked.

"For our next date, why don't we go on a double date? That way we can see each other in action. Of course, it will have to wait until I'm feeling better. But let's start looking at prospects."

"All right," he said. "That could be interesting. But I'm still unclear about something you said. Did you say you didn't want to date anyone who is divorced?"

"No, that's not what I meant. I understand that when you get into your thirties, most guys are going to come with some baggage. We're not spring chickens anymore. So, yes, divorced is okay—I'd be a bit hypocritical if I ruled out all divorced men. Actually, what scares me more at this point in the game is the ones who have never been married. There're usually issues with them, too."

He nudged her with his knee. "Need I remind you that I've never been married? I don't have issues."

"I hate to break it to you, but you have more issues than most guys."

He made a face as if he was offended. "I don't have issues. I just know what I want."

"You never want to get married."

They sat in silence for a moment, her words ringing in the air.

Finally, she turned to him. "Jake, I know your mom left your family and it was hard on you boys. I saw what you went through. I lived it with you. Even as bad as it was, you, your brothers and your dad were always close. I really don't understand how you can let her leaving your family rob you of one of the most wonderful experiences of life. It's made you so dead-set against getting married. Most women out there aren't going to be like your mother. They'll be faithful and loving wives. A wife is someone you can count on. It goes beyond the sex and having kids. A husband and wife are a team. Your spouse is someone you can count on when nobody else in the world has your back. Forgive me for saying this, because I know your mom is gone, but she was wrong. She took the easy way out. And you shouldn't have to keep suffering for her bad decision."

The day his mom left the family, she'd tried to take the kids with her, but of course his dad had put up a fight. His dad had told her, "It may be your choice to divorce yourself from this family, but I'll be damned if you're going to take my boys."

Two days after she'd moved out, his mom had crashed her car over on Highway 46. The police report indicated her car had drifted off the road and she'd overcorrected and lost control of her car. It had flipped several times.

She'd been pronounced dead at the scene.

Anna knew this part of the story. What she didn't know was the part Jake had learned three years ago, when his father died. It had changed everything.

"What?" Anna asked. "You looked so far away there for a minute. We were talking about how I'm sure the right woman can help you see that your family history shouldn't turn you against marriage."

He wasn't sure why he was going to tell her this, but how could he make her fully understand? But the words were spilling out before he could stop himself.

"When my dad died three years ago, you couldn't come for the funeral."

She frowned. "I know. I'm sorry, Jake. Hal was just so impossible when it came to you."

"God, he was obsessed with the notion that you and I had something going on. It was kind of crazy, huh?" He shook his head as he remembered the no-win situation. "I've never told you this, but after my dad died, I learned something that floored me. It changed me. In fact, it turned my entire childhood and upbringing into a lie."

Anna sat up, grimacing as she did so, but she turned her full attention on him.

"What was it, Jake?"

He took a deep breath, suddenly regretting opening up this line of conversation. But they'd come this far and Anna was the one person he'd always trusted with all his secrets. He'd managed to keep this one to himself for three years.

"My mom didn't simply leave our family out of the blue. She had a good reason—my father had been seeing Peggy for at least a year when my mom found out about their affair. He kept their relationship hidden for two years, or at least he kept her away from my brothers and me, but he married her. You know how she made our lives hell when we were growing up. And then after the funeral, she couldn't rest until she made sure that my brothers and I knew about her affair with our father."

Anna's jaw dropped.

"All those years, we thought my mom was the one who'd walked away from us, and my dad let us believe she was the villain, even after she died, when all that time our father had been living a double life. I just can't get over what a screwed-up situation it was, and then there's the added guilt of how my brothers and I vilified our mother because we believed she'd walked out on us.

"That's why I don't want to get married, because their bad marriage and my dad's deceit ultimately turned our childhood into one big lie."

She sat there watching him, taking it all in. "I'm so sorry that happened to you and your brothers. With both of your parents gone, I'm sure it must feel like a whole lot of unresolved business. But, Jake, I am imploring you not to let it continue to rob you of something that could be incredibly good for you."

* * *

The following week, Anna was definitely on the mend. Her sprained wrist was still tender, but it was feeling remarkably better. She'd done light duty to give it a chance to heal. Now she was nearly back up to speed. Since she'd only been at the hospital for a little over a month, she wanted to make sure she pulled her own weight. She didn't have time for an injury, but she was heartened when her coworker, Patty, had assured her that she and the others on the OB floor were happy to pick up the slack, such as carrying heavy supply baskets and equipment.

Even if they leaned a little heavy on the gossip sometimes, Anna believed that they truly had her back, even in the short time she'd been working at Celebration Memorial Hospital.

Of course, nothing came without a price. They were more curious than ever about what was happening with her and Dr. Lennox.

"Nothing is happening," Anna told them.

And Patty maintained that the jazz festival lip-lock certainly didn't look like *nothing*.

"Sorry to disappoint you, but he and I are just friends. I've known him all my life."

Patty and Marissa exchanged dubious glances. "Looks more like friends with benefits to me," Patty said.

"No. It's not like that. If you don't believe me, maybe this will change your minds—we both have dates tonight. In fact, we are double-dating."

"Are you dating each other and going out with another couple, or..." Marissa asked.

"Or. He has a date and I have a date. Since our dates are both this evening, we thought it would work if we all went out together. You know how blind dates are. Anything to make them easier."

Patty's eyes grew large. "Did you fix Dr. L up on a blind date?"

"I did." Anna had the sinking feeling she'd better steer this conversation in another direction. It was getting a little too personal; Jake wouldn't be very happy if word got out and he traced it back to Anna as the original source.

"If you're looking for candidates, keep me in mind," said Marissa.

"Hey, I have dibs," cried Patty.

"You're both crazy," said Anna. "But only in the best way."

That evening as they walked into the bar inside Bistro St. Germaine to wait for their dates, Vicki Bright and Burt Jewell, Anna was hyperaware of the light pressure of Jake's hand on the small of her back. It was more possessive than if he'd simply walked beside her, but not quite as intimate as if he held her hand or put his arm around her. But why was she even thinking about that kind of closeness?

The bistro—where Emily worked, but she was off tonight—was an upscale spot with floor-to-ceiling glass doors that folded open so that the bar and casual dining area spilled out onto the sidewalk outside the restaurant. The more formal dining room had tables in the back that were covered with crisp white linen tablecloths and sported small votive candles and vases hosting single red rosebuds.

As they approached the maître d' stand, the soft strains of a jazz quartet and muted conversation buzzed in the air.

Anna was glad she'd worn her black dress—it wasn't too dressy, but it still had an air of sophistication.

They were meeting their dates at the restaurant. The one thing to which Anna had held firm during this bet with Jake was that she would meet her blind dates at the location. She didn't want strangers picking her up. What if the guys were real duds? Or turned out to be stalkers? Still, Anna made no apologies about playing by her own rules.

Vicki had driven herself tonight, too. Because of that, Jake and Anna had ridden together.

The bar was buzzing with people. Jake and Anna managed to grab the last two open seats. Anna ordered a glass of merlot and Jake had a beer.

As they waited for their drinks, Anna asked, "What do you need me to do to help you with the Fourth of July party? Because you're going to be out of town next week, aren't you?"

"I leave tomorrow."

"Oh, really? I didn't realize the conference was so soon."

Hospital CEO Stan Holbrook had personally asked Jake if he would attend a medical conference on research and development and bring back the information to share with the rest of the staff. It was proof positive that Jake was on Stan's radar and it seemed like another step toward securing the chief hospitalist position.

"Yes, I decided to fly in a couple of days early so I could spend some time with Bob Gibson, my mentor from med school. He's retired and living in New Orleans now. I haven't seen him in years."

"Sounds like fun. Are you boys going to tear up Bourbon Street?"

Jake laughed. "Hardly. That's a little too spring break for me. Besides, Bob hasn't been doing very well lately. He's been having some health problems. But he sounded good when I talked to him. He suggested we grab some dinner and then go listen to some jazz over on Frenchmen Street. It's quite a bit lower-key than Bourbon Street. After that, it will be all medical conference all the time and I won't have time for much sightseeing. But I'll bring back some Mardi Gras beads for you if you want."

"That's sweet of you, Jake. Only if you have time to get them. Please don't make a special trip into the drunken debauchery just for me."

"I would go to the ends of the earth for you."

There was something in his eyes that made her melt a little inside. It was an odd feeling because this was *Jake*. She wasn't quite sure what to say. They'd always kidded around, but somehow this didn't feel like a joke. A lot of things had felt different in the month since she'd been back in Celebration.

Or maybe she was reading too much into it after that kiss, which certainly hadn't felt like a joke—

"I see Burt," Jake said, staring at a point over Anna's shoulder. "That must be Vicki."

Anna turned around and saw her friend Vicki— actually, she was Emily's friend. Emily had suggested Jake and Vicki might hit it off since she was smart, pretty and a busy, professional woman who seemed to be more committed to her work as an attorney than hunting for a husband.

Vicki was standing in the restaurant's entryway, engaged in deep conversation with a bald man who was a little on the short and pudgy side. The two of them were already engaged in conversation, talking and laughing animatedly like old friends.

"Is that Burt in the brown jacket?" Anna said. "If so, the woman he's hugging is my friend, Vicki."

"Yep, that's Burt. Do they know each other?" Jake slid off of his bar stool and extended a hand to help Anna down.

"I hope so. If they didn't before they do now."

Come to find out, they did know each other. They'd dated in high school, but had lost touch. What a small world, they marveled. It was a wonder that they hadn't crossed paths before this since they both lived in the Dallas area and Vicki was an attorney who practiced family law; Burt was a psychologist specializing in family counseling. They may even have had clients in common.

Anna watched the years melt away for them right before her eyes. And she was happy for them, even if all branches of conversation seemed to lead back to *remember that time when...* or legal/family counseling shop talk. Even when Anna or Jake tried to steer the conversation toward something more inclusive, it managed to wind back around to a precious moment Vicki and Burt had shared.

Finally, after they had finished their entrées, Anna and Vicki excused themselves to the ladies' room.

"What a small world, isn't it?" Vicki said. "Burt was my big love back in the day. We lost touch after I found out that he'd gotten married. He's divorced now."

"*Whew*, what a relief," Anna joked. "Since he's here for a blind date. You know, the two of you should get together. Seems like that old spark is still there."

She was sincere and she certainly hadn't meant to sound snarky or jealous—God, no, she wasn't jealous. She was inspired by the sweet rekindling of long-lost love. But Vicki must have interpreted it as a dig because she turned and looked at Anna, her mouth forming a perfect, soundless O.

"We have been so rude tonight," she said. "Anna, I'm so sorry. The way Burt and I have monopolized the conversation tonight is just inexcusable."

Anna put a hand on Vicki's arm. "You have nothing to apologize for. I would love nothing more than to see you and Burt get to spend more time together. Really. I mean it. There's nothing like a second chance at love."

"Well, I feel just terrible. You went to all the trouble to fix me up with your friend, Jack—"

"Actually, it's *Jake*."

Vicki covered her face with her hands. "I'm sorry. I'm really batting a thousand tonight, aren't I?"

"The heart wants what the heart wants." Anna smiled

at her reassuringly. "You have absolutely no reason to be sorry."

As they made their way back to the dining room, Anna wasn't sure if the relief she felt was because she wouldn't have to make excuses at the end of the night about why she couldn't see Burt again or if it was because Vicki and Jake would not have a second date.

Chapter Seven

Jake had gotten back into town late the previous night after his trip to New Orleans for the weeklong medical conference. He hadn't slept well. Actually, he hadn't slept well the whole time he was gone. His mind kept wandering to places it had no business dwelling.

And then, *dammit*, once he'd gotten back into town, he was tempted to drive straight over to Anna's house, because all he could think about was how he'd missed her.

Thank God common sense reigned, because he'd gone home and crawled into his own bed instead of going to her.

The first thing this morning, he'd texted her and asked her to meet him for lunch in the hospital courtyard.

Our table on the patio? he'd asked.

The table that was shaded by a large oak tree. The day was mild and clear, the perfect opportunity to sit outside and get some fresh air.

I'm so there, she'd responded. I've missed you. But then she'd qualified it with, We need to firm up July 4 party plans.

Now, as he walked toward her, he couldn't get over how beautiful she looked, sitting at the table, soaking up the sunshine. Her auburn hair was pulled back off her face and when she looked at him and smiled, he saw that she wore hardly any makeup. She didn't need it. She looked fresh and gorgeous without it.

"Hey stranger," he said as he set his tray on the table. "Anyone sitting here?"

"I was saving that seat for someone very special," she said.

He leaned in and kissed her on the cheek. "How's it going? How's your wrist feeling?"

"No problem," she said, moving it in a circle. "It's pretty much back to normal now. What's in there?" Anna nodded toward the white plastic bag he carried.

"I brought you something." He pushed it toward her. "Open it."

She cast a questioning glance at him and he smiled at her.

"I think you're going to like it."

She opened the bag and peered inside. Then reached in and pulled out several strands of Mardi Gras beads and a CD.

"What's this? Wait a minute—is this what I think it is?"

"You won't believe this, but that reggae-jazz fusion group we saw at the jazz festival was playing at The Spotted Cat, a music club on Frenchmen Street. What are the chances? Here's the CD they were talking about at the jazz festival."

Anna held up the CD and examined it. "Are you kidding me? That's crazy. And I love it."

She was scanning the back cover of the CD. "'Love is in the Air' is on it." He noticed a flicker in her eyes.

"Yeah, there it is. I like that song." He noticed that she didn't meet his gaze. Suddenly, she was acting a little shy.

Keeping it light, he said, "I had to drag myself through the drunken debauchery to get those beads for you."

"Thank you for compromising yourself for me," she said, fingering the beads. She set the CD on the table and looked thoughtful as she traced the letters spelling out the name with her finger.

For a moment, the craziest thought crossed his mind—he would do anything in the world for her. What was happening between them? Because suddenly everything seemed different and the weirdest part was, it didn't scare him. Neither did the fact that, right or wrong, he wanted to explore it a little more. He'd realized that over the week that he was gone.

"Oh, my God, did you get a card from Vicki and Burt?" she asked, suddenly seeming more like herself.

It took a moment for the names to register. "Oh, right, Burt and Vicki. Hearing their names together threw me."

"Well, wait until you hear this. Did you get anything in the mail from them this week?"

"I had the post office hold my mail while I was at the conference. They're delivering it today. Why? What did you get from them?"

"You have to see this." She fished in her purse and then handed him a peach-colored envelope that was nearly the same hue as her scrubs. "I'm sure you got one, too, but I want to see your face when you read this."

He squinted at her, hoping for a hint about what was inside. She looked as if she could hardly contain herself.

"Open it," she said, gesturing toward the envelope.

Jake pulled out a white card and blinked at the picture on the front. It was Vicki Bright and Burt Jewell. Underneath the black-and-white photo, spelled out in bold, black letters, it said,

We're getting married!
Save the Date: December 24, 2015.

Jake's mouth fell open. Then he laughed. "Is this a joke? They just reconnected with each other *a week* ago. Can you even get printing done that fast, much less propose, address cards and mail them out? They obviously had a lot of catching up to do after we left them at the restaurant."

"Funny thing is, I thought Vicki didn't want to get married," said Anna. "Emily told me she was too immersed in her quest to make partner at her law firm. But it's not as if they just met. They were high school sweethearts. Maybe she was waiting for him?"

His stomach tightened in a weird way and as he looked into her beautiful blue eyes, there was that feeling again. The two of them had been separated for a decade and Anna had only been back in his life full-time for one month, but after all these years it seemed as if a lot had changed. Changed for the better. And he wasn't quite sure what to do with these feelings. One thing that remained constant was they wanted different things from life. She wanted marriage and a family. He…wasn't so sure.

"Well, we know we can set up the perfect couple," he said. "Apparently just not for each other."

"Don't count me out just yet. I have someone in mind to fix you up with for the July Fourth party. Cassie Davis, that nurse on the second floor."

"Cassie? Oh…she's nice. And pretty. She sort of reminds me of you in a way."

Anna threw him a look.

"Oh, well, poor Cassie. I guess that means you're not interested."

Why had he said that? Or at least, why had he said it that way? It wasn't a slam. Any guy would be lucky to have Anna. Unfortunately, the jackasses of the world, like her ex, always seemed to come in and mess things up for the good guys. Jake wondered if in her eyes he fell into that jackass category, dating beautiful women who weren't marriage material, so, a few months down the road, he could walk away with his bachelorhood intact.

"I didn't mean anything bad by it," he said.

Tell her. Tell her that a man would be lucky to have her love.

But the words stuck in his throat and then he convinced himself that he'd better quit while he was ahead, or at least before he dug himself in deeper.

"I don't know if it's a good idea to date someone I work with. Look how messy it got after people saw us together at the jazz festival."

Anna's right brow shot up the way it always did just before she made a smart-mouthed comment about something. But then, it was as if she stopped herself before she said what was on her mind. He realized what he'd said might've sounded as though he was calling their night at the jazz festival a date.

It wasn't.

Not technically.

God, he didn't want to pressure her.

No, if it had been a date…what would he have done differently? He might've asked her if she was available earlier, rather than just showing up at her house. But one of the things he loved about her—about *them*—was that they were spontaneous. They didn't have to schedule fun. Fun seemed to follow them wherever they went. It was as natural as—

"You're welcome to invite her, if you'd like," he said. "But how about we don't bring dates to the party? It's a lot of pressure."

He hoped that didn't sound wrong. Even though he didn't know how else it could sound.

"I mean, you can bring a date if you want. But I think I want to go solo to this one. Since we're cohosting. It might be easier."

"If I didn't know better, I might think you were asking me to be your date."

Her eyes sparkled as she sat there watching him. She was baiting him, but he wasn't going to bite.

"Even better, I was thinking Cassie could be your date for the wedding. Really, she's perfect, if you think about it. Stan Holbrook knows her. He thinks highly of her. Everyone does."

"If everyone loves her so much, why is she still available?"

She clucked her tongue at him and wrinkled her nose.

"Watch what you say there, buddy. You make it sound like she has some sort of defect. She's a good catch. Don't forget, you and I are *available*. Does that mean we're defective, too?"

"Of course not."

"Okay, then. Take Cassie to the wedding?"

"If it will get you off my back." He smiled at her to make sure she knew he was joking.

Sort of.

"Okay, good. That's one thing off my plate. You do realize I'm a step ahead of you here. Even though the dates with Vicki and Cheryl didn't work out, Cassie is a keeper. Or at least someone you don't need to toy with."

"I don't toy with women. Especially not women I work with."

She shrugged as if she were giving him that point. "You need to fix me up with someone decent. I mean, Joe and Burt are nice guys, decent guys, but they weren't for me. Obviously. So you'd better bring your A-game for this one. I don't want to be the third wheel on your wedding date."

He wouldn't mind her being the third wheel. No, actually it crossed his mind that maybe it would be a better idea if they went to the wedding together. But he knew what she would say to that. By the grace of God, things had not gotten weird after the kiss. He needed to rein it in a bit before his luck ran out.

Sitting here, looking at her, fresh-faced and lovely, his body was telling him exactly what he wanted—her, in her bed, with nothing between them but their feelings. But then reality crashed the party, reminding him that she wanted—she *deserved*—so much more than he could offer her.

For a moment, he let his mind go there. He was crazy about her in a way that he had never felt about any other woman in his life. Would it be so bad? Of course it wouldn't. But he had to stop pushing the envelope with her. If he kept on, he was bound to hurt her. Ruin everything between them.

And that was the last thing he wanted to do.

"Let me think about a date for you," he said.

Dylan Tyler came to mind. He had a good career and he and Anna had both found each other attractive—as they'd stated at the jazz festival. But he wasn't going to lie to himself. The fact that Dylan and Anna might be just a little too perfect for each other made him uncomfortable. Did he really want to tempt fate?

What the hell did it even mean, that he was thinking that way?

If he knew what was best for both of them, he would say goodbye now.

* * *

At least forty people had turned out for the party. Apparently, Jake's annual shindig had become something of an institution. One of the reasons his house was the perfect place for this party was that fireworks from at least three different local shows were visible over the water.

Since Anna had been in San Antonio until last month, and because Hal had been so funny about her friendship with Jake, this was the first year she'd been able to attend his infamous party, much less be involved in helping him host.

"Hey, Anna, you and Jake throw a great party," said her sister, Emily, who was sitting around a fire pit with Ty and Ben, two of Jake's three brothers, roasting marshmallows for s'mores. "I think they make a good team. Don't you, Ty?"

Emily could be such an instigator sometimes. She flashed a smile at Anna, then turned her charm on Jake's youngest brother, Ty. She could be a flirt *and* an instigator. Anna sat down on the arm of the Adirondack chair Emily was in. Her sister's long brown hair hung in soft waves around her tanned shoulders. The aqua halter top she wore accentuated her blue eyes. The glow of the fire made her cheeks look rosier than usual. Or maybe it was simply the fact that she was in her glory, enjoying the sight of the younger Lennox brothers engaging in a subtle tug-of-war for her attention.

"I'm glad you're having fun," Anna said.

"She's right, you know," said Ty. "Jake's Fourth of July parties are always good, but you've helped him kick it up another notch this year. I think there's something to this pairing."

Anna nudged her sister's leg, in a thanks-a-lot-for-getting-this-started gesture. "Well, what you see is what you get. You know Jake and I have always been good buddies."

"I think you two are good for each other," said Ben. "He seems so much happier lately—since you moved back."

The idea sent Anna's spirits soaring, despite the fact that she sensed a conspiracy.

Ty was a good-looking guy. He was an EMT, the kind who might be featured on the cover of a first-responders calendar. He'd always had a thing for Emily, but she'd always viewed him as a brother. Maybe that was the thing about knowing somebody since their paste-eating kindergarten years. Sometimes it was hard to see past the old and into the possibilities.

"Where is Luke tonight?" Anna asked. "I thought he'd be here."

She glanced at her sister. Emily had always had a thing for Luke Lennox. Wasn't it just the grand irony that Ty seemed to be attracted to Emily, but Emily was interested in Luke? And Luke… Who knew where Luke's head and heart were these days? He'd been pretty scarce since Anna had been back. He was nearly as bad as his older brother when it came to loathing commitment.

"Are they giving you a hard time?" As if on cue, Jake walked up beside Anna and rested a hand on her shoulder. Her skin prickled under his touch, and she held her breath, hoping Emily wouldn't start asking why she and Jake were trying to fix each other up...when the obvious answer was right there in front of them.

Well, that's what Emily would say.

And Anna couldn't believe she was even letting her mind go there. She and Jake were obviously wrong for each other. They wanted completely different things out of life, even if this attraction did seem to pull them both toward a middle ground where they could meet... but for how long? And to what end?

"Do you really think I'd let them get away with that?" Anna said.

She'd been working on the decorations and setting up for the party since midmorning. She'd strung stars-and-stripes bunting along the back of the house and festooned the tables with red, white and blue tablecloths, and napkins and centerpieces made of white hydrangeas and small flags arranged in vases that looked like mini-washtubs.

This was the first chance she'd had to slow down all day. She'd worked up until the guests had started arriving. Then she'd quickly changed from her shorts into her red sundress and she'd played hostess, greeting everyone, fetching drinks and doing her best to make them feel at home. Her stomach growled a stern reminder that she hadn't eaten much that day.

Now dusk was settling over the backyard. It was just about time to bring out the giant flag cake she'd made—a sheet cake with whipped cream icing, adorned with strawberries and blueberries to form the stars and stripes on the flag. She'd have just enough time to grab a bite and serve the cake before the fireworks started.

"I'm starving," she said to Jake. "I have got to get something to eat. Would you care to join me?"

"I'd love to," he said. "Let's grab some food and go down to the dock."

"The dock, hmm?" Emily muttered. "That sounds romantic."

Anna stepped on her sister's foot as she stood.

"Ouch!" Emily said. "That hurt."

"Mmm-hmm." Anna shot her sister a sweet smile. "I intended for it to. Mind your manners."

As they walked toward the food table, Jake asked, "What was that about?"

Anna shrugged and pretended to be much more focused on the barbecue than was really necessary. "Oh, you know how Emily can be. I was just keeping her in line."

"What's she getting you all riled up about now?"

Jake's voice was deep and ridiculously alluring. Anna slanted a glance at him.

"She's gotten it into her head that we shouldn't fix each other up."

Jake raised a questioning eyebrow, but something in his gaze seemed to say he knew what she was going to say next.

"She thinks you and I should date," Anna said. "She always has."

Jake shot her a lopsided smile that reminded her of the times when he used to triple-dog-dare her to do things she would've never tried on her own.

Or maybe she was simply imagining it.

Anna looked away, training her focus on the food, inhaling the delicious scent of barbecue and trying to ignore how her stomach had suddenly twisted itself into a knot. She helped herself to the barbecued ribs Jake had spent all day slow-cooking, a scoop of potato salad and some baked beans.

"Want a beer to go with that?" Jake asked.

He looked *good*, standing there in his blue jeans and bright blue polo shirt. Her stomach did a little flip, which she tried to convince herself was hunger.

But hunger for what, exactly?

The flames from the tiki torches cast shadows on his face, accentuating his strong jaw line and full lips. He was sporting that sexy-scruffy five-o'clock shadow that Anna had become inexplicably fond of. He fished a bottle of the micro-brew he'd picked up for the party out of the cooler and held it up for her to see.

"Yes, please. That sounds wonderful."

They'd been so busy facilitating that they hadn't had a chance to say much to each other, much less enjoy a beer together.

Jake grabbed another bottle out of the cooler and turned toward the dock.

She took her plate and followed him. It was one of the few unoccupied spaces, probably because it was set away from the food and festivities. Their friends were clustered in groups under the canopy of trees that stretched protectively over the large backyard. All the seats and places at the tables appeared to be occupied. In fact, people were sitting on the ground amidst the tiki torches and fire pit; everyone was talking and laughing and seemed to be having a great time. But right now, all Anna wanted was to find a quiet place away from the crowd where she could eat, and if that place happened to be on the dock, alone with Jake…all the better.

This was what she'd been missing all the years she'd been away. A lot of things had changed, but one thing that had become a tradition was that people loved to gather at Jake's house. She hadn't asked him, but she wondered if over the years his various girlfriends had played hostess. She made a note to rib him about it later.

But not now.

There wasn't time.

The sun was setting, and Anna knew if she didn't eat while she could, soon everyone would be shifting out from under the trees, toward the dock and the lakeshore to watch the fireworks. She didn't want to spend what little alone time they might have conjuring the ghosts of exes past.

For the first time that evening, as Anna sat there with Jake, she inhaled a full deep breath and relaxed.

On the dock, they sat side by side on the bench that overlooked the lake. The warm summer breeze must've blown out the tiki torch that Jake had lit earlier, because the only light came from the dusky twilight reflecting off the water.

He was sitting so close to her that his muscular biceps grazed her when he lifted his beer to take a sip.

All seemed right with the world as they sat next to each other listening to the symphony of cicadas, just as they had so often before. But this time, something felt different. There was a charge in the air. No matter how Anna tried to ignore it or explain it away or put herself on notice, she didn't care that it was a bad idea to allow herself to be drawn in by this strange, new magnetic pull that was so strong between them.

"It seems like everyone is having a great time," said Jake.

She was acutely aware that his knee had drifted over and was pressing against hers, and she was doing nothing to put some much-needed space between them. She didn't intend to do anything.

"Yeah, they are. We should do this more often."

"Do what? Have a July Fourth party?"

She was just about ready to swat his arm for the sarcastic remark, but he said, "Or should we do *this* more often?" He gestured between them. "I'd vote for this, myself."

She felt shy all of a sudden, as if he were testing her wit…and she couldn't come up with a good comeback. All her words felt clunky and strange and wrong.

Or maybe he was calling her bluff?

It sure seemed like it when he trailed his finger along the tender underside of her arm. The feel of his hand on her was her touchstone, her anchor, the one thing in this world that simultaneously frightened her and made perfect sense.

He set down his beer and turned his body to face her. He was looking at her with an intensity that had her gripping the edge of the bench to keep from reaching for him.

Despite the summer breeze blowing across the lake, the heat between them flared. He was playing with her hair, and she reached out and touched his hand. It was just meant to be a passing touch—something to anchor her, but it seemed to ignite that spark.

She wasn't sure who moved first, but suddenly they were kissing each other.

He kissed her exactly the way she hoped he would: deliberate and intense, as if he wanted to prove to her that they were *that* good together. That it really was electric. That it hadn't been a fluke that night when he'd first kissed her at the jazz festival. Right there in front of everyone. In front of their coworkers and their neighbors and God. In the moment, she hadn't worried about who saw them or questioned them or talked about them. She didn't think she would ever worry about it. This was Jake. The guy who had always looked out for her. Protected her.

She was sure he was still that guy who cared about her more than the man she'd married had ever done. But she wasn't the blindly foolish woman who'd convinced herself for years that her feelings for her best friend were purely platonic.

No. She definitely wasn't that woman anymore.

In this moment, she was just a woman who wanted a man. *This man.* And the sizzling hot, extraordinary kiss he was giving her. She would consider the consequences later.

Or maybe she wouldn't.

Maybe she'd pretend there were no consequences to worry about.

Maybe she worried too much.

Jake was kissing her and nothing else mattered. This

dock was their own world for two, their own universe. It was vast and amazing. This kiss wasn't about weddings and children and happily-ever-afters that she could never have with him.

Stop thinking so much, Anna.

This kiss wasn't about friendship and history and knowing each other inside and out.

The only thing that mattered was that this felt amazing. It worked. *They worked.* They were good together.

She wanted it, and he did, too.

She fisted her hands into his shirt and felt the warm, solid weight of his body against hers. He leaned into her, even closer, his hands moving across her back, down her to her hips, then sliding back up her sides and pushing against the weight of her breasts. He lingered there, liking it, she hoped. As if silently answering her, he shifted his body just enough to move his hands in so he could explore and caress.

He made a low, deep sound in his throat and she felt the vibration of it all the way through her own body, like fireworks on the Fourth of July or the rumble of a night train steaming its way through the heat of summer.

She wanted to live in that dark, rich sound; she wanted it to pick her up and carry her far away from every thought or intrusion of reality that might come between them.

But then, without warning the kiss ended. He pulled those delicious lips away. It was so abrupt it was disorienting, like soaring through the inky, starry sky one moment and then free-falling back down to earth the next.

"I'm so sorry." He moved back, raking his hand through his hair, putting some distance between them.

"Why are you sorry? Don't be sorry, Jake."

"This wasn't supposed to happen again," he said. "I promised myself I wouldn't kiss you again."

"So you've been thinking about kissing me again?"

He nodded. "I haven't been able to get those lips of yours out of my head." He seemed a little subdued. Maybe even a bit contrite.

"It's okay. It's fine, really. Would it make a difference if I confessed that I was hoping you'd kiss me again?"

She just blurted out the words. It was only the truth, and why shouldn't she tell him the truth?

Why? Well, she had a long list of why's for not confessing this particular truth, but they didn't matter right now.

"You deserve someone so much better than me, Anna." He leaned back and seemed to be trying to put even more distance between them.

"I've never met anyone who treats me better than you do."

He shook his head, looking so remorseful that it nearly broke her heart. "Believe me, you could do *so* much better. You *should* do better than me…than this. Especially after Hal."

No. She wasn't having any part of that.

"Don't be so hard on yourself, Jake. Remember, I've had two years to work through my failed marriage. I didn't rush right into dating the day after it happened. Not even the day I signed my divorce papers. It took you to get me back out into the world, albeit kicking and screaming, but I'm glad you nudged me out there."

"Even though the two dates I've fixed you up on have been complete and utter failures?"

"That's right. I sprained my wrist with the first guy and the other one married my sister's friend. If I didn't know you better, I'd think you were setting me up to fail. Is that what happened? Or was it leading me here?"

His right brow shot up. She loved the way he looked. It made her smile. *He* made her smile.

"I guess you have conquered your fear of getting back out there in the dating world."

If not for him, she'd still be hiding away.

"And you're the one who helped me do that," she said. "You've reminded me that romance isn't necessarily synonymous with pain. Thank you for that."

"But God, what are we doing, Anna?"

"Jake, why won't you let me in?"

There was a full moon tonight and the reflection of it rising over the water flickered in his eyes. He looked at her for a long moment and she could almost hear the jumbled thoughts churning in his head as he tried to put them in order.

"You're such a good person, Anna." He sounded preoccupied and she might've jumped to the conclusion that he was trying to let her down easy, but his expression and his body language told a completely different story. He was leaning in again. "You deserve someone equally as good."

"Shut up." She pressed her finger to his lips. "Don't ruin this moment."

His gaze, smoldering and intense and completely at odds with his protests, locked with hers.

"You just have to promise me one thing," he said.

Running the pad of her index finger over his tempting bottom lip, her wrist rubbed against the sexy stubble on his cheeks. Her body reacted with a warming shiver. He opened his mouth and gently caught her finger between his teeth. Nipped at it and sucked on it for a moment.

It felt like she'd been waiting her entire life for this moment. Despite his words, he certainly didn't seem to be in a hurry to get away. *Yeah*, he wasn't going anywhere.

Not right now, at least.

"Anything," she said.

She wasn't going to let him tell her he wasn't good enough for her.

She knew what she wanted, and he'd just slipped his arms around her again.

"No regrets," he said.

"No regrets," she answered. "But tell me something. How do you know that you're not good for me—that we're not good together—if we've never…tried it out?" She whispered the proposition inches from those lips of his, letting the promise tease his senses. "I'll bet we could be very good…together. The only thing I'd regret is if I never knew for sure."

He drew in a ragged breath and she scooted onto his lap, feeling the rock-solid proof of his interest underneath her.

"God, Anna, you're killing me," he murmured. His

breath was hot and he seemed more than a little *bothered* by the way he adjusted the angle of his hips so that their bodies aligned through their clothing.

He murmured something under his breath, but it was lost when he closed his mouth over hers and kissed her with a hunger that had him deftly turning her body so that she was straddling him.

It felt perfect, and dangerous, and maddeningly, temptingly delicious, awakening in her a hunger that she feared she might have to satisfy right here on the dock—with the guests behind the trees, only a few yards away. All someone had to do was walk down the path and around the corner and they would be discovered. But she didn't care. She wasn't thinking of problems or reasons why not, or second-guessing her actions or his reactions. It just felt so darn right, and that was all she cared about.

That thought cut the line that tethered her to reality and she let herself drift out on the tide of his kiss.

A few minutes later—or maybe it was hours, who knew?—Jake's phone rang. At first, he ignored it, but then it rang again.

"You'd better get that," Anna murmured. "It sounds like someone is trying to get you."

He wasn't on call, but if there was a big emergency at the hospital, Jake would've been among the first to be notified. Still tingling with awareness, Anna eased herself off of Jake's lap to give him some room. He fished his phone out of his pocket, but by the time he'd pulled it out, the phone signaled a voice mail.

"It's a 504 area code. That's New Orleans. Sorry, but I should pick up this message."

"Of course," she said.

As Jake listened to the voice mail, Anna watched his features contort into a mask of shock and disbelief. Then he stared at his phone for a moment before looking up at Anna.

"Is everything okay?" she asked.

He shook his head. "No. It's not. Bob Gibson passed away this morning."

Chapter Eight

Despite how strong Jake had tried to be, he'd ended up asking Anna, Emily and his brothers to tend to the guests while he stepped out for a few moments. Anna empathized with what he must've been feeling after receiving the news of Bob's death. Even though Jake was no stranger to personal loss after the death of both his parents, it never got easier.

After the fireworks ended, the guests began saying their goodbyes and calling it a night. It was a Saturday, but some of them, including Anna, had to work tomorrow. After all, the hospital was open 24/7. It didn't operate on bankers' hours.

Since she had to work, Emily, Ty and Ben had offered to tend to the basic cleanup—gathering trash and extinguishing tiki torches and the fire pit so that Anna could go home and get some sleep.

Her lips still tingled from his kiss. She didn't want to leave. She wanted to be there for Jake when he returned, but after thinking about it and weighing everything that had happened that night, she decided that maybe it was better to give him a little space. She'd call him tomorrow. Maybe ask him to go for a run after she got off work.

She was supposed to have Sunday dinner at her parents' house. Maybe she'd see if he wanted to come along. Lord knew he'd spent more than a few Sundays at her family's dinner table when they were growing up. Maybe going back to the comfort of the past would help him feel better.

The last thing she expected when she turned onto her street was to see his car in her driveway. But there he was, sitting in the car. It was almost eleven o'clock.

By the time she parked and let herself out of the car, he was standing there.

"How long have you been here?" she asked.

"Not too long," he said. "I'm sorry I bolted. I needed to clear my head."

She held up her hands. "No apologies needed. Come on in."

He nodded.

Once they got inside, he sat down on the couch and she went to the refrigerator and got two beers.

"Are you okay?" she asked as she handed one to him and settled herself on the couch next to him.

He rested his hand on the back of the couch and stared up at the ceiling, looking thoughtful.

"It's strange," he said, "to think that Bob is gone. He was so alive last week." Jake shook his head. "Being a doctor, you'd think I'd get used to the fact that people die and life goes on. But it never gets easier."

"I guess that's why it's important to live in the moment and appreciate the people in your life while they're there," she said.

"You're right. As I was driving around, I was thinking about what you said. About why I won't let you in." His voice was a hoarse rasp. "I don't know why, but I want to try. I mean, your strength humbles me, Anna. I've been running from my monsters for so many years. You don't run. You face your biggest terrors head-on. I don't know if I can be that strong—but..." His voice trailed off.

"Jake, listen to me. You need to hear what I'm saying to you." She cupped her hand under his chin and turned his face toward hers. Staring into his eyes, she said, "You're a good man, Jake Lennox. You need to accept that and believe it."

He caught her hand and brought it to his mouth, pressing a kiss into her palm. Then he slid an arm around her and closed the distance between them, brushing one light, hesitant kiss on her lips.

"This is different for me, Anna." His lips were mere inches from hers. "You are different for me."

"Are you saying that because you're trying to seduce me?"

He was familiar, yet different, for her. They were

picking up from where they'd left off on the dock, but at the same time, it felt brand-new. This was still Jake—the same big frame, the same dark hair setting off blue eyes as inviting as the Mediterranean. But he was changed. His body was tense; his face was flushed and way too serious. Desire laced with a little sadness colored his eyes a deeper shade of blue.

"I'm just picking up where we left off earlier. If that's okay…?"

She rested her hand on his shoulder, not saying it wasn't okay, but not giving him the green light either. Despite how she wanted to stop talking and just lose herself in him.

"Jake, I need to know… I know that this is different for us. But we can't seem to keep our hands off each other. And that's not a problem. It's definitely *not* a problem. I just need to know… Really, it's not. I just need to know…what are we doing?"

He looked her square in the eyes.

"I'm exactly where I want to be, Anna, and with the person I desire. Doesn't that tell you what we're doing… or what we're about to do?" His lips were mere inches from hers. "I want to make love to you, Anna Adams. Tell me that you want that, too."

"Oh, I want you, too, Jake. You have no idea."

She kissed him, wanting to make sure there was absolutely no doubt in his mind exactly how okay it was.

Then he leaned in and closed the rest of the distance between them. Then they fell into a kiss, arms wrapped around each other; his hands trailing down her back to cup her bottom, her hands in his hair, desperately pulling him closer, both of them impatient and ravenous as they devoured each other.

Anna had unleashed a want in him that rendered him desperate for something he never knew he needed. This was exactly how he imagined her body would feel. Now, he was greedy for her, needing to know every inch of her, eager to bury himself deep inside her.

She took his hand and led him to the one place in her house he had never been—her bed. Her bedroom was feminine and fashionable. A king-size bed sported a blue-and-yellow bedspread, turned down over soft white cotton sheets. There was a dresser and matching nightstand that held a table lamp, but he didn't turn it on after they stumbled into the room, clinging to each other as if their next breath depended on it.

How many nights since she'd been back in Celebration had he held her in his dreams, subconsciously breathing in her scent, taking possession of her body, loving her with his mind and his heart as he slept?

How was it that he was just admitting this to himself?

He unclipped her hair and dug his hands into the heavy auburn mass of it. Then he walked her backward until he could feel the bed behind her legs. As he eased her down onto the mattress, he buried his face in her hair, breathed in the scent of her—that delicious smell of flowers, vanilla and amber. A fragrance that was so intimate and familiar. Yet the newness of it hit him in a certain place that rendered him weak.

Smoothing a wisp of hair off her forehead, he kissed

the place where it had lain; then he searched her eyes, needing to make sure she was still okay with this.

"Make love to me, Jake," she answered before he could even say the words.

He inhaled a shuddering breath. As he pulled her into his arms, a fire ignited and he melted into the heat of her body. Relishing the warmth of her and the way she clung to him, he cradled her face in his palms and kissed her softly, hesitating, as he silently gave her one last chance to ask him to stop, to leave, to walk away from what was about to happen.

As if she sensed his hesitation, she pulled him into a long, slow kiss.

"Relax," she said. "I won't break. I promise. *No regrets*, Jake. Remember?"

For a moment, he looked at her in the dusk. The only light in the room was cast by a slim slice of light from the other part of the house and the glow of the full moon filtering in through the slanted blinds.

"Your lips drive me crazy," he muttered. "They have since that night I first kissed you. How is it that we've known each other for so many years and it took all this time for me to realize this addiction? Now, I look at that bottom lip of yours and it just makes me crazy."

He drew her lip into his mouth and she kissed him with urgency and demand as she tugged at his shirt, yanking it free from his pants. The move sent a rush spiraling through him. He felt the silk of her hands as they slipped under his shirt and up his back, turning his skin to gooseflesh. He couldn't stifle a groan.

He pressed his lips to her collarbone, exploring the

smooth, delicate ridge, and lingering over the hollow between her shoulder and throat. He stopped when he reached the top of her dress.

She made an impatient noise. So he found the hem of her skirt and began pulling it up, easing her body up and slightly off the mattress so that he could rid them of one of the barriers that stood between them.

"You're so beautiful," he whispered as he eased it over her head.

She lay there in just her panties, since she hadn't worn a bra beneath her sundress.

She tugged off his shirt. He sank back down beside her, tracing his fingertips down the slender column of her throat, splaying his hand to touch both beautiful breasts and then sliding it down to gently graze her stomach with his fingertips. When he reached the top edge of her panties, he slid his fingers beneath the silk to find her center. She gasped as his fingers opened her and slipped inside her. A rush of red-hot need spiraled through him and he nearly came undone with her as he watched her go over the edge.

As he slid her panties down, it was as if she sensed his own need. She made haste of unbuckling his belt and unbuttoning his jeans. Before he tossed his pants away, he pulled a condom from his wallet and sheathed himself. When they were finally free of the last barrier between them, his arms encircled her. He held her so close he could hear her heart beat. He shut out everything else but that sound and the need that was driving him to the brink of insanity.

All he wanted was *her*.

Right here. Right now.

Not the past.

Not the future.

The present.

Right here. Right now.

She pulled him even closer so that the tip of his hardness pressed into her. He urged her legs apart and buried himself inside her with a deep thrust.

As his own moan escaped his lips, his gaze was locked on hers. He slid his hands beneath her bottom, helping her match his moves in and out of her body until they both exploded together.

He held her close, both of them clinging to each other as the aftershocks of their lovemaking gradually faded. As they lay there together, sweaty and spent, Jake was still reveling in the smoothness of her skin, the passion in her eyes, the way they'd fit together so perfectly... She took his breath away. What they had right now was damn near perfect. And if it weren't for the fact that it scared him to death, he might've felt like he'd come home.

Had Hal been right? Had she been in love with Jake all along but just hadn't realized it?

Because Anna had never felt fireworks the likes of which she'd just experienced with Jake.

Her body still thrummed.

She lay with Jake in her bed for what seemed like hours, lost in the rhythm of his breathing. He was sleeping on his stomach with one arm thrown protectively over her middle, sacked out, sound asleep. Anna lay there frozen, the realization of what had just happened taking on gargantuan proportions in her brain.

Now what?

Looking back, she knew they'd been on a trajectory for what had happened tonight ever since Jake had come to San Antonio to rescue her. He'd packed her up, moved her back to Celebration. Now they'd crossed that line and she feared her worst nightmare might be waiting to jump out at her with dawn's first glimmer: that everything would be different now between Jake and her. That Hal had been right all along.

Had he somehow hit on something to which Anna had been so clueless? Or worse, had she simply been in denial all these years? She'd always prided herself on knowing herself—who she was, what she wanted and how to get it. She'd always known what was *real*.

How was it that she was here with Jake, feeling this dichotomy of emotions? She wanted to be here, there was no doubt about that. But *should* she be here? That was the question that turned everything on its axis.

She shifted her body so she could turn her head to the right and look at him as he slept. Jake's face was inches from hers. He was sleeping soundly, the sleep of the innocent, as if he didn't have a care in the world. Based on the pleasant look on his features, he might open his eyes and smile at her and tell her this thing that had happened between them was good. Hell, it wasn't just good; it was great. They were great together.

But one other thing Anna knew about herself was that she was a realist. She never kidded herself about important matters. She may have been the last to know

about Hal's affair, but once she'd learned the truth—
saw the proof in black-and-white in front of her eyes on
that computer screen—not once had she tried to pretend
it was anything else other than what it was: betrayal.

So, now, as she lay here watching this beautiful
man—this man who was her best friend, this man who
was *Jake*—sleep with his arm thrown over her middle,
she knew she couldn't ignore the truth: life as they'd
known it had just irreparably changed.

A swarm of butterflies unfurled in her stomach, but
she wasn't sure what she was supposed to do about
them.

It took Jake a couple of seconds to remember where
he was when he opened his eyes. He rolled over onto
his elbow and saw Anna. He was with her. In her bed.
She was sleeping peacefully beside him.

And it all came back to him.

He'd fallen asleep, but he wasn't sure how long he'd
been out.

He glanced around the room and located a digital
alarm clock that glowed cobalt blue in the darkness.

Five minutes until four. In the morning.

Awareness of her sleep-warmed, naked body so close
woke every one of his senses. He fought the urge to
move closer, pull her to him and make love to her again.
God, how he wanted to, but—

God, if he didn't know what was good for him—
or maybe he should focus on how bad it would be for
him…for *them*—he'd give in to this weakness and stay
right here next to her.

But he couldn't.

He should leave now before the sun came up and he and Anna were forced into saying awkward good-mornings and goodbyes. He gently eased himself off the bed, moving slowly so as not to wake her. He gathered his clothes and went out to the hall bathroom where he dressed.

When he stepped back out into the hall, he saw Anna clad in a robe and framed in her bedroom doorway.

"Where are you going?" Her voice sounded small.

"I was going home."

"You don't have to leave." His arm settled around her middle again and he nuzzled his nose into her neck.

"Anna… I have to go."

Oh, hell. This was the awkward moment he'd dreaded.

"Are you okay?"

"Yes. Fine. Great, I mean."

Liar.

"Jake? Were you just going to leave without waking me?"

"Why would I wake you?" He knew she had to work in a few hours. She might have a hard time falling back asleep.

The look on her face was equal parts horror and disbelief. Obviously, he hadn't given the right answer. Crap.

"No regrets, right?"

That's what they'd promised each other. Now he wondered if in the heat of the moment she'd meant it, but now she was having second thoughts.

He cared about her.

He thought those protective feelings would edge out any possibility of regret. Kissing her had certainly erased the word *regret* from his vocabulary. Now, not only was the word back, but it seemed to be swimming in his blood. Yet he had no choice but to keep his word or risk ruining everything. In the moment, he'd had no idea that it would be so difficult to have *no regrets*.

She just stood there, blinking at him with sleepy eyes, clutching the lapels of her robe. She looked as if she wanted to shove the word *regret* up his left nostril.

"I didn't wake you because I know you're on the schedule tomorrow—er, later today—and think about how everyone will talk if you show up looking sleep-deprived."

She was still doing that frown-squint thing.

"I guess they wouldn't necessarily know I'd spent the night with you," he said.

He was trying to be funny. But somehow his words were making it worse. They sounded like excuses… that were full of regret. But for a fraction of a second, a traitorous part of him wanted to take her back to bed and show her the meaning of "no regrets."

Instead, he raked his hand through his hair as he stared toward the door.

Regret, the bastard, wasn't so easy for him to ignore either.

Standing there watching Jake walk toward the door, Anna felt very naked and exposed, and not just in the physical sense. But now was a heck of a time to worry about that, wasn't it?

Don't make this any weirder than it has to be.

Don't look back, only forward. Because if you're not going to let this one night of indiscretion ruin a perfectly good friendship, you're going to have to leave it in the past.

As she watched him walk away, she tried not to wonder if he'd ever spent the entire night with Miss Texas. How in the world could she have left without her underwear? And why did it feel as if she were the one doing the walk of shame?

"Will you at least let me make you some coffee?" she asked. "It will only take a few seconds."

He turned back to her, his hand on the front doorknob. "No. Thanks, though. You should go back to bed and get a little more sleep before work."

Sleep? Was he serious?

She glanced around her living room to keep from looking at him. Anywhere but him. Funny, how her own house could look both familiar and foreign at the same time. Would everything look different now that this had happened?

"I intend to," she said. But suddenly she was tired of tiptoeing around the crux of the matter. "Jake. We don't have to talk about this now, but we both know this shouldn't have happened. What were we thinking? No, just—"

She gave her head a little shake and held up her hand to indicate she didn't want him to answer that. Not right now.

She found the courage to hold his gaze, wanting to make sure he understood the gist of what she meant.

He nodded. "I need to go. Let's talk later. After we're both rested and thinking with clearer heads."

Her heart lurched madly, but then it settled into a still ache beneath her breastbone.

He already had the front door open, but he stopped in the threshold and turned around. She wasn't prepared for the pain she saw in his blue eyes.

"Anna, it's still me. We are still us. Let's not let anything change that, okay?"

That's exactly the point.

Jake was still Jake—the man who grew tired of lovers after a few months.

They were still them—chums who should've left well enough alone, keeping relations firmly in the friend zone.

When he stepped outside, he lingered on the porch and Anna moved to the door, unsure about whether she should give him a goodbye hug as she always used to do…or a kiss?

No, definitely not a kiss.

And apparently not a hug either, since he was already making his way down the stairs. The reality of this mess made her heart hurt.

Trying not to think about it, she gazed out the front door at her neighborhood bathed in the inky predawn. She didn't see it like this very often: still and peaceful, and, besides Jake, not a soul in sight.

Across the street, there was a basketball hoop on a stand. It stood like a sentry along the side of the driveway. In the manicured yard of the house to the right of that, kids' toys lay lifeless and untouched. In the distance, someone had left a porch light on. As Jake walked to his car, Anna inhaled a deep breath and smelled the scent of late-night laundry that lingered in the air. Fabric softener perfumed the muggy summertime air.

This was her life, not Jake's. Mr. Don't-Fence-Me-In would be an anomaly in this cozy, family-oriented neighborhood. He didn't want a wife to tie him down or kids who would complicate his bachelor lifestyle. He didn't even own his own house because he was still convinced that he would be leaving Celebration for bigger and better things in the future. Even if he got the chief hospitalist position, it didn't mean he would stay. In fact, he could parlay it into a better position elsewhere.

If Anna fell in love with him, she was doomed. He would never marry her and that meant—well, that meant he could break her heart. She'd been there, done that. She'd let Hal break her heart. She wasn't opening herself up to that kind of hurt again.

So that was that. End of story.

They'd made a mistake. Now it was time to salvage what was left.

They both just needed some space.

The car chirped and she could hear the locks disengage. The sound seemed to echo in the still of the night.

Before he got into the car, he repeated, "No regrets, right?"

"I know, Jake. Good night."

Chapter Nine

In less than twelve hours, Jake's life had gone to hell.

First, the news about Bob Gibson's death and then the ridiculous stunt with Anna. Word of Bob's death had come as such a shock—he'd looked fine last week. Sure, maybe he was moving a little slower than he had in the past, but everyone slowed down. How could it be that a person was on this earth and seemingly fine one minute and then the next minute…they were gone?

He'd turned to Anna for comfort. Because some-times—most of the time—she felt like the only thing in his life that was real and solid and true. Now, he might have screwed that up, too.

He knew he'd been playing with fire when they'd kissed the first time. Then, not only had he kissed her again, but he'd ended up in her bed.

Three strikes and you're out.

But just as with the first time they'd kissed, attraction seemed to take over. When the magnet of her pulled at the steel in him, resisting seemed futile—for both of them.

Man up. When have you ever not been in control?

Maybe that's what scared him the most.

When had this change in the chemistry between them happened? Growing up, they'd edged close to that line once, but they'd decided right away that they made more sense as friends. Then they'd each gone away to separate colleges and it always seemed like one or the other of them was involved. Then Anna met Hal, married him and moved away. That had seemingly sealed their fate—even if they hadn't been consciously aware of it. After all, they'd been away from each other for the past ten years—four years of college and six years that encompassed Anna's marriage, separation and eventual divorce.

Now that she was free and back in Celebration, she was the same Anna he'd loved his whole life. Yet even thinking about the platonic *love* he'd had for her his whole life, everything had felt different in the weeks that she'd been back.

For a crazy split second, Jake wondered if he'd dodged long-lasting commitment with the women he'd dated because he'd been waiting for Anna. But the thought was ridiculous. How could he have been waiting for her when she was already married?

He shook off the absurd notion.

Thoughts like that were pinging around in his head,

keeping Jake awake long after he'd gotten home. He'd lain there in his cold, empty bed, tossing and turning, feeling the phantom touch of her on his skin, smelling her and alternating between mentally flogging himself for jeopardizing his relationship with the most important person in his life and trying to digest the reality of Bob's death.

His mentor was gone. Anna was upset.

And rightfully so. What the hell was wrong with him?

If anyone else had tried to take advantage of Anna that way, they would've had hell to pay. Jake would've made sure.

After tossing and turning for what seemed like hours, he'd showered, made a pot of coffee and dragged himself out to the dock for some fresh air. As the sun overtook the lifeless, gray sky, bringing it to life in a blaze of variegated splendor, the lake shone like pieces of a broken mirror reflecting his misery back at him.

So, what now? He still hadn't found the answers he was seeking. Everything was still as messed up and disjointed as it had been since he'd walked out the door of Anna's house this morning. She deserved more than he could offer, more than one night as friends with benefits. Because even if he wanted to try to give her more, he just couldn't trust himself for the long haul.

He'd been a product of a broken marriage. He'd been led through his parents' maze of lies—his mother leaving, but shouldering all the blame, his father turning out to not be the man Jake had thought he had been all those years. Hell, for his entire life.

Marriage had taken something good and drained all the life out of it. Even though it might've seemed as if he were copping out on Anna by taking this stance, she would thank him in the long run. She still believed in happily-ever-after and he'd damn sure see that she got nothing less.

He would make things right between them.

Somehow he would make things right.

Judging from where the sun was sitting in the eastern sky, it had to be well after eight o'clock. He needed to quit brooding and get up and do something constructive with his Sunday. Since Anna was working today, he'd see if she was free for dinner tonight. Then he'd check on flights back to New Orleans for Bob's funeral.

As he walked from the dock through the yard, he surveyed the evidence of last night's party: the canopy was still up, tables and chairs needed to be put away and there were still a few stray beer bottles. Not that he was complaining; he was grateful that someone had stepped in and done the majority of the cleanup…while he'd been with Anna.

And damn if she hadn't fit perfectly in his arms.

At that moment he hadn't given a rat's ass about anything else. She was the one person in the world who'd always been there for him—even across the miles and years, during the time they'd been apart. She'd never let him down.

Now, he had a sinking feeling he'd let her down in the worst way. He needed to talk to her and make sure she was okay. Because he wouldn't be okay until he knew she was.

Jake grabbed a couple of empty bottles that were in his path and threw them into the recycling bin that sat just outside the back door. He'd clean up the rest later, but now, he needed to talk to Anna.

He let himself in the back door of his house and found his phone on the kitchen counter. He started to text her, but he thought a voice mail might be better. Texts were so impersonal. Meaning and intention could get lost or misconstrued.

He clicked over to his phone's keypad and dialed Anna's number. He didn't expect her to pick up since she was working, and he was in the middle of composing a message when Anna answered.

"Jake?"

It took him a beat or two, but he pulled his thoughts together.

Keep it light. Keep it upbeat.

"Hey, stranger. I was calling to leave you a message, but I'm glad you picked up. What do you say to dinner tonight? I'll cook for us."

There was a pause on the line that stretched on a little longer than it should've.

"That sounds great, but I can't tonight. I'm busy. Besides, you don't owe me a consolation dinner, Jake. Really, you don't."

He leaned his hip against the kitchen counter, trying to decide if she was joking. He detected a hint of truth in her words.

Busy? As in a date?

Despite how badly he wanted to know, he wasn't about to ask her.

"What a coincidence, because I hadn't planned one single bite of consolation on tonight's menu. How about a rain check?"

She laughed and he was so relieved to hear that sound he closed his eyes for a moment to savor it.

"Yes, of course. That would be great. But, hey, I'm going for a run this afternoon after I get home from work." Her voice was soft and she sounded a little vulnerable. "You can join me if you want. Unless you're busy."

"You just turned down my invite to dinner. Of course I'm not busy.

"We can run and then I'll fix dinner for us. Consolation-free, you have my word," he said. "How can you say no?"

She was quiet for longer than she should've been and that made Jake uncomfortable.

"Oh, come on, Anna. Don't make me come to the hospital to do the Sadness Intervention Dance. Because I will. It will be humiliating as hell, but I will march right up there to the third floor and dance in front of the nurses' station. Then you'll get to explain it to Patty and Marissa."

"Look, I really do have plans later this evening, but come run with me. We need to talk. Meet me downtown in the park at four o'clock."

"By the gazebo?"

"Perfect. But I have to go now. I'll see you later."

He exhaled a breath he hadn't realized he'd been holding. This was definitely a step in the right direction. All he needed was the chance to make it right, and this boded well.

He'd taken some orange juice out of the refrigerator and was pouring it into a glass when his phone rang again.

Grabbing it with his free hand and still pouring with the other, he glanced at the caller ID, but it came up *number unknown*. Sometimes calls from the hospital registered like that. Since he wasn't on call this weekend, he wondered if it might not be Anna calling back from a landline to say she'd changed her mind about running this afternoon.

He pressed the talk button and held the receiver up to his ear. "You'd better not be calling to beg off."

Silence stretched over the line. After a moment, he almost hung up because it seemed as if no one was there.

"Yes, good morning. I'm trying to reach Jake Lennox." The voice was male, decidedly not Anna's.

"This is he," Jake said.

"Hello, Jake. It's Roger James. I hope I'm not calling too early."

Roger was Jake's landlord. The man and his wife lived in Florida. Since Jake paid his rent on time, he rarely heard from the home owner.

"Good morning, Roger. How are you?"

The two men made small talk for a few minutes—about Jake's career, about Roger and his wife June's plans to travel in the years ahead.

"Which brings me to my reason for calling," Roger said. "June and I are excited about our cruise and one of the things we're most excited about is streamlining our responsibilities. We wanted you to be the first to know that we're planning on putting the house you're living in on the market. Since you've been such a great tenant for so long, we wanted to offer you first right of refusal. Are you interested in buying the house? Since you've lived there for so long, seems like you might be ready to make that commitment now."

The park was crowded for a Sunday afternoon. Jake passed joggers and mothers pushing small children in strollers as he made his way across the grassy area to meet Anna. The weather was perfect, one of those cloudless robin's-egg-blue-sky days that should've had him feeling a lot better than he was when he finally spied Anna near the gazebo.

She was dressed in running shorts and a pink tank top that hugged those curves that were so fresh in his memory. Her hair was knotted up on top of her head and her long legs looked lean, strong and tanned as she did her prerun warm-ups.

He remembered how those legs felt wrapped around him and his body responded.

"Anna," he said, falling into sync with her as she performed lateral lunges to warm up her glutes. He did his best not to think about her glutes, and especially tried not to think about how his hands had been all over them as he pulled her body into his.

"Hey." She virtually pulsed with tension. Was that anxiety tightening her lips? He ached to touch her and had this mad vision of kissing her until she relaxed, but he knew that would only make things worse. So he kept a respectful distance. And tried his best not to think about her glutes.

"How was work?" he asked.

"Good," she said, going into the next sequence of stretches. Her movements were sharp and fast. Normally, she would've waited for him to start, maybe even stopped stretching to talk to him for a couple of minutes, but today she didn't.

And she was giving him one-word answers. Had he missed something here? Was she mad at him?

"Thanks for making time to get together," he said, immediately hating how he sounded so stiff and formal. For God's sake, this wasn't a business meeting. No, it was much more important. Thirty years of friendship was hanging in the balance here.

I mean, come on. We need to talk about this.

"Not a problem," she shrugged.

This was ridiculous.

"What's wrong?" he asked.

"Nothing," she said. "Just a long day…after a night rather short on sleep."

"If it makes you feel any better, I didn't get much sleep either."

"Why would that make me feel better?"

"Look, can we talk about this, please?"

"Jake, really, what is there to talk about?" she said.

He attempted a smile, but it didn't quite make it. As she brushed a strand of hair off her forehead, he saw her hand was trembling.

"Anna," he said. "Talk to me."

She took a deep breath. "Things got a little intense

last night." She shook her head. "You were vulnerable and I was so determined to help you feel better. I'm always trying to get you to open up." She lifted her shoulder, let it fall. "I guess I pushed it a little too far last night. Because you still won't let me in. I mean, there's the physical, and then there's letting me *in*."

She put her hand on her heart.

Jake shrugged, unsure what to say.

"Are you upset because I didn't spend the whole night with you?"

Apparently that was the wrong response, because she pinned him with a look that was almost a sneer, then turned away without answering.

"I wish letting you in were that simple. I mean, I'm not purposely keeping you at arm's length."

"Obviously not." She sat on the bench that was behind her and retied her shoe.

"Okay, so maybe we did get a little carried away last night. But when all is said and done, you don't want me, Anna. I'm not the man for you. You deserve so much more than I can give you."

"You already said that, Jake. I told you I disagree."

Wait. What was she saying? Did she think he was the man for her?

She turned and with a quick jerk of her head, she motioned for them to start their run.

Hell, he should've known this was going to happen. He was such an idiot.

"You said what we did, what happened between you and me, mattered to you, too. It does matter. I can't be *that girl*, Jake. The one who has casual sex with you and then goes out with someone else the next night."

"Anna, I know that—"

"Just, please let me talk," she said. Her voice was barely a whisper.

Jake went silent, waiting patiently, watching her.

Emotions seemed to be getting the best of her. Jake reached over and took her hand, but she pulled away, balled her hand into a fist and quickened her pace.

"Talk to me," he said softly. "It's me, Anna. It's still me."

"That's exactly what you said last night, and you're right—you are still *you*. I'd never expect you to change. You don't want to get married. Jake, I want a family someday. I know you don't. But I can't be your friend with benefits, hanging around and pretending we want the same thing."

"You may have noticed that I'm not the most experienced…woman in the world. I haven't been with a lot of men."

"Notice? Of course I didn't notice. You were great. Everything last night was great, except today you're upset and that kind of ruins everything."

She stopped running and stood there looking at him.

"You're only my second lover, Jake." She stared down at their hands. He was glad because he couldn't bear seeing the hurt in her eyes. He would never purposely hurt her for anything in the world. Not even for the best sex of his life— and what had happened between them last night was paramount.

If Hal had been her only other lover, she was a natural.

Or, Jake thought, maybe he and Anna were *that* good together.

God, he had to stop thinking like that. He'd caused her enough pain.

"You haven't had a lot of experience. It's not a big deal." He wanted to tell her that last night had taken him to places he'd never been, but he was afraid that would sound as if he wanted them to do it again. He wanted to. Damn, how he wanted to—he wanted to pull her into his arms right now and show her how much he wanted her and how good they were together—but then what?

All he had to do was look into her gorgeous blue eyes and he could see the hurt. He couldn't lead her down a dead-end path.

"You were married and faithful and that didn't give you a lot of opportunity for experience." *And some things simply came naturally.* "Plus, it's taken a while for you to get back on the dating path."

The dating path?

"Is that what this is?" she said dully. "The first step on the dating path?"

Her heart sank. She resumed jogging, hoping her inner anguish wasn't showing through in her eyes. Jake picked up the pace alongside her.

Of course this was the *dating path.* That's why Jake was fixing her up with his friends. If he was interested, he would've kept her for himself. He would've stayed the entire night rather than bolting like a stallion that had discovered a break in the fence.

After all, hadn't he told her before they'd crossed that line that he was still the same old Jake? He was who he was. She realized now what he probably meant was that making love wouldn't change him. It wasn't supposed to change anything. She'd promised him there would be no regrets and here she was on the verge of falling apart.

Get a hold of yourself, Anna.

Get a grip, girl.

Their relationship had been built on a solid foundation of friendship. She couldn't dig up that foundation now and replace it with a glass house. Because that's where a friends-with-benefits relationship would live, in a glass house that was likely to shatter as soon as one of them decided to slam the door.

In a split second that she saw the shattering glass in her mind's eye, she realized that even though she was sad, she needed to get a hold of herself and turn this around.

She had two choices: mope and lose, or cope and move on.

It wasn't hard to choose.

"You're right," she said. "It has taken me a while to get back on the dating path. I'm so glad you're okay with what happened between us and you won't let it change anything. No regrets, right? So, we're good, right?"

A look of relief washed over Jake's face and he reached out and squeezed her hand, holding it tighter than he should've. "That's exactly what I was hoping you would say."

Of course it was.

"Anna, you are amazing."

Of course she was. And if she told herself that, she might start to believe it. Because despite the cool-friend thing happening on the outside, on the inside the message that was echoing was, *He doesn't want you.* How had this gone so wrong? How had she not kept herself firmly planted in reality?

Somehow, she'd miscalculated. Somehow she'd misread the signs. She'd been turned on; he'd been vulnerable after the news about Bob. She'd been there, an easy refuge to temporarily unload his sorrows.

She imagined she could still feel the weight of his body on hers, feel the way he moved inside her.

"Okay, I'm glad we got that settled." Her voice was brisk. "I should get going, really."

"Anna? Are you okay?"

She was so pathetic that she thought for a moment she saw a flicker of worry flash in his eyes.

Well, Jake, you can't have it both ways.

But then it hit her; maybe it wasn't worry as much as it was pity.

Had it really come to this?

No. She wouldn't let it.

Jake Lennox might not be able to love her the way she wanted him to. But if it was the last thing she did, she'd make darn sure he didn't pity her.

"Of course. I told you. I'm fine. We're fine. No regrets."

She forced a smile, despite the fact that all she could think about was escaping to her house only a few blocks away. If she could get away from him and inside, she'd be okay.

"You don't look fine."

She conjured another smile. This one felt too big. "I told you I'm fine." *Liar, liar, pants on fire.* "I'm glad we're fine. But really, I need to go. I'm sure we both have things to do."

She knew she was smiling a little too widely and a very tiny part of her that she didn't want to acknowledge hoped Jake would see that she was so not okay, that she was drowning in it, actually. She'd fallen backward down a black hole that negated everything she wanted, and all that was left was this Cheshire cat smile and this need to run. God, she had to get out of there. Get somewhere she could think and make everything inside her feel right again. Because if she didn't, nothing in her world would be right.

Jake looked just as uncertain as she felt.

"Can I share something before we leave?"

Anna nodded.

"My landlord, Roger James, called me this morning. He's putting the house on the market. He gave me first right of refusal. What do you think about that?"

"What *I* think doesn't really matter," she said. "What do you think? Are you going to buy it? Plant roots?"

He shrugged and offered her a smile that wasn't really a smile.

"Who knows? Though I guess I need to figure it out pretty soon. Roger needs an answer soon. I've spent a lot of good years in that house. I've got my boat and a place to dock it. Where would everyone spend the Fourth of July?"

His smile was wistful.

"So what's the problem?" Anna asked. She hadn't meant to sound like such a witch.

"I haven't bought the place because I never intended to stay in Celebration. Not this long. But here I am. All these years have gone by…what am I doing?"

Anna felt her insides go soft. He was hurting and maybe she was being too hard on him. He'd lost a good friend, his home was being sold and last night they'd managed to jumble the only thing that made sense in either of their lives. She needed to cut him some slack, even if her own heart was breaking.

"Why are you always so hard on yourself? Look at all you've done. Not only do you have a good job, but you're in line for a promotion at the hospital. You're a valuable part of this community and you have friends who adore you."

She stopped short of saying, "And you have more women after you than you know what to do with." Clearly, he knew what to do with women.

"It's unexpected. I guess I just need some time to think about it. Buying a house is a big step."

"Maybe if you're eighteen."

Jake winced.

God, shut up, Anna. If you can't say something nice, don't say anything at all.

She bit her bottom lip to keep another snarky-sounding comment from slipping out.

"You're right. I'm thirty-four years old. I guess symbolically…buying this house feels like…" His voice trailed off and she gave him a couple of beats for him to finish the sentence, but he didn't.

So, she finished it for him. "Commitment?"

His eyes got large, like she'd just uttered the name "Bloody Mary" three times or spouted some other unmentionable.

"Touché," he finally answered.

Way to go, Anna. You made your point. Are you happy now?

She needed to leave so she could get herself together. Taking snipes at him, *especially* when he was clearly feeling bad about everything, wouldn't do anyone any good.

Besides, she'd been steering them toward her car, which was along the side of the park. Now they were there.

"Well, this is me," she said, pointing to her yellow VW Beetle. "I need to go. I have to be somewhere."

She clicked the key fob and heard the locks tumble. As if she didn't feel like enough of a heel for the way she was acting, Jake reached out and opened the car door for her. Why did he have to be nice when she was trying so hard to hate him right now?

Well, not *hate*. That wasn't the right word. She could never hate him.

In fact, what she was trying to feel was exactly the opposite…she was desperately trying not to fall in love with Jake Lennox.

"Thank you," she murmured as she slid behind the wheel.

He closed the door and she rolled down the window.

"I'm sure they don't need an answer tonight," she said. "Take some time to think about it. But, Jake, try not to overthink it. Just go with your gut."

He reached through the window and put his hand on her arm, snagging her gaze.

"You're right," he said. "I think we both need to stop overthinking things."

She watched him walk away. Damn him for being such a fine, fine man. And not just on the outside, but also inside.

She sat in the car for what felt like ages, long after Jake had disappeared from her line of sight, alternately feeling like an ogre and perfectly justified for pushing him away. This was exactly why friends didn't cross that line. It rendered things awkward and confusing. Despite how they'd promised each other that it would change nothing—that there would be no regrets—it had changed *everything*.

She needed to talk to someone who could help her put things into perspective.

She took her phone out of her glove box and texted her sister.

Need to talk to you.

Call me? Emily responded.

I'd rather talk in person.

Everything okay?

Anna didn't want to open the conversation over text. So, she answered with the only word that seemed to fit without going into detail.

Meh.

Is this about a guy?

Emily was so good at reading her.

Maybe.

I thought so. What are you waiting for? Get over here.

On my way.

Emily lived in an apartment just north of downtown. Anna arrived there in less than ten minutes and that was only because she hit every red light between the park and her sister's place.

When Emily answered the door she handed Anna a steaming mug of Earl Grey. Normally, Anna would've preferred iced water on a day like today, but hot tea was the sisters' ritual—just like she and Jake had the Sadness Intervention Dance.

Had was the operative word.

Anna's heart hurt at the thought of it. When they made each other sad, who was supposed to intervene with the dance now?

"Thanks, Em," she said as she accepted the mug and stepped inside. "What smells so good?"

"I'm baking cookies for tonight, but I think we need to do a taste test. There's oatmeal and chocolate chip."

"At least your apartment smells good. I'm sorry I don't. I just finished my run and wanted to come over before I went home to change to go to Mom and Dad's tonight."

"You don't smell bad, but just to be safe I'll hold my breath when I hug you."

Emily wrapped her arms around her sister. Anna was careful to not spill the tea. Then Emily took her sister's hand and pulled her toward her tiny kitchen. When Anna stepped inside, she could see a plate of deliciousness waiting for her atop her sister's glass-top café table.

"You're an angel, Em. This is exactly what I need."

Emily squinted at her sister, the concern obvious on her face. "What's going on?"

They sat down. Anna placed her cell phone on the table and took a sip of tea. It was supposed to fortify her, but instead it burned her tongue.

"I slept with Jake." As she blurted the confession, she set down the mug a little too hard. The table rattled and tea sloshed over the rim. Anna grabbed her phone to save it from the tea tidal wave and braced herself for her sister to call her a bull in a china closet or something equally as snarky. But when she looked up, Emily was staring at her wide-eyed and slack-jawed. She stumbled over her words for a moment, sputtering and spitting sounds that didn't form a coherent sentence.

"Oh! Uh. Well. Hmm. Ummm… Wow!"

Emily popped up and grabbed a paper towel and wiped up the spill with quick, efficient swipes. By the time she'd disposed of the soaked paper and returned to the table, she seemed to have collected herself. She smoothed her denim skirt and reclaimed her place at the table.

"I like that blouse on you," Anna said, suddenly feeling the need to backpedal. "You look good in magenta. I can't wear that color."

"Don't change the subject," Emily said. She gave her head a quick shake and a smile broke out over her pretty face. "This is the best thing I've heard in…maybe ever. Did I call it or what?"

"Stop gloating. It's not like that."

"Not like *what*?"

"It's not like however you're imagining it. Because if you knew how it really was, you wouldn't be smiling."

Emily's hand flew to her mouth. "No! Oh, no. Is Jake bad in bed?"

Anna squeezed her eyes shut for a moment, trying to block out the memory of exactly how far from the truth that was.

"No… Jake is actually quite good."

Emily's mouth formed a perfect O and her eyes sparkled. "*Ooh!* Do tell."

God, she couldn't believe she was talking about this. Even if it was Emily. She didn't kiss and tell…well, actually, with Hal there hadn't been much to talk about. So…

"Tell me everything," Emily insisted.

"I'm not going to give you a blow by blow—"

Emily snorted. She *actually* snorted.

Anna cringed when she realized her unfortunate choice of words. She couldn't help but think how gleeful Joe Gardner would've been if he'd heard that pun. He probably would've bowed down in reverence.

Anna frowned at her sister. "Are you thirteen years old? Get your mind out of the gutter."

"Well, this is a conversation about sex and according to you, it was mind-blowing. I'm not seeing the problem here."

Ah, the problem. Right.

Anna took a deep breath and, using very broad terms, she brought her sister up to date on the situation.

"I will not allow this to degenerate into a friends-with-benefits pseudo-relationship. But I'm so attracted to him, sometimes I can't seem to help myself. I knew exactly what I was doing last night, and I knew exactly how I would feel afterward, but I did it anyway. And I'm afraid I might do it again if I get the chance."

"Wow" was all that Emily could offer.

Anna plucked a chocolate chip cookie off the plate. It was still warm and gooey. Sort of like her resolve with Jake—unless she turned into the superwitch she'd been at the park.

"I'm mad at myself, but I'm taking it out on him. I mean, I know he feels bad because I'm acting like this and his good friend just died, and now *this*. What is wrong with me, Em? Was Hal right? Could he see all along that I was attracted to Jake? You saw something. Am I as much to blame for the breakup of my marriage as Hal was?"

And now she was babbling—because this wasn't about Hal. It was about Jake and her and how everything was now upside down.

"Don't be ridiculous," Emily said. "You weren't the one who cheated. I'm sorry to bring that up. But it's true. How can you be guilty of feelings you never knew you had. I mean…unless these feelings aren't new?"

"No! I promise you, this is as big a surprise to me as it is to you. Come on, this is *Jake*."

"Well, sis, I hate to break it to you, but Jake is pretty darn sexy."

"Tell me about it." Anna raked both hands through her hair and stared up at the ceiling.

"I am not going to play a game of 'Don't. Stop. Don't. Stop.' I just need to know how to get things back to where they were before. How do I do that, Em?"

The refrigerator motor hummed and, overhead, one of the fluorescent lightbulbs blinked a couple of times.

Emily sipped her tea, looking thoughtful. "First, if you're sure this relationship isn't good for you, you can't sleep with him again."

"I know that," Anna said. "I wish I could promise you I won't do it again."

"Hey, don't promise me. That's all on you. Personally, I think you two would make the perfect couple."

"Emily, stop. Jake and I want different things. He doesn't want to get married. He definitely doesn't want kids. I hate to admit this, but I'm not getting any younger. I do want kids. I never thought I'd be one of those women lamenting her biological clock. But here I am."

"God, you two would have gorgeous children."

"Emily. Have you heard a word I said?"

"Of course I have. But it's true."

Anna *tsk*ed. "*Really?* Are you going to torture me after I turned to you for help?"

Anna resumed her tea-gazing, and Emily reached out across the table and took her sister's hand.

"Even though it's my prerogative as your younger sister, I won't tease you. The next time you're alone with him, if you're afraid you're going to be tempted, text me an SOS and I'll come and rescue you."

"Actually, that's not a bad idea," Anna said. "The only thing is, unless I fix things with him, it's a moot point. I was so mean to him this afternoon, I'm ashamed of myself. I wouldn't blame him if he didn't want to talk to me. I don't even like me after the way I acted."

"Then that's all the more reason you need to talk to him," Emily said.

Anna grimaced.

"Don't be such a baby," Emily said. "Based on what you said, he was trying to meet you halfway this afternoon and you were a total B. You need to reach out and make this right. Tell him exactly what you told me. Except for the part about being in love with him."

Anna jerked ramrod straight in her chair. "I did *not* say that."

Emily tilted her head and smiled. "You didn't have to, sweetie. It's written all over you. You're oozing *Jake love* out of your pores."

Feeling her cheeks burn, Anna buried her face in her hands. "Am I that obvious?"

Emily nodded. "Sorry, hon, just calling it as I see it."

"Then I definitely can't…"

"You can't what?" Emily's voice sounded impatient in that way that only a sister could get away with.

"I can't call him. I certainly can't see him."

"So you're just going to let him walk away? You're essentially going to set a match to a thirty-year friendship and watch it burn? Is that what you want?"

"No." Even though the word came out as a whisper, Anna nearly choked on it.

"Then call him, for heaven's sake." With a manicured finger, Emily slid Anna's phone across the table. Anna recoiled and fisted her hands in her lap as if the cell would burn her if she touched it. "The longer you put it off, the more difficult it's going to be."

"I don't know what to say."

"Invite him to dinner tonight. You know Mom and Dad would love to see him. And Mom always cooks enough for fifteen. Think about it. A family dinner will take both of you back to your roots. How many times did he have Sunday dinner with us when we were kids? He was like a part of the family."

Hence the problem. Only he certainly didn't feel like a brother. Anna wondered if he ever had. She sighed. "Funny you mention it. I'd intended to invite him before everything got so weird."

"Then do it." Emily stood, pushing back her chair with the bend of her knees. The wrought iron scraped a mournful plea on the tiled kitchen floor. She picked up Anna's phone and handed it to her. "I'm going to go put in a load of laundry."

In other words, her sister was going to give her some privacy.

Once Emily cleared the room and before Anna could overthink it, she opened her phone address book to the

contacts that were saved as favorites—all six of them—
and pressed the button to call Jake's phone.

He picked up on the third ring.

"Hey, Jake, how about dinner tonight with the Adams
family?"

Chapter Ten

"Jake, honey, it's so good to see you," said Judy Adams. "It's been far too long."

"Thanks for letting me come to dinner tonight," he said, offering Anna's mom a smile.

"You have a standing invitation. Please don't wait for that daughter of mine to invite you."

Judy gave Anna a pointed look and Jake smiled at the way she blushed.

"Thank you," he said. "I appreciate that."

"Would you care for more lasagna?" Judy offered. "Hand your plate to Norm and he can dish it up for you."

"It's delicious, but I'm stuffed. In fact, everything was fabulous."

"I'm sorry we couldn't make it to the party yester-day," Norm said. "We'd promised my folks that we would take them to see the fireworks over in Plano. Now that they are in the retirement community, we have to get over there every chance we get."

Jake nodded. That was the thing about the Adams family; they seem to have longevity in their genes... and in relationships. Both sets of Anna's grandparents were still alive and together. This move to the retirement community for Norm's folks was a new turn of events. Earlier, Judy had mentioned that her parents were on a cruise around the world.

The Adamses' world was different from—in fact, it was polar opposite to—the one he'd grown up in. While the Adamses had always been generous to include him, more often than not he'd felt like an outsider looking in. That was all on him, though. It was nothing they'd done. They'd always been as warm and welcoming as they were this evening.

Jake glanced at Anna, who had been quiet for most of the dinner, allowing her sister to entertain with tales of crazy customers at the restaurant and a few sidebars about customer woes at the bank. As he listened to her talk, he wondered why his brother Luke had never shown an interest in Emily. The woman made no secret about her affinity for him. No doubt Luke had his reasons, and far be it from Jake to interfere.

Anna caught him staring at her. She gave him a shy smile and turned her attention back to the lasagna that she'd been pushing around on her plate. He'd been so glad to get her call. After the way they'd left things earlier in the park, he wasn't sure what to do next. He would've figured it out, because there was no way he was going to let this indiscretion come between them. He was simply going to give Anna some room until she was able to realize that, yeah, they may have feelings for each other—and there was nothing more that he wanted than to have her in his bed every night—but he wasn't the man for her.

The only conclusion he'd come to was he would make the ultimate sacrifice by putting a lid on his feelings for her to make sure that, eventually, she ended up with a man who deserved her.

They'd arrived at Judy and Norman Adams's place in separate cars. So they hadn't had a chance to talk. Yet here they sat in the same dining room, at the same table, in the same places that they'd occupied on all those Sundays all those years ago.

Judy and Norman each sat at each end of the table; Jake and Anna sat to Judy's right, Emily across the table from them. The dining room still had the same traditional feel and furniture set—a large table in the center of the room, a sideboard and china cabinet on opposite walls, blue-and-white wallpaper depicting old-fashioned scenes of men and women courting on benches and under trees. What did they call it? Tool or toile—something like that. It didn't matter.

What was important was that despite how everything had changed between him and Anna, there was still that connection, that lifeline that kept them from drowning. Sharing a meal with the Adamses felt as if they'd stepped back in time nearly a decade and a half. Suddenly, what he needed to do was as clear as the crystal goblet on the table.

He was going to let bygones be bygones and fix her up with Dylan Tyler. The guy had asked about Anna several times since he'd seen her at the jazz festival. Jake had had his trepidations about fixing up the two of them—if he was honest with himself, the feelings probably stemmed from his being afraid that Anna and Dylan might actually be a good fit. Not that he thought the dates he'd arranged for her wouldn't work, but it just took a few go-rounds to realize who would work—who would be the best person for her.

Jake mulled it over as he helped clear the table. That was one thing about the Adamses; they all pitched in and it made him feel even more like family when Judy and Norm didn't excuse him from doing his part—even after all these years.

During cleanup, he and Anna made small talk and, to the untrained eye, nobody probably realized any-thing was different. God, he hoped not. All he had to do to set himself straight was think of looking Norman Adams in the eye and telling him that he'd had a one-night stand with his daughter.

Yeah, that put everything into perspective.

When they finished washing the dishes, he said to Anna, "Want to take a walk around the old neighbor-hood?"

The unspoken message was "It's time we talked about this." He could tell by the look on her face she understood and that she was ready to talk.

Outside, twilight was settling over the old neigh-borhood. Fingers of golden light poked through the branches of the laurel oaks and the sun had painted the western sky with broad strokes of pink, orange and dusky blue.

It was always bittersweet coming and going from the Adams house. Because the house he'd grown up in was right next door. After leaving for college, Jake had only been back for Christmas and to visit his dad occasionally when he wasn't taking classes over the summer. When his dad had married Peggy—two years after Jake's mom had died—the house had gone from feeling discombobulated to cold and unwelcoming. Peggy, who was only twelve years older than Jake, had no interest in being a mother to Karen Lennox's children. The moment she moved in, it was apparent that the countdown clock had begun for when she could get the four boys out of *her* house and out from under the obligation of caring for them. At the time, Jake didn't realize what she was doing—even worse, he didn't realize that his father was allowing this woman to push his sons out of their own home. But that was because his father had always played the victim, making his wife out to be the villain who had walked out on her own family.

As Jake and Anna stepped out onto the sidewalk, Jake tried not to look too hard at the house next door to the Adams family. It looked cold and haunted and only dredged up the worst memories. As far as Jake knew, Peggy still lived there. He and his brothers hadn't had contact with her since the day of his father's funeral, when somehow Peggy had managed to let all four Lennox brothers know that she and their father had been together a lot longer than they had realized. They'd started seeing each other the year *before* his mother had left the family.

That was when everything had clicked into place. His mom hadn't just randomly left the family as his dad had led them to believe. She'd left because her husband was involved with another woman, and just a few days later she died in that accident, unable to defend herself or let her voice be heard—that she fully intended to come back for them once she was able to get herself established. Even though Jake had no hard evidence of this, he felt it down to his bones. It was so out of character for his mother to abandon her home and the children she adored. She had probably been flummoxed by the realization that the man she'd trusted with her heart was in love—or under the spell of—another woman.

The only good thing Peggy had ever done for Jake and his brothers was to tell them the truth, which had vindicated their mother. Of course, it had also revealed their father for the weak, henpecked, poor excuse of a man that he really was—letting Peggy dictate the fate of his family, turning a blind eye and simply going along for the ride because it was the path of least resistance.

If Jake had had trepidation about marriage and family before his father's death, Peggy's revelation was the wax that sealed the deal. Jake would never let himself be that influenced by a woman. After living with Peggy for years and seeing what she'd done to their father and family, Jake vowed never to let a woman render him weak like that.

As he turned his back on his childhood home and walked with Anna in the other direction, a warm evening breeze tempered the fierce July heat, making it almost pleasant to be outside. Still, Jake felt the heat of apprehension prickle the back of his neck because of what he was about to do. He just needed to figure out how to say it. He could go all corny and sentimental opening with the old saying, "If you love something, set it free." But that was a little dramatic. So he opted for taking the more direct route. But before he could find the words, Anna spoke.

"You might have wondered why I asked you here tonight."

He smiled because that was a line from some corny black-and-white television show that they'd been obsessed with one summer a long time ago.

"Actually, I think I have a pretty good idea. Anna—"

"No, let me go first. Please?"

He nodded. "Okay."

"I owe you an apology for how I acted this afternoon... and this morning."

"You don't have to apologize."

"Yes, I do. Because you don't deserve to be treated that way. No wonder you're afraid of commitment if women turn into needy, beastly creatures. Or am I the only one who acts like that? I'm so bad at this."

"Stop," Jake said. "You aren't being unreasonable. Don't ever compromise what's important to you. Okay?"

She nodded.

"Funny, how you and I had a better time with each other than any of the blind dates we've been on," Jake said after they'd cleared the Adamses' white colonial-style home. "But I've thought a lot about what you said, and you're right. You're not the kind of woman who sleeps with one guy and dates others."

Realizing that this preamble might sound as if he was going in a completely different direction than what he meant, he quickly added, "I would love to be with you, Anna. In fact, if I could create the perfect woman for me she would be someone just like you—"

"Only someone who didn't want the ultimate commitment, right?"

"I know that sounds ridiculous. Anyone of your caliber deserves everything she wants. I'm sorry, but I don't see myself ever getting married. That means no kids, which is probably a good thing, because if I got married and had a family, I'd probably screw up worse than my parents did."

Anna shook her head. "Are you really going to let your parents' mistakes steal the happiness of family from you? Isn't that just adding to tragedy on top of tragedy?"

"This is where you and I differ. We have completely different takes on what constitutes happiness. Family and happiness are not synonymous in my book."

"What about your brothers? You guys are pretty close. How can you say they don't bring you happiness?"

He thought about it for a moment. "My relationship with my brothers is so different it's hard to explain. Of course, I wouldn't trade them for anything in the world, but that relationship doesn't do anything to convince me that marriage is the right path for me. It's completely different. Anna, you have to remember that growing up I was more of a caregiver to my brothers, a parent rather than a sibling."

He was starting to feel hemmed in, cornered, having to defend himself. And that feeling made him want to run. But he couldn't. He and Anna needed to work through this. He had things to say to her, and he wasn't going to leave until those things were said and they were okay.

As he tried to cool his jets and regroup his thoughts, the question of what he might be capable of that would be worse than cheating and vilifying a dead spouse—the way his father had—niggled at the back of his brain. Of course, he didn't make a habit of lying and cheating. That's why he broke up with women when the relationship had run its course.

He glanced at Anna as they turned the corner off their childhood street. He did have a modicum of self-control. Except when it came to Anna, apparently. But Anna wanted both marriage and kids. As much as he wanted her—needed her—it wouldn't be fair to lead her down a dead-end path.

"There's still the bet," she said, sounding more like her old self. "Now that we've had a couple of warm-up rounds and we know the kinds of people who aren't right for us, maybe we should regroup and get going on that again. I'm going to win, you know."

Yes, thank you, that was his Anna. Her spirit had returned. Or at least she was trying. If he was completely truthful with himself, he wasn't convinced that Anna's too-broad smile was completely sincere. It called to mind those people who believed projecting the emo-

tion that they wanted to feel would make it a reality—
or something like that. But this was a start in the right
direction.

"No, you're not. Because there's someone I want to
fix you up with."

She groaned. "Who?"

"What do you think of Dylan Tyler?"

"The new doctor who works at Celebration Memorial?"

"The one and only."

"Dylan Tyler... Since the first time I heard his name,
I wanted to ask, is he a good Southern boy with a double
first name, or is that his first and last?"

"Very funny," Jake said.

Anna gave a one-shoulder shrug. "I don't know. He's
handsome. I guess. I've not had the chance to get to
know him."

"Now's your chance. I have it on very good author-
ity that he would love to ask you out."

There was that too-wide smile again. It didn't match
the dullness in her eyes.

"Oh. Goody."

"Wow. Your enthusiasm is overwhelming. Could you
tone it down a bit?"

Anna shrugged again. "I don't know. You know how
I feel about dating doctors. Do you think it's a good
idea, since we work together? I mean, you saw how
rumors flew when people thought you and I were..."

The same pink that had colored her cheeks earlier in
the dining room was back. He knew exactly what she
was thinking, and damned if his body didn't respond.

The primal, completely base part of his brain kicked in. God, if he didn't have good sense, he'd pull her into his arms right now and remind himself how much he wanted her.

But sparks faded and then you were left with real life.

What had happened between them was a cautionary tale, and if he really cared about her, he wouldn't lead her on.

Dylan Tyler called Anna the following day and asked her to be his date to the Holbrook wedding.

And she'd said yes.

Really, it wasn't as daunting as it seemed at face value. Given the circumstance, there would automatically be a barrier between them. The daughter of Celebration Memorial Hospital's CEO was getting married. Everyone would be on their best behavior.

Not that she expected Dylan to bring anything less.

This date felt safe. Like going to prom with the friend of a friend...even though her prom had happened more years ago than she cared to admit.

Tick...tick...tick...

Darn that biological clock.

Jake would be there.

Now she just needed to remind him that he'd agreed to ask Cassie Davis to be his date, and make sure he didn't revert to his old ways and ask someone like Miss Texas.

She hadn't given it much thought since they'd been otherwise occupied...with him being away at the conference...and them planning the Fourth of July party…and, well, everything else. But they needed to get back to their original plan. It was the only way to get their friendship back on track.

She jabbed the up button and tried to ignore the cold, hollow emptiness in the place where her heart should be. As she stood there, she tried not to think about how Jake had said his perfect woman would be someone like her. If she didn't know that he meant well and didn't believe that he would never purposely hurt her, she might think he was playing her.

Someone just like her, but not her.

Was that supposed to be a consolation prize? Because it sort of felt like a slap in the face.

She gave herself a mental shake.

Come on, Anna. You know the rules. It would be fruitless to try and change them.

Anna adjusted her grip on her insulated lunch bag, which contained a turkey sandwich on whole wheat with lettuce and tomato, an apple and some carrots. She had to go light since she had no idea whether or not she could fit into the cocktail dress she was going to wear to the wedding. It had been so long since she'd had a fancy occasion to wear it, she wasn't sure how it would fit. When she and Hal were married, it seemed as if there was something or another every other night, but the dates Jake had arranged had been informal and the dresses she'd purchased for them had been casual and not suitable for a wedding.

Funny, she hadn't missed the stuffy occasions at all. She didn't mind getting dressed up, but the so-called friends who really weren't friends at all… She didn't even want to give them a second thought. She hoped Hal's girlfriend was better suited to inane cocktail chit-chat than she was.

You know what? On second thought, no. She didn't hope she was better at it. She hoped the woman was twice as miserable as she had been and that the so-called friends made it even harder on the girlfriend than they had on her.

Wow. That sounded really bitter.

She didn't want to be that way. Really, she didn't. But after all she'd been through, couldn't she simply get a break?

A little voice inside of her told her that maybe Dylan was her break. Or at least a step in the right direction. He was a good-looking guy. Light brown hair with sun-streaks that looked natural. They'd better be. She refused to date a man who spent more money on his hair than she did. And if they were natural, at least that meant that he liked to spend time outside. That was one thing they'd have in common, besides working for Celebration Memorial.

Anna wasn't prepared to list the fact that they were coworkers in the pros column just yet. In fact, she was very nervous about it. At least he worked on the second floor and rarely, if ever, got up to the third floor, which was why she hadn't had a chance to get to know him.

But Jake had handpicked Dylan for her. That had to mean something, didn't it? Especially given the delicate nature of their own relationship right now.

She decided she owed it to herself to approach it with an open mind. She'd given Jake the advice that "if you keep doing what you do, you'll keep getting what you get." Maybe she needed to borrow a page from her own book.

The elevator chimed and Anna waited for the people who'd ridden down to step out. Then she got in and pushed the button for the third floor. As the doors were closing, she heard a woman call, "Hold the elevator, please?"

With a quick jab of her finger, Anna managed to re-open the doors before the car lifted off.

As if fate had conjured her, Cassie Davis rushed inside, uttering a breathless "thank you so much. You know how slow these elevators are. If you hadn't waited for me, I'd be late. As it is I'm cutting it close."

"No problem," Anna said. "I'm glad I could help."

She was glad they weren't clock watchers up on three. Then again, she was usually early or right on time like she was today, but she understood how missing the elevator could cost you a solid five minutes, and it always happened at the most inopportune times.

"I guess I could've taken the stairs," Cassie said. "But given how my morning has started, I probably would've fallen on my face. I just hate being late."

"Me, too," Anna said, studying the woman with her pretty peaches-and-cream complexion, blue eyes and auburn hair. Yes, she would remind Jake that he'd agreed to take Cassie to the wedding. Cassie was perfect for him. Maybe even a little too perfect, but she couldn't think about that right now.

The elevator dinged to signal its arrival at the second floor.

"Cassie, I don't mean to be nosy, but are you dating anyone?"

The woman did a double take as she started to exit the elevator. Anna jabbed the door open button again to give Cassie time to answer.

"No. I'm not. Why do you ask?"

If it was possible to be simultaneously happy and disappointed, that was how Anna felt hearing the news. But of course she wasn't involved with anyone. She'd been practically drooling over Jake that day Anna had filled in on the second floor.

"Because I have someone I want to fix you up with."

Cassie smiled. "Oh? Do I know this person?"

"You do. It's Dr. Lennox. Are you interested?"

Cassie's jaw dropped for a moment. "Absolutely."

"Good. He's going to call you soon. Today probably. Can he find your number in the hospital personnel directory?"

"Yes."

"Good." She looked so happy and Anna tried to convince herself it was a good thing. It *was* a good thing. Jake would have an appropriate date for the wedding and Anna would…just have to be okay with that. At least she got to pick his date.

When the door started to close, Cassie reached out and stopped it. "I need to ask you a question, though." Her brows were knit. "I thought you and Dr. Lennox were involved."

Anna mustered her best smile. "Jake and I are good friends. He's like a brother to me."

Cassie looked even more confused. "Oh. Okay…?"

"I need to run. Neither of us wants to be late."

Anna waved and Cassie pulled her hand away. As the doors closed, she looked as if she were trying to decide whether Anna was playing a practical joke on her. Anna knew that because that was what she would've been wondering if the tables were turned.

Poor Cassie.

Actually, no. Not poor Cassie. Lucky Cassie.

Just don't fall in love, she wanted to warn Cassie.

The elevator chugged slowly up to the third floor and when the doors finally opened on the maternity ward, Anna's heart skipped a beat when she saw Jake standing at the nurses' station. His back was to her. But she'd recognize those shoulders anywhere.

She drew in a deep breath to steady herself.

"I didn't know you were pregnant," she said as she approached, trying to use humor to cover her own nerves. He turned around at the sound of her voice.

He ran a hand over his flat stomach. "Oh, am I showing?"

Anna laughed as she reached over the counter that defined the nurses' station and set her lunch bag, keys and phone on the desk.

"What are you doing up here in baby-land, Dr. Lennox? Are you lost?"

She spied the personnel directory, looked up Cassie Davis and wrote her name and phone number on a piece of note paper that was next to the computer.

"I just happened to be in the neighborhood."

"Is that so? Well, then, you are lost. Walk with me and I'll help you find your way."

Good grief, if there were a ship called *The Mixed Messenger*, Jake would've been the captain, because one minute he was making love to her, and the next he was fixing her up on a blind date. Before the fireworks on the Fourth of July, she wouldn't have thought twice about him dropping by like this…for no reason. Now she just needed to put what had happened out of her mind and remember how things used to be.

"Will you cover for me for a few minutes?" Anna asked Patty and Marissa.

"Sure thing," Patty said, looking up from the patient charts she'd been pretending to be engrossed in.

Anna could feel her coworkers watching her and Jake as they walked toward the elevator bank where they would have the most privacy, at least for the five minutes that it took the elevator to chug its way up to the third floor.

"Did Dylan call you?" he asked once they were out of earshot.

"He did."

"Good. And you two have a date?"

"We do. And so do you."

"No I don't."

"I'm fixing you up with Cassie Davis."

"I'm going out of town tomorrow. I'm going back to New Orleans for Bob's funeral."

"I'm sorry. I'm glad you're able to go, though."

The stress showed around his eyes. There was a tightness in his lips and in the way he held himself that had Anna wanting to give him a shoulder massage… and offer other means of stress relief—that she couldn't even believe she was thinking about, given where cross-ing that line had gotten them.

She blinked away the thought and held out the piece of paper with Cassie's number.

"Here, take this. She can be your date to the wed-ding this weekend. You will be back in time for the wedding, right?"

Jake nodded, but he looked as if he were about ready to balk at her suggestion to call Cassie. Anna preempted his protest.

"Look, you're the one who agreed to let me find you a date for the occasion. Cassie is nice. And appropri-ate. The chief knows her and will instantly realize that you have good taste in women. Besides, it's not like you have a lot of suitable options."

He took the paper and shoved it in his lab coat pocket.

"I know you have a lot of your mind, but will you call her before you leave for New Orleans?"

Jake shrugged, obviously not very enthusiastic about the date.

"I don't know that I really even need a date. I can just go to the ceremony and give my congratulations. It's not as if a date is mandatory."

"Yes, it is mandatory. You and I have a bet going on. If I'm going with Dylan, then you have to go with Cassie."

Technically, she knew he didn't have to do anything he didn't want to do. For that matter, he didn't have to go to the wedding either. But it was in his best interest to do so. And so was bringing a date like Cassie.

"You told me that you'd do anything to get things

back to normal between us. Taking Cassie to the Holbrook wedding will go a long way toward that end."

He shot her an incredulous look and she knew that he knew that she was making this up as she went along. But there was some substance to it. Because maybe if she saw him with another woman—a woman who was good for him, who might possess whatever it was that she lacked to change his mind about commitment— maybe they could get back to being just friends.

But what if he really fell for Cassie?

Didn't it always happen that way? A man swore he'd never get married, until the right woman came along and turned his entire belief system on its head. Whether or not Cassie was that woman, Anna hoped that seeing him with someone else would shock her own system enough to stop her from falling in love with Jake.

Because it seemed no matter how she tried to put on the brakes, her heart just kept careening toward disaster.

Chapter Eleven

Jake hated funerals.

Not that anyone loved them, but he'd developed a particular aversion since attending his mother's all those years ago.

Funerals weren't for the dead; they were for the living, a means to say goodbye, or maybe it was more apt to say that they were a reality check to make you aware that everyone's clock was ticking, that every day that you were fortunate enough to wake up and see the sun rise, you were also one day closer to death.

Funerals were a stark reminder to stop putting off the things you wanted to do and to handle everyone you loved with care, because death spared no one—it was the one thing that all humans had in common, Jake mused as he stood in sober contemplation and looked around.

The turnout at Bob Gibson's service was overwhelming. Standing room only.

Jake's plane had been delayed. By the time he'd arrived in the church and squeezed in among the latecomers standing along the back wall, one of Bob's sons, who looked to be about Jake's age, was already giving the eulogy.

"There are so many things in life that are uncertain, but love—unconditional love—is one of the few things you can invest in and get a return that far exceeds the outlay. My parents' marriage—the example they set—always had a profound effect on my life."

Lucky guy.

"Love isn't easy. In fact, by nature, it's complicated and messy, but without it, what do we have? A career? A fancy car? A big house? But what does it all mean without someone to share it?"

Jake's shirt collar was beginning to feel a little tight. He reached up and loosened his tie. The sun was streaming in through the stained-glass windows and the effect gave the sanctuary an otherworldly feel. A large portrait of Bob sat on an easel in front of the podium from which his son spoke. The way one shard of light hit the frame, it seemed to cast a halo over Bob's image.

Jake shifted his weight from one foot to the other, alternately looking at Bob's son, who looked a lot like him, and his friend's photo.

"I'm sure Mom won't mind me sharing that there were times in their marriage when the obstacles seemed nearly insurmountable, when both of them, in turn, had to sacrifice what each wanted for the other. But they always put each other's wants and needs ahead of their own. My parents rode out the storm when it got tough. My dad always told me you don't give up on the people who matter."

During Jake's internship, Bob had been more of a father figure to him than his own dad. Jake recalled a couple of times when Bob had to exercise some tough love, calling him on his own BS and giving him a reality check when he got too full of himself. Even though Jake didn't believe it at the time, it was now clear that his mentor's high expectations were one of the driving forces that saw him through the challenging years of becoming a doctor.

You don't give up on the people who matter.

How many times had Bob said that to him? More important, how many times had he demonstrated it?

The last time he saw Bob, they'd talked about marriage and family. Bob had seemed perplexed when Jake had told him he had no plans to get married. In fact, he'd urged him not to close his mind. And much like what his son was saying today, he'd warned Jake of the shallow trappings of succees. And also, he'd advised him to not let his career consume him because the body aged and success was a fickle mistress who didn't offer a whole lot of warmth in your golden years.

What does it all mean without someone to share it?

As the choir began singing "Amazing Grace," Bob's son returned to the church pew. He sat between his mother and a younger woman, who Jake guessed was his wife. He put an arm around each of them. Something in that protective gesture—or maybe it was the picture of his mentor bathed in that holy light—evoked a feeling that was strange and foreign.

Just last week Bob had been so alive. And now he was gone.

Something shifted inside Jake.

Feeling a little light-headed, he tugged at his collar again. It was just the heat—and possibly the prospect of ending up alone...or even worse, dying without allowing himself to love.

The rest of the week went by in a blur. Even though he'd only taken off one day, Thursday, flying to New Orleans and back on the same day, he just couldn't seem to get everything back in sync when he got to work on Friday.

To compound matters, he also realized on Friday morning he hadn't called Cassie to ask her to the wedding. He only remembered when she said hello to him as he passed the second-floor nurses' station.

He was surprised that Anna hadn't been on his case about it. But what was almost more disconcerting was when he realized how little he'd seen of her this week.

He paused in front of Cassie, not quite sure what to say, uncertain if it would be insulting to ask her to a big event the day before it happened or—"Hi, Cassie."

It was one of those rare moments when they were the only two at what was usually a hub of activity.

He figured he might as well ask. She could always say no and call him a cad for waiting until the last minute. If he ended up going to the wedding stag, at least he could tell Anna that he'd tried.

Cassie was cute, he supposed. Auburn hair—similar to Anna's—with large, sparkling blue eyes that seemed to light up when he stopped in front of her. He hated to admit it, but even though they worked on the same floor, he'd never really noticed her unless she spoke first. Not that he meant to be rude or disrespectful, but he was usually so focused on patients and their charts that sometimes he navigated the hospital on autopilot.

"Hey, so," he said, stumbling over his words, "I'm sorry this is such late notice. I meant to ask you earlier. Actually, I meant to call you, but I— Anna gave me your number. You know Anna Adams, right?"

Cassie smiled at him enthusiastically as she bobbed her head. "Right, she mentioned that she would like to give you my number."

Wait. Should he be doing this here? The hospital didn't have a no-fraternizing policy. So officially, he wasn't breaking a rule. But something just didn't feel right.

"I'd love to get together sometime," Cassie offered, seeming to sense his hesitation.

"Good. Are you free tomorrow night? Stan Holbrook's daughter is getting married and I, uh, RSVP'd for a plus-one."

Wow, that sounded enticing.

But it didn't seem to dull Cassie's shine. "That sounds lovely."

She jotted something on a piece of paper and handed it to him. "This is my address. I wrote my phone number down in case you need it. What time should I be ready?"

* * *

The next day, Jake had picked Cassie up at five-thirty for the six-thirty wedding. Even though she looked lovely, he couldn't seem to take his eyes off Anna, whom he'd picked out in the crowd in the hotel ballroom. She was with Dylan, of course. They were sitting two rows ahead of where he and Cassie were seated. Upon seeing them together, Jake instantly regretted setting them up.

What was wrong with him? He couldn't stand the thought of being tied down, but he hated the thought of her with someone else. The thought of Dylan possibly putting his hands on her the way he had the night they were together had him fisting his hands in his lap as they waited for the bridesmaids to finish parading down the aisle.

Cassie reached out and touched his hand. "You okay?"

Jake relaxed his hands. "Yeah," he whispered. "Fine."

Of course, that was the moment Anna made eye contact with him and smiled.

"She looks beautiful, doesn't she?" Cassie said.

Was he that obvious? Apparently so, since most of the guests were turned in their seats watching the bridal party parade, but Jake was facing forward, staring at Anna.

He was relieved when Stan Holbrook and his daughter finally appeared and everyone stood up and gave the bride their attention. Even Cassie stopped asking him questions and stood silently as the bride floated by.

What had happened to him over this past month since Anna had been back? She was Anna, through and through, but she was different, too. Or at least he was different.

In the good old days, the one thing Jake disliked almost as much as a funeral was a wedding, but tonight as he listened to this man and woman that he didn't even know exchange their vows and promise to love and honor and cherish each other until death did them part, something similar to what he'd experienced at Bob's funeral stirred inside him again.

What does it all mean without someone to share it?

Jake wished he knew the answer to the question, because it seemed as if it held the key to eternal happiness... or a life sentence without it.

After the ceremony was over, he lost sight of Anna as the guests filed out of the ballroom into another lavishly decorated room that was twice the size of the first.

A server with a tray of champagne stopped in front of them.

"Would you like something to drink?" Jake asked.

"Yes, thank you."

When he only took one flute off the tray, Cassie asked, "Don't you like champagne?"

"Oh, I forgot to mention I'm on call tonight. So I can't drink. It's your lucky night. I'm your designated driver."

Cassie lifted her glass to Jake and sipped the golden liquid.

It was in that moment of brief silence that Jake spied Anna and Dylan across the room. They were just entering the ballroom. Dylan had his hand on the small of Anna's back, causing the same possessive force that had driven Jake to fist his hands to consume him again.

"When did Anna start dating Dr. Tyler?" Cassie asked.

"They're not dating." Jake realized his tone might have been a little brusque.

"Well, that's good for you. Isn't it?"

"Why would you say that?"

Cassie cocked her head to the side and smiled up at him. "It's pretty obvious that you have a thing for her."

Oh, hell.

"So, is it that obvious?"

"Pretty much," she said with a sweet smile.

Out of respect, Jake did his best to avoid looking at Anna—since he was that obvious. One of the great things about Cassie Davis was that she was exceedingly easy to talk to. She was great at making conversation. As the various courses of the dinner were served, they not only made lively conversation with the other guests at their table—some of whom they knew from the hospital—but they also talked to each other about neutral subjects, like recent happenings at the hospital and the food they were served for dinner, such as the merits of the steak versus the salmon. She was funny and quick-witted and quite enjoyable, but there was absolutely zero chemistry between them.

Cassie was the kind of woman who would be fun to hang out with, but she was definitely 100 percent in the friend zone, and he had a feeling the feeling was mutual. She shared a lot of the same qualities that he found so attractive in Anna—they were both nurses, they both had a similarly unpretentious way about them that cut through the nonsense and went straight to the heart of the matter. Cassie was also fun to dance with when the music started and an all-around nice person, but that was as far as it went.

As the night went on, it became clear that Anna was either otherwise occupied or avoiding him, too. Because other than the smile that they exchanged before the ceremony, they hadn't had any contact.

And then the unthinkable happened. The wedding band decided to change things up. The singer said, "This one is by special request." The band broke into the first strains of "Don't Worry, Be Happy."

Immediately, his gaze snagged Anna's across the ballroom. He wasn't so sure it was an appropriate request to make at a wedding, but he was glad Anna had done it. Of all the icebreakers—well, aside from taking Cassie to the wedding at Anna's insistence—Jake hadn't been able to think of any that would get them back to the other side of the line that they had crossed. It had actually started to feel like a futile battle—a one-man war with himself.

What does it all mean without someone to share it?
Don't worry. Be happy.

Cassie must've noticed, because she said, "Go ask her to dance. You can't ignore her all night. Good grief, I think I need to be your romance coach. And I mean that in the most platonic way possible, just in case there was any question. But somehow I don't think so. Go dance with her and then I need to think about leaving. I have to be at work early tomorrow."

* * *

"I can't believe you requested this song," Anna said once she was on the dance floor with Jake.

"Don't Worry, Be Happy" was one of those songs that was too slow to fast-dance to, but too fast to slow-dance to. So they did a modified version of the swing dance where Jake alternately sent her spinning out in turns and pulling her back in close.

"I didn't request it," he said as he reeled her back in and held her for a moment. "I thought you did."

Anna pulled back and looked at him. "Are you kidding? The guy in the band said someone requested it."

"I wish I had," Jake said. "Looks like fate intervened and requested for us."

"I guess so. How was New Orleans? I haven't had a chance to talk to you since you got back."

He looked so handsome in his suit and tie. The deep charcoal of the merino wool fabric echoed his dark hair and offset his blue eyes in a way that made her a little breathless. Good thing she could blame it on the dancing.

"It was a quick trip, and you know how I feel about funerals—"

"Yeah, the same way you feel about weddings."

He arched a brow and nodded solemnly. He really was taking Bob's death harder than she'd realized. She had the urge to pull him in close and hug him until all the anguish melted away.

But she knew better than that.

"Looks like you and Cassie are getting along well," Anna said.

This time when he reeled her in, he pulled her in close, slipped his right arm around her waist and held her left hand, guiding her to a slow sway. Her curves molded to the contours of his lean body, making her recall what had happened a week ago tonight.

"Cassie's a lot of fun," he said.

If Anna didn't know better, she might've thought the muddy feeling that washed over her was her heart sinking. But she was happy for her friend; really, she was. She wanted Jake to meet someone who could take his mind off all the ick that had happened lately. Someone who was just in it for the fun. He really was due for an upswing, and Cassie sounded perfect.

"Does that mean there's going to be a second date?"

He stared down into her eyes and she felt the connection all the way down to her soul.

"No, I don't think Cassie and I are suited to date. But we should definitely put her on the list to invite her to the Fourth of July party next year."

Oh. She knew she shouldn't read too much into that comment. He was just making conversation, not future plans. A lot could change in a year. He could meet the woman of his dreams. She could meet…someone.

"I'll make a point of adding her to the guest list."

She could feel the warmth of his hand on the small of her back, and for a moment she lost herself in the feel of it. Even though other people had joined them on the dance floor, for a moment it was just them. And it was so nice.

"So, how about you and Dr. Tyler? You are looking pretty cozy over there."

"Cozy? I wouldn't call it that. He's nice."

Jake's eyes widened. "You're perfect for each other. He's a great guy, Anna. Really, he is. I'm happy for you. I'm sensing that I'm getting closer to winning the bet?"

"You're getting a little ahead of yourself there, bucko. It's kind of hard to get to know a person at a function like this. It almost feels more like going through the motions with a rent-a-date—or maybe *arrange-a-date* is a better way to put it. In fact, maybe you should consider that before you write off Cassie. Keep an open mind."

Jake had a funny look on his face. Maybe he was considering Cassie in a different light.

"What are you thinking about?" she asked.

He was gazing at her so intensely, it was obvious that he wanted to say something—

"What, Jake?"

Their song ended and the band started a set of Southern rock 'n' roll, but Jake didn't move his hands and Anna stayed in his semi-embrace.

"Bob's funeral had a stronger impact on me than I realized. Life is short and there's no time to waste. It hit me like a train."

Wow. This was news. Where was he going with it?

She had to lean in closer because the music was so loud. She could smell his aftershave and that heady mix of sexy that was uniquely Jake. For a fleeting moment, she thought she could stay right here, breathing him in the rest of her life. But then there was a cold hand on her shoulder—a hand that wasn't Jake's—and it made her jump.

"Hey, guys," said Dylan. "Mind if I cut in and dance with my date, buddy?"

No. She wanted to hear what Jake had to say. But the moment was over, ruined. It was probably way too noisy to have that conversation now anyway.

"Sure thing, buddy," Jake said, stepping away from Anna and extending his hand for Dylan to shake. Dylan gave Jake's hand a hearty pump.

Ahh, the international man-sign for *I hear you, I see you; no harm, no foul.*

"Cassie and I need to leave anyhow. She has to work early in the morning and I'm on call. You know what it's like to be the only sober man at a rollicking party."

He winked at Anna.

"Hey," she said before he turned to walk away.

"But they haven't even cut the cake yet," she said.

"Have a piece for me, okay?"

Dylan put his hand on her shoulder, and she had to fight the urge to take a step away from him to reclaim her personal space.

"Call me later so you can finish telling me what you were saying about Bob's funeral. It sounds important."

There was that intense look again. It had her stomach flipping all over again.

"Okay," he said. "Don't you kids stay out too late. Anna, we will talk later."

Chapter Twelve

Anna was surprised when Jake's text came through. She didn't think he'd contact her since it was after ten o'clock, much less ask if he could come over.

Dylan had dropped her off about fifteen minutes ago and she was glad she hadn't immediately changed out of her cocktail dress and scrubbed her face free of makeup. All that she'd had time to do was kick off her shoes, take down her hair and brew herself a cup of tea.

After she'd texted Jake back, she remembered he was on call. So she added some water to the kettle so she could offer him a mug of something nonalcoholic when he arrived.

As she bobbed her own tea bag up and down, more for something to do with her nervous energy rather than to hurry up the tea, she couldn't help but wonder what was so urgent that he needed to talk to her tonight.

Unless he'd been worried about Dylan putting the heavy pressure on her and was dropping by to make sure she was in for the night, safe and sound. Dr. Tyler had tried to make a campaign for a nightcap, but Anna had nipped that in the bud right away. And to Dylan's credit, he hadn't pushed. Although he had told her he'd like to see her again. That was the part of dating that never got any easier—how did you let someone down easy and tell them you just weren't feeling it?

He was a great guy. Any woman in her right mind would be thrilled to spend an evening with him. He was good-looking—even if he wasn't her type. But why wasn't he? He was handsome, successful and funny. He didn't chew with his mouth open. Yet that indefinable je ne sais quoi was missing, and no matter how Anna tried to concentrate on the good, all she could think about was that she just wasn't that into him.

He wasn't Jake.

Damn you, Jake Lennox. Have you ruined me for all men?

If Anna could've slapped herself, she would've. She was sitting here pouting like a petulant child who was moping because she didn't get exactly what she wanted.

Buck up, buttercup. You don't always get what you want.

Sadly, she couldn't even convince herself that Dr. Tyler might be what she needed if she just gave it time.

No, what she needed was to be on her own for a while. This dating bet with Jake had started out as fun, but suddenly it had turned so serious. And that wasn't fun.

Or maybe what wasn't fun was the possibility of Jake changing his mind about Cassie. It had dawned on her that maybe he could tell how down she was at the wedding and didn't want to completely ruin her night with the confession that he actually was feeling it with Cassie.

Okay, now she was just assessing.

But just to be safe, maybe she should fix Cassie up with Dylan. They'd make a good couple.

Anna had gathered the flowers from the Fourth of July centerpieces and put them in a large vase, which sat in the middle of her kitchen table. The flowers caught her eye and took her back to that night one week ago. It hadn't been too much later than it was right now when things began to heat up with Jake.

Anna's heartbeat kicked up as she remembered the way he'd leaned in and kissed her on the dock, pulling her onto his lap and then coming back to her house to finish what he'd started.

Her breath hitched in her chest. What if that was why he was coming here tonight? He might not even realize that was what he was doing.

And that was exactly how things *just happened* between two people who knew better, who swore that they wouldn't fall into that friends-with-benefits trap. They started dropping in for late-night visits and—*Oh! Oops! Gosh, I didn't mean for that to happen...* And pretty soon they'd established a pattern of *Oh! Oops!*

Gosh! I promise it'll never happen again…after this one last time.

And damn her all to hell. She wasn't going to call him and tell him not to come over.

For a split second—actually, it was more like a good several minutes, a fantastic several minutes—she played out her own *Oh! Oops! Gosh!* production in her head.

What was she doing? The only thing that might be worse than having slept with Jake was to continue sleeping with Jake, knowing full good and well how he felt. He was her drug, and she needed to go cold turkey if she had any self-respect at all. Good grief, this wasn't only about that; it was about self-preservation.

She grabbed her phone and pulled up Emily's number. Before she could change her mind, she texted, SOS! It's urgent! Need you to come over now and save me.

She'd just pushed the send button when Jake knocked at the door.

So, he was still choosing to knock and wait, rather than doing their special knock and walking in the way he always had in the past. Then again, it was pretty late. She had locked her door behind Dylan, not that he would come walking in uninvited, but it just felt like an extra barrier between her and her date and the night.

And now Jake was here.

She padded to the door in her bare feet and looked out the peephole. There he was—all six foot four of him, with his perfect hair and perfect face and those perfect arms that had held her so close she didn't know where her body ended and his began.

Oh, dear God, Emily, please get here as soon as you can.

As she unlocked the dead bolt and pulled open the door, it dawned on her that she and Emily had never seriously talked about the SOS call. In fact, they'd sort of joked about it. Emily was probably working tonight. Of course she was on Saturday night.

Oh, crap.

Oh, well... Maybe she should ask for a sign from fate. Toss it up to the heavens. If she should sleep with Jake just one more time, Emily would *not* show up. If it was a bad idea, her sister would come to her rescue.

In the kitchen, the teakettle whistled, as if calling her on her BS.

I know, I'm a weak, weak woman. So shoot me.

Well, she would probably want to be put out of her misery if she let it happen again... But others had died for much less.

"Good evening, Dr. Lennox. Won't you come in?"

That was corny, she thought as she stepped back to allow him inside. Oh, well, that was what they did sometimes. That was why they were so darn good together—

But Jake wasn't moving. His feet were planted firmly on the front porch, and Anna was sobered by his stiff demeanor. He didn't look like a man who'd come to seduce a woman who would be oh-so-easy to take.

Oh, God! He's going to marry Cassie.

Anna actually took a step forward and looked out on the porch to see if maybe Cassie was waiting there to deliver the happy news with him. But no, he was alone.

"Are you going to come in? Or are you going to stand there and let the mosquitoes in?"

Jake flinched. "Sorry."

He moved inside like a man on autopilot—or maybe someone who wasn't feeling well.

She shut the door behind him and turned the lock. "Are you okay?"

"No, not really—" He made a face. "What's that noise?"

"Oh! It's the teakettle. I put on some water to make you a cup of tea since you're on call tonight."

Anna hurried back to the kitchen to stop the racket.

"What kind of tea would you like? I have English Breakfast, Earl Grey and peppermint. The peppermint is caffeine-free, but the bergamot in the Earl Grey supposedly has properties that will lift your spirits."

"I don't care," he called from the other room. "Whatever you have handy."

She glanced at her phone, which was lying on the kitchen counter, to see if Emily had responded. Nothing. Not a single word in response to her SOS.

Hmm. Okay, then.

They'd have a cup of tea—she opened a package of Earl Grey, just in case Jake needed the caffeine—and see where fate led them.

Anna carried the two mugs of tea into the family room, set them on the trunk that she used as her coffee table, and took a seat on the couch next to Jake, leaving just enough room to be respectable, but not enough room to send the keep-your-hands-off-me signal.

Careful, Anna...

Oh, shut up. Loosen up. Maybe Jake was right; maybe she needed to stop overthinking things.

"Is this about the house?" *Of course it wasn't. Although she was curious and it was a neutral subject.* "Have you made a decision about whether or not you're going to buy it? I love that house. I can't imagine you living anywhere else."

"Good, because Roger accepted my offer today."

"Jake, that's fabulous news. I'm so happy for you." She threw her arms around him and it felt so right. "And selfishly, I'm glad because that means you're staying put. Because I can't imagine being that far away from you again."

He pulled back slightly and looked at her. For a heart-rending moment, she couldn't read him.

God, had she said the wrong thing?

"I mean…since I just moved back. And all."

He was just frozen. Looking at her. She'd always known what he was thinking. Sometimes better than she'd known her own mind. But now…? Not so much.

"What's going on, Jake? I'm worried about you."

"Don't be," he said. "Or maybe you should be. Because I don't know what's happening to me. One minute, I was so sure where my life was going and what I wanted and what I didn't want. The next, everything was different. I just started seeing my life from a whole new perspective."

Uh-oh. Maybe this is about Cassie.

They had looked awfully cozy at the wedding, talking and laughing.

Oh, my God. He is here to break the news to me

gently. Of course, it wasn't as if Cassie was a complete stranger. Not even really a blind date. They worked together. He'd said it himself, he wanted someone like Anna, but not Anna… Jake was getting ready to settle back into another stretch of monogamy. Only it was with Cassie, and if anybody had the potential to move mountains and change his mind, she was the woman. And Anna had insisted they go out.

Oh, what have I done?

Jake scrubbed his face with his hands and gave his head a quick shake. "I'm sorry I came barging in here so late, and I start right in with what's on my mind and I didn't even ask you how things turned out with Dylan."

"That doesn't matter. I need to know what's going on with you."

Her heart was hammering so fast and loud that she was afraid he could hear it.

"Well, I can't say anything else until I know how everything went with Dylan. I need to know—are you going to see him again? It's important, Anna. Because whether or not you are could have a direct bearing on what I'm about to say."

Why? "What difference does it make?"

The look on Jake's face was so serious, she decided to quit playing games.

"He's fine. He's nice. I guess. A little possessive for my taste. Ha! I feel like I'm channeling you."

Then, the strangest thing happened. Jake was smiling at her in a way that made her lose her breath and she knew, she just knew that he was going to lean in and—

But at the sound of the front door opening, he flinched and diverted his lean toward his tea.

What?

Emily bounded into the room. "I got here as soon as I could."

Maybe it was because of Emily's abrupt entrance or maybe it was because she was giving him the look of death as she all but escorted him out, saying that she and Anna were having a girls' night and no guys were invited.

For the second time that night, Anna did not get to hear what Jake needed to tell her and seemed to be having so much trouble saying.

Damn her sister.

Damn that SOS text. Why had she been such a chicken, when in the end all she wanted to do was make love to Jake?

She'd followed him out to the porch, trying to ignore the fact that Emily was lurking in the living room. Anna had reached out and shut the door, putting a barrier between them and Emily.

"Jake? What were you going to say?"

Jake glanced back at the door and then at Anna. "Not now. Go back inside with Emily and I'll talk to you tomorrow."

Then his phone rang.

"It's the hospital. I need to take this. I'll talk to you later."

Rather than leaning in to kiss her, as she was so sure

he was going to do before Emily arrived, he picked up the call, saying good-night with a distracted wave.

She'd asked for a sign from fate and if this wasn't as clear as crystal, she didn't know what was. Still, all day Sunday, she waited for Jake to call as he'd said he would. She didn't want to call him since she wasn't sure how late he had been at the hospital dealing with the emergency.

Finally, at a quarter past two, she got a text. From Jake.

I know this is short notice, but are you busy tonight?

Defying common sense and her better judgment, Anna's heart leaped.

She didn't even wait a respectable amount of time to text him back. She grabbed her phone and typed, No plans, why?

Good. I've made arrangements for you to have one last date. I'm sure this guy is the one.

What? Was he kidding? He had nearly kissed her last night and now he was fixing her up on another blind date?

She typed, Sorry, I don't think so. I'm just not up for it.

How humiliating. Obviously, he was trying to pawn her off on someone to get her off his case.

She started typing again, Look, Jake, you don't need

to pair me up with someone to get me off your case.
I get it. I understand.

As she hit Send on the second message, a message
from Jake came through.

Please, just do this for me? This is the last date. I promise. I will never try to fix you up with anyone else again
after tonight.

Oh, for the love of God. Was he really doing this?
She was about to type No and then turn off her
phone. Instead, she opted for the path of least resistance.

I will meet him for a cup of coffee and that's it. And
I'm driving myself. Then I'm off the hook. And just so
you know, in case he doesn't want to waste his time,
I'm giving him fifteen minutes max. And the clock will
start the minute I walk in the door.

She probably sounded like a major B about it, but
this hurt. And Jake was clueless. Or maybe he wasn't.
Maybe he knew exactly what he was doing. If he'd come
over last night to disengage, this date from out of the
blue had completed the job for him.

A couple of moments later, Jake texted back, Actually, he has a seven o'clock reservation at Bistro St.
Germaine. I guess you could have coffee in the bar. So,
maybe get there a little early so they can give away
the reservation if you really don't want to have dinner
with him.

Really? Bistro St. Germaine?

She texted Emily, Are you working tonight?

But Emily didn't respond. She was probably tired of coming to her sister's rescue. Especially since, after Emily had scared Jake away last night, Anna hadn't been very gracious.

Anna had been in such a snit that Emily had opted for going home about half an hour later, once she knew that Jake was at the hospital and there was no risk of him coming back.

In fact, since he was going to such great lengths to pair her up with somebody—anybody, it seemed— it was pretty darn clear that there was no risk of him coming back at all.

It was just as well. She would give him space and maybe in a little while they could figure out how to be *them* again.

Even so, in that half hour last night, Anna had endured her sister's lecture of why she should avoid guys who didn't want to commit.

Hello? Wasn't that why she'd called in the first place? But she just let Emily say her piece.

It was just as well that her sister didn't return her text now.

To clear her head, Anna decided to go for a run. With each step, with each pounding of the pavement, she took out her frustrations and let off steam. Until she'd worn herself out, until she was so numb she felt nothing.

As she dragged herself back home, exhausted and emotionally spent, she vowed to take care of herself for a change. She'd spent so many years contorting and configuring her life to appease Hal, and in the time she'd been home, she'd let herself fall for another man who didn't want the same things she did—

She stopped herself.

Really, Jake hadn't done anything wrong. He hadn't lied or cheated. He may have led her on a bit, but she'd gone willingly, knowing what he wanted didn't align with what she wanted. So really, if anyone should shoulder the blame in that regard, it was Anna.

But that was where she was going to take care of herself.

She wasn't going to beat herself up.

Facts were facts: she and Jake were magnetically attracted to each other, but it simply wouldn't work.

End of story.

Around five-thirty, Anna freshened up, and prepared to make herself presentable. She washed her hair and blew it dry.

She kept her makeup very light, because she didn't wear much anyway.

Then she surveyed her closet and decided on a cute little shift with a bold blue and white print. It seemed brighter and happier than she felt.

The run had helped her let go of some of the sting of Jake's rejection-disguised-as-a-fix-up. It still hurt, but it had subsided to a dull ache. By that time, she'd decided she couldn't take it out on the guy who was meeting her tonight. Sure, she was only going to give him fifteen minutes, but she wasn't going to be rude or mean or vent her frustrations to him. After all, his only sin was that he wanted to meet her.

She would let him know that while she appreciated

his interest, this meeting had been a mistake. It wasn't a good time. She simply wasn't available right now. Not when her heart belonged to another.

A man who couldn't return her feelings.

When she got to Bistro St. Germaine, there was a space open on Main Street in front of the restaurant. It must have been her lucky day.

She glanced at her clock on her dashboard. Right on time. The sooner she went in, the sooner the meter would start ticking and the sooner she could leave. As she let herself out of the car and approached the restaurant, she rehearsed her preamble about bad timing and leaving early and being sorry to waste his time.

Wait. What was his name?

Oh, great. In the haze of her hurt and fury, she hadn't even asked Jake for the guy's name. He should've told her that up front. She thought about texting Jake to ask, but she really didn't want contact with him right now.

The way she felt right now was proof-positive that she needed distance. She didn't want to hate him. The only way she could stop that or any more damage from happening was to let her wounds heal. Right now, contact with Jake only tore them deeper.

She took a deep breath and squared her shoulders. She centered herself by reminding herself that the hapless, nameless man who should be waiting for her in the bar would not bear the brunt of her sorrow.

The floor-to-ceiling doors that opened onto the sidewalk in front of the bar were open. A few of the outside bistro tables were occupied, but nobody looked as if he might be waiting for a blind date. Anna circumvented the hostess stand, where Emily would be if she was indeed working tonight, and entered the bar via the open sidewalk doors.

The bar was virtually empty, save for a man and a woman making eyes at each other at a cozy corner table and four middle-aged women who occupied a four-top. Okay, so he wasn't an early bird. She pushed the button on her phone: six forty-six. Their reservation wasn't until seven. So technically she was early...as Jake had suggested.

What if her mystery date didn't show until seven?

So not only was it an inconvenience, it was awkward. *Now what?*

Anna turned in a circle for one more look to make sure she hadn't inadvertently missed him. She hadn't. Great.

She decided to sit at the bar and order a cup of tea—chamomile tea. She couldn't drink coffee because that was too much caffeine too late in the day, and she was already wound up as it was. She certainly didn't want to order a glass of wine because that would send the wrong message. When the guy arrived, she would simply tell him there had been a miscommunication and she had to leave at seven o'clock.

If she were thinking about Jake, she would want to strangle him. But she wasn't thinking about him. Nope, not at all. He was the furthest person from her mind.

The bartender had just brought her tea—she felt a little silly sitting at a bar drinking chamomile tea...but who cared? The bartender had just placed it in front of her when she heard Emily say, "Oh, my gosh, there you are. How did I not see you when you passed the hostess stand?"

That was an odd choice of words.

"How did you know I'd be here to even walk past the hostess stand?"

Emily opened her mouth to say something but then closed it quickly and glanced up at the ceiling, before she said, "I don't know what you're talking about. But I have something to show you, so come with me."

"What? No, Emily. I'm meeting somebody and, well, it's a long story, but this is not a good time. I just got my tea, and you know if I step away for even a second, my date will arrive."

"Hey, Porter," Emily said to the bartender, "watch my sister's tea for her, okay? If someone shows up looking for her, tell him she'll be right back."

Emily winked at him. She actually winked. But that wasn't the only thing that was odd. First of all, she hadn't said anything about Anna being on a date tonight after she'd had to come rescue her last night, and completely let slide the fact that Anna was drinking *chamomile* tea at a bar. God, the mileage she could've gotten out of that one.

Instead, she was all but pulling Anna off the bar stool and herding her toward the dining room.

Then the cherry on top of all the prior weirdness happened when Emily stopped suddenly and turned to her. "Look, don't be difficult tonight." She looked deadly serious. "Just go with this. Trust me, you'll thank me later."

"What?"

Emily gave an exasperated shake of her head and continued leading Anna out of the bar, across the entry and into the dining room.

What the heck was Anna supposed to say to a warning like that? When Emily got serious, which wasn't very often, she always meant business.

So what was going on?

Whatever it was, Anna decided to heed her sister's advice and just go with it.

Emily paused in front of the door to the private dining room. It was closed, but the room was partitioned by a wall with dark wood wainscoting on the bottom and leaded, beveled glass on top. The glass was fogged to give the diners privacy. Anna could see a flickering light coming from the other side, but she couldn't see who was inside.

The sudden frightening thought that the mystery man was somehow in cahoots with Jake—and had gotten her sister involved to trick her into having dinner—nearly had her hyperventilating.

Well, she wouldn't stay. He couldn't make her. And neither could Jake.

Fifteen-minute rules still applied, and she pulled out her phone, clicked the button and saw that the guy had exactly five minutes.

He can always take home a doggie bag. Give her meal to Jake, the louse. She'd made it perfectly clear she would only stay for fifteen minutes and then they'd agreed that Jake would never fix her up on a blind date again.

Would he really go to these lengths to win this absurd bet between them?

Anna didn't have time to ponder it because all of a sudden Emily threw her arms around her and said, "I am so happy for you."

Then she opened the door to the private dining room, grabbed her hand and tugged her inside.

It took a moment for Anna to register what was happening because the room was filled with red roses and candlelight and Jake was there and he was thanking her sister...for her help?

Then, after Emily left the room and shut the door behind her, he said, "God, you can be so difficult sometimes. I thought you weren't going to come."

"What are you doing? Jake, what's going on?"

They were the only two in the room. There was no mystery man and now Jake was reaching for her hand.

"I've tried twice now to tell you something important, but we keep getting interrupted. So, I figured I needed to go to drastic measures to get you alone.

"Anna, I'm your date. I'm the one. You're the one. That has become so clear to me since you've been back in Celebration. I guess sometimes it takes a lifetime to see that the love of your life has been right in front of you all along."

A peculiar humming began sounding in Anna's ears and her knees threatened to buckle beneath her. Was this really happening?

"I lost you once to a man who didn't deserve you, and I'd be an idiot to let you get away again."

Was he saying he wanted a *commitment*? *But Jake didn't, not the kind she needed.*

But maybe she needed to stop overthinking it. Stop making everything so blasted heavy and just go with it.

She loved him. She'd been in love with him her entire life. So what was the problem? Marriage hadn't given her the happily-ever-after she'd expected. So, just—

But then Jake was down on one knee and he had a small black box in his hand.

"I love you, Anna. I don't want another day to go by that I don't wake up and see your face first thing when I open my eyes. Will you do me the honor of being my wife and building a family with me? If you say yes, I promise I will make sure you have no regrets."

With tears streaming down her face, Anna was so choked up that all she could do was nod, but that was enough of a go-ahead for Jake—her mystery man, the last man she'd ever date, the one man she'd spend the rest of her life with—to take the ring from the box and slip it on her finger.

The gorgeous, classic round diamond sparkled in the candlelight as if it were celebrating with them. The sight of it on her finger and her hand in Jake's was instantly sobering.

"I love you so much," she said.

He pulled her into a deep kiss, the magic of which was only interrupted by Emily's voice. "So, I gather she said yes?"

Tears glinted in her sister's eyes.

"I did. I don't think I've ever been this happy."

Emily put her hands on her hips. "Sorry, but I have

to ask. If you two are marrying each other, who won the crazy bet?"

"We both did," Anna and Jake answered together.

* * * * *

**Don't miss Sarah Morgan's
next Puffin Island story**

Some Kind of Wonderful

Brittany Forrest has stayed away from Puffin Island since her relationship with Zach Flynn went bad. They were married for ten days and only just managed not to kill each other by the end of the honeymoon.

But, when a broken arm means she must return, Brittany moves back to her Puffin Island home. Only to discover that Zac is there as well.

Will a summer together help two lovers reunite or will their stormy relationship crash on to the rocks of Puffin Island?

Some Kind of Wonderful
COMING JULY 2015
Pre-order your copy today

Join our *EXCLUSIVE* eBook club

FROM JUST £1.99 A MONTH!

Never miss a book again with our hassle-free eBook subscription.

★ Pick how many titles you want from each series with our flexible subscription

★ Your titles are delivered to your device on the first of every month

★ Zero risk, zero obligation!

There really is nothing standing in the way of you and your favourite books!

Start your eBook subscription today at www.millsandboon.co.uk/subscribe